# THE KING MUST DIE

**ALSO BY KEMI ASHING-GIWA:**

*A Splinter in the Sky*

*This World Is Not Yours*

# THE KING MUST DIE

KEMI ASHING-GIWA

LONDON NEW YORK TORONTO
AMSTERDAM/ANTWERP NEW DELHI SYDNEY/MELBOURNE

1230 AVENUE OF THE AMERICAS, NEW YORK, NEW YORK 10020



First Saga Press trade paperback edition November 2025



Interior design by Yvonne Taylor

Manufactured in the United States of America

1 3 5 7 9 10 8 6 4 2

Library of Congress Control Number has been applied for.

ISBN 978-1-6680-6101-5
ISBN 978-1-6680-6102-2 (ebook)

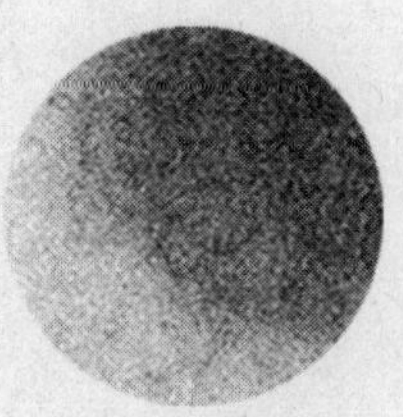

I'M DEDICATING THIS BOOK, A STORY ABOUT FOUND FAMILY, RESISTANCE, AND HOPE IN TIMES OF DISASTER, TO MY FRIENDS.

AT THE BEGINNING OF 2025, MY FAMILY'S HOME BURNED DOWN IN THE EATON FIRE. MY FAMILY AND FRIENDS IN THE AREA MADE IT OUT UNSCATHED, BUT MANY OF US LOST ALMOST EVERYTHING WE HAD. WHOLE NEIGHBORHOODS ARE GONE. ONE HUNDRED AND FIFTY THOUSAND PEOPLE HAVE BEEN DISPLACED.

BUT MY LOVED ONES ARE SAFE AND WELL, AND FOR THAT I AM GRATEFUL. I WAS TOUCHED TO RECEIVE CALLS AND MESSAGES FROM SO MANY OF MY OLD FRIENDS ASKING IF MY FAMILY WAS ALL RIGHT AND IF THERE WAS ANYTHING THEY COULD DO. IT MADE ME FEEL A LITTLE LESS ALONE AND HELPLESS TO DO THE SAME. IN THE MIDDLE OF THIS CATASTROPHE, I RECONNECTED, HOWEVER BRIEFLY, WITH PEOPLE I'D FALLEN OUT OF CONTACT WITH FOR A DECADE.

LIFE CAN BE HARD, BUT GOOD FRIENDS MAKE IT WORTH LIVING.

*The Makers saved us, the Accusers slay us, and the Executors find the balance.*

—old Ataa saying

# THE KING MUST DIE

# BOOK ONE

# AN ENDING

"DO YOU REMEMBER THE WORLD WHERE DIAMONDS FELL LIKE RAIN?"

That was what the Maker asked Its companion, after the human emperor had begged It for Its aid. The imperial Accuser, a levitating tangle of limbs, did not answer immediately. For a long moment, the pair floated beside each other in silence, alien and construct, creator and created. They had both been worshipped; they had both been reviled. They had crossed half a galaxy together, had seen hungry stars swallow planets whole. They had forced lush forests to sprout from barren desert, had transformed frozen tundras into tropical paradises. They had seen civilizations rise and crumble to dust—and they had saved humanity from its own folly.

"OF COURSE I REMEMBER," said the Accuser at last. "IT WAS AN UGLY WORLD."

What they had done to it had been ugly, too. And what they'd do here would be so much worse.

Fen walked through the camp as the darkening sky bled fire, picking up after the man she was guarding. Newearth's dusty rings arced above her in gleaming white lines, slicing the firmament apart.

"Oy, Fenyyang!" barked the nasal, now-familiar voice of Talaat Nagi. "Hurry it up. The faster we move, the sooner I can sleep in my own bed."

If her parents' lives had not depended on her deference, Fen would've stomped over and smacked Talaat across his wrinkled, bearded face.

"I'm going as quickly as I can, sir," she replied, bending down to stab her trash picker into yet another food wrapper. "If I miss a single piece of refuse, it's my back that'll get beaten. The punishments for environmental defilement are severe—"

"I know that," Talaat snapped.

Did he really? As an imperial messenger, he could get away with anything short of murder. In any case, she didn't mention that if Talaat hadn't littered in the first place, she wouldn't have to do this at all. "Then let me finish. Sir."

"Fine. I'm going to lie down." Talaat cursed under his breath as he stalked back to his photovoltaic tent, his spindly arms crossed over his chest.

Fen had realized this mission would be horrendously boring less than two hours in. Though it wasn't as if she would've been doing anything particularly exciting back at Onath's estate otherwise. What precious little free time she possessed was primarily spent deciphering the mail of the magistrate of Talishminn—her lax captor, reluctant guardian, and not-so-gracious host. Even though the messenger she'd been ordered to guard was tasked with delivering a missive of utmost importance to a high-ranking official, she already knew—from decrypting the correspondence itself one hour in—that it held nothing of consequence to her. Unlike some of Onath's letters, the missive had little to do with the only two things she cared about. Namely, the condition of her parents, and of herself.

And even if the letter Talaat carried had been interesting, the whole mission was to protect him while he delivered it. She'd never gotten the chance to use the fighting skills she'd honed to a sharp edge under Onath's instruction. No one ever attacked imperial messengers like Talaat—or any of Onath's clients. The dictates of Enkaiia stated that criminal tendencies were genetic, and typically three or more familial groups were executed for the treachery of one. Her presence was just a formality.

As the sun sank beneath the horizon, Fen tied up the biodegradable trash bag she'd been lugging around and threw it into the trunk of the messenger's transport to dispose of later. The floatcar was a sleek matte-gray vehicle, as much a symbol of the empire's might as its heraldry. She picked up her quarterstaff from where she'd reverently rested it on the grass. She spun it experimentally before moving through a few forms. The weapon whistled through the air, the weighted copper bands at the ends winking in the fast-fading light. She didn't have a license to carry a blade or a stinger, but even if she did, she wouldn't trade her quarterstaff for the world. It was a work of art: tensile graphene and resilient realwood, embedded with parallel strips of titanium to turn aside cuts.

"Sir?" she called. "I'm done now."

"Finally." Talaat emerged from his tent like an ursus that had just completed its hibernation cycle. He wore his professional mask now, plain gray with holes around the eyes, nose, and mouth. Once they hit the road, he'd technically be on official business again.

He pulled a small round commandisk from his coat pocket. At the press of a button, the solartiles atop the tent folded up. The structure deflated like a popped balloon and shrank into a fist-sized cube. A few burrowing eryxes chirped nervously at the sudden commotion. Talaat, unbothered, tucked the habitat under his arm and headed for the floatcar. Fen climbed in after the messenger, the levitating transport dipping momentarily as she added her weight.

Like most of Onath's clients, Talaat had paid Fen little attention for most of the mission. In fact, he'd fully ignored her on their three-day trip to Hollmigorn, a city of spires and tall grass. But the successful delivery of his message to the ruling magistrate there had put him in high spirits, and now he wouldn't shut up.

After inputting a destination and activating the floatcar's autodriver, he reclined his seat and turned it to face her. "So how long have you been living with Onath?" he asked.

"Twenty years," Fen said stiffly. Most clients began interrogating her less than an hour after meeting; she'd naively thought that Talaat's former silence meant he wouldn't ask the same obnoxious questions everyone else did. Now she hoped her sharp tone would dissuade further attempts at conversation.

Talaat whistled. "So much of your life, then. Though you look much older."

Fen sighed through her nose. Her hair had prematurely grown gray when she was a teenager, due to a combination of stress and a genetic predisposition.

"How old were you when you . . . ah . . . "

"When my parents were placed under house arrest and I was

handed off to Onath?" *When everything good in my life was wrenched from me? When I became a hostage?* Fen gripped her quarterstaff a little tighter, bitterness seeping into her gut like poison as memories flooded over her. "I was six."

Not old enough to remember her fathers in great detail, but just old enough to remember what happiness and safety felt like. To ensure she'd feel her family's loss like a torn-out tooth every day.

Talaat's narrow, lined face softened. "House arrest is the most merciful punishment they could've gotten for inciting rebellion."

"They were ambassadors." Fen swallowed down a mouthful of resentment and forced the words from between clenched teeth. "All they did, *sir*, was unintentionally encourage a few people to raise their concerns to the late emperor."

She couldn't see his face under the mask, but she could imagine that Talaat was giving her a flat look. "You strike me as a clever young woman. You know very well that 'concerns' were not all that were raised to the Sovereign." He laced his bony hands over his stomach. "Tell me, if your parents' lives did not depend on the preservation of mine, would you kill me and run?"

Fen sat frozen, her heart hammering against her rib cage. Was this a trap? She considered keeping her mouth shut, but Onath had taught her that silence was an answer, too. It didn't seem like a particularly good one to Talaat's inquiry. "You're only the client of my captor. I'd probably just leave," she said honestly. "I've never killed anyone."

"When Onath sold me the protection of his supposedly best bodyguard, I assumed you'd be more . . . experienced." Talaat took off his mask to get a better look at her. Curiosity and surprise had lifted his bushy eyebrows. "Onath has his fair share of enemies, even for a magistrate with, let's say, unorthodox methods. I'm shocked you've never ended a life."

Fen snorted. "Unorthodox methods" was putting it lightly. Most imperial officials had obtained their positions through some combination of nepotism and flattery. Onath's path to his current administrative post, by contrast, was littered with bodies and bribes. But much like his brethren, his ambition was far from sated.

"I *am* Onath's best bodyguard," Fen protested. "I've dueled his entire guard of lictors. And won, every time."

Talaat waved a dismissive hand. "Defeating someone on the training mats and drawing blood on the battlefield are two very different things."

"Battlefield?" echoed Fen, forcing a chuckle. "There is peace. And even if there were not, I doubt anyone would do battle over you. Sir."

Talaat scoffed. "Peace?"

"The uprising died two decades ago, with Kira Moru." Fen spoke slowly, as if to a very small child.

"And yet, people continue to fight and die over the matter of her demise alone."

The only thing anyone in the empire of Enkaiia could agree on was how the bloodbath had begun and ended. Moru, great leader of the insurgent Broken Masks, and Yaryun Akitsuro, niece to the honored late Sovereign, had met to sign their marriage papers. Omiko Gatasan, daughter of the chief imperial advisor, had taken Moru's head. No one knew—and would ever know—what happened in between.

Imperialists proclaimed that Omiko was only defending herself and the princess from an assassination attempt. The Broken Masks—those that remained, anyway—declared that the noblewomen had attacked first. Whatever the truth was, to argue either in certain lands was to invite death.

"The leaders of revolutions are like the heads of a noboa," the messenger continued. "They always grow back. Moru was not the first great insurgent general, and she will certainly not be the last. And with this unending drought . . ."

Fen swallowed thickly. They were fast treading into dangerous waters. The drought did not exist. And if it did, it was just a turn of nature. A normal environmental phenomenon that would soon pass. Or the rebels were at fault for the drying riverbeds and the burning winds. Somehow. To insinuate anything else was tantamount to treason.

"The drought will pass," she said carefully. "In the meantime, every city has a storehouse. We have more than enough water and food rations to last the empire a century."

"Have you any idea how many of those storehouses are empty?" Talaat shook his head. "A thousand nations throughout the ages have fallen for lack of food."

Fen's stomach plummeted. This was sedition. She glanced out the window, the urge to flee swelling as a terrible itch between her shoulder blades. The land rolling by outside looked like a sweetcake that had been frying for too long: cracked and brittle and grayish brown.

"The Makers left the Accusers for a reason," she said, her tone flat. "We'll be fine."

Talaat snorted. "What do you know of the Makers?"

"I know they saved us. I know they gave us a new world."

"Yes, and then they watched as we made a ruin of that one, too." Talaat snorted. "Their Accusers are half myth, made real only when we step out of line. What reason have they to aid us?" His voice rose. "Those . . . *creatures* were sent to enforce the aliens' will, nothing more and nothing less. They're not even really sentient, you know. They say one once let a settler scientist take a sample—their cells look almost identical to our own, all bound by some sort of bioelectric network, but in culture they behave like viruses."

Fen shook her head, trying to throw off the messenger's rambling words as if they were drops of water. "They wouldn't just let us starve. Not after their masters saved us." She sounded as unconvinced as she felt. But if this man was a spy as well as a messenger, she wouldn't risk her life by revealing what she knew to be the truth.

"Perhaps I was wrong about you," Talaat said, frowning now. He donned his mask. "Perhaps you aren't clever at all. Why do you think Moru started a revolution with your parents? For excitement? So a few particularly fearless singers would dedicate an album or two to her? The people have been starving for decades. Moru might have been an idealistic fool, but she carried on the rebellion so that she'd never have to see another child waste away while the emperor held feasts that lasted a fortnight—while the rich and titled destroyed what little living land is left to us."

If Fen had been unsure that the man was a spy, she was certain now. He was far past mere insinuation. No true rebel would be bold or foolish enough to say such things aloud. Her heart beat faster at the thought of what Talaat might ask next.

"I suppose it's unfair to expect you to know all this, though." He crossed his arms. "You're an Ataa prisoner a thousand leagues from home."

It was a testament to the discipline of her training that Fen did not breathe out a sigh of relief. He believed her. Or at least he pretended to. Either way, she'd said nothing incriminating—and if his robes concealed a recorder of any kind, he'd have nothing to show the imperial spymaster.

"War is coming, Fenyyang," Talaat continued, "and there is nothing you or I or even His Majesty can do to prevent it."

## ALEKHAI

Alekhai had been having a just-okay week when his sister's assassins arrived. He'd been making the taxation rounds at his eldest brother's behest, a nothing job leagues beneath a chosen grandson of Oldearth. It was a task meant to get him out of the palace so the great and lordly Sovereign, beloved emperor of Enkaiia, could rule for a few days without Alekhai huffing down his neck. Or so Akrysanth had said. Fine, the forced outing gave Alekhai the chance to follow up on more interesting things than taxes and levies and tribute.

And now, finally, he was on his way back home from Bakrai, a minuscule shithole of so-called artisans who'd fallen far behind on their taxes. It hadn't taken long to figure out that the local chieftain had been pocketing most of the region's yearly profits, but getting her to admit it had been a royal pain in his royal ass. But he'd submitted his findings to the minister of finance, and hopefully someone who wasn't Alekhai would set things right.

For now, though, he was lounging on his personal barge, relishing the burn of the desert beneath the shade of an embroidered tarp. Though he rarely imbibed, he was nursing a crystal glass of iced vodka, turning his head every so often to nibble anata seeds from the painted fingers of the new friend he'd picked up on the journey.

Kacper was saying something particularly funny, Alekhai nipping at his thumb, when the skiffs appeared. The assassins had picked a good spot; the barge was trapped on both sides by two massive walls of sand, and the only option was to go forward or turn back. The skiffs slid down from the dunes like serpents, the hum of their engines echoing off the ancient rock. There were six or seven in total, each a rusted patchwork of ostensibly stolen parts. They hit the road just behind the royal barge, only meters away. Hoots of laughter grew as their vehicles closed in. One caught up to their right side.

The driver, a masked man with golden hair, spun the steering wheel and slammed his skiff into the barge. Kacper went right over the edge with a scream. Alekhai tumbled to his hands and knees with a hissed curse.

"My lord!" A Senmavar—one of only four guards Akrysanth had seen fit to lend him—helped the prince to his feet. Alekhai couldn't see her face through her mask, but there was real terror in her voice. "Are you all right?"

"I'm fine!" He spun around. Another ship was gaining on them. Fast. The royal barge was a predator, and the skiffs were prey. Why hadn't the captain shattered them by now? He yelled over the growl of the skiffs and the jeering of their drivers: "What are you waiting for? They're going to cut us off!"

At the bow, Captain Yuen Hua-Ambar gripped the steering wheel. Repairbots swarmed the controls. "The defenses have been deactivated, sir! We're working on it!"

Well, fuck. That explained why the assassins were still alive. No doubt Alekhai's little sister Sona had thought she could skimp on contract killers if she was certain his barge would be rendered a sitting mochen when they attacked.

"How long?" Alekhai barked.

Hua-Ambar jabbed a complicated pattern of buttons, her fingers moving lightning fast. "I just need a few minutes, my prince!"

"I'll buy us time!" Alekhai grabbed the nearest Senmavar. "Hand me your stinger."

They yanked the stun weapon from its holster and slapped it into his hands.

Alekhai spun toward the blond man and fired. He ducked as a fusillade of golden beams burst against the skiff's mast. The sails unfurled as a series of well-aimed shots undid the rope binding them, and the vehicle spun away, caught between the thrust of its engines and the push of wind. The crashed ship was soon replaced by two larger vessels, this time crammed with armed warriors. The skiffs scraped against the barge's gilded hull, sending sparks into the air.

"Prepare to board!" rasped a bald figure, drawing a stinger from their charcoal robes.

Enemy fire nearly skimming his hair, Alekhai dashed forward with the four Senmavari, shooting wildly as the assassins began to clamber up the sides of the ship. One managed to throw a grappling hook over the side of the barge, binding the vehicles together. Alekhai shot him in the shoulder before he could climb all the way in. Blubbering his pain, he went flying back onto the sands.

The barge slammed to a stop. Two rows of folded blades slid out from its sides, dislodging a quarter of the climbing assassins. Alekhai looked back at Hua-Ambar. She gave the command. The nearest skiff burst into a shower of scrap metal as the blades unfurled and whirled into the hull. The two ships behind it were cleaved in half. The remainder fled with almost comical haste, billows of sand puffing up behind the skiffs as they sped off into the desert.

"Excellent work." Alekhai handed back the stinger. "I'll be sure to recommend you all for promotion."

Hua-Ambar beamed at him. "Thank you, my prince. I would not have been able to get the blades online if not for your aim."

"Of course not," quipped Alekhai, striding back to his tent.

Hua-Ambar snorted; after years of service, she knew him well. "So what now, my lord? To the capital?"

"Not quite yet. We need to figure out who fucked with the defenses and skin them alive." Alekhai plucked up his fallen glass, refilled it with liquor, and flopped back onto his pillow heap. "But first, let's turn back and see if Kacper survived."

He really, really hoped the man had nothing to do with the assassination attempt. The bowl of anata had somehow managed to remain upright, and he needed someone to feed him the rest of his fruit.

The floatcar reached Talishminn on a cold, bright day. It was the end of the rainy season, though scarcely a few drops had fallen from the unforgiving cerulean sky. The floatcar carried them through the last few kilometers of the withered landscape surrounding the city.

Abandoned villages dotted the gray-green grassland, occupied only by ghosts. Hard times had forced many into the bigger settlements in search of food and work; Fen and Talaat passed growing parties headed for the same destination. There were commoners of all sorts: merchants and farmers, artisans and scholars. The only constant features were the state of their tattered clothes and the hollow looks on their faces as they watched the floatcar fly by.

As the sun reached its zenith, the pair passed the small salt lakes that had once attracted scores of tourists. Microbial pigment turned the open water of the lakes a scarlet as rich as blood, and the shallow fringes a deep gold-orange. Buildings painted in once-bright shades of blue came into view, curved frames hunched against the parched winds.

Without a word, Talaat dropped Fen off at the front gate of the magistrate's estate, one of the few structures that still retained a gleaming cobalt shine. She grabbed her satchel and hopped out of the floatcar without bothering to bid him farewell, her heart rate already picking up. The magistrate would be expecting her.

A silver beam from the gate ran up and down her right forearm, scanning the subcutaneous omnichip implanted there. It was the latest model sold by the imperial family, powered by the body heat it converted into electricity. After a moment, the gate swung open before her. Fen strode across the outer courtyard, her path curving around empty stone-lined ponds.

The magisterial estate was a tightly organized collection of round buildings with angular roofs, encircled by porticos and connected by narrow colonnades. The autonomous security measures—stun fields and metal spikes that would impale anyone with an unauthorized omnichip—were running at full power since she was the only guard home. Like the rest of the magisterial staff, Onath's official lictors were assigned by the palace. He trusted them about as far as he could throw them, and so he banished them on fool's errands across the empire.

Fen laid her quarterstaff against the wall, toed off her boots, and dusted off her coat before entering the magistrate's office. Though the room was small and low-ceilinged, it was uncluttered, and the glass doors on each wall were open to let in a breeze. A latticework screen stood before a row of large windows, slicing the afternoon light into golden ribbons as it fell upon the smooth wooden floor.

And at the center of it all was Magistrate Onath himself, draped in a simple tunic of brown cloth that shaded to yellow around the collar. Seated at an elegantly carved desk, Onath looked every part the imperial magistrate. He was a tall, thin man with a gaunt face that held deep-set eyes and a prominent nose many a sycophant had called aristocratic.

"The mission was uneventful, hm?" There was a datachip in his hand.

"Quite," said Fen, not moving from her place by the door.

With a pang, she recognized the seal on the datachip's gleaming surface. When had Talaat sent it? Yesterday? This morning? And with what, a courier drone? But she wouldn't have missed it; those things could drown out thunder. And did it say anything about her? Her palms dampened with nervous sweat. Even with all her frequent missions, she was unused to seeing information in her captor's hands that she hadn't gone through herself beforehand.

"Talaat tells me your presence was reassuring, at least until you told him exactly how untested you are." The magistrate shook the datachip at her. "He's probably already told half the realm. How am I supposed to convince these cowards they need my protection now, you little fool?"

Fen sat before the desk while he berated her. She stared blankly at his official mask, hanging behind his high-backed chair. It was a gleaming confection of black stone inlaid in bleached realwood. The destruction of a tree—even part of a tree—must have been extremely costly.

When he was done ten minutes later, she met his furious gaze and said, "Talaat said far worse than I. He spoke sedition."

"And you have proof of that?" the magistrate demanded.

"Well, no—"

The magistrate spat out a disgusted sound. "Then be quiet." He steepled his hands over his desk. "Keep your head down, do as I tell you, and *nothing* else." The corner of his mouth slanted upward. His smile was almost sympathetic. "The emperor who imprisoned you may be dead, but his son has not forgotten you."

Fen was dimly aware of her hands curling into fists, of her blunt nails digging deep into her palms. "I know, sir."

Of course she *knew*. Her parents' lives were on the line, and a very thin one at that. If she ever wanted to see them again, she'd do her job and do it well.

"If you say so." Onath stood. "I have errands to attend to. I'll be back at sundown. Have dinner ready."

Fen didn't ask what or who might be involved; she'd learned long ago that with much of the magistrate's work, it was safer not to know. She collected her quarterstaff and boots as Onath gathered up his things. Fen swung by her small house at the back of the estate to stow her things, and then headed for the kitchens.

Paranoid to a fault, Onath didn't have any house servants, believing them a liability on top of an unnecessary drain on resources. Why hire a cook and cleaners when he could extort free labor out of his hapless Ataa prisoner? Fen stomped to the fridge and started grabbing squishy orbs of raw ingredient paste from their carefully labeled drawers: vegetable matter, protein matter, carbohydrate matter, sugar, and so on. She input the proper commands for a three-course meal into the food printer, and then popped the ingredient spheres into the device one by one. The device beeped cheerfully and informed her supper would be ready in an hour.

Instead of heading back to her quarters, she sat on the edge of one of the empty ponds, dangling her legs over the side. Up until a few years ago, right about this time, the trees in the courtyard had begun to bloom, filling the air with delicate perfume. But now only bare, bent trunks sat in their enamel pots, and the air carried nothing but dust and decay.

Someone pounded against the gate. The structure was opaque from the outside but perfectly transparent from within; Fen turned to find an imperial messenger at the door. Her unfamiliar figure was tall and broad, but she wore a gray mask that would've been identical to Talaat's but for its paler hue.

Fen opened the gate. The messenger stared down at her from a humming floatcycle, a small parcel clutched in her left hand.

"Are you Lord Onath's . . . ward?" she inquired hesitantly. "Is the magistrate home? May I see him?"

"Yes to your first question, and no to your second and third. He'll be back at sundown." Fen leaned against the side of the gate. She held out a hand. "I'll put whatever it is on his desk."

The messenger shifted in her cushioned seat. "Perhaps I should come back later."

"Onath will be having dinner then, and he does not like to be disturbed," Fen warned. She cursed inwardly; she should've said he was in a meeting. But the chances of the messenger staying until the "meeting" was over had seemed too high to risk.

"I was ordered to ensure that Lord Onath read the missive myself." The messenger shook her head. "It's important. It *cannot* fall into the wrong hands."

Fen rolled her eyes. Obviously. The whole purpose of having human messengers, besides their ability to provide context, was safety. The imperialists were overcautious by nature; it was probably why they'd held on to power for so long. Any official letter that couldn't be sent over the omninet—secure though it was—held information that was both very important and very sensitive. Perhaps so important and sensitive it held intel about Ata, about her parents. The need to read its contents crawled over Fen's skin like an itch.

"Sundown, you said?" The messenger made to tuck the package back into the floatcycle's trunk. "I—"

"Look," Fen interrupted, pushing off the gate wall. Her gaze fell on the packages crammed into the trunk. "I'm sure you have at least three cities to hit before morning. You won't make it in time if you circle back, and then you'll have to explain to the imperial postmaster why you didn't deliver all this stuff when you were ordered to."

"But—"

"If you recognized me as Onath's ward, then you know exactly who I am," Fen said slowly.

"I do," said the messenger, just as carefully. "I know you're

Ataa. If this letter were to end up in the possession of your chieftains, I'd lose my head."

"The pompous fools in Ata are not *my* chieftains," said Fen. She pulled in her shoulders, made herself look meek. "If you know who I am, you know why I could never betray my host."

For many reasons beyond her parents. She had no one in the world to turn to for protection but the magistrate, despite not being here by choice. And in her own strange way, she trusted him. She'd always gotten the sense that he'd never been overly fond of her, but that he hated everyone else more.

"The postmaster didn't even tell *me* what was in it, only to ensure that the magistrate received it." The messenger's grip tightened on the package, but after a moment, she handed it over. "It's important," she repeated, before speeding away.

The gate slid shut behind Fen as she made her way to the office. She tapped her forearm twice and the omnichip dutifully spat out the time. Nearly four hours until sunset. That was more than enough.

Fen hadn't the slightest clue what was in the parcel, but she'd never left a single delivery to Onath untouched if she could help it. She set the package on Onath's desk and plucked up a letter opener. The surface was a perfect, unblemished white, marred only by tiny ripples where the wrapping met. With painstaking slowness, Fen sliced along the seams. She pried apart the covering and untied the ball of black spidersilk within. Familiar stabs of anxiety racked her body as her eyes fell on the strange creature emblazoned on the datachip inside: a sphinx in shimmering blue. Of all the imperial seals, only the royal family was permitted to use this one. Fen forced herself to continue. She'd done this a thousand times, though only twice with letters straight from the palace.

She held the datachip over her forearm until the omnichip replicated the information within. A holographic panel popped up above her bent arm. Fen spoon-fed the program a series of files that would satisfy the biometric protections: a scan of Onath's thumbprint she'd saved on a piece of glass, a three-dimensional image of his face, and finally a render of his irises she'd painstakingly stitched together from several dozen holoimages. She was rewarded for her efforts by the appearance of another screen. Now she could get to work.

The missive had been written in code, as much of the magistrate's official mail was. But she'd been decrypting since before she was old enough to print her own breakfast. What set her nerves afire was that the letter was written in a simple character-replacement cipher, nearly the exact same one she'd seen in a handful of other messages from the palace. Anyone could crack such a code by checking the frequency of each character. So the letter had come straight from the desk of the emperor himself. A more sophisticated encryption method might have required the involvement of technical staff. So whatever was in the missive wasn't official business. It was personal.

The cipher was a simple one: The letters had been shifted down three Standard alphabetical letters for vowels, and six for everything else. She typed in a few short commands with her other hand. A moment later, the complete deciphered letter appeared on the panel.

**My loyal servant Onath,**

**Former ambassadors Juma and Kagiso Mekantai suffered a tragic accident this morning. My personal physician detected small amounts of poison in their bodies. Unfortunately, the chemical composition of the toxin is such that all traces of it will vanish by the time their corpses reach Ata.**

**See that the daughter joins them.**

# 4

Fen felt something die within her.

Her arm trembled so violently that she could no longer read. Dread flowed into her, transmuting her limbs to lead. She doubled over the desk, her mouth open in a silent cry. Rapid, panicked gasps inflated her lungs as if her torso were a paper bag. She squeezed her eyes shut, gripping the edge of the desk. She breathed in, long and hard, through her nose.

*I'm not dead.*

*I'm not dead.*

*Yet.*

And if she wanted to stay that way, she needed to *do something*. She opened her eyes. The fear began to dissolve, leaving her shaking like a leaf in a tempest. Another feeling trickled down her throat, as the knowledge that she'd never see her parents again sank in. Not sorrow. *Rage.* Rage flared inside her gut, pulsing through the rest of her like a heat wave. Rage so hot and solid she nearly choked on it. Senmavari—the emperor's elite soldiers—had dragged her from her fathers' arms when she was only six. She hadn't even had the chance to develop strong memories of them. Gentle hands, laughter like tinkling bells, the warm softness of a realcotton blanket. That was all she had of them. That was all she would ever have of them. The emperor's people had promised her that after another five years of dutiful service to the crown, she'd be reunited with her fathers. And now that life—the life back in Ata she'd fantasized about, the life she'd thought she would live once she finally got her family back—was dust.

Without the threat of her parents' deaths, Fen was as free as she had ever been, and yet she felt as if a whole colony of myrma were crawling over her, biting every centimeter of skin they could find.

"What does it say?"

Fen jerked back as if punched. Blood leapt to her face and rushed furiously in her ears. "You're early," she whispered senselessly, as if she could change this, change anything. "You're never early."

The magistrate had moved so quietly she hadn't even noticed the door swinging open. He was looking not at Fen, but the mefabo set on his shelf. It was his favorite game and the very first thing he'd taught her. They'd spent hours playing at the end of each day, until the morning he'd decided she was old enough to pick up a weapon.

"What does it say?" Onath asked again.

When Fen didn't respond, he stepped a bit closer. Outside the window, Newearth's rings had just started to redden, tinted a blushing orange by the slowly sinking sun. The entire room was cast in deepening crimson light.

"*What does it say?*" Now his voice was very, very low.

He arched a brow at her, serene as the worthless, rainless cirrus clouds now drifting over the courtyard. "Judging by your expression," he murmured, "either your parents are dead or I've been instructed to kill you."

She said nothing.

The second brow lifted. "Both, then?" He dipped his head in what appeared to be genuine sorrow. "My deepest condolences."

Fen tensed, every muscle winding up for a fight as fear flooded over her. The magistrate had run all of her combat lessons himself; she knew very well how this would end. But instead of challenging her, he stepped back and threw the door fully open.

"Leave, then," he said. "I won't stop you."

What game was he playing? "You'll just hunt me down," Fen rasped, the words scouring her bone-dry throat.

"Why would I do that, when I could just snap your neck where you stand?" He chuckled pleasantly. "Flee now." He moved away from the exit, hands raised placatingly.

Fen took a single step toward the door, fear and hope warring within her. The magistrate stayed completely still.

She was almost over the threshold when he spoke again.

"Flee now," he repeated, "if you want to end up impaled on the capital gates. Or you can help me help you."

Though everything screamed at her to run away, Fen turned halfway around. "How?"

"We'll fake your death, and I'll give you the directions to your parents' allies. They'll help you escape to the very edge of Ata, where no imperialist will be able to find you."

"Allies? What allies?"

"The Broken Masks, of course."

Fen stared at him. When his expression remained perfectly serious, she let out a burst of strangled laughter.

"I am serious," Onath said. "Do you have a better idea? Or any ideas at all?"

The familiarity of his irritation snapped her out of it. He was a cruel, vindictive man; Fen knew that. But he'd never been that way with her. With her, he'd been all bark, no bite.

Was this truly her only option? Was she so helpless? But as the precious seconds ticked by, no alternate plan surfaced in her mind. She'd been preparing for this her whole life. But she saw now that every plot she'd spun up till this day was as thin as a length of spidersilk. If she tried to escape to Ata, as she'd originally thought to, the Senmavari would run her down before she was even within ten kilometers of the border.

"What first?" she asked.

Onath smiled. "Get your things, then go to the garage. I'll be there shortly."

And he let her leave unobstructed.

Fen rushed to her quarters. She stuffed all her worldly possessions into her leather satchel. In went two sets of clothes identical to the ones she now wore, a brown tunic over brown trousers; the pair of matching engagement bracelets Onath had told her he'd found tucked into her pocket when the Senmavaris had handed her over; a spare medkit; and a tiny green jar. And though she knew it'd take up valuable space, she tossed in a pouch of datachips with a few holobooks and pictures downloaded onto them. She dug through her hoard of the emergency ration packs she kept for long missions, and stuffed as many into her satchel as she could. After a moment of consideration, she twisted her quarterstaff until the segments loosened and slid together into a small cylinder. Extending it again would take a few seconds, crucial moments she might not have if this was all a trap. But some part of her, bone deep, knew it wasn't. She knew when Onath was lying: She'd seen him do it a thousand times, had learned each and every one of his tells.

She went to the garage. The magistrate was already there, along with three items: a corpse, a syringepad, and a commandisk. The floatcar's doors were open.

"Oh, good, you're here," he said. He pointed to the cadaver. "Help me get that in, would you?"

Fen gaped at the body. The dead woman was phenotypically very similar to her, unnervingly so. They were both tall and toned, with skin the cool umber of polished realwood. If Onath had told her this was her long-lost sister, she would've believed him. They had the same round, dark eyes and the same scowling mouth, so at odds with the rest of their soft facial features. The only obvious difference was their hair; the woman's was black and wound into very short twists, whereas Fen's storm-gray hair puffed down to her shoulders.

"Whose body is that?" she choked out.

"Does it matter? Grab the legs and I'll take the shoulders."

Tasting stomach acid at the back of her throat, Fen rolled up her sleeves and took hold of the corpse's ankles. The skin was like ice, the limbs unnaturally stiff.

*Oh, Eternal Mother.* Fen nearly dropped the woman. "Did you kill her?"

"Will it make you feel better if I say no?" Onath replied easily, as they dragged her onto the floatcar's smooth floor. "She stabbed an entire family to death and got away with it. No witnesses besides my spies, and I couldn't expose them. A model citizen besides, but no one gets away with murder in my city."

"And where exactly were you keeping her?"

Onath gave her a deeply unimpressed look. "The freezer in the kitchen isn't the only one on the compound, my dear."

Knowing the woman was a murderer did not ease the churning in Fen's gut. How long had Onath suspected he'd need a corpse to replace hers?

Onath stepped back out of the floatcar and picked up the syringepad. "I need a blood sample to fool the bioscanners. If we're lucky, and I always am, then they'll be set to confirm only your identity."

Fen ground her teeth together but held out her arm. "So you'll say I tried to hijack your floatcar? No one's going to believe I'd be stupid enough." Everyone knew government-issue craft were automatically set to self-destruct if tampered with.

"You'd be surprised what people will believe about their perceived enemies." Onath wrapped the syringepad around her wrist. Fen felt a small, sharp pinch as the white surface of the device darkened with her blood. Meanwhile, Onath's fingers flew over the floating, translucent screen his omnichip produced.

"There." He waved away the display. "I've disabled the tracking and information-gathering program on your omnichip and transferred your identifications onto our friend's." He threw an unsettlingly satisfied grin back at the body.

Onath peeled the syringepad off and tore it into a dozen tiny crimson pieces.

"So where exactly are my fathers' allies?" She couldn't bring herself to admit aloud that she was headed for the Broken Masks.

Onath jumped back into the floatcar and began scattering bloody bits of syringepad over the floor and seats. "There's a secret rebel base called Kanoh. One of many such hideouts, and far from the largest or strongest, but it's less than a week's hike from here—"

Fen drew back. "*Hike?*"

"I'd give you the floatcycle, but that'd be far too conspicuous. Plus, there are thousands of starving peasants wandering around the grasslands. You'll fit right in." Onath gave her a considering look. "You won't even have to dye your hair or cover your head, since gray is popular among you young people again for reasons I shall never understand." He chuckled to himself. "The emperor truly chose a fortuitous time to order your death. Give me your fathers' engagement bracelets."

Fen drew back immediately.

Onath rolled his eyes. "Come now. If I wanted those, I'd have them already." He held out an expectant hand. "And hold up your omnichip again."

Fen made herself reach into her bag and hand the bands over. She watched, tense, as Onath slid the two pieces together, forward and then backward and then forward again. There was a little beep, and then two matching rings of hidden lights lit up between the enamel segments. As the magistrate held the glowing bracelets over Fen's forearm, a shimmering beam slid over her face before she could blink.

Her omnichip chimed. The second she activated it, a new file popped up. A map, with a blinking red light indicating her current position and a solid green dot over her destination. Even reduced to a simple illustration of tiny tents tucked into a forest, Kanoh seemed so achingly far away.

Her heart flung itself against her ribs. Her fathers had made this map for her. It had been right there waiting for her this whole time. And yet. "I can't do this," she croaked.

Onath reached out, a comforting hand closing around her shoulder. Fen tried not to flinch; though the touch was soft, the magistrate had rarely treated her with such affection. She tried not to resent him showing this kindness only now.

"Very well," Onath said sweetly. "If you can't do it, you can take her place in the car. It's all the same to me."

That was more like it. Fen trailed behind him as he strode toward the back gate, which opened into the desiccated steppe.

"What about you?" she asked quietly.

Onath beamed at her. The last time she'd seen him smile that big was when he'd received the news five years ago that the rival candidate for his current position had been gored by a wild emerino on a safari. "What about me?"

"What if they find me before I reach Kanoh? If the emperor discovers I'm alive—"

"*If* His Majesty discovers you're alive—which he won't—I'll be long gone by the time he calls for my head." He clasped his hands behind his back. "I've been planning to leave Talishminn for a long while now, though the time for my exit has not quite arrived."

"Truly?"

"You've always been a decent student." Onath's voice took on a pedagogical cadence. "Tell me, what is Enkaiia?"

"Shall I tell you what the emperor declares, or what I believe?"

Onath sniffed. "Which do you think?"

Despite everything, Fen smiled. On this nightmarishly strange day, here was something she was used to. "The tribes were forced together long before I was born, and the empire spent its first years mired in a civil war. And things haven't gotten better, the clans within each tribe squabbling over matters smaller than grains of sand all as the world dies around us."

"And yet our esteemed leader calls himself *the Sovereign*. His predecessors conquered for glory. For the greatness of it all, so that their names would be remembered for a thousand myriads. But greatness is not the same thing as power, and what the imperials have is fragile." As they reached the gate, Onath made a rough, derisive sound low in his throat. "So I am a man whose power comes from what may soon be a powerless dynasty. What does that make me? The Synedria, the emperor's so-called 'guiding hands,' is elected by the people, but our rulers have heeded the councilors' words as much as they might heed the chirping of a newly hatched eryx. What does that make this new world of ours?"

His knowledge of her fathers' allies, the relative nearness of the rebel base to Talishminn, the casual treason of his speech just now . . .

"Are you a Broken Mask?"

"*Eternal Mother*, no," Onath gasped in affront. "But why have few friends when you could have many?"

"Then why—why are you helping me?"

"You're of more use to me alive, obviously. And now you're very much in debt to me." Onath smirked at her. "The more pots one has a hand in, the more likely one is to be fed. You're an investment, another sign of my, ah, acquaintanceship with the rebels, should they rise up again and somehow succeed in striking down our great Sovereign."

"So I'm just fresh meat. A sacrifice."

Onath laughed. "I'd say I'm sending you as more of a 'friendly gesture,' but yes. I *did* teach you well." He opened the gate before turning around to face Fen. When he spoke again, there was a roughness to his voice. "I knew your fathers, Fenyyang, better than I've let on. We were never *friends*, but . . . we had an understanding. If they were captured, if your life was at stake, I would take stewardship of you."

With a slow, careful movement, the magistrate cupped her cheek. Fen stiffened in surprise, her eyes stinging as she stared at the one person who'd ever come close to resembling family since she'd been taken away. This was so much in so little time.

"You should've told me."

"I know," Onath said. His gaze fell away with his hand. It was the first time she'd seen shame in the man's eyes. "But you know that I couldn't."

Before Fen could get another word out, he pressed the commandisk. On the other side of the estate, the entire garage exploded, flame fountaining into the deepening sky with a booming roar. A deluge of heat smacked into Fen, and she took a few stumbling steps back. Onath steadied her as sharp fragments of metal rained down a safe distance away. He let her go, but not before gently brushing stray hair out of her eyes. This time, Fen did not flinch.

"And that, my ward," said the magistrate, "is your cue to leave."

Scorching air scraped against Fen's skin as she trekked through a rustling sea of grass. Adrenaline had kept her awake all night, but as the distance between her and Talishminn grew, her heart gave up trying to tear itself from her rib cage and flee.

Sunlight stretched through the sky, striking flecks of useless white cloud. There would be no rain this week. Or the next. The waves around her glowed an eye-searing yellow. Not a speck of green. She couldn't recall laying eyes on anything truly green in the last decade.

Many people trod upon the same path as her, heading in the same direction. They had gray, grim, determined faces, and they kept their heads down as they tugged floatwagons over the terrain. Fen kept her quarterstaff collapsed and hidden within her satchel. The titanium-embedded length wouldn't pass for a walking stick, and she couldn't very well go gallivanting about the wilds with such a conspicuous weapon. She wished she could don a mask or dab on face paint to hide her visage, but only nobles and servants of the realm regularly sported such ornamentation, and commonfolk only wore either on special occasions. Rebels were known for throwing on masks and face paint to both mock the highborn and hide their identities, but it wasn't worth the risk. Even a dully painted face would stand out here. She couldn't imagine that a mob of starving commoners would be particularly kind to what looked like a roving official, or that an undercover Senmavar wouldn't hesitate to put a blade in the heart of a suspected insurgent.

A hundred fears filled her gut, wriggling over each other like worms and eating away at her insides. Her parents had been killed quietly; she could assume the emperor would want her death to be equally discreet. It was obvious now how little Ata cared about the affairs of anything that happened beyond its traditional borders, even if its own people were being killed off. The palace-appointed Ataa chieftan was as useless as the Synedria. She had to know what had happened to the ambassadors, but she'd continue to pretend otherwise so long as the emperor didn't have the bodies paraded about. At least Fen wouldn't have to worry about holoposters of her face going up on everyone's omnichip—yet, anyway.

Any of the migrants around her could be imperial spies, waiting for the perfect moment to strike. Or watching her, letting her lead them to the rebel base. Even a party of particularly desperate commoners might just gut her for what little she carried. She could take on perhaps five or six fighters at once, but any one of the larger groups she'd seen would beat her to a pulp. What if no one even had to lift a finger to see her dead? She could starve out here, die of thirst.

The sun no longer felt like a blessing on her skin. It was a curse now, scorching tendrils falling upon her face, her neck. Sweat spilled down the ladder of her spine, plastering her tunic to the small of her back.

Fen's vision flashed black for one terrifying second. Her breaths were coming fast. Her chapped hands tightened around the strap of her satchel as she stumbled, dizzy and disoriented.

"I have to stop," she said aloud.

Speaking felt good, even if there was no one close enough to catch the words. Just hearing her own voice was enough. It reminded her that she was alive. And to stay that way, she needed to take care of herself. There were no rocks or trees to provide shelter, so she sat down where she stood. She stuck a hand into her satchel, hoping the tall, crisped grass would shield her from prying eyes. She pulled out a hydration sphere from a ration pack and popped it into her mouth. Her teeth pierced the edible skin, and electrolyte-enhanced water burst over her tongue. She chewed through the skin, swallowing as she dug around for a nutrient bar.

Her hand found leather instead, and she drew out a pair of sturdy gloves. They'd come in handy when night fell and the heat of day fled. Or if she wanted to avoid leaving a trail of fingerprints across the empire. Onath must've slipped them in, the sneaky bastard. Fen caught herself smirking and wiped the expression from her face.

She found a bar and tore it open with her teeth. While she ate, she tapped her omnichip so she could take another quick glance at the map. But this time, when the implant spat out its holographic interface, her identity had been replaced. Her omnichip now identified her as a mid-level bureaucrat, important enough to move throughout the realm without being questioned, but low-ranked enough that any traveler she met wouldn't remember her. And there was money, more than enough for her to live comfortably once she was in Ata.

Fen silently guffawed. Was this the magistrate's way of apologizing to her for keeping her captive? She'd never faulted him for that; if not him, she would've been handed off to another official. And perhaps they wouldn't have allowed her chambers of her own, given her the run of the estate, handed her a weapon and trained her to fight. Granted, Onath had trained her so he could loan her out as a bodyguard. But the emperor's people could've found a much worse use for her. He'd treated her as well as any ill-tempered cutthroat of a government official could. And then he'd saved her life.

Fen chewed down the wrapper and set the gloves back in her bag. As she did so, her hand brushed the engagement bracelets she'd slipped in.

Two silver bands, decorated with bits of yellow enamel. This was all she had left of her fathers. Her fingers closed around the jewelry. The loss of her parents as a child was like a terrible splinter, embedded too far under her skin to ever dig out. The agony had faded with time, leaving her with only the stinging certainty that something in her life was *wrong*.

For a long time, Fen could do nothing but kneel there and breathe, staring at the fading enamel pieces. She was so, so alone. She covered her face with trembling hands, her whole form convulsing with a deep sorrow she didn't understand. She could barely remember her parents; why did their death agonize her? But she knew the answer, had known the answer even before the question had been posed. She'd worked for Onath, serving as ornamental protection for his clients for years upon years, to keep her fathers alive. To keep the hope of seeing them—of having a family—alive. As a child she'd promised herself that everything would be all right once they were all together again, and the years since had done nothing to dull that naïveté, only bury it. Deep down, she'd really believed they'd had a chance.

Rage and resentment; those were emotions she was well-acquainted with. Sorrow was an unwelcome stranger. She tried to dredge up a memory of her parents but found that for all her trembling efforts, she could gather no more than crumbling fragments sanded down by age. Images flickered into her mind, ephemeral: outstretched fingers, the curve of a smile. The visions vanished as quickly as they came, slipping from her grasp like handfuls of ash.

Fen stared at her clenched fists. There wasn't time for this. Slowly, slowly, she wrestled down her despair, shoved it away. She'd mourn later, when she was safe.

So she walked.

And walked.

And walked.

When the sun sank in the sky, she collapsed into the grass and threw an ultrathin thermal blanket over herself. Dark-shelled tshekar clicked angrily at her as she settled down under the stars, fingers gloved against the coming chill of night. Two of Newearth's tidally locked moons dominated the sky. This far from Talishminn, the two natural satellites didn't have to battle light pollution to be noticed. They hung bright and beautiful on opposite ends of the sky, one a waning crescent, the other a waxing gibbous perched just within the outer ring—a perfect match, two pieces of a celestial puzzle. Stars shone between them, the light of better worlds gracing the planet's skin.

There were fewer people traveling alongside Fen on the second day. As she crossed the unofficial border between the realm and the untamed wilds, she took out her quarterstaff. She swung it in a great, sweeping arc to extend it. Out here, between the cities and the forest, the imperial guard held about as much sway as the rebels: none at all. Large groups were few and far between now, and the fear of being arrested for waving around an unregistered weapon was fading fast. Anyone who tried to harass her would find nothing but a frayed temper and the blunt end of her quarterstaff.

Vast cenotes dotted the landscape. Limestone bedrock had collapsed here and there, leaving sinkholes that had once exposed groundwater. Massive semiaquatic carnufex, Newearth's version of Oldearth crocodiles, had once inhabited the shadowy pits. But their numbers had evaporated with the water, leaving only bones to tell their tale. Meter-high ribs surfaced from the grasses here and there, bleached white by the sun. Fen found them lovely in a melancholic sort of way. She couldn't imagine the grasslands supporting many of the great beasts for long. Had the skeleton to her right been the last of its species? Had it wandered the grassy oceans alone, crying out for its dead brethren as its world dried up? Her sympathy for the fallen creature took her by surprise as it melted into her self-pity.

Even a hundred kilometers from any of the many active wildfires, smoke hung heavy in the air as she lay down to sleep that night.

By the third day, the heat, unending trek, and bloodsucking bugs had left Fen dizzy, sore, and itchy. Every step felt like torture. She spotted ever fewer signs of human activity as she went on, bits and pieces of stories not her own. A circle of campfire ashes, soon to be swept up by the wind. A tattered scarf, undulating through the air. A shard of a glazed plate, its blade-sharp point peeking out of the sand. A pile of assorted detritus, dumped by a passing floatwagon.

At first, she'd been surprised by the refuse; she hadn't exaggerated the penalties of littering to Talaat. But she supposed the people she'd seen eating young grass to fill their stomachs didn't have the energy to care. And it wasn't as if the emperor would feign concern about the environmental state of lands overrun with rebels and worse. Fen had read gut-churning reports about a powerful new bandit lord violently absorbing rival gangs in the region.

At night, she spotted a flash of silvery blue bioluminèscence. She hadn't seen much in the way of fauna until now. She crept closer and closer, only to find that the source was a trail of myrma, their tiny backs coruscating with chemical light. She'd tried a handful of the candied insects at a festival years ago, but the bugs were notoriously poisonous if they weren't prepared correctly.

Fen followed the trail anyway, her stomach already rumbling. Another thing myrma were known for was finding the sweetest fruit. In less than half an hour, she came upon a clutch of dark purple anata bushes. Glossy cobalt blossoms unfurled under a trio of smoke-shaded moons. Fuzzy pollinators with iridescent compound eyes poked curling proboscises between the blue petals, while myrma dug into the rotting fruit below. At least five different species feasted together here. Life would survive the changes Newearth was suffering, Fen thought. Just not all life, and perhaps not the life that had brought about the changes in the first place.

When the Makers had whisked Fen's ancestors away from Oldearth half a millennium ago, they'd left terraforming technology to complete the transformation of humanity's new home. But the first settlers were impatient, and they'd forced an acceleration of the process. The consequences, unfolding over hundreds of years, were proving dire. The strict environmental protection rules placed upon everyday citizens did little to help the situation, not when the palace let noble-run corporations do whatever they pleased with the planet, and punished anyone who suggested the situation was getting worse. Not that there was anything Fen could do about it.

Six fat, shiny berries hung on the nearest anata bush. They were a delicacy she'd only heard about from officials who'd attended royal feasts. Fen twisted one off and flicked away the insects already inspecting it for harvest. With a grin, she broke open the bumpy skin to reveal one great clump of bloodred seeds, each bursting with sugar and vitamins. After three days of tasteless nutrient bars that left her whole mouth feeling gritty, she dug in with gusto. It was delicious, slightly acidic with floral notes.

As she tore open another, a whisper of wind ran through the grass. Fen pulled her mouth from the fruit and glanced around, eyes narrowed. When nothing happened, she returned to her meal, albeit a little warier. But though she tried to convince her brain not to imagine things, she couldn't help but feel there really was something moving out there, watching and waiting. She scarfed down the rest of the fruit in her hands and plucked as many berries from the bushes as could fit in her satchel.

She tapped her forearm. With only the omnichip's built-in flashlight to fend off the dark, she used her quarterstaff to draw aside a wave of grass. A dark blur of movement so fast she could barely detect it snagged her attention like a hooked blade. She whirled around, breath quickening as the steppe around her shivered. Perhaps the carnufexes weren't as extinct as everyone believed. A mature one would be too large to hide in the grass, but an adolescent might be able to. Ice pierced her heart as she imagined serrated teeth sinking into her skin. Her muscles seized up—

*No, no, get it together,* Fen snapped at herself. She exhaled slowly, fingers flexing around her weapon. She angled her quarterstaff so she could deliver a crushing downward blow, or, as a last resort, shove the middle of it between open jaws to keep her throat from getting ripped out.

The grasses right in front of her rustled. Before she could move, before she could even breathe, a flock of eryxes scuttled out, chirping madly. Fen breathed out a sigh of relief as the burrowing birds ignored her in their haste to partake of the fruit.

And yet, even as she curled up to rest soon after, she felt eyes on her.

On the fourth day, Fen saw no humans at all. Only desiccated shrubs and grass kept her company as she pushed on. Her thighs and calves screamed with exhaustion. Her shoulders ached horribly, and switching her satchel from one side to the other helped not at all.

Her movements could hardly be called walking anymore; she stumbled and swayed like a drunkard as the sun fried her back. She knew she should be taking more breaks, shut her eyes for a few moments, but she couldn't shake the vertiginous vulnerability that overcame her whenever she did. She felt detached from herself, like she was a distant spectator watching the Mother pull the strings of her puppet body.

Five white-feathered corags circled high above her, drawing steadily closer as if they expected her to keel over and die any moment. They were probably right; her fatigue had swelled into a mind-numbing ache. With the ache came nausea. She floundered whenever her boots struck even the smallest of stones, her gut trying to escape through her mouth.

On the second-to-last day of her journey, Fen came across a temple. She spotted the edge of a dark, peaked rooftop poking out from behind a hill to her left. She recognized the building for what it was. For a couple hundred years, everyone onworld had loosely worshipped the same god, the universe itself: the Eternal Mother. Religiosity had declined after the imperialists began cracking down on rebellious clerics, though the people of Eira in the east remained generally devout.

Newearth's sun lounged upon the slanted shingles; if Fen hurried, she'd make it there before sunset. Since the temple was almost certainly abandoned, she probably wouldn't find any edible food or potable water, but she still had more than enough, and at least she'd have shelter for a night.

Upon her arrival, she saw that the temple had once been a masterpiece of seamless white marble and pale-yellow realwood. Small buildings in various states of disrepair were scattered around the central worship hall. The walls were cracked, and many had crumbled under collapsed roofs. Broken solartiles dangled precariously from once-elegant eaves. Paint peeled off splintering gray doors. The pavement stones of walkways and staircases were fragmented and caked with dried mud. Fruit trees that had once shaded the grounds and sweetened the air were withered husks of cellulose and rot.

Fen made her way onto the veranda of the worship hall, avoiding the treacherous patches of soft, age-rotted realwood. Inside, a thick cloak of reddish dust wrapped itself around broken furniture and carved statues. Her sluggish footsteps stirred up the grime as she crossed from the first chamber into the next. Dry, crushed petals littered the floors; garlands of the seasons' brightest blooms had once been strung up on the exposed beams above. Stars were etched into every ceiling, though many chambers had been built without a roof.

The first six rooms lay stark and mostly empty—a glass goblet here, a painting there—but the last two were full of items both religious and secular. Thick tomes sat in neat stacks, alongside a small shelf of datachips in the corner. Scrolls draped themselves over low tables. Worn pallets with insect-nibbled blue quilts stood in careful stacks by the walls. Fen could almost imagine clerics going about their daily work, preparing to lead service or transcribing some sacred text.

It wasn't long before she reached the nave of the worship hall. Her eyes danced over solar-powered holograms flickering under the sinking sun. At the center was Oldearth, distant and fabled and dying. Fen passed a hand through a holographic fleet of tiny angular spaceships—the abandoning of Oldearth by the only ones who could afford to leave. She moved on, disrupting each transparent floating mural as she went. The biopods of Mars, the fragile habitats on distant moons, the floaters atop the rings of gas giants. Migratory stations tucked within the asteroid belt. Toward the far end of the room shimmered a row of oblong ships: the Makers. Next was the wormhole they'd summoned, its exit suspended just above Newearth.

And then there was the bestowal of the Benevolent Directives, the dictates meant to protect the fledgling human population. The Makers had known simply ordering humans not to kill each other would be ineffective. Instead, they'd tried to mitigate the inevitable bloodshed that would occur after they left by forbidding the weapons they deemed most offensive. Had they bothered to define whatever a "defensive weapon" was? No. But trial and error with trigger-happy Accusers lurking around meant that using projectile or high-powered deadly weapons was itself a death sentence. No slingshots, nor javelins, nor bows and arrows, nor trebuchets. And certainly no firearms. While far fewer died of intentional violence on Newearth than on ancient Oldearth, people had quickly resorted to using just about everything else. It hadn't taken long for someone to develop the stinger, a nonlethal stunning handgun.

Fen stepped around a holographic video. It was a growing record of the first hard decades on a half-terraformed Newearth, beginning with the establishment of the initial border. The Makers had decided to restrict humanity's expansion, but every few decades they extended the boundaries humans could live within. Then came the splintering of the progenitor colony into the four tribes, fracturing further throughout the centuries into countless clans. First the great democracies: Ophthia to the south, Ata to the west. Fen paused before the second hologram, sliding her fingers through the display. Her parents' birthplace was a land of gilded dunes and purple mountaintops, bone-white salt flats and glittering oases. If the Mother looked upon her with merciful eyes, then one day she'd see those sights herself.

She moved on. Theocratic Eira lay to the east. And finally Makhan to the north, once the laughingstock of the four tribes and now their master. Ever since his ascension, the old Sovereign had treated the constitution meant to bind him as a list of suggestions. The Synedria had stood by and watched their influence wane, and private companies had encroached into every aspect of life, following the example set by the emperor. The imperial family loved to brag about how the first Sovereign had invented omnichips, turning minor jewel dealers into billionaires almost overnight. But their true wealth and power came from selling the data their technology wrung from its users to other technocrats. And so it went.

By the time Fen reached the end of the worship hall, moonlight had begun to slip between jagged gashes in the outer screen doors. She passed the altar and stepped into the sacristy. She brushed her hands over the back wall, searching for the telltale seam of a hidden door.

Ah, there.

Fen smiled; she'd never thought Onath's obscure lesson on temple architecture would come in handy so soon. Or ever. She dug her fingers into the seam and pulled it open a crack. The wall split apart with a low groan, the two sides swinging on hidden hinges. The sacristy was still crammed with treasures. The clerics must've been forced to flee, to leave such relics behind. Silver-gilt offering dishes. Translucent spidersilk tapestries, woven from the fibers spun by a native arachnid-analogue. Vestments with semi-precious stones sewn into the hems. Tiny golden apotropaic statues of the Makers, or at least what clerics thought the aliens looked like. There were seven-armed tubes and serpents with three eyes, tentacled orbs and gaseous blobs. What a waste of precious metal. The aliens had never responded to such adulation.

Not that the first settlers hadn't tried. They'd hoped worshipping their saviors ardently enough would ensure that Newearth, humanity's last hope, would remain their home. The Makers had vanished after Makhan conquered the other tribes, leaving the world in the first Sovereign's hands. But their promise to return without warning left the tribes steeped in the fear that they might one day be pried from their home and shipped back to Oldearth, where they'd suffer the mercy of the warring corporate clans now ruling the old solar system. It was partly for this reason that few had ever dared to break any of the Benevolent Directives.

But mostly, it was the brutal justice of the Accusers that dissuaded rule breakers; those who broke the Directives never lived to tell the tale. Like most people, Fen had never seen an Accuser in the flesh. Alien constructs left behind by the Makers to enforce the Directives, the Accusers tore apart anyone found in violation of their masters' sacred laws, even if the victim had acted unwittingly.

Fen yawned, closed the hidden door behind her, and sat on the floor mat with a grimace. The woven fibers smelled as if something had crawled under it and died. And given the state of the place, something probably had. But she knew better than most that beggars couldn't be choosers.

She crawled into a corner, wrapped a holy tapestry around herself, and fell asleep to the susurrus of the smoke-smothered wind outside.

Fen awoke many hours later, head stuffed with spidersilk cocoons and mouth tasting like socks that had been worn for a week straight. The fuzziness faded as she stretched, but an itch soon crept up her back to take its place. The sort of nervous tingle that warned someone they were no longer alone. Or at least, that was how Onath had explained the feeling, because anxiety was either a flaw to overcome or a tool to utilize.

Immediately alert, Fen sat up and reached for her quarterstaff. She waited, tense and already starting to sweat. Nothing happened.

*Eternal Mother.* She settled back onto the ground. Her eyes had begun to flutter closed when she heard them.

Floatcraft.

At least four of them, judging by the volume, though the sound was still fairly low. For now. They'd be on her in minutes.

Fen rolled to her feet. She couldn't just wait around for whoever it was to find and slice her open like an anata, so she pushed out of the secret chamber, slipped through the sacristy, and crept into the nave. She ducked low and crawled over to the nearest window.

The hairs on the back of her neck stood at attention as she peered into murky morning darkness. She was right: Four floatcraft were parked in the temple courtyard. Twenty or so shadowy figures snuck around the buildings. The nearest wore a brocaded surcoat of deep gray over pleated black trousers. A sword hung at his side, sheathed for now. Blood curdled in Fen's veins as he turned in a slow, sharp-eyed circle.

His mask was blue. Pale, nearly white, but blue all the same. They were Senmavari, and the man prowling about just outside—no doubt their leader—was a prince. Judging by the pallor of his mask, he was a very minor royal, probably only a distant nephew of the emperor, but still.

Her grip on her quarterstaff tightened as anger welled up in her, sharp and burning. For all she knew, these could be the same people who'd murdered her parents, on their way to tie up one last loose thread.

But why in the Eternal Mother's name would the emperor send a *prince* after her? Fen gritted her teeth. The answer, whatever it was, didn't matter. If she'd managed to find this secret chamber, the empire's elite soldiers would, too. There was nothing to do but head to the back of the temple and make a run for it. She tore a scrap from a nearby tapestry, beat it against her leg to shake off the dust, and wrapped it around her face.

As she tied a knot at the back of her head, she heard the prince snarl, "Do whatever it takes to capture him, but I want him alive. Split up."

Him.

They weren't after her. The relief that shot through Fen was so powerful it was almost painful. But the danger was far from over. If they found her, they'd no doubt have questions for which she had no good answers. They might detain her, and all it would take would be a quick transmission to the capital of Ivytra to see her imprisoned for good. Or murdered, like her parents—

Footsteps.

Fen froze.

Someone was running clumsily along the side of the corridor outside, as if needing the cracked walls for support. As if winded or wounded. She'd bet what precious little she owned that this was the person the Senmavari were after.

Fen extended her quarterstaff and waited with bated breath. The door swung open with a screech, and the dusty toe of a boot peeked through the gap. Before the intruder took a second step inside, Fen swung her weapon at his legs. He managed to dodge the blow, stumbling away with his gloved hands held high.

Fen narrowed her eyes. She couldn't see a single trace of skin. He was tall and broad, clad in a loose, high-collared coat concealing everything from the neck down. What flesh that was not covered with cloth was plastered with elaborate red, white, and black facial paint.

Fen breathed in, blood pounding furiously in her ears. He was either a Broken Mask, a fugitive official, or a villager celebrating his birthday. Somehow she doubted it was the last.

The man's gaze skimmed down the length of her body before returning to her eyes, no doubt searching for weakness. And then, brazen as the stars themselves, he pushed her weapon aside and circled her. Perhaps he thought Fen might make a run for it herself, maybe even try to yell to the guards. The distance he maintained made her think he wasn't sure if he should try to stop her or let her go without a fight.

Well, she wasn't going to let him decide her fate. He took a single step forward but remained still after. A surrender?

No.

A challenge.

Before he had a chance to raise his hands again, Fen lunged at him and slammed her quarterstaff into the side of his head. Or at least she tried to. He spun aside in a blur, and her blow merely brushed his nose.

Fen took an involuntary step back when he looked up at her

with a scarlet smile. It was impossible to tell whether the red around his mouth was blood or paint.

"I could use your help," he whispered. There was a slight rasp to his voice, as if from a lifelong cold. Or perhaps she'd successfully broken his nose.

"What?"

He pushed back the shoulder-length brown hair framing his wide face. "I could use your help," he said again, wiping a rivulet of red from his nose. Blood, then. For someone on the run, he sounded absurdly insouciant, and as far as Fen could tell, the levity in his voice wasn't forced. Was he drunk?

"Absolutely not," Fen said. And then, because she couldn't help herself, "Why should I?"

"I was once a cleric," he said. His brown eyes held their bright, amused glint, even as blood crept down his chin. "And though that was a lifetime ago, my vows remain. I can do no harm."

"Try again," said Fen.

"Because you're a good person," replied the man, sotto voce. "And if I'm caught, they might want to know who whacked me in the face."

So if the imperialists found him, he'd make sure she went down, too. She could probably knock him out, but what were the chances that she could do so before he screamed? Fen breathed out through her nose, eyes closed. She didn't have a choice.

"Fine." The word leapt from her mouth before she could snatch it back, like a civerm wriggling out of clasped hands.

The fugitive let out a puff of air, like he'd expected her to argue.

"Follow me," Fen ordered. "There's a place we can hide—"

"Not on my watch."

Fen's heart pitched violently into her throat as she whipped around. A Senmavar stood at the end of the nave between them and the exit. A short sword was clenched in each hand.

"He's here!" the soldier yelled. "With a woman!"

Fen heard boots thudding against the wooden floor. Louder and louder and louder.

Sweat beaded on her face as the Senmavar drew nearer. She was balanced on the very knife-edge of terror. She couldn't panic. If she panicked, she couldn't fight, and if she couldn't fight, she was dead. But fear wrung her insides as her heartbeat quickened.

The Senmavar stepped closer. The stomps of approaching soldiers swelled. Fen squeezed her eyes shut for a second, though a part of her that sounded awfully like Onath screamed how unwise that was. *Breathe,* she willed herself. *Breathe.* She imagined her actions before taking them. Her eyes flew open.

She kept her eyes straight ahead, but she gave the fugitive behind her an order: "*Run.*"

He didn't move. With terrifying speed, the Senmavar leapt toward him. But her blade sank into the silk of a tapestry and not the sinew of her target, for Fen had yanked the fugitive away. It'd been like trying to move a boulder. *All that muscle,* she thought, *and for what?* She took the opening the stray blow made and struck out with her quarterstaff. The weapon slammed into the soldier's gut. She let out a gush of air as the wind was knocked out of her.

As the Senmavar sank to a knee, Fen swung the end of the quarterstaff into her head. With a groan, the soldier slumped to the ground and went motionless.

The fugitive grabbed Fen's arm and yanked her toward himself. Dragged forward, she stumbled over the woman she'd downed.

"Where?" he demanded.

Fen made herself swallow. "Follow me."

She took off, the fugitive right behind her. Soldiers rushed in, shouting a flurry of orders. Fen sped up, forcing herself past her limit. Military-issue boots thundered on tile as Fen and the runaway fled for their lives.

Then armored arms tackled her from the right. Fen dropped her staff out of sheer shock. *Stupid, stupid!*

She flailed desperately, her wild kicks striking nothing but air. The arms were crushing her. She gasped in pain. Just ahead, the fugitive spun around, mouth twisting. His fingers flexed indecisively as another soldier stormed in. Fen couldn't count on him to save her. She couldn't count on anyone. But that was hardly new.

She drove her free elbow backward, striking the hardened surface of the chest plate. The grip tightened on her. Her assailant panted harshly into her ear. She tried again. This time, she twisted her torso, pulling away with a sudden spasm, then drove her fist into the soft flesh of a throat. Her captor wheezed in pain. Their hold loosened, just for a second. Fen wrenched herself free. The soldier tried to make another grab for her, but she was faster.

She dove, grabbed her quarterstaff, and twisted around to jam the end into their neck. They flew back, gurgling in agony. Another Senmavar took their place in the next breath, and his sword clashed against her weapon. With a roar, Fen unleashed a storm of blows upon him, too fast to block or parry, and he collapsed, joining his fellow soldiers on the dusty floor.

If only Talaat Nagi could see her now—

A silent bolt of eye-searing light lanced across her jaw and sank into the floor at her side. Fen pressed a shaking hand against her cheek as the entire left side of her face went horrifically slack. A stun bolt. For the first time in her life, she was acutely grateful for the Benevolent Directives. If that had been lethal . . .

She shook off the numbness and scanned her surroundings, to no avail. The shooter was outside, aiming through one of the windows. Another guard ran in. He lunged at her, swinging an axe toward her neck. Fen parried his first four blows, stun bolts slicing through the air around her. Then she pivoted and swung her quarterstaff into his stomach. He was better armored than the others—the blow did little to incapacitate him. But it did push him right into the line of fire, and a beam landed square in the middle of his temple.

She looked up, panting hard. Stun bolts bursting at her heels, she rushed toward her useless new ally, now pressed against the wall by the doorway. The shots cut off abruptly; she was out of either sight or range for now. Hopefully both.

"I told you to run," she panted.

"I can't," he growled. "Four or five are lying in wait outside."

*Shit.* They'd have to hide after all. She shouldn't have snuck out in the first place. *Stupid, stupid, stupid.*

She ran past the altar and toward the sacristy.

The runaway spun and looked at her askance. "It's a dead end!"

"Not quite." Fen drew open the hidden chamber.

He shot her a brilliant grin before diving inside. He poked his head out when she didn't follow. "Come on!"

"Shut up!"

Fen shoved open a window on the wall opposite the doorway, hoping it would throw the Senmavari off their scent, and jumped in. The moment the door swung shut, she pressed her back against the wall. She slid to the ground as she tried to slow her breathing. Hard stone dug into her shins as she sucked in gulp after gulp of air.

The runaway sat slumped on the opposite side, staring at her and breathing heavily as the sound of enraged voices rose. He tilted his head up, pinching the bridge of his nose to stop the flow of blood as footfalls sounded outside the hidden room.

"Mother damn it," a soldier swore. "They went out the window."

Then the soft chime of someone activating an omnichip. "Run another perimeter search," another voice ordered.

"Sunan is going to be pissed," muttered the first Senmavar. "If I lose my promotion, I'm going to stun *someone's* ass off."

*"His Highness,"* corrected the second, but their voice was weary, like this wasn't the first time they'd had to remind their companion. "Let's just go out into the courtyard, pretend to poke around so he doesn't know we're the ones who lost him."

They left, dragging their feet as they went. Fen barely managed to swallow the wild peals of laughter bubbling into her mouth. She'd nearly died two, three times back there.

The minutes crawled by. The fugitive straightened. He lifted his hands in a placatory gesture when Fen gripped her quarterstaff, useless as it would be in such a confined space. When she didn't try to smash his face in again, he plopped down beside her on the floor.

After a moment, he turned a bit and reached a hand toward her shoulder.

Fen immediately smacked him away. "What do you think you're doing?"

The runaway lifted his brow, the picture of innocence. "You're injured."

Fen brought an unsteady hand to her shoulder. Sure enough, her fingers came away red. As the adrenaline thrumming in her veins drained away, pain sank into her muscle. The cut was shallow, but if she didn't deal with it soon, it'd get infected. She winced as she rummaged around in her satchel for the medkit. She popped it open and pulled out an antibiotic restorative patch. She pulled down her collar, tore the wrapper open with her teeth, and slapped the patch over the cut.

Fen looked back at the former cleric, pondering why a small army of imperial guards, led by no less than a prince, was after him. But Senmavari were after everyone, and she was too tired to wonder in silence for long. Getting some idea of what he'd done would help her figure out how to deal with him.

"So you're a bandit."

Suddenly, the amused glint was back in his eyes. "That's rude."

"Well, you look like a bandit."

"Hasn't anyone told you that you shouldn't judge a holobook by its coverscreen?"

Fen sighed. "So what did you do?"

When the runaway wiped at his face, some of the paint came off with the blood and sweat, though not quite enough to reveal skin. Some of the mischief in his eyes bled into his smile. He drew in a deep, long-suffering breath and shook his head.

"Nothing, really," he said, resting his chin on the palm of a wide gloved hand.

"Really?" Fen deadpanned.

"Really," he confirmed. "I stole from a magistrate. Her people were starving, and yet she somehow managed to keep herself and her husband glittering with silver."

"That's punishable by execution. Death by a thousand cuts is the standard method, if I remember correctly."

The fugitive shrugged and swept a hand through the air, waving her words away as if they were biting insects. "I robbed a robber. That makes me a hero," he concluded.

"Sure, but it'll also make you a corpse," Fen replied, even as her lips curved into an involuntary smile.

It was then that she realized how close her face was to his. At this distance, she could pick out some of his features, even under all the curling crimson and black pigment: thick brows above high cheekbones above an angular jaw.

The hum of retreating floatcraft filled the space before rapidly fading away.

"I think," said the fugitive, "we can go out now."

Fen might've been inexperienced, but she wasn't a fool. "There's only steppe outside. We'd be completely exposed. It makes more sense for them to leave a couple behind to catch us when we come out."

The runaway shook his head. "They have a deadline. It was

now or never. And the prince is an idiot. He'll want to return to the palace to lick his wounds. They won't be back."

They stood and headed for the secret door.

Fen wouldn't have risked it ordinarily, but the hum had been just as loud as when the vehicles first approached, so she was fairly sure all four transports had left. Hopefully with the whole Senmavaris squad inside them.

The runaway pushed through the door and used a foot to flip an overturned chair upright. He draped himself over it as if it were a throne.

Fen strode past him toward the window to scan the temple grounds. Finding them empty, she moved toward the exit.

"Oh, you're going?"

Fen fixed him with what she hoped was an appropriately incredulous look. "Well, yes. I didn't see anyone, but they could circle back at any time."

He caught her wrist as she reached for the door handle. Fen twisted around and quickly broke his hold with the quarterstaff.

"I owe you my life," he said, voice perfectly serious as he shook out his wrist.

Fen swallowed a groan. In the northern tribe, a life saved was a life owed, and that sentiment had spread across the empire. Stupid Makhanish and their stupid honor. "I want nothing from you," she said.

"I owe you my life," the former cleric repeated stubbornly, "a debt I mean to repay in full."

"Oh, I'm sure." Fen opened the door. "I don't want your life."

"I'm serious," he insisted, rising from his seat. "My mother raised me with honor. To not repay you would sully her memory."

Fen swung her quarterstaff between them, keeping the fugitive at bay with his back to the window. Outside, beyond the temple's low outer walls, the sun had clambered up the faraway mountain ridge. Its glare slowly but surely warmed the planet, burning through the smoke hazing the summit. And below the mountains, Fen glimpsed a long stretch of gray-green treetops. Between her and the woods were kilometers of rolling, dying fields.

She met the fugitive's gaze and said nothing.

"Please," he whispered.

Eternal Mother. She didn't have the energy for this. "Fine," she said. She ran her tongue over her teeth, thinking. Onath's words blew over her like a winter breeze.

*You're very much in debt to me.*

"If we ever cross paths again and I ask for your aid, you cannot refuse," she said.

*There.* They'd never meet after this, so she could go on her merry damned way, and he could run off to whichever crumbling village would shelter him, patting himself on the back all the way.

The runaway held out his wrist and waited expectantly for her to do the same. Custom dictated that oaths be sealed by a kiss on the wrist, just above the vulnerable ulnar and radial arteries, as a sign of trust.

"No."

"But—"

"I said no."

Thankfully, he relented. He bowed low and stepped over the threshold. Outside, he ducked under the worship hall's stairs and dragged out a floatcycle. He turned it on with a few rapid taps to the forearm. Lights blinked on in quick succession as the front wheel slid out from under the frame. Once the vehicle was back to its regular size, the fugitive dropped a boot atop a foot peg. He levered himself up over the seat in a single elegant motion.

Fen descended the steps. "Why did you stop here if you had *that*?"

"Couldn't outrun them. This baby's saved my ass more times

than I can count, but it's an old model." The runaway patted the handlebar lovingly. "I can't get rid of it, no matter how slow it gets. Also, Oldie was retrofitted from a Senmavar floatcycle, so it's hidden from their scanners."

*Good grief.* She didn't care.

The runaway revved the engine. "Safe travels, friend!" he called.

"I'm not your friend!" she yelled back.

But he was already driving away, yellow dust puffing up in farewell.

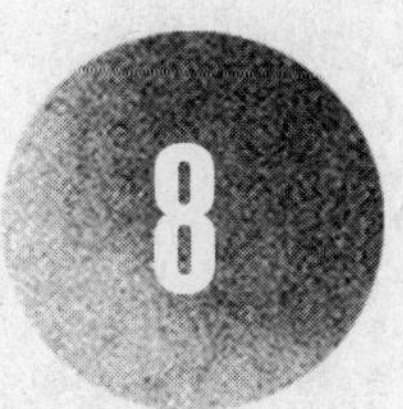

The sky was dark when Fen reached the edge of the woods, even though nightfall was still far off. The air was swirled with bitter gray smoke, hazed by the distant brushfires as they grew further out of control. Still, the sun managed to beat down on her, the blaze still finding its way through the blurred atmosphere. At least the view directly ahead was clear.

Thousands of trees clawed their way up from the dry dirt, their once-proud trunks now shriveled and bleached. Ominous shadows cavorted in the expanding darkness between them.

Fen stood before the forest, trying to scrub away the itch of sweat breaking out over her entire body. A sense of dread completely unrelated to the wildfires filled her gut. According to her map, she was practically on the Masks' doorstep. What if the rebels didn't take her? What if they decided she was more trouble than she was worth? They might very well slit her throat and be done with it. No one would ever know. No one was left to care. If Onath found out, he might even mourn her in his own way, but his way was brief and sharp and bloody. With every second Fen spent standing there, a hand tightened further around her throat.

She almost turned around. She wanted to go back, but there was nowhere to go back to. She had no home beyond the one she was promised in Ata.

She walked into the woods.

The world here was even quieter than on the steppe. There was no birdsong, nor the chirp of tshekar. The trees, shrunken though they were, quickly smothered any wind that found its way in; not even the hiss of a thirsty breeze snuck through.

A few hours' trek took her to the bottom of a massive cliff face. Besides the hardy yellow shrubs poking up here and there over its dolomite haunch, there was nothing of note. Fen's heart gave a nervous squeeze behind her ribs. A third, and then fourth, glance at the map confirmed she had reached the rebel base. She jumped when she heard a soft peep, the first sound she'd heard that she herself hadn't made. A spiny tapcrab launched itself off the cliff with its ten spindly limbs.

It was only by tracking the creature's scuttling path into the dirt that she caught a glimpse of a figure between the trees. Her heart flew into her mouth. Shadow hid their features, but they were taller than her, broader than her.

"Hello?" she called, pushing aside a thin wasted branch for a better look. Her other hand tightened around the quarterstaff.

No answer.

They were gone a heartbeat later, dissolving into the darkness, silent as death. It was as if they'd never been there at all. She pressed a hand to her temple, her stomach giving a nervous kick. A hallucination? But this time, her intestine-twisting fear was not misplaced.

Fen barely caught the glint of a broadsword flashing through the air. She swung her quarterstaff just in time to block a blow clearly intended to behead her. Her injured shoulder roared with pain.

Eternal Mother, she was tired of meeting people like this.

"Who are you?" she demanded.

Her attacker's only response was to shift their weight down

upon her through their blade, still braced against her quarterstaff. Fatigue had already worn Fen down. Her arms were still buckling from the initial strike; she couldn't keep this up.

She slipped out from under them and swung down toward their exposed ankles. Her assailant dove to the right, avoiding her blow. They struck out again with their sword. Fen deflected with the end of the quarterstaff, but only barely. If her weapon had been any less than it was, their sword would've shattered it.

Hidden fauna began to hoot and screech, jeering at her. Fen leapt away from her attacker, putting as much space between them as possible in a single move. They didn't close the distance immediately. Instead, they began to circle her. Pinned at the epicenter, Fen crouched low and searched for any vulnerability she could exploit with her weapon's longer reach.

*There.* Their posture was slightly hunched, as if curled in around an injury, though she couldn't pinpoint the exact location. On the offensive, Fen threw herself forward and swung her quarterstaff with all the strength she could muster. Her assailant moved, but not fast enough. Her weapon caught them mid-jump, sending them tumbling to the ground. The broadsword slipped from their grasp as they fell. Fen kicked the weapon away. She jabbed her quarterstaff at her attacker's neck in a strike meant to crush their trachea. She stopped right before the blow landed.

Panting, the stranger lifted their hands, their fingers spread in surrender. "You're quite good." Their voice was perfectly flat, but she saw blood rush to their tawny cheeks.

"I know," Fen snapped. "I'll ask once more. Who. Are. You?"

They paused, pushing a handful of brown curls from their brow. "Who're *you?*"

"*I'll* be asking the questions here. Why did you attack me?"

Their gaze darkened. "You're an imperialist. And if you're here, you already know far too much."

"I'm no imperialist," Fen growled.

"Don't bother. Your peasant disguise could use some work; the cut of your clothes gives you away. I know you're a spy, and I'm not going to give anything or anyone up." They lifted their chin, leaning over to press their neck to her weapon. "So go ahead. Do it."

That confirmed it. "No need for dramatics, I won't hurt you. You're a Broken Mask." Fen stowed her quarterstaff and stuck out a hand.

They scoffed, ignoring her gesture. "What I'm *not* is a fool," they said carefully.

She took a measured breath. "My name is Fenyyang Mekantai."

The rebel looked at her blankly. "Am I supposed to know who that is?"

"I'm—I'm the daughter of the Ataa ambassadors."

A kernel of recognition surfaced on their face. "Show me your biofile."

Fen did as they asked. But instead of her information, up popped the ID of the imaginary mid-level bureaucrat Onath had fabricated for her. *Oh, Eternal Mother.* She'd forgotten.

Still on the ground, they shifted back, gaze flicking to their blade.

Before they could make a grab for it, Fen blurted, "Wait, it's fake! So I could escape." Her free hand flew over the holographic screen, trying to access some other proof. *Shit, shit, shit.*

The rebel's eyes narrowed.

Fen gave up. "I swear. Just look up my parents."

Their shoulders tensed. They were going to lunge for their sword, and Fen would have to fight them all over again.

"Please," she said, "just do it."

"Either you're telling the truth and an idiot, or you're a spy and an idiot."

Against her better judgment, she held up both hands instead of grabbing her quarterstaff. "The palace doesn't employ idiot spies."

They looked thoughtful for a moment. "A good spy can play a fool."

She let out a humorless laugh. "Don't overestimate me."

With a sigh, the rebel activated their omnichip and summoned up a profile of the ambassadors. Fen flinched as their faces appeared. She'd looked up her fathers on her own only once since their murder; why torture herself with something she could never have again? But now she found every fiber of her being focused on those hauntingly familiar features: faces and eyes in varying shades of brown; a square jaw and a round chin; a gentle brow and a heavy one. The white river line, the ceremonial symbol of adulthood, ran across each of their noses. Facial markings were an important part of Ataa culture, not that Fen's parents had been around to show her.

The imager had captured two men who looked like they could take on the world. They had. And they'd died doing it.

The rebel lifted their arm and passed the hologram over her face so her fathers' features flickered over hers in turn. Both omnichips gave a happy chirp, confirming that both of the ambassadors' biofiles had a partial match with Fen's, wherever it'd been stored.

"All right, you're their kid," the rebel said. "So what?"

Fen offered her hand again. After a moment of hesitation, they took it, and she helped them up.

"I need you to take me to your leaders. I have to ask them to—"

They cut her off with a sharp shake of their head. "You can't just waltz in and demand favors. Your *dads* are sympathizers. They helped the cause when it suited them and were imprisoned for it. The Masks are all very grateful, I'm sure. But that doesn't mean you aren't an imperialist pet." Their brow furrowed. "I don't trust you."

Fen bit the inside of her cheek. "They *were*."

"Pardon?"

"They *were* sympathizers. The emperor just had them killed." She swallowed thickly. "My guardian told me that if I came here and asked your comrades to help me, they would. My parents aided you, and now I'm asking you to do the same for me."

The rebel pursed their lips, tapping their foot in thought. "Give me my sword back, and we'll see."

Fen gritted her teeth. What choice did she have? She snatched up their blade and held it out to them hilt first. They reached out slowly, as if about to pet a feral lema. When Fen didn't yank the weapon back, the rebel pulled it from her grasp. They didn't sheathe it right away. For a long, blood-chilling moment, they just held it where it was, the glinting point positioned at the center of Fen's chest.

"Go ahead," Fen rasped, echoing their words. "Do it."

"You're insane, Fenyyang Mekantai." They stared at her. "My name's Ihazan. I'll take you to the captain, and you can bring your case to him yourself." They held up a warning finger. "If you *are* a spy, then we'll figure it out. And you should know we don't take prisoners."

"Fair enough." Fen crossed her arms. "So where is it?"

With a sly grin, Ihazan—if that really was their name—used that same finger to point upward. Of course. Onath had once told Fen that people looked around and under but rarely upward. She'd never considered that the same rule might apply to rebel strongholds.

Ihazan reached over and tugged aside one of the shrubs clutching the cliff face, revealing a horn hooked beneath the foliage. They lifted the instrument to their lips and blew hard. Once, twice, thrice, and then again in a long, low tone. What followed was a complex array of notes Fen could barely follow. And then, as if that weren't enough, Ihazan reactivated their omnichip and entered a long string of symbols into a flashing holographic box.

After a few tense moments, two ropes with looped footholds at the ends came tumbling down though the leaves.

"Grab on," Ihazan said, gripping the nearest cord. "They go up fast."

Fen stuck her right boot into the loop on the next rope. "What's all the music for? Aren't you worried someone might hear?"

"It's an extra layer of security," they said. "The imperialists love using Oldearth techniques, but they'd never suspect us of doing the same. And no; as I'm sure you've discovered, the woods drown out sound almost immediately. Something about the trees. The only place sound travels is up. You could have a whole concert here, and someone ten meters away wouldn't hear a thing."

Fen wasn't convinced; that sounded just like the foolish traditionalism the Broken Masks lambasted the imperialists for. But she wasn't about to fight anyone over it, not when they had just agreed to help her.

"Ready?"

Fen nodded, bracing herself. Ihazan tugged thrice on their rope, and the pair went flying upward, Fen yelping in surprise. In seconds, they were cutting right through a tunnel in the canopy, leaves whipping past them in a dark blur. Though the foliage was withered and thin, there was so much of it that after a few moments she could barely spot a single patch of ground below.

Their ascent slowed gradually, and they came to a surprisingly gentle stop before a platform of bound branches and wooden planks. Fen's jaw fell as she took in her surroundings. The rebel base was a huge lattice of reinforced realwood, dozens upon dozens of lopsided buildings connected by a rickety web of walkways and ramps. Each structure had a low roof with extendable ladders going up the sides. And there were people everywhere, all armed to the teeth. They dueled on platforms and hammered planks of wood together, pitched tents and dragged crates she could only guess the contents of.

A man in mismatched bits of armor stood on the platform. He gave Ihazan a sharp, questioning look as the young rebel stepped onto the platform.

"A friend of friends," Ihazan said, tilting their chin at Fen. "That, or our new training dummy."

Fen, still gripping the rope, swallowed hard when the man let out a rough laugh. He nodded and let them aside.

Ihazan turned around. "Come on!" They offered her a hand—a truce?

Fen made herself take it. "How—how did you build all of this?"

Ihazan grinned proudly. "Our ancestors called necessity the mother of invention. They were right."

Together they wove over branch-framed gangways and bridges, ducking and diving under a sky of fluttering leaves. Fen squirmed under the gaze of Broken Masks going about their business, nervous anticipation trickling into her gut like a handful of hot sand. The anti-imperialists wore all manner of dress: probably purloined spidersilk tunics; improvised armor made of high-strength synthetic fiber; and even robes fashioned entirely of hastily stitched scraps. The whole thing yanked at Fen's nerves. The rebels didn't look like some great army of liberation. They looked like angry people who'd suffered a lean year or five. They looked like they'd dragged themselves from the edges of the empire in search of bodies to sheathe their blades in.

They looked like bandits.

Fen tugged on Ihazan's sleeve. "How many armies are there?"

"That depends on your definition of army, but not many." They gave her an odd look. "You've heard of others?"

Fen gaped at them. "But Moru commanded thousands of people—tens of thousands!" The handfuls of sand in her stomach were more like buckets now. "How many are here? A hundred people? Two?"

"Two hundred and fifty," Ihazan said tightly. "For the daughter of the ambassadors, you've missed much. The emperor hunted down Moru's allies."

"I know that, but—"

"But what? All you know was probably forced down your throat by the imperialists' so-called historians. The former emperor promised to spare rebels that surrendered, but it wasn't long before he went back on his word. Did you know he eradicated whole bloodlines? Nine familial groups were executed for each captured rebel."

"How is that even possible?" Fen whispered.

"In addition to the normal parents, grandparents, and children killed, they murdered their siblings and cousins, their spouses and all their in-laws—"

"All right, I get it," Fen said. "Sorry."

"The point is, the ones that escaped hid themselves so well that we were never able to find them. And even if we could track them down, they'd never risk fighting again." Ihazan bit their lip, sliding out yet another ladder so they could clamber up to the next level. "There won't be another standing rebel army, not until we show we can take on the Sovereign and his forces. But we can't do that until we have . . . well, a standing rebel army."

"Then what are you all doing? I've seen the official reports. Magistrates whisper about you all like you're truly a threat."

"We *are* a threat. Just a small one, for now. We're limited to guerilla fighting, cutting off supply lines, picking off stray bands of soldiers, that sort of thing, while we rebuild our strength."

*Oh, Mother.* They really were bandits.

"Up here." Ihazan scurried up a rope and pulled themself up onto a level that stood above Fen's head.

She followed them up. A large octagonal tent had been pitched on the platform ahead. Baked clay amulets dangled from black ribbons looped along the roof. A pennant was pinned above the painted door, a sinuous dragon clawing apart the imperial sphinx over a field of anti-imperialist green. Two cloaked Broken Masks stood guard outside the entranceway. They nodded in welcome.

One of them, a short woman with a knife-sharp blond bob, cocked her head at Fen. "Ihazan, who is this?"

So that *was* their real name.

They gestured at Fen. "This is Fenyyang Mekantai. She's—"

The other guard lifted his bushy brows. "Mekantai, as in the daughter of the imprisoned Ataa ambassadors who just killed themselves?"

Fen flinched.

Ihazan glared at the guard. "Don't mind him. We always find him with his foot in his mouth." They looked back at Fen. "Well, I see I'm almost as ignorant as you, Fenyyang."

"Is that what they're saying?" Fen asked the guard, ignoring Ihazan. "They were assassinated by order of the Sovereign!"

"Well. Barra will certainly want to see you." The first guard pushed open the door, revealing a collection of shadowed, shifting forms. "Go on in."

Surprise dropped into Fen's gut like a stone, despite her former eagerness to finally come face-to-face with the leader of the Broken Masks. She took a startled half step back. "Wait, right now?"

"Yes, Mekantai, right now," said the second guard.

She forced herself to focus on her heartbeat, carefully measuring the rapid thumping of her pulse until it calmed. "It's just Fen." She handed her quarterstaff to Ihazan before they could demand it.

Ihazan still extended a hand. "Any other weapons?"

"No, that's all. Don't lose it." Fen drew herself to her full height and walked through.

It was stiflingly warm inside the tent, despite the windows cut into the cloth walls. The interior was illuminated by archaic globelamps, solar powered and fireproof but infamously inefficient. War masks of steel and bronze lined the tapestried walls, leering down at her from makeshift stands. Below them sat nineteen rebels lounging in a half circle around a realwood throne. And upon that throne reclined the man who held Fen's life in his hands.

The room swayed. She staggered forward, dragged a few desperate breaths into her shrinking lungs, and knelt on the floor.

Fen choked down the great lump in her throat and spoke. "Sir, it is an honor to make your acquaintance. My name is Fenyyang Mekantai—"

"Yes, yes. It's a tent; the walls are thin. I heard some of that." The captain grinned down at her, baring all his teeth. The expression stretched the scars crisscrossing his chiseled face. He thumped his broad chest. "Captain Barra Jin Sherida of the Broken Masks. My condolences. Juma and Kagiso Mekantai were good men. Rise." His voice resonated through the room, his words heavy with command.

She did as he bid. "Thank you, sir."

Even seated, Barra towered over Fen. She made herself meet his gaze, even as she felt the interest of the other rebels sink into her like claws. His blue eyes were unfocused, and despite the distance, she could smell his alcohol-sour breath. The glass wine gourd in his mighty fist was nearly empty. *This* was the leader of the Broken Masks? He looked like a soldier, certainly, but the pleasant blankness of his expression worried her more than anything else she'd seen that day.

Barra sat back in his seat, scratching at his chin. His jaw could probably shatter iron. "So what, exactly, do you want?" The words were slightly slurred.

"After my parents . . . after they were *murdered*, my guardian advised me to ask for your aid," she said, trying to keep her voice steady. "Sir, I need help getting to Ata. All I ask is that you help me evade the Senmavaris until I reach it."

"There are songs about how your parents saved the life of our beloved Kira Moru." Barra drained the rest of his wine. "Not any songs you would know, of course." He blinked blearily down at her. "A life saved is a life owed, young Fen. We can spare two from our forces, small though they are."

"No, we can't."

Every head in the room snapped around as if yanked by a puppeteer's strings. A tall figure stood at the tent's entrance, silhouetted by the canopy-piercing daylight outside.

Barra guffawed, running a hand through his salt-and-pepper hair. "That would be my second-in-command, Lieutenant Ruiha Khotol."

Ruiha sauntered forward. Her gait was confident, and something told Fen that the confidence was more than warranted. The assembled rebels shied away from her on their cushions, parting like fabric before a pair of scissors. She came to a hard stop at Barra's side and leaned against his throne.

She possessed dark skin and silver-touched curls that framed her face just so. Black eyes glittered beneath graceful brows. She wore a military-style green coat, with segments of simple laminar armor sewn into the front with black thread. A sword was tucked into either side of her belt.

"You said a guardian told you to come here. What guardian?" Ruiha's voice was colder and sharper than honed steel.

"A magistrate."

"What. Magistrate."

"Onath Siullu."

Ruiha threw back her head and laughed. "That old goblin? I'm shocked he didn't hand you right over to the Senmavaris. The emperor would pay *very* well for your capture if he knew you were still alive."

A chill scraped up Fen's back. She found herself wishing she hadn't given up her weapon.

Ruiha marched over, swords bumping against her hips.

"You won't make it to Ata. Nobody gets in, and no one gets out. Its borders are guarded tighter than the royal granaries." She shot a sharp look at Barra. "We cannot risk it."

Fen stared at her, slack-jawed. But she had seen the signs. Of course they couldn't spare anyone, not with their numbers shrunken as they were. Not with the Sovereign drowning every whisper of dissent in blood.

Fen stared into the lieutenant's narrowed eyes. There was only one thing she could do to save her own skin.

"Then let me join you."

Ruiha snorted. "No."

One word. And with it, all of Fen's hope shattered like a vase thrown against a wall. Her heart sank low in her chest. For several shaky breaths, she was unable to utter a single sound.

"What do you mean?" she finally asked, her voice cracking.

The lieutenant gave her a look that could've withered a thriving forest, if they'd still existed. "I mean, you can't join."

Fen felt horribly, utterly weak. She felt betrayed, but by whom, she could not say. "I have nowhere else to go."

Ruiha shrugged and looked around at the assembled rebels. "My esteemed fellow officers," she said. "Who here thinks that's our problem?"

Blood roared in Fen's ears. "Please," she choked out. "I can fight—"

"Eternal Mother, now she's begging." Ruiha shook her head, as if at a pitiful child. Fen certainly felt like one. "Get out."

Desperate, Fen looked to Barra. He shrugged helplessly. She tried to move, but her wobbling legs wouldn't budge. She was going to die. The Broken Masks wouldn't really let her go, not with the knowledge she had now. Ihazan had said as much. But she'd been dismissed; she had no choice but to leave.

No.

She had a choice. And she'd pick dying here and soiling the tent with her blood over a rebel knife in the back or slow starvation in a royal dungeon any day. Shapeless fury sparked to life in her gut, lit by resentment and bone-deep fatigue. What was it Onath had always said, when one of his rivals had miraculously vanished?

*No fruit that falls into your hands is worth eating.* Nothing easy was ever worth doing. All things that were good in the world were painful, and you knew they were good because of the pain.

Fen couldn't just let herself die. She wanted so much. To avenge her fathers. To destroy the Sovereign. But more than any of that, to *live*. Fuck the Broken Masks. Fuck the empire. Truth be told, she didn't much care about getting tangled up in the failed revival of her fathers' uprising. The rebellion had killed them as much as the imperialists had. But if joining these idealistic fools was the only way she'd see another sunrise, then so be it. If she found staying here intolerable, she'd just bide her time until she could desert.

She could feel the pump of her heartbeat in her temples. It was fast, but strong. "You *will* let me join you."

She braced herself for an attack, but Ruiha merely smirked. "Oh? And why is that?"

"I want revenge," Fen said.

Ruiha sighed. "You, me, and everyone else. You think you're special?" The faint wrinkles at the corners of her eyes deepened as she gave Fen a long, considering look. "And I don't think you really want vengeance. I think the only thing you really want is your family back."

The lieutenant's words tore through Fen like a knife through paper. It wasn't quite right—there was no point in hoping for what one would never have. But at least Ruiha hadn't called her a parasite. At least she hadn't called her a coward. In that moment, both would've been true.

Fen forced a smile even as heat rose up her neck and pooled in her face. "Is that so wrong? Perhaps one day I'll dig up an Executor."

If the room had been quiet before, now it fell as silent as a tomb. Sometimes, when a very lucky—or perhaps very unlucky—child was born, an Accuser would present itself. The construct would bless—or perhaps curse—the babe with the power to bring back the dead, an ability meant to balance the Accusers' merciless executions. Such people were called the Executors of the Makers' will. They were extraordinarily rare.

Ruiha let out a little puff of air, not quite a laugh. "Executors are a thing of the past. And even if they hadn't died out, they never helped the likes of us. If they had, we might've won." She crossed her arms. "Try again."

Fen tried not to fidget overmuch under Ruiha's sharp gaze. "Even if I did reach Ata, there's nothing for me there." The words rang true as she said them, and they hurt. She reached into her satchel and pulled out her parents' engagement bracelets. She held them high. Light scattered off them, and for a moment they seemed to glow. "This rebellion is my fathers' legacy. It's all I have left of them. And I could tell you right now that I want to make them proud, but they're never coming back." She took a deep breath, struck by the simple truth of the words and trying not to show it. "I do want vengeance, yes. But I also want to help you finish what they started. So if I have to die by the blade, *sir*, then I want my death to mean something. I have nothing to lose. Give me the chance to prove myself."

They obviously needed all the help they could get, too, but pointing that out probably wouldn't be a good idea. Barra's eyes were pinched shut, a muscle in his wide neck flinching. Fen would get no support there. Ruiha's face was brushed with a sort of soft menace. Fen shifted on the balls of her feet, hope and resolve withering in her chest. Her fingers curled into fists as the lieutenant exhaled long and forcefully.

"All right," Ruiha said, to Fen's surprise. "You're in. For now. Worst comes to worst, we'll use you as leverage."

Tension sloughed off Fen like mud in a landslide. She let loose a breath she didn't know she'd held in the first place.

"Go tell Ihazan to take you to the first-year barracks. You'll report for training at dawn." Ruiha grinned menacingly. "Now seriously, get out."

Ihazan was waiting outside, hands tucked into their armpits. "Yeah, yeah," they said, when she opened her mouth. "I heard all that. I'll give you the grand tour." They handed her quarterstaff back. "I'm glad you fought back. We would've had to kill you otherwise."

"I know."

"Ruiha denies *everyone* the first time," Ihazan continued. "She says those truly devoted to the cause will always fight to join it."

But the way their gaze slid away from hers told another story. Ruiha had really considered dooming her.

"Sure." Fen was still trying to keep herself from shaking.

The barracks for new recruits were on one of the middle tiers of the base, a short trip down from the captain's tent.

"Like Ruiha said, training starts at dawn. If you want to eat, you'll have to visit the mess before then. Training ends at dusk, with a couple short breaks in between." Ihazan led her down a rope ladder.

"Are all the people I saw with Barra commanders?" Fen asked, hopping down from the last two rungs.

"Indeed," Ihazan replied, their smile vanishing for a moment. "Fifteen of those are sergeants, and they each command their own squad of fifteen. We have five lieutenants in total—they lead platoons of three squads each, but the only lieutenant that really matters is Ruiha."

"That leaves about twenty-five people without a squad." Fen followed Ihazan onto a bridge. "What about them?"

"You've got a sharp ear, hmm?" Ihazan paused, leaning against the side of the bridge. "Twenty-one of those are strategists, medics, people who can't run around stabbing other people in a skirmish. And then Ruiha leads her own squad of four—which includes yours truly—in addition to her platoon. But she mostly leaves leading the latter to her sergeants. All the officers attend training so they can pick out new recruits for their own commands." They started walking again. "Last but not least, newbies like you have extra duties."

"Such as?"

"Cooking, cleaning, that sort of thing. You'll be stuck with them unless you go into medic training or until you're a second-year, like I am. *Finally.* Then you get to pick a single chore—here we are!"

They stopped before a large rectangular tent. Ihazan threw the door open with gusto and ushered Fen inside. The interior was plain, with twenty nondescript cots shoved side by side, rough-woven mats layered over the floor, and a couple globelamps hanging from the ceiling. A few low shelves stood in the corners, empty save for a stack of playing cards and a couple carved figurines.

"Dinner's at sundown." Ihazan pointed out the door, at a large platform attached to seven different trees. "All the first- and second-years eat there." They planted their hands on their hips. "Any questions?"

"Only one. Which bed is mine?"

"Have your pick." Ihazan laughed. "There are only two of you. No one's stupid enough to join up these days."

Fen arched a brow but held her tongue. Stupidity had nothing to do with it. She imagined that rebels usually joined up for reasons like hers, no matter what the second-in-command had told her. And if not for revenge against the empire, a person would've had to lose everything before pledging themself to the Masks. This wasn't a powerful military force; it was the last dregs of a defeated revolution. The way Ihazan spoke made it sound as if this was a vocation one was funneled into after their declaration of self.

Ihazan headed for the door. "Now, if there's an emergency or something, just ask for me. Otherwise, I'm going to act like you don't exist. It's not socially savvy to hang around the newbies. Remember, dinner at sundown!" They shut the door behind them.

Fen set an alarm on her omnichip and threw herself down on the nearest bed. She let her eyes drift closed. Sleep found her quickly.

☾

Fen jerked awake to something poking at her ankle.

"Hey, you're in my bed."

The words were very close. Fen threw herself upward and swung her legs off the cot. She scrambled for her satchel and the quarterstaff inside it.

"Whoa! It's okay! I'm your roommate!"

Fen blinked blearily at the shape reclining against the wall. She took her hand out of her bag. "Sorry. I'm Fen."

"Don't apologize. I shouldn't have woken you. I promise I'm not usually an asshole." The shape stepped into the light of the nearest globelamp. The youngish, clean-shaven stranger before her was tall and reedlike, with ivory features. His eyes were jet black, the exact same shade as his long, straight hair. He seemed strangely familiar, but she couldn't quite place him in the annals of her memory.

" . . . Are you going to tell me your name?" prompted Fen.

"Right, sorry! Mettan," he said. "Pleased to meet you." His stomach grumbled loudly, and his face flushed red. "I missed breakfast. And lunch."

Fen chuckled. "I'm starving, too."

Mettan smiled hesitantly. "Do you want to go up for supper?"

"Mother, yes."

"Good. Great."

He followed her out the door.

"Where are you from?" she blurted out as they headed across the bridge.

"Sohanashan. You?"

"Talishminn." Fen waited until a rebel with wild red curls hopped off the nearest ladder before she started climbing. "Did you ever visit? I feel as if we've met before."

"We definitely haven't," said Mettan. "I never left Sohanashan, not until I came here."

"I suppose you just have one of those faces."

Mettan smiled. "I get that a lot, actually."

They scrambled onto the shared dinner platform. Lights hung above the level, pulling long shadows from everything their glow touched. Forty or so people milled about the space, impaling tshekar with skewers and roasting the beetles over cracked-open globelamps.

Suddenly the lights were too bright, the burble of conversation too loud. Fen's mouth went dry. Mettan was saying something. She couldn't hear. The seconds sped by too swiftly, time spiraling sharp and wild around her like a sandstorm. And then, like a boulder suspended by the thinnest of strings, the weight of all she'd been carrying for the last days fell upon her. Fen staggered off to the side of the platform and crept behind a folding screen. She fell against the low protective wall bordering the level, her body heaving with airless sobs.

Someone grabbed her by the shoulders. "Fen! Are you all right?"

"I'm fine—I just . . . I . . . " She folded over and hugged her knees as the sharp tang of copper coated her tongue. She was not all right.

She was very, very far from all right.

Mettan's voice rose, but his words were raindrops against the roar of a fabled river.

Fingers wormed their way under Fen's chin and forced her head up. Fen stared at the round, expressive face right in front of her.

"I'm Ying," said the black-haired woman holding Fen's chin. She looked to be about Ruiha's age, somewhere in her forties. There was a realwood mask under her arm, rough and unpainted, a clear work in progress. "I'm a medic. You're having a panic attack."

Fen knew. She'd been having panic attacks almost yearly for the last five years. But she couldn't speak, could barely take in air.

Ying smoothed Fen's hair away from her face. "I want you to breathe with me, up to ten and then down again." She began to rub small, comforting circles on Fen's back. "One, two, three, four . . . "

There was something about Ying's voice that carved a hole in Fen's panic, just large enough for her to squeeze her way through. Fen breathed. And breathed. After six repetitions, the blinding lights dimmed and the taste of iron faded.

"Thank you," she croaked.

"You're welcome." Ying sat down against the screen in front of Fen. Her voice was startlingly kind. "What brought this on?"

"I don't know." Fen let her head fall into her hands. "Nothing, I think."

Ying smoothed her copper-brown hands over her wave-patterned tunic. Its hem was stained with a dark red-brown, the color of old blood. Fen hoped it wasn't the woman's own. "For some people, anxiety attacks can be triggered for no reason at all. But I think you have an abundance of reasons."

Fen tried and failed to summon a smile. "I think . . . these last few days have been a bit much."

"I imagine so," said Ying. She cocked her head, her brows arched. "I was astonished to learn that you found your own way here. Most of us were recruited in towns and cities over the course of months, and then guided through the steppe."

"Ruiha might not show it, but I think she's almost impressed." Mettan plopped down next to Fen, a ceramic platter of roasted tshekar in hand. After a moment and a half of hesitation, he slung an arm around her. "You'll fit right in. Eventually."

Fen shrugged, unsure how to manage all the attention. "Well, I had help. An old friend of the Broken Masks gave me a map."

"Still." Mettan gestured to the charred insects. "I knew I wouldn't be much help, so I got you some food. Feeling better?"

"A little. Thank you." An odd, warm feeling filled Fen's chest. Her eyes began to burn. She squeezed them tight.

"What's wrong?" Ying asked gently. "Specifically, I mean."

Fen's hands tightened into fists as she pressed them firmly against her thighs. She still couldn't hold back the onslaught of tears. She was exhausted. Everything hurt. She would never see her fathers again; her entire life had been taken from her. And yet, these two were here guiding her through a panic attack, bringing her food, holding her.

"It's just—" Her voice broke. Sniffing hard, she scrubbed away the moisture on her cheeks with the back of a hand. She wanted to say how kind she thought they both were, but to do so would be a weakness she couldn't bear. "You didn't have to do this for me."

"*This* is just basic common decency," said Mettan. "Do you not have that in Talishminn?"

Fen laughed, though her throat was sore from sobbing. "I'm sorry. I didn't plan on ruining your evening."

Mettan made an incredulous noise around the tshekar he was crunching on. Ying rolled her eyes and linked her left arm with Fen's right. Music began to play; one of the rebels had picked up a twenty-one-stringed duruqin, and another sang.

Fen recognized the song from the first three notes. It was a ballad about how a fourth moon had once ruled the night sky, only to be shattered into stars by its warring lunar kin. Once, while drunk, Onath had mentioned it was her parents' favorite song. After that, Fen had listened to the same lyrics until she couldn't bear to hear them any longer.

She wasn't sick of the words now.

## ALEKHAI

The door chimed as it read Kacper's omnichip and let him inside. Alekhai, sprawled over the lumpy hotel couch, arched a brow when the man gave a cry of alarm. Kacper shoved himself back against the plaster wall, breathing fast.

"My lord, I wasn't expecting you, I—"

"I know." Alekhai inspected his fingernails. "How are you, Kacper?"

"Fine, my lord—"

"Do you know how hard it was to find you?" Alekhai asked amicably, fingers drumming on the arm of his seat.

A bead of sweat was already trickling down the side of Kacper's face. But he managed to put on a faint smile. "Very, I hope."

"No, not at all," Alekhai said. "But I had other business to attend to. I hope you'll forgive the delay."

Kacper's throat bobbed. One hand inched toward the door panel.

"Don't," said Alekhai. "The hotel's crawling with Senmavari."

"What do you want from me?"

Alekhai rose but strode to the far side of the small room. "Information."

It was the lifeblood of his family's empire. The golden thread that bound every other sniveling technocrat to the throne; the silver garrote that had strangled every rebellion in the crib until Kira Moru had put the right programmers together and they'd figured out a way to fool the data harvesting function on omnichips. Alekhai's ancestors had been rich enough by the time most humans on Newearth had one of their implants. Winning the long fight to start putting omnichips in infants had made them gods. (Plus, child mortality had practically vanished after, thanks to the constant monitoring.)

But Alekhai was here to learn one simple thing. "Why'd you do it?"

"What?" Kacper choked out.

"Please. Wasting my time is the worst thing you can do right now." Alekhai turned his back to Kacper as he traced a finger along a polished countertop. "What did my sister offer you? Money? A title? Or was it simply the chance to off a royal?"

"I'm so sorry, my lord. Please, I—"

Alekhai heard the thump of knees hitting the cheap flooring. He sighed. "Get up, Kacper. I didn't come here to see you grovel."

"I . . . You know I was a fisherman, my lord. But the oceans are dying. Half our staple species have vanished, and the rest have fled toward the poles. Posedao owns the best remaining waters, and they're not accepting applications anymore. I had to move to Bakrai, but with Lady Maheka pushing us out to make room for her villa . . . " A sniffle. *Eternal Mother.* "The princess said she'd take care of my family if I was caught."

Alekhai's finger paused on the counter. "You have a family." He knew that. But he couldn't remember if Kacper had told him or if he'd uncovered that tidbit while hunting the man down. They'd been traveling together for weeks; had he simply never bothered to ask? Or had Kacper kept that information private on purpose? Alekhai whirled around. "I told you to get up."

Kacper wobbled to his feet. "My partner and two children, my lord."

Alekhai sniffed. "Well, that changes nothing."

"I didn't expect it to." And now there was a hint of steel in Kacper's voice. "But I beg of you to spare them."

"I never had the intention of killing anyone," Alekhai said. He waved a hand. "Go see to your family, Kacper. There are enough credits in your account to carry you all through the coming shit-storm."

"Why?"

"Because I'm a generous man, especially with my friends. All I ask is that they don't stab me in the fucking back." Alekhai swept past him and opened the door. "If you'd asked me for help earlier, I would've given it to you."

And then, without another word, he left.

# 10

Fen rose with the chill glow of dawn. As sunlight crept over the distant mountaintops, she dressed. Ihazan had been right about one thing: Her old garb stuck out like a broken thumb, so she'd traded her clothes for a nondescript tunic and pair of trousers. Though her bodyguard uniform had been sturdy and thick and would no doubt be recut into several new garments, she'd definitely gotten the better end of the deal. Her travel clothes were caked with so much dust and sweat, they could probably stand up on their own.

Excitement spiced the air as she and Mettan scarfed down a quick breakfast. The cooks served fried discs made of—as far as Fen could tell—dried fruit and ground insect flour. Second-years milled around the platform to collect their own meals, leveling wary and curious glances at the pair.

The morning bell summoned the two newbies plus the fifty or so second-years up to the training grounds right after. Mettan was vibrating with anticipation, shaking harder than the leaves clustered around them when a breeze cut through. This would be his very first training session. He'd arrived about a week before Fen, and the rebels had been waiting for an expected batch of fresh recruits to show up. But fear and common sense had gotten the better of the prospective revolutionaries, and the recruiters had returned empty-handed. There was only Fen. She and Mettan quickly lined up in the center of the first-level platform, eyes forward, spines straight, feet spread, and hands folded firmly behind their backs. No sooner had they taken their places than a chorus of laughter went up behind them.

A short, stocky woman with faintly graying hair and freckled brown skin took her place at the center of a raised dais at the platform's edge, arms crossed over her chest. Her hard brown eyes homed in on the newest arrivals.

"I'm Lieutenant Oran," drawled the woman, one corner of her thin mouth tipping into a thin smirk. "And we don't do that here. We don't drill in neat little lines. You will all be assigned to three pairs, and you will fight in three five-minute rounds with your partners." Her eyes narrowed. "Fighting sequences have their place in martial arts schools and in formal duels. Not in true combat. If you seriously think you'll go into battle against an enemy who'll attempt the seven steps of the Striking Reed sequence such that you can perform the Hidden Viper form to counter them, then do us all a favor and just jump off the platform."

Despite her embarrassment, Fen had to stifle a laugh of her own as she and Mettan stepped back into the throng of new rebels. She saw now that faint white circles had been painted onto the rough realwood floor, each with a large number carved in the center—obvious fighting rings. If Onath were here, he would've smacked her upside the head for failing to notice.

"Take up your weapons," Oran continued. "Partner assignments are being sent now." She activated her omnichip and flicked an impatient wrist.

Fifty chimes echoed across the training grounds. Fen tapped her forearm and opened the notification. Three numbered fighting rings. Three names. By the Mother's grace, none of them were Mettan's. She suspected that beating him up probably wouldn't help their budding camaraderie.

Mettan clapped her on the shoulder. "Good luck, buddy. Kick some ass."

Fen chuckled. "You, too."

Some of the older rebels had weapons of their own, but most headed for the makeshift racks set up against the protective walls, stuffed with all manner of deadly instrumentation. As Fen walked toward the fifth ring, she watched a pale man with a scruffy auburn beard heft a two-handed broadsword. She gulped but stayed where she was with her quarterstaff in hand. Blades could slice through skin as if it were paper, but weapons like hers had reach. As long as she stayed out of range, she'd be fine. She was probably also the best fighter here.

Onath had made her and the lictors learn the proper flashy sparring sequences to impress his clientele, guests, and enemies. But as soon as they'd memorized the moves, he'd encouraged them to beat each other to a pulp on the training mats. No rules. Fen had earned her fair share of bruises, cuts, and broken bones, but pain had forged her into a honed weapon. She didn't think she'd find much of a challenge here.

A bald, ebony-complexioned woman picked up a double-pointed spear of reinforced iron. She whirled it around expertly, slicing the air apart with incredible precision. She grinned.

Fen couldn't tear her eyes away until she came to a stop at the edge of her first ring. It was then that she realized: Everyone here was already a fighter. The imperialists could draft legions of peasants for use as human shields; the Broken Masks couldn't. A weak link could destroy them all.

Another bell rang, a slightly deeper tone than the one that announced the time. Fen looked toward the dais. The other lieutenants sat behind Oran on threadbare cushions. One seat was glaringly empty. Fen didn't even have to look around to see who was missing: Ruiha.

"Shame we have to meet like this."

Fen's attention snapped to the woman across from her. She had spiky brown hair and beady eyes. Fen extended her quarterstaff with a swing of her arm.

"I'm Riyan."

"I'm Fen."

Riyan smiled. "Oh, I know."

Oran clasped her hands behind her back. "Oh, and one last thing," she called, "lose all your rounds, and you're out."

Fen froze.

Oran lifted a hand for silence as panicked murmurs erupted from the crowd. "You'll be assigned to somewhere you'd be more useful, like the medics' tent. Or stationed in an outlying village, to serve as our eyes and ears in an official's household."

Her eyes met Fen's for a half second, brows lowering fractionally, and Fen immediately understood: If she failed here, she wouldn't be mending broken bones, nor would she be quietly dumped somewhere for a thankless espionage assignment—she'd be sent to her grave. She looked back at Riyan, and suddenly the women seemed a far more formidable opponent.

"Begin," Oran barked.

Fifty bodies slammed together, filling the air with low thuds and the clanging of metal.

Riyan's dual swords cut through the air in a whirlwind. For a split second, Fen was taken aback by her opponent's ferocity. The woman was out for *blood*. Fen swung her quarterstaff and blocked at the last moment. The thud of graphene against steel made her teeth ring. Riyan lunged again, blades whirling. Fen dodged. And so they went, twisting and turning around and toward each other like nobles in a court dance. Their feet hit the wooden floor in time with the rapid beat of their thudding hearts.

But it was just that, a dance. Fen realized within moments that for all her opponent's fierceness, they were severely mismatched.

When Riyan swung wide, Fen took a gamble she prayed would impress the lieutenants. She slipped in close, boldly sacrificing the advantage her longer weapon gave, and cracked the side of her quarterstaff against the other woman's ribs. Riyan hit the ground. She flipped back up, but Fen knew she'd done damage.

Riyan sliced at her twice before Fen spun and delivered a punishing blow to the stomach. When Riyan toppled to the floor again, she stayed there, chest heaving rapidly.

"I yield," she wheezed, and a high-pitched bell rang.

Fen offered the rebel a hand, relief thrumming in her veins. *One down, two to go.* "I hope I didn't hurt you too much."

Riyan rolled her eyes. "You wish," she said, but Fen caught her wince. "I'm fine. It was a good match."

Fen was thrown off by how laid-back she was. The lictors back in Talishminn had never taken defeat well.

Fen's second adversary was a slender, smirking man with a thin mustache and a beard as pointy as his sword. His hair, tied back from his face, was bound in three large braids. A dark purple bruise pooled over the pink curve of his cheekbone.

When Oran called for the second round to commence, he did not immediately go in for the attack. Instead, he merely watched Fen, the veins in his neck pulsing.

"Well?" he sneered. "Come at me."

Fen rolled her eyes when he tossed the hilt of his saber from one hand to the other. She sighed, and then obliged. The man immediately drove her back. He was as vicious as the woman before him, though with far more control. His smooth maneuvering, coupled with the slick speed of his blows, would've made Onath weep.

When he twirled on his heel, Fen's attention was on his flashing blade, not on the foot that swung out to strike the back of her knee and sweep her onto her back. She choked back a yelp, just to refuse the man some small measure of gratification. He grinned down at her anyway, eyes gleaming like oiled steel. Before he could react, Fen smacked him in the gut with her quarterstaff. He wheezed and wheeled backward, a hand clutching ineffectually at his belly.

"You'll pay for that!" he roared. He was so crimson Fen half thought smoke was going to start puffing from his ears.

He advanced again, unbalanced in more ways than one. His smirk had vanished, replaced by a savage snarl. Fen just barely managed to drive him back. Teeth gnashing, he aimed a slice at her head. She dodged and leapt forward to return the attack.

The bell sounded. Fen cut off her swing and jumped back in relief. A tie. She was safe. Safe as she could hope to be, anyway. "Um, good match?"

The man spat at her feet, glaring daggers.

Well, perhaps Riyan had been an outlier. Fen looked around for her last ring but saw that one fight was still going. Oran herself stood at the edge of the eighth white circle, stroking her chin as she watched the pair within duel. Mettan, armed with a short sword and a dagger, was fighting a heavily muscled, axe-wielding woman who, while a handspan shorter, had to be almost twice his weight. If Fen and her first opponent had fought like a pair of dancers, Mettan and the woman battled like lifelong companions. When the woman struck, Mettan slipped away. When he dove forward, she dodged. Fen couldn't look away; Mettan was breathtaking.

He fought like he was a stinger. Release him, and he was a bolt of pure, simple power. But Fen could see that he was evenly matched with the woman, if not in mass and height. Oran seemed to have come to the same conclusion minutes ago; she was just enjoying the show. Finally, she shook her head, as if snapping herself out of a stupor.

"All right, all right. Next round!" Her lips twitched, as if she was trying to maintain a stern frown.

The fighters broke up, and Mettan bowed at the woman. With a grin, she returned the gesture. When Fen caught Mettan's eye, she nodded approvingly at him before heading toward her final ring.

"Not so fast!" called Oran.

Fen turned around. "Sir?"

"Fresh recruits always fight each other for the last round," the officer said. "There was an error in the lineup." Her smile was anything but innocent. "Ready yourselves."

"Yes, sir," Mettan said sharply.

Oran didn't say a word as the other rebels left their own circles, abandoning their assigned matches as Mettan stepped back into the ring. His eyes were narrowed. Focused. He didn't jeer at Fen. He didn't make faces or taunt. He didn't have to. She shot him a friendly look, but his expression didn't change. Unease pricked at her.

"Begin!"

Mettan launched himself into the air. Fen swung up with her quarterstaff, parried his down cut, and sliced her weapon toward his temple. He sprang aside, landing in a smooth crouch. When he leapt toward her, Fen managed to strike his underarm, but he shook off the blow as if it was nothing. He dodged her next attack and kept coming.

Eternal Mother.

If she could just throw him off-balance, knock him down hard enough and keep him there . . . Fen planned her next blows in her head: a strike at the chest, then the stomach, finally the knees—

Mettan stepped aside. He feinted, slashed at her wrist, and swung the dull flat of his sword up into her rib cage. The blow wasn't hard enough to break something, but it still sent Fen careening several steps back, huffing in pain.

She recovered, switched tactics, and swung low to knock him off his feet. Impossibly, Mettan hopped up over the blow and landed right on top of the quarterstaff. The weapon ripped down through Fen's fingers, nearly snapping them. She pedaled backward, jaw clenched, sweat streaming down her forehead.

Expressionless, Mettan tossed aside his sword, and then his dagger. Fen's lungs stuttered violently in her chest as he stalked closer, unable to get enough oxygen through her veins fast enough. Her hands tightened into fists. If Mettan could do this, so could she. He had to be worn out, too.

Wrong. Before she could take another too-shallow gulp of air, Mettan was on her again. He punched. She parried, miraculously. By the grace of the Mother alone, Fen blocked or dodged every single blow he unleashed upon her. Until he started using his feet, anyway. Mettan's boot connected with her shin in a savage kick.

Fen flailed backward and her body crumpled. She worked desperately to regain her balance, even as something in her ankle gave a sickening twist. For all her efforts, she landed hard on her back. She looked up at Mettan, incredulous. He looked at her blankly, eyes cold and dead as he stalked toward her. Her place here was guaranteed; she'd secured a win and a tie. But that didn't matter if her roommate snapped her neck.

"I yield," she croaked. She couldn't believe the words were leaving her mouth. She couldn't even remember the last time she'd used them.

Something came over Mettan. He snatched up her weapon and dove for her. Fen would've rolled over and kicked him in the chin if she hadn't seen the absolute horror swallow his face.

"Eternal Mother, are you okay?" He handed her the quarterstaff with one arm, slipping the other around her waist to help her up. "Oh, Fen, I'm so sorry—"

"Sorry?" Fen cut him off, struggling to collapse her quarterstaff with one hand—the other was around his shoulders. "What are you sorry for? That was amazing!"

"I—I don't know what came over me," Mettan rasped. "I just, I can't go back out there, Fen, and I—"

She wasn't listening. "Where'd you learn to fight like that?"

"Where indeed," murmured Oran, her eyes so narrowed she might as well have closed them.

"My eldest sister taught me, sir," Mettan said quietly. His concerned gaze didn't leave Fen.

"Hm," was all Oran said at first. "Enjoy your lunch. You've earned it, both of you. And Fen?"

"Yes, sir." She held her breath.

"Get that ankle checked out."

The second Oran turned back toward the dais, the afternoon bell rang. Mettan messaged Ying via omnichip to meet in the corner of the first- and second-year dining platform. While Ying bound Fen's ankle in a meshbrace, Mettan scampered off to get them all lunch: grub stew, some forest herbs baked to almost inedible crisps, and more of the insect-fruit discs.

Crammed between Mettan and Ying, Fen tucked in with gusto, despite everything tasting like oversalted mud.

Mettan nudged Fen's shoulder. "So . . . no hard feelings?"

Fen lifted her brows. "Of course not! Honestly, the fall was more my fault than yours."

The moment the words were out of her mouth, she realized how insulting they might've sounded. But Mettan only looked relieved.

Ying, on the other hand, looked anything but. "Mettan, you did this?" She made an aggravated sound. As she circled her spoon through her stew, a raw, beady-eyed grub bobbed to the surface. It didn't look any happier about the situation than she did. "You're supposed to maim the imperialists, not your friends, you ass."

"I know! I really am sorry."

Fen snorted. "And *I* really am getting tired of your apologies.

Seriously, I've been hurt far worse while sparring, and by good friends, too." The lictors back in Talishminn certainly hadn't been anything close to *friends,* let alone good ones, but the lie made Mettan visibly brighten. Then she thought of how dull his eyes had looked when they'd sparred. How vacant his face had been, his features frozen into a mask. "Are *you* all right?" she asked quietly.

Mettan blinked. "Of course I am. Why wouldn't I be?" He didn't give her a chance to answer. "Anyway, I'm still going to make it up to you. Somehow."

"My monthly quota of honor-bound oaths has been filled already."

"Oh?" Ying quirked a brow. "Sounds like you have a story to tell."

Fen groaned happily. "It's a long one."

"Well, until the imperialists try to transport another water shipment out in the open for us to steal," replied Mettan, "we have time."

☾

By the time Fen and Mettan had dragged themselves back to the first-year tent, bodies spent and aching and sore, she'd almost forgotten about being sorted into a squad.

She was reminded the moment she saw Lieutenant Ruiha Khotol seated upon Mettan's bed with Ihazan. Two men flopped over the end of Fen's cot, and another woman had her feet propped up on Fen's pillow. Out of all the beds they could've chosen, Ruiha's team had selected theirs.

"I never take first-years. But I'll be damned if I let Oran snap you two up. So." Ruiha gestured lazily at the person beside her. "You've both met Ihazan already."

"I've met Ihazan's sword," corrected Fen.

The men laughed, one louder than the other. Ruiha gave a

sharp, amused snort. The other woman's mouth tipped into the slightest of frowns.

Ruiha pointed at the men on Fen's cot. "And here are our identical twins, though I'm half sure it's a jest. The sunbeam is Hahru, the shadow is Naijima."

The description really fit. The sharp lines of Hahru's features were severe, but his expression was bright, honest, and open. His lips were naturally bent so he looked as if he was always smiling. Loose black curls framed his burnished bronze face, which held slightly heterochromatic eyes: one a warm brown, the other lucent hazel.

The man beside Hahru looked exactly like him—if Hahru had lost a concerning amount of weight, died, was buried, dug up again, and then dragged back to life by an Executor. Hahru's fine features were striking on his own face, but somehow, though the structure was the same, Naijima's cold visage might as well have been carved from smoky quartz; he looked almost translucent around the edges. His hair, yanked back in an unforgiving bun, was held in place with a modest two-pronged pin in the shape of a flower bud. It was the sort of bauble that friends and lovers would snap in half if they were forced to part. When they were reunited, the hairpin would be bound back together with the finest metal the companions' families could afford. The ornament atop Naijima's head was missing its other half. All in all, he looked like he'd never smiled a day in his life.

"And this," said Ruiha, nodding at the other woman, "is Sijara."

If looks could've killed . . .

Sijara lifted her chin, jaw firm. Fen shot Mettan a look; he just shrugged. It was a shame Sijara clearly wasn't fond of Fen, for several reasons. Sijara was exactly the sort of woman she used to fantasize about during particularly tedious missions. Her complexion was a deep, smooth brown. Her thick black hair was braided into an immaculate crown around her head. There was a dangerous spark in her eyes, and Fen was willing to bet she could slice a sheet of paper in half on the other woman's cheekbones.

"Really? That one?" Sijara asked coldly.

It really was a shame.

Ruiha's expression remained cuttingly pleasant. "Yes, that one."

"She's a magistrate's lackey," Sijara ground out, but said no more.

Despite the insult, Fen couldn't help but find that—to her chagrin—Sijara's voice was as rich as fine wine.

The lieutenant nodded. "Really."

"We already know your names, of course." Hahru cut right into the awkward silence that followed, grinning lopsidedly at Fen and Mettan. "Welcome to the squad!"

Fen saw Ihazan smother a laugh. "There's booze in Ruiha's command tent." They hopped to their feet. "Let's celebrate."

"Thank you for the invitation," the lieutenant said, dry as desert dust.

Naijima patted Sijara on the shoulder and followed Ruiha and Ihazan out. Fen and Mettan waited patiently for Sijara to exit before them, out of respect, but she only snapped, "Well, *go*," and shoved them out, none too gently.

Ruiha's command tent took up a small platform a brief stroll away. It was just large enough to fit all seven of them comfortably. Woven grass rugs littered the floor, with colorful characters painted along the edges. As promised, the lieutenant did indeed have a great deal of booze. A few of the vessels, beautiful long-necked amphorae, had definitely been looted from a noble caravan. Most of the stash, however, were jars of foamy homemade beer. The squad sat down on the mats and passed around ceramic bowls, along with shallow dishes of roasted, spiced grubs that would sharpen the alcohol's taste.

Before the drinking began, Ruiha lifted her bowl. Wine that might've been intended for the emperor's own table sloshed onto the floor. "From now on and forever," she said, the blade of her gaze digging into Fen and Mettan, "you are Broken Masks. Our lives are bound. From this day forward we live and fight as one. The death of a single soldier is a death for us all." A smile. "Congratulations, you're stuck with us."

"To the end," said Naijima, raising his bowl. His words were soft, but the sentiment behind them was not.

Fen's stomach clenched with nerves. She prayed it didn't show on her face as she and Mettan held up their own bowls. "To the end."

They each picked up a fat grub, tossed it into their mouths, knocked back the first round of drinks, chewed, and swallowed.

"Eternal Mother, that's disgusting," wheezed Ihazan. "Isn't this supposed to be His Infernal Majesty's wine?" They held up an amphora, carefully painted with the imperial sphinx.

"It's the taste of all the lowborn blood, sweat, and tears that went into making it," said Naijima, perfectly serious.

When the bottle of wine came by Fen again, she topped off her cup. She had a feeling she was going to need it. And she did. They spent the next few hours airing their many, many grievances about the imperialists. Even though the conversation never quite veered into personal territory, there were still mountains of bitterness and anger left over to explore.

"The worst people . . . " Ihazan began, slurring the words, "the worst people are the commoners that actually support the king."

"Don't get me started," growled Naijima, who'd gotten started long ago. "I don't understand how someone can get kicked senseless and then turn around and kiss the boot."

"Oh, you understand fine. It's the cultural significance," Hahru said quietly. Fen noticed that despite the introduction Ruiha had given and his previously chipper mood, he was capable of a truly grim countenance. "The myth of a single line of Maker-chosen kings is an alluring one, and the sentiment spread out of the northern tribe."

Naijima looked shocked to hear his brother speak those words. "*Alluring?* Makhan was a laughingstock. It should've *stayed* a laughingstock," he growled.

Hahru lifted a placatory hand. "You know I agree with you. I'm just saying that Makhan's chieftains have been kings for so long, most of the tribe can't imagine another way."

"Any other way than fear and oppression and hunger?" Ihazan rolled their eyes. "And what of the other tribes?"

Ruiha plucked the stopper from another amphora. They'd all stopped complaining of the taste by then. "The other tribes surrendered for the second time two decades ago. No one remembers a time when we governed ourselves. Change, even for the better, is terrifying." She pressed her fingers to the imperial seal. "But the people can be convinced, turned to the cause. The worst, Naijima, are the ones actually profiting off lowborn blood, sweat, and tears. The emperor and his court, the aristocrats and their corporations." She passed the wine to Sijara. "Their days are numbered."

After four bottles, Sijara met Fen's eyes for the first time. Fen cursed her heart for beating that much faster.

"Here's some advice," Sijara drawled. "Bind your hair or cut it. Shoulder length, no longer than that."

Fen looked over at Mettan; she'd glimpsed him clambering out of bed an hour before dawn to comb his lustrous locks. But he nodded obediently. Though her own hair was poorly cared for, Fen was less than willing to chop half of it off.

"Why?" The second the word was out of her mouth, Fen knew she'd basically asked for it.

Sijara grabbed a fistful of Fen's ash-gray hair and pulled. Hard.

Everyone laughed except for Mettan, who gave Fen a concerned look. The smile Sijara flashed at her, meanwhile, was that of a predator trying to figure out how long it could toy with its prey before killing it.

Ruiha lifted her gaze to the ceiling. "Save the roughhousing for tomorrow. There'll be more than enough."

Though Ruiha trained her squad apart from the rest of the militia—and Fen was struggling to call it even that—their day would still begin at dawn. And so, sighing with the pleasure that could come only from a full belly and probably too much alcohol, they headed for their beds—Ruiha to her private quarters, Ihazan to the second-year tents, Hahru and Naijima to the main barracks. Sijara was about to follow the twins when Fen stopped her.

"I think we should talk." She wanted to be certain that Sijara would have her back in a fight, not be the one to drive a knife into it.

"What do you want?" Sijara's tone was like a heavy stone lobbed into a still pond.

Fen felt her tongue stick to the roof of her mouth. She was suddenly very aware of the hammered bronze dagger fastened to the other woman's belt. Mettan stood at the doorway of the tent, one cautious hand on the tent flap.

"Go ahead," Fen told him. "I'll see you back at the barracks."

He pressed his lips together but left.

"I know your parents were the Ataa ambassadors," Sijara said.

Fen shrugged, feigning nonchalance. "By now, who doesn't?"

Sijara crossed her arms. "That's the question I keep asking myself. Because I don't believe that everyone knows, *really* knows. I don't believe they're all just ignoring the fact that your fathers started the rebellion."

Fen drew back, anger flickering to life within her. "The bloodshed began long before my parents were sent to Makhan."

"There's a difference between a hopeful insurgent executed

once a year and an entire family getting wiped out once a month." The pain in Sijara's voice was so raw it was bloody to the touch. "My parents are dead because of yours."

Fen's gaze dropped to her feet. "I'm sorry for your loss," she said quietly, "but that wasn't my fathers' fault. They only wanted to help—"

"Call it what you like," snapped Sijara. "But I don't see how mocking the emperor until he started murdering innocents was helping the cause."

A harsh, disbelieving laugh bubbled up Fen's throat. She forced it back down. "You know that's not what happened—"

"Your fathers flew in with their fancy floatcraft, set up shop in the palace just long enough to insult the entire ruling class, and then went around the empire wailing about how every tribe would be better off if the Sovereign were struck down." Sijara's voice was so thick with disdain that Fen was surprised she didn't choke on it. "The embers were there, but your beloved fathers turned what might've been a controlled flame into a conflagration not even the rebels themselves could manage. This," she hissed, spreading her arms wide, "is their fault, and I know you know it."

Fen swallowed hard, trying to erase the hurt she knew was written on her face. She must not have scrubbed away all of it, though, because Sijara smiled at her, beautiful and condescending and brutal.

Lightning shot through Fen's veins at the sight of that smile. She clenched her jaw, tight-knuckled hands rumpling her tunic. "If you truly believe that, then why are you here?" She snapped off each syllable, each word a burning branch on the blazing tree of her anger. "You don't fight conflagrations. You flee from them."

"Because someone has to clean up your parents' mess," Sijara said, in a tone that would've been pleasant had it not been accompanied by a sneer.

Fen knew she shouldn't say the words that surfaced in her head just then, but she couldn't stop herself. "Do you hate me because you genuinely think my parents bewitched yours into rebelling," she whispered, "or because your kin couldn't mind their tongues, and you're just looking for someone to blame?"

Though the curve of Sijara's lips did not change, her eyes certainly did. The shiver of dread that went up Fen's back was the only warning she had before Sijara closed the distance between them. She moved with the silence of morning mist, with the speed of death on a battlefield. In one moment, Fen was standing in the middle of the tent, hands fisted. In the next, Sijara had her pushed up against the tree trunk at the platform's center, forearm pressed to Fen's throat. Fen swung up an arm to break the hold, but Sijara grabbed her wrist and pinned it down by her side. The pressure on Fen's throat tipped over into painful territory. Still, she refused to look away as Sijara loomed over her, eyes wild.

Fen quashed the urge to apologize. Instead, she said, "The only reason you're taking your anger out on me is because you can. I'm here, and I can take it, and you know it. But you don't really hate me—"

"Let me guess, you think I really hate myself, deep inside, because I survived. Who do you think you are?" Sijara's tone was mocking, but her eyes narrowed dangerously. She leaned forward, bringing her lips to the shell of Fen's left ear. When she spoke again, it was tortuously quiet, even though everyone else had already gone to bed on the lower platforms and couldn't possibly hear her. Her words were a promise brushed against Fen's cheek, a secret for just the two of them. "But you're wrong. I *do* hate you. We may follow the same commander, but you'll keep your distance," she murmured in her wine-rich voice, "or I will make you wish you'd died with your fathers."

Fear dampened Fen's palms. "Let go."

Sijara let go. Without another word, she stalked off. Fen licked her dry lips, touching three fingers to the base of her neck.

Once she got her breathing under control, she went straight to the first-year barracks. Inside the tent, even the globelamps slept, but she could tell Mettan was awake.

"You're all right?" he whispered.

She stared at him, uncomprehending for a moment. "Yes. Thanks for asking." Fen shed her tunic, shrugged on her sleeping clothes, and collapsed on her cot. But not before she swapped her threadbare pillow for another, remembering where Sijara had put her boots.

She rubbed at the sore spot where Sijara had tugged her hair. In the darkness, she finally noticed that all that remained of Mettan's treasured mane were short, uneven black patches.

"You chopped it all off!"

He sat up. "Are you really all right?"

"Can I borrow whatever you used to cut your hair?"

Mettan, Mother bless him, didn't call her out on her pathetic attempt to distract him. He wordlessly handed her an oblong instrument. A simple switchblade. She got to work over the trash bin, sawing off sections handful by handful.

"If you're that good in the training ring," Fen said, after she'd returned the switchblade and sprawled back on her bed, "then your eldest sister must be unbelievable."

"She's dead," said Mettan.

The hand idly massaging her scalp froze. She hadn't known him for long, but the apathy in his tone was obviously forced. She turned on her side to face him. "I'm so sorry," she managed. "What was her name?"

"Dayana. She's . . . she was a magistrate," whispered Mettan. "She was one of two native appointed officials from the whole eastern tribe, but our family fell out of imperial favor remarkably quickly. She took a couple bribes that seemed harmless enough, and then a couple more. But she couldn't hold up her end of the deals she made, and the gang paying her wanted their credits back. She, uh, she tried to wed me to a wealthy family, hoping I'd be able to help cover her debts. That was the Korawan way; we married out of problems." The soft, broken sound that left his mouth was not exactly a laugh. His voice took on a bitter edge. "Not like I'm good for much besides fighting. And then we found out that the in-laws' riches were all for show. We thought we were getting money, they thought they were getting power. So I guess we all deserved each other." He paused. "I . . . Sorry, I didn't mean to dump that all on you. I just—"

"Mettan, I'm happy to listen," Fen said. "But only if you want to tell me. You don't owe me your pain."

She knew what he'd say next, anyway. She'd finally figured out why his face had seemed so familiar; his family's story had popped up in an article on the omninet years ago, along with a portrait. Onath had once spoken of the entire Korawan family as a cautionary tale for magistrates.

"No, I want to. Talking about it helps." Mettan made a sound that sounded awfully like he was trying to hold back tears. "My father-in-law got to my sister before the gang did. Turns out, being a warrior of her caliber doesn't mean much when your opponents have an unregistered stinger and sharp knives." Another not-quite-laugh.

Fen rubbed at the frayed hem of her sleeping tunic. Sorrow had tossed her into a great jagged pit, but she'd never bothered to consider that others might be trapped in chasms even deeper than hers. She'd never known her fathers. Perhaps that had been a mercy; they'd never gotten the chance to disappoint her.

She got out of bed, pushed her cot up beside Mettan's, and wrapped her arms around his middle.

She let herself fall asleep shortly after he did.

On the training platform reserved for Ruiha's squad, Fen left Mettan's side and strode into the sparring ring. Naijima stood at the epicenter, short sword in hand. He fought with a two-meter weighted chain as well, but he'd set it aside for their match, thank the Mother. Fen had no idea how she would've defended against *that*.

Ruiha, seated cross-legged on a mat, set down the mug of tepid beer she was nursing. "Begin!"

"Ihazan told me you're graceful in victory," Fen said, smiling sharply. "I wonder if you'll be graceful in defeat as well."

"I wouldn't know. I've never been defeated." Naijima's grin was just as vicious. He swung his sword in a lethargic arc. He crooked a finger at her with his other hand. "Come on, then."

Fen didn't need to be told twice.

By now, she'd rethought her earlier hubris. She knew she was by far the least skilled in Ruiha's squad. In the last week, she'd won only six of the fourteen matches she'd fought in. She'd sparred with Sijara once and had been put on her ass in seconds. The woman was a superior fighter, beyond even what Fen had imagined. She didn't merely wield her sword, it *was* her—a deadly extension of her arm.

Like Onath, Ruiha was the sort of instructor who clearly

delighted in her students' suffering. The lieutenant tolerated questions that weren't stupid, but she thought every question was a stupid one. Fen learned to simply obey.

So she kept her mouth shut when Ruiha extended their training hours, despite the fact that they were still expected to spar with the other first-years. She bit her tongue when Ruiha made them skip lunch every other day. She even choked down her protestations when Ruiha told them they'd start sparring in matches where only one of them had a weapon.

After supper, new recruits normally worked cleaning shifts before spending the evening hours as they wished. Not Fen and Mettan. They had to suffer through the same exercise regimen as the other squad members before and after dinner, and *then* attend to their chores.

But perhaps Ruiha knew what she was doing. Fen had to admit that she was getting better. Nowhere near as good as Sijara, certainly, but she was getting her ass handed to her less frequently. Six matches out of fourteen was actually better than her results in the first week.

Sijara and Hahru tied twice after a win by the former. Then Ruiha made them all do handstands while she smacked at their arms with a thin rod. When training finally, finally ended, Fen and Mettan limped away to their domestic duties.

Fen's omnichip directed her to the kitchens. Today she was supposed to prepare the next day's meal with the cook, a bald lieutenant with night-black eyes and freckled brown skin. When Fen walked in, he was stirring a great vat of what one could only begrudgingly call soup.

"You're Fen, right?" he asked, throwing in a handful of ground insect flour for protein. "I'm Zepha."

Fen smiled. "I know."

Zepha snorted. He'd been with the Broken Masks for seven

years now, and he'd accumulated quite a few stories in that time. Ihazan had told Fen that Zepha had once killed a man with only a spoon. If Fen had needed any further proof that the Masks ran themselves differently from any other army, it was that the officer with the second-highest kill count made everyone lunch.

Zepha passed her the massive ladle he was dragging through the soup—perhaps the fabled murder weapon itself—while he went to grab another jar of flour. The soup, which was thickening at an alarming rate, belched foul steam into Fen's face. Apparently, Zepha had nominated himself for this job, but by the time complaints had reached a critical mass, he was too respected to replace.

"I have a suggestion," she said as Zepha dumped the whole jar in.

He nodded encouragingly at her.

"What if we let this firm up? Maybe until we could roll it up into balls and, I don't know, drown them in pepper sauce. Or anything, really." She'd much rather burn her taste buds off than subject them to whatever was taking shape in the vat.

Zepha fixed Fen with a venomous look. "You don't like my cooking?"

"The fried discs were nice," Fen said quickly, though by "nice" she meant "vaguely edible."

The glare vanished as Zepha chuckled. "You don't have to lie. *No one* likes my cooking. I'm not a chef, I'm a nutritionist. Or at least I was, professionally, when there was enough food for people to care about what they were eating." He tucked the empty jar under his arm. "My first and only goal is to ensure you all don't die of nutrient deficiency."

"Nutrients and good flavor aren't mutually exclusive, sir," Fen said gently. She'd thought Zepha must have heard this before, but apparently not, given his genuinely wounded glance. Quickly, she added, "Perhaps a secondary goal could be taste. Sir."

He sighed a long-suffering sigh before stepping back, hands raised. "All right. We'll try it your way. I'll turn up the heat and get another pan for the sauce."

☾

Supper the following day was a success. Thirty minutes into the dinner hour, Fen found that all her chore shifts had been switched to the kitchen.

☾

Though Fen was the weakest link in the iron chain Ruiha had welded the squad into, she had no intention of remaining as such. At least, she had to become strong enough not to be her unit's downfall in battle—or, more likely, in a skirmish. Though the Broken Masks were expanding their recruitment efforts again after the last batch of prospectives turned tail, they simply wouldn't have the numbers to wage war traditionally, not for a long time.

Midnight found Fen on the main training platform. But she was not alone. The moment she set foot on the realwood, she recognized the lithe form of the woman weaving between the practice dummies.

When Sijara's gaze fell upon Fen, there wasn't just bitterness in her eyes; there was full-blown fury. And under it all was the wet, pained gleam of years' worth of unshed tears. Fen felt an odd pang of pity for her.

Sijara paused her drills for a moment, her back facing Fen. Her sword glinted as it fell to her side. "What part of 'keep your distance' wasn't clear?"

"I'm trying to," Fen said evenly. She extended her quarterstaff as she made her way to the farthest fighting ring. "But I need practice."

Sijara narrowed her eyes at the dummy to her right. Then she whirled around and sliced its torso into two perfect halves, post and all. Any pity Fen felt evaporated. Sijara turned around and, maintaining eye contact with Fen, took a step forward.

Fen immediately took a step back.

"There's not much point," said Sijara. "Even if Ruiha were willing to embarrass herself by bringing you on a mission, no amount of training would help you."

Fen's face heated with anger, as well as a healthy dose of embarrassment. Sijara's haughty smirk from that morning was seared into her memory.

"What do you want from me?" Fen snapped.

Sijara's laugh was thin and dry and sharp, a yellow blade of razograss. "Honestly, Fen? I want you to jump into a well."

With most boreholes around the kingdom as empty as they were deep, it would be a particularly quick death.

Fen tried again. "What would it take for you to work with me?"

"I already have to," Sijara said coolly. "To take down the imperialists that took our families away. Or have you already forgotten?"

Fen's vision flared red. She squeezed her eyes shut, pressing her lips into a thin line to trap a retort. Or just a scream. She didn't know. When she opened her eyes again, she wanted to throttle Sijara a little less. "What would it take for you to at least respect me?" She hated how plaintive it sounded.

"Nothing." But Sijara's lips curved into a vicious smile. "Though if you spent the night checking the perimeter in person, that could be a start."

"Pardon?" The hackles on Fen's neck rose. The carnufexes might be dead and gone, but the same couldn't be said for the apex predators of Newearth's forests.

"Just the inner boundary." Sijara's grin stretched. "We're not approved to venture farther than that."

"Still—"

"Are you a coward," Sijara asked, "on top of everything else?"

Fen gave an incredulous scoff. "Why should I care what you think of me? You've already said there's nothing I can do to earn your respect."

"And the rest of the squad?" Sijara arched a nicked brow. "Their regard for you will evaporate if you walk away from this. Consider this your rite of passage."

The challenge was immature. Ridiculous, even. Fen knew now that the forest was monitored night and day with an extensive camera system. She should laugh in Sijara's face, then turn around and go to bed, her planned training for the evening be damned.

"Fine. I'll do it."

Fen headed for the rope ladder that went back up to the first-year barracks. She'd need a few things—

"Take only your quarterstaff," Sijara said sweetly, stowing her sword. "With any luck, I *won't* see you again at dawn."

The path down to the forest floor was a short one. Fen cursed when her boots hit the hard, desiccated soil mere minutes after she'd begun her descent. She looked up at the meager patches of sky that shone through the leaves. She couldn't spot the moons, but she caught glittering, foliage-framed glimpses of the debris-spun rings, eight parallel arcs two hundred thousand kilometers across.

Kanoh was encircled by three perimeters, each more intensely surveilled than the last. Fen stopped right before the six-hundred-meter line, where the jury-rigged, outward-facing scanners wouldn't cry of an imperialist invasion every time she moved. Gritting her teeth together, she set off at a brisk pace, keeping her eyes on the shadowed woods beyond. Completing her first pass took far less time than she'd thought. So did her second, more methodical run. By her fourth go, repetition had dulled her nerves, and she was getting bored.

It had been some time since Fen had run through the traditional Newearthan quarterstaff forms. As Oran had said on her very first day of training, set sequences would be less than useless in a real fight. Nevertheless, going through the familiar motions was a comfort.

She'd just completed the sixteenth form—a series of upward slices with quick twists of the hips for leverage—when she heard a branch snap. A chill raced up her spine, spearing through what little peace of mind she'd accumulated in the past days. Genuine panic, familiar and ice cold, wrapped its gnarled fingers around her neck.

"Who's there?" she called.

There was a range of responses she could've gotten, going from a wild, inhuman growl—bad—to the shout of a person about to attack—very bad—to the sharp clink of Senmavaris armor—very, very bad. The response she got was silence, which was somehow worse. A prickling sense of terror filled her lungs as the seconds slithered by.

Something hissed, loud and lethal and far too close. Fen spun around, swinging her quarterstaff at whatever had made that cursed sound. She was half a breath too slow. The end of her weapon slammed into the triangular head of a noboa. But the strike didn't land before fangs punched through her right boot and into her calf.

A scream ripped out of Fen's throat as she stumbled backward. The noboa slumped beside her, writhing frantically as it hit the dirt in a cloud of dust. The creature might be dead, but a single bite was enough to doom her. A tide of horror flooded over any attempt at cogent thought. Feeling faded from her face, and then her hands. Her quarterstaff slipped from her fingers. She didn't even hear it strike the ground. The blood thundering in her ears swelled to a crescendo before trickling into nothing.

Her knees buckled. The ground thrashed wildly under her, as if she were a chunk of driftwood caught in a typhoon. She tried to regain her balance and failed. She couldn't breathe; she felt like a band of hot steel was tightening around her rib cage.

Fen slid bonelessly to the dirt. Her face struck the ground hard, but she barely felt it. She couldn't feel anything but the crushing weight of her own body pinning her down. Her last thought was of her parents, and of how she'd failed them one last time.

And then, like a rising sea of shadows, darkness swallowed her whole.

☾

When Fen woke on a hard realwood floor, she was in agony. But the pain meant she wasn't dead, and that almost made up for the screaming sensitivity of her skin, so raw she felt like she'd been flayed alive. She writhed and trembled under a thermal blanket, rattled by her own breaths. Voices called out to her, but they were muted and distorted, as if she were under the surface of a deep pool.

She didn't stay awake. Sometime later, she found herself under the white cloth roof of the medical tent, swaddled in thick covers and watched over by warm globelamps. Day and night bled together. She drifted. She saw shifting faces, felt gentle hands she wasn't sure were really there. Now and then her temples would throb from thirst. She'd whisper out nonsense, but then the cool rim of a bowl would kiss her lips and she would drink. At some point, she fell into a long, fitful sleep.

When consciousness came again, it stuck. Her left hand ached as badly as her bitten calf. She opened her eyes and saw that Mettan was gripping her fingers. Ying sat on the edge of the cot beside him.

Fen's mouth was so dry her lips bled when she opened them. Her swollen tongue felt far too leaden to form words. She tried anyway. "You're going to break my hand," she croaked.

Ying let out a high, brittle sound, and Mettan dragged Fen up into a hug. Ying wrapped her arms around them both. It hurt more than the hand-holding, but if Fen was being honest with herself, she needed it.

"Thank the Mother," Mettan whispered. "It's been three days!"

"What were you thinking?" Ying demanded, once the pair had set Fen back against her pillow.

A serrated blade pressed into the inside of her throat when she spoke. "It was a dare."

"Is that so?" asked a stone-cold voice.

Ying and Mettan whirled around to face Ruiha. The lieutenant stood on the threshold of the tent, arms crossed over her chest.

"Give me a moment with her," she said. It wasn't a request.

Mettan squeezed Fen's hand, softer this time. Fen cringed when Ying fixed her with a stern look. She'd no doubt get an earful the second they left. And from the look on Ruiha's face, it wouldn't be the first tongue-lashing she'd get that day.

"Who dared you?" Ruiha sat on a nearby bench, dropping her elbows onto the table behind her and leaning back on them.

"It was my fault," said Fen. No one had *forced* her to scarf up Sijara's easy bait.

"Sijara, then." Ruiha gave Fen a flat, unimpressed look when the younger woman flinched. "How do you feel?"

"It's just pain," said Fen, trying to force nonchalance. "Nothing new."

Ruiha, on the other hand, threw back her head and laughed. Then she squinted hard at Fen, the lines of her unforgiving face no longer apathetic but curious. "You don't know what true pain is." She tilted her head. "But you *will* if you keep up this little pissing contest, and not because of dangerous fauna. I've already exceeded the limits of my patience for this month."

The temptation to backtrack and complain that she hadn't, in fact, done anything wrong rose in Fen like burning steam. She fanned it away with some effort. "Didn't the Month of Copper just begin?"

"How perceptive." Ruiha reached out and took hold of Fen's shoulder. Her touch was firm, but gentle. "As I said, I never take first-years. I don't have time for the typical shenanigans of a new recruit. Is that clear?"

Fen nodded once. "Yes, sir."

"Get some rest. I'll tell your friends to leave you be." Ruiha's eyes crinkled, her mouth twitching into the shadow of a smile. "For now."

☾

When Fen limped outside on the fourth day, the squad was waiting for her.

Ihazan clapped her on the back. "Aren't you a tough one?"

"She has to be," said Hahru. "Only four out of ten people survive a noboa bite."

"*Three* out of ten," Naijima corrected with an impressed look.

Mettan handed Fen her quarterstaff. "How are you feeling?"

"Good as new." Fen winced when Ihazan smacked the space between her shoulders again.

"Excellent."

Fen glanced over at Sijara, whose fingers were drumming the pommel of her sword. For the time being, it was sheathed.

"Ruiha said to bring you up for exercises as soon as you were back to normal," Sijara said.

Fen bit back a groan as she followed her squadmates toward the nearest ladder. She should've stayed in bed. "So who saved me?"

Sijara looked down at Fen from where she hung on the ladder. Her glittering brown eyes ran Fen through, though not altogether unpleasantly. "I did, obviously."

# 12

## ALEKHAI

Dealing with the assassins and taking care of personal business had taken far longer than Alekhai had anticipated, and so home would have to wait. The Sovereign had already retreated to the imperial hunting lodge, and Alekhai had to make his report there before returning to the capital.

It was probably for the best; his party had run into a storm, and they needed immediate shelter. The clean line of sandy crests that'd once marked the horizon had since flared up into a furious blur. The vanguard winds had all but reached his barge, and it was hard to get a good look at the storm without getting a mouthful of sand.

The hovercraft approached a small mountain of bloodred stone at a speed that would've smeared the riders if the mountain had been just that. Instead, section by section of the great rock slid away, revealing a set of massive carved doors. They were solid bronze, four meters wide and twelve meters tall, but so well balanced they could be pushed by a single person with ease. Now they slid open with scarcely a whisper, and Alekhai's somewhat reduced entourage zipped through into a pitch-black chamber, the storm chasing after them in glinting whirls of sand.

The rock slammed shut the moment the barge was clear, plunging them all into complete darkness for a heartbeat. Then the walls around them fell away in thick slabs, lighting the way as the vessel glided through a vast hall of crystal-clear, reinforced glass. The wan light of sunrise splashed over the smooth floor.

What appeared to be misshapen lumps of rock from far away gradually revealed themselves to be a complex system of buttresses and beams, crenellations and columns. The lodge was a massive boulder, just hollowed out and sumptuously furnished. Alekhai hopped out halfway through the hall, pausing only to give the captain a sharp salute before heading up to his brother's office.

The interior of the lodge was fashioned from blocks of pale-yellow sandstone and creamy travertine. Gleaming braziers stood along the walls, flames flickering in their copper bowls. Above, artificial lights inlaid into the rectangular ceiling illuminated the places the fires did not. Still, Alekhai strode carefully; the complex was threaded with traps, most of them pitfalls, and the low windows had no bars to keep unfortunate souls from tumbling to their death far below.

He didn't bother to knock at Akrysanth's intricately carved door. He simply commanded it to slide open with his omnichip and strode in. Below a shuttered, deep-set skylight sat a low marble dais, over which floated two hoverchairs and a round table. Samite tapestries hung from columns of rust-red laterite, nearly brushing the triangular tiles of the chamber. A carmine rug ran the length of the room, edged in gilded thread. And at the far end, a pile of cushions lay beneath a tasseled canopy.

"Little brother!" Akrysanth practically leapt from the plush seat behind his desk and dragged Alekhai into a hug. "How are you? I heard the collection rounds were particularly eventful this season."

Alekhai suffered the too-tight embrace, counting the seconds as his hands curled into fists. "No more so than last," he said. "Sona doesn't know when she's beaten."

Akrysanth snorted, finally releasing his brother and returning to his seat. Alekhai slumped into his own. He activated his omnichip and transferred the last of the records to Akrysanth.

"How are *you*?"

"Oh, everything's been just wonderful." The Sovereign scrolled through the files, lips pursed. "Except for our guest's latest complaint."

Alekhai had always found it incredibly petty that his brother still called the Maker their guest, as if the aliens hadn't rescued humanity and gifted them the planet. "What's the problem?"

"You know the Oldearth lampreys I had the labs whip up? Well, I starved them and tossed a few dozen traitors into their pit. The Maker thought it unnecessarily cruel to both the beasts and the betrayers." Akrysanth's fingers tapped on the arm of his chair. "The hypocrite. You can't imagine the horrendous things Its species has done out there in the starry black. Whole systems gone, brother." He snapped. "Just like that."

The Makers had always proclaimed that their great purpose was to spread life across the galaxy. Terraforming Newearth and settling it with humans had been just one small part of that sacred mission. But Alekhai had gleaned enough from Akrysanth and his own Accuser to suspect the Makers destroyed nearly as much life as they created or protected. Any perceived threat to their particular vision of a vibrant, flourishing, peaceful galaxy was exterminated without mercy.

"Well, no matter. I had the pool filled in and served the poor pets at yesterday's feast." Akrysanth sighed and deactivated his omnichip, evidently exhausted by the records. "Anything of note?"

"We traced the assassins back to Lady Maheka. She arranged the attack at Sona's bidding, in exchange for a slice of the yearly tribute."

"How certain are you of that?"

"Almost entirely."

"Is Maheka still alive?"

"For now."

"Good. She'll stay that way." Akrysanth laced his fingers over the tabletop, a slab of fossilized trunk. The tree it'd been cut from had been living once, only for silica to swallow its decaying innards over millions of years. "I have no interest in appeasing Maheka's extended family if we execute her."

"Then banish her to the desert," Alekhai said. "Maheka's been making the lives of everyone in Bakrai a living hell. She wants them out so she can build her own personal resort on the ruins of the old city. Financing future construction is half the reason she stole the taxes in the first place."

"Let it go, little brother."

Alekhai looked down, biting the inside of this cheek until he tasted iron. Whether he lived or died, it was all the same to Akrysanth, and everyone knew it. He hadn't missed the pleased gleam in his brother's eyes right before that bone-crushing hug.

Akrysanth heaved a sigh. "Do you not trust me, brother? Do you not trust that I have the best interests of my heir at heart?"

Alekhai had always wondered whether Akrysanth had been the one to poison their father. The former Sovereign's death had been quietly ruled a suicide, but Alekhai knew better. Now, inexplicably, he was sure his brother had helped the old emperor to the grave. "Of course I trust you."

"Good. Anything else?"

"No, my lord."

"Hm." Akrysanth stood and walked to the edge of the chamber. Three high, thin windows dominated the right wall, dripping with gauzy curtains. The sky was utterly occluded by the stone walls, save for paper-thin gaps of knife-sharp blue. The storm had evidently died down. "Bakrai fell behind on its taxes this year, no? With that new loom, we should've gotten twice what we've collected from the whole clan."

Alekhai joined Akrysanth. Tiled landing bases sprouted up around the lodge, rising from the sandy waves. Shimmering vessels in a rainbow of hues flew in and out of circular pod-bay doors.

"That's right," Alekhai said carefully. "But only because Maheka stole the rest. I ordered her to hand it over. I'm going to dispatch an official to oversee the return."

Akrysanth waved a bored, heavily ringed hand. "Don't bother."

Alekhai stiffened. "Pardon?"

The middle of Akrysanth's mouth remained the same, but the corners bent upward. "You know I don't like repeating myself," he said pleasantly. "Leave Maheka be."

Alekhai kept his eyes on the desert. "As you wish."

Akrysanth placed a cold, heavy hand on his shoulder. To an outsider the touch would appear affectionate, perhaps even an apology. "The day I get sloppy and die, you'll be Sovereign," the emperor said. "And you'll learn soon enough that terror is power's closest companion. The commoners will never love us—they're too stupid to see we know best. We rule only as long as they fear us. Or better yet, fear what happens without us. Do you hear me?"

Alekhai forced himself to hold the Sovereign's gaze. "I hear you."

"Good, good." Akrysanth beamed. He released Alekhai with a few hard pats. "You're dismissed, little brother."

Fen awoke to Mettan gently shaking her awake. "Come on, it's time to be tortured for sport."

She sat up with a yawn and slithered out of bed. "We're always tortured for sport."

"This time's different. We're going on a scavenging expedition, a couple klicks outside the security perimeter. Barra's leading it."

Fen blinked at her roommate, the last of her drowsiness fading fast. "What? Why now?"

"Our mineral resources are running low or something. Iron for weapons, salt for curing food." Mettan shrugged before slipping on a tunic. "Beyond that, anyone's guess."

"But why us?" Fen hopped as she yanked on her boots. "Feels like we just arrived here. Did something happen?"

"I know as much as you." Mettan pushed open the door, letting in the dawn as it announced itself with brushstrokes of scarlet and indigo. "But we're about to find out."

As it turned out, exactly nothing had happened. With the imperialists and their hoards holed up in their cities, easy pickings for food and other necessities were few and far between. And even if anyone were willing and foolish enough to sell to them, the rebels had barely a credit to their name. As for why Fen and Mettan were being dragged along, Barra had simply woken up and decided that it was high time the newest recruits left the perimeter.

Their target was an untouched resource rig a scout had happened upon a few days ago. Built by the aristocratic companies that'd sprouted up in Makhan and spread to the other tribes post-unification, the rigs were designed to suck up anything they could—water, oil, minerals—and send a signal back to whoever owned them when they were full. They were almost never abandoned, but there was the rare exception. Sometimes they broke down before their owners deemed their contents worth the effort of extraction, other times they fell off records during corporate takeovers. Whatever the reason, the rebels weren't going to pass up the opportunity.

Fen and Mettan walked side by side as the rebels hiked toward the rig, swapping stories they'd collected from the more seasoned Masks. At least until Fen turned, and the words were stolen right out of her mouth. To the right of the path, at the center of a half-overgrown clearing, was a sun-blocking steel behemoth. A massive orb perched on four rust-caked legs, vine-like appendages dangling from its center.

"*That's* a resource rig?" The holopictures Fen had seen didn't do it justice.

Naijima pushed between Ihazan and Hahru and strode up beside her, eager as always to show off. "Abandoned long ago." His mismatched gaze narrowed. "Just another company that stole more from Newearth than it could handle, leaving the excess trapped in their machines rather than returning it to the planet or, Mother forbid, donating it to the people."

"They did donate it," said Ihazan, smirking. "Just not intentionally. The Broken Masks gutted this one when they first settled here. The rig we're after is up ahead."

Fen's jaw tightened as they passed the ruin. Imperialists said that the unification allowed the four tribes to better address widespread problems, but all it had seemed to do was allow nobles to exploit the whole empire more effectively. Nevertheless, the lie persisted.

"You know, an official I guarded years ago insisted it was the Makers who made a mess of the planet," she muttered.

Mettan pursed his lips. "Naturally. Blame the aliens no one alive has ever seen while you botch the terraforming and destroy whatever's left."

"But what of the environmental protection laws?" Ihazan exclaimed in mock surprise.

No one could muster up a laugh. These days, corporations spent more on ads celebrating their quarter-assed efforts to undo damage than on undoing the actual damage.

Naijima shook his head angrily. "The rules don't exist for the technocrats. They—"

"I know. We all know. It's why half of us joined up." Fen arched a slightly irritated brow. Lately Naijima's lectures had begun to grate. "Welcome to Enkaiia."

"We're here!" Barra called as the squad entered the clearing. He scrambled up a rock near the middle. Behind him lay a toppled rig, its bulbous head dented but whole. It was much smaller than the monster they'd seen on the way here, but judging by the expressions on some of the more seasoned rebels, it was still a find.

The squads crowded around Barra, lieutenants taking their places at the foot of the rock. The sun shone brutally, and without any tree cover in the clearing, heat flooded over the rebels. Fen ineffectually wiped sweat from her brow.

Ruiha came up beside Barra. "We're going to explain this once for the new recruits, and once only, before we give it a try. The rig here malfunctioned before it could alert its owners that it was full. It's broken, but still dangerous." Her mouth quirked, as if the prospect of a challenge thrilled her. "This model is typically booby-trapped, with solar-powered sensors and a pressure-triggered incendiary device."

Barra took a swig from his flask before clearing his throat. "I have no intention of dying today. So here's what we'll do—"

Something crashed in the forest behind the rock. Then came the creaking snaps of desiccated trees smashing into the ground. Then the huffs of a panting, heaving animal. And then the gargantuan snout of a beast that should've been long extinct.

A carnufex.

Fen's mouth went desert dry with fear.

The predator lifted its mottled head, bellowing a roar felt and heard in equal measure. The beast paced back and forth, sizing up the prey before it. The carnufex was massive, twice the size of a hut, but it was starving. Each of its forty ribs showed clearly through its dull, matted fur.

"Fall . . . " Barra dropped his flask, eyes bulging. "Fall back!"

The carnufex's five eyes latched onto the captain as the rebels scattered. Every muscle in its depleted form tensed. Shrunken sinew slid and tightened beneath sagging skin. And then the creature charged.

"*No!*" Ruiha leapt to take Barra's place.

She wasn't fast enough. There was scarcely an emotion upon Barra's face as countless curved teeth encircled him. He looked horrifically calm in the seconds before two fangs punctured his skull. Ruiha's mouth opened in a silent scream.

Air snagged in Fen's throat, choking her.

"Get to the base!" Oran yelled, just as Ruiha roared "Die!" and drove her swords into one of the carnufex's legs.

The predator screeched in pain, its pointed tail lashing furiously. The wicked edge caught Oran across the middle. She was sliced into two neat halves, blood fountaining as she fell to the dirt.

Stomach acid shot up Fen's throat. She was too shaken to make sense of the rapid orders filling her ears. Dimly, she felt a hand grab her by the shoulder and shake hard.

"Snap out of it!" Mettan screamed. "We need to move!"

He pulled her toward the trees.

Barely managing to hold on to her quarterstaff, Fen stumbled after him, her whole body going numb with panic. Chaos reigned in every direction. Terrible sounds filled the air—flesh being torn from bone, screams being torn from throats. Lieutenants barked conflicting commands as the carnufex pounced from victim to victim, propelling itself on enormous limbs. Great claws tore through armor and cloth, skin and bone. The few rebels not petrified with fear launched futile attacks against the creature. But it'd learned its lesson after tasting Ruiha's steel. It knocked aside spears and dodged maces as it set about crushing the last of the Kanoh rebels.

And then it vanished into the yellow grass.

"Where is it?" Ruiha roared, a green-bloodied sword clenched in her right hand. "*Where is it?*"

Sijara adjusted her grip on her blade. "I think I—"

The carnufex burst out of the ground, soaked and screeching. With a cry, Sijara collapsed into the space it left behind, arms flailing.

"Eternal Mother." Mettan had stopped dragging Fen.

"A cenote," she whispered, her stomach pitching with terror.

The carnufex flung itself at Ruiha, but Sijara was still screaming. Of course—she didn't know how to swim. Few had access to enough spare water to learn. No matter. She couldn't keep her head above for long. She'd drown.

Heart hammering against her ribs, Fen wrenched her arm from Mettan's shock-loosened grip and ran.

"Fen, no!" he shrieked, but she didn't stop.

The carnufex was too distracted eviscerating a lieutenant to notice Fen as she dashed to the spot where Sijara had vanished. Blood rushed in her ears, drowning out the whole world as she flung aside her quarterstaff and leapt over the edge.

Stars exploded behind her eyes as she hit the water. Pain lanced through her. The impact was so much worse than she'd expected. This was nothing like the pool Onath had made his guards train in before the wells ran dry. Her body felt like it was weighted down with stones. She began to sink, but then she forced her arms to move in the motions the magistrate had drilled into her.

Just as she was getting the hang of it, a hand clamped around her leg and yanked her down. Fen choked as she went under, water flooding her mouth and throat. A second hand grabbed her calf, and she sank farther. Sijara was going to drown them both. Panic thrummed in Fen's veins. She pedaled desperately, squeezing every last drop of energy she could coax from her muscles. Her lungs burned white hot.

They broke the surface.

Gasping for air, Fen grabbed Sijara's waist and propelled them both toward the side of the cenote. They clung to the rock, vomiting water. Fen felt like she'd thrown up her guts by the time she finally stopped hacking.

The sounds of battle had stopped. Without turning to look at Sijara, she climbed up and heaved herself over the cenote's side. Dark, bloodied shapes littered the clearing. At the center of them all, slumped over the rock where Barra had been eaten, was the carnufex. Its tongue lolled out of its mouth, stinking green blood trickling from countless slashes across its belly.

Fen let herself fall back against the dirt, her skin screaming from where it had struck the water. She drew her knees in, rocking herself until her ragged breaths slowed. After a moment, Sijara crawled out and collapsed beside her, trembling.

Two familiar pairs of boots entered Fen's vision.

"You could've died!" Mettan cried.

"I know," Fen said, forcing the words through her burning throat. She rolled onto her side and looked up at him.

He looked like he had half a mind to start kicking her. Beside him, Ruiha gazed down at the pair of women at her feet. Her eyes were glazed. She bent down, kneeling before them. Fen and Sijara sat up immediately.

Ruiha began wiping carnufex blood from her swords with a dry handful of grass. "You did well, Mekantai." Then she stood again. "Come with me, Mettan."

She walked away, emerald ichor dripping in her wake. Mettan shot Fen one last poisonous look before he followed. Fen watched as they passed what remained of Barra. Ruiha paused, her shoulders shaking. But then she forced herself onward. The wounded were moaning in agony. There was work to do.

Fen made to stand, but a hand grabbed her wrist.

Sijara's lips twisted. "I—I don't want you dead, Fen."

"Oh, thanks," Fen snapped. "Let go."

"I will, just—" A hundred emotions flickered over Sijara's features, too fast for Fen to identify. "I'm sorry."

Fen froze. "What?"

"You weren't entirely wrong that day," Sijara said. "It's easier to be angry at you than the emperor. I can't get even with him, so I always settle for someone closer—" She coughed up a little water. "I thought I'd outgrown it, but it looks like joining a rebellion doesn't exactly solve anger issues. Who would've thought?"

Those words slid right through Fen's defenses, a knife between the ribs. She offered Sijara a tiny smile. "You, evidently."

The corners of Sijara's lips tipped upward, though there was no mirth in her eyes. "My rage was like a boiling pot. I thought if I let off a little steam killing imperialists, I'd keep myself from exploding."

It was a bad metaphor. Still, Fen wrestled with the sudden, sharp desire to reach out and hold her. She knew—Eternal Mother, she *knew*—what it was like to lose family and any chance at a future. She knew what it was like to feel completely, utterly alone.

But Fen clasped her hands together and stayed where she was. "That's not very healthy," she said, as if she had any idea what a coping mechanism was.

Sijara's answering laugh was fragile. "Oh, believe me, I know."

☾

There was no formal funeral for Barra.

None of the surviving lieutenants showed up for training the next day. In fact, no one seemed to know where any of them had gone. Fen and Mettan helped Ying and the other medics patch up the wounded rebels lucky—or unlucky—enough to survive. There was no official proclamation announcing Barra's successor, either. The choice was obvious. His right-hand lieutenant would take up the mantle.

Ruiha and the other officers returned to the camp two days later. They ignored the soldiers who ran up to them, vanishing into her tent. Only one lieutenant, Jurek, would speak to the gathered Masks when the commanders finally reappeared. He explained that they'd gone back to crack open the rig and collect the cenote's water. But first, they'd buried the dead. He wept as he spoke.

Ruiha remained in her tent for the next two days. When she finally emerged, it was to announce that Zepha would be her second-in-command. As the following weeks coalesced into months, the fine lines on Ruiha's face deepened. Dark shadows grew under her eyes. Her shoulders began to curve inward. It seemed as if she were shrinking into herself—that one day she would truly disappear.

She didn't, and the Masks thanked the Eternal Mother for it, but she was never the same.

## ALEKHAI

Alekhai tightened his scarf before the wind could snatch it away, scooting farther down along the slowly baking rock of a low hill. With the other hand, he adjusted the binoculars pressed to his face, trying to find the best angle as he looked out over the vast broken landscape before him. This close to the equator, a pale band cleaved the sky neatly in two, the rings layered into a single gray-white line. In the far distance was the dark, angular smudge of Boğazkesen, perched in the plummeting dip between two great mountains. Built by Alekhai's ancestors to block Ophthia's access to trade pre-unification, the fortress's name meant "cutter of the straits" in Oldearth Turkish. But the only seas here were made of sand, sand that had soaked up the blood of two armies. So perhaps the more literal translation fit better: throat-cutter.

Alekhai's contact hadn't failed him: The windows of the fortress were black as the vacuum of space. Akrysanth had set about restationing Senmavari at their father's old outposts, but the soldiers had yet to reach Boğazkesen. A mercy, as the only other way to Bakrai would require dragging his skiff over the mountains or losing a week driving around them.

Darkness was falling like an axe, cleaving warmth from the sand and stone and air as Alekhai scrambled down the rock to the skiff. Stars winking sleepily into existence above him, he hopped inside the vehicle and drove onward. Bakrai wasn't very far, but it snuck up on him all the same. Though its ancient walls were high, typically the glow of the settlement shone for kilometers out. But when he parked his skiff behind a pile of rough-cut stone at the foot of the great wall, there was nothing but shadows and silence. Alekhai hadn't expected a bustling metropolis; a century had passed since Bakrai had last been worth putting on a map. And Lady Maheka's efforts to further depopulate the once-great city to make way for her gargantuan new estate had been, by all accounts, successful; only a handful of villagers remained. But still.

The front and only gate was shut fast. There was no one on duty to open it, either. He'd have to use one of the imperial overrides. Doing so would reveal his location to the spies Akrysanth had no doubt assigned to monitor him, but his options were limited. Alekhai activated his omnichip and commanded the gate to open.

Nothing happened.

Gritting his teeth together, Alekhai stared up at the wall. There was nothing for it; if he couldn't go though, he'd have to go over. If only he'd brought all his gear. But this little excursion was supposed to have been a vacation. Or as close to a vacation as he ever had. He rolled up his sleeves and found the first set of handholds.

Alekhai was a chosen grandson of Oldearth, born and bred for war despite finding physical combat distasteful. (It was just so . . . messy.) He was much stronger than the average human, but by the time he was halfway up, his limbs were shaking from the strain, lactic acid burning like fire in his muscles. Only once he was safely atop the wall and searching for the stairway down did he realize he was bleeding. Some sharp bit of stone had sliced through the meat of his shoulder on his way up. Bright red rivulets snaked down his arm, jewellike drops of blood beading up at his elbow and falling in slow succession across the dusty platform.

Alekhai ripped a length of cloth from the bottom of his tunic and wrapped the wound as he finally located the stairs and ran down. He'd seen nothing from above the city, only more swirling black. But as he hit the last step, he encountered the first living thing he'd seen since entering Ophthia: a selach, also known as the common land shark. It whirled around to face him, its attention snapping from the citizen it'd been digging into. The victim's face was unrecognizable, and so was the rest of him. The only thing identifying the corpse as human were the scraps of clothes framing the mess.

Fuck.

Alekhai faced the selach calmly. Unblinking, unnaturally pale eyes. A pointed nose that could sniff out blood from hundreds of meters away. Two overlapping rows of curved fangs. Pebbled yellow skin. The creature looked very little like its aquatic Oldearth namesake, save for a bony back ridge that almost resembled a fin. With a breathy roar, it sped over to him on its seven-toed feet. Alekhai flung himself backward, yanking a stinger from a hidden pocket. He fired twice. Both shots went wide. He landed among a clump of thorny bushes, the selach atop him. The beast's maw clamped down hard on his forearm. Blood gushed.

He cried out. What had he been thinking? Eternal Mother, he'd spent so long hunting enemies inside the palace he'd forgotten he was essentially prey outside it. The selach wrenched its flat head from side to side. If his flesh hadn't been reinforced, the creature would've taken his arm. Snarling, he drove his free fist into its mottled face. The selach shuddered, a roar scraping from between the fangs buried in his skin. Alekhai punched it again, but its whole head was armored. Saliva flew from its mouth in great blood-pinked globules.

Alekhai sucked in a breath, made his fingers a flat blade, and struck. His hand went right in, stabbing into the small pocket of soft white flesh beneath a beady gray eye. The beast let out a strange, whistling scream and thrashed, releasing his arm. Thick blood pouring from its eye, the selach leapt off him and skittered away into the darkness. With a deep, shuddering breath, Alekhai wobbled to his feet. The movement, gradual as it was, sent bolts of searing pain down both arms. Hissing through his teeth, Alekhai tore off another strip of fabric and carefully tended to his wounds as best he could. If fortune was on his side, Kacper would have a proper medkit, and he'd be able to take care of himself without having to expose himself to a physician.

He snatched up the stinger, activated his omnichip, and summoned up the light feature. A bright white beam shot from his wrist, illuminating—

Alekhai's stomach crawled up to his throat. He jabbed Kacper's address into his omnichip. And then he was running, scrambling over corpses and splashing through pools of blood. Bodies, bodies, bodies, hacked and torn in all manner of ways. Alekhai had seen enough carnage to drive most mad, but it all paled in comparison to what was before him now. One might almost call the variety of butchery creative. And yet, despite the gore painting the walls and flowing through the streets, there was no smell. No rot. It was as if the people of Bakrai had died only a moment ago, with a hasty wind following to sweep away the copper tang of blood. But there wasn't so much as a breeze. Only one sort of being could have carried out such a slaughter.

And only one person could have ordered it.

Alekhai crashed through the front door and into the living room. They were all there: Kacper, his partner, their daughter and son. Holding on to each other. They hadn't let go, even as they'd been torn apart. Alekhai crumpled to his knees. In the far left corner, something shimmered. The thing responsible for all this bloody destruction, all this terrible loss.

"Why?" Alekhai rasped. The word was a whisper in a typhoon.

He received no answer. He hadn't expected one. He reached into his tunic, this time for his trusty knife, designed to mimic an Accuser's blade-tipped limbs.

Now the alien construct that had haunted him all his life spoke, thundering, "ALL OF THEM? BUT YOUR BROTHER JUST—"

"Yes," Alekhai demanded. "All of them."

He grasped Kacper's cold hand with his free one. And then he got to work.

☾

"How did we—?" Kacper asked, after he'd woken, gasping and weeping, beside his partner and their children.

Alekhai could not look at him. "My brother. He had the imperial Accuser do it." Even to his own ears, his voice sounded like two rusted plates of iron grinding together.

"He commands an Accuser?" Kacper choked out.

"He believes he does. It was assigned by a Maker to assist him upon his ascension."

Kacper's mouth fell open. "There's still a Maker on Newearth?"

"Very rarely," Alekhai said. "It visits a few times a year, only to refuse to repair the planet."

"Is that why your family hides It from the rest of us?"

"That, and to keep complaints from reaching It," Alekhai spat. "My family's done a great job of convincing It we've always worked in humanity's best interest."

Kacper's eyes pinched closed. "Why . . . why would the Sovereign butcher his own people like this?"

Alekhai turned then, made himself stare at Kacper's open, trusting face. Akrysanth was not so cruel, nor so petty, that he would massacre a village simply because Alekhai had found a friend in one of the inhabitants.

Or was he?

No, there had to be another reason.

"Before this, the emperor's Accuser always refused to attack enemies, let alone regular citizens. Or do much of anything, which is why we never advertised its existence. I'm going to find out how and why this happened." He stared at the knife still in his hands. Any trace of what he'd just done had vanished, as it always did, but he couldn't stop seeing golden blood splattered over his fingers. "How many dead? Do you know?"

"They murdered half the village. Fifty, about. But you can't possibly—"

"I can." Alekhai's hand tightened around the hilt. "And I will."

"Thank you."

Alekhai laughed. It was a bitter, broken thing. "Don't thank me."

He stepped outside, Kacper beside him. Up above, a silent flash lit up the darkness, painting deep red shadows over the roofs and walls. Smaller bursts of light followed, flickering across the constellations, skipping past the ring.

Fifty.

So be it.

Alekhai found the nearest corpse. He drew in a long, deep breath as Kacper took his hand. This time his fingers were warm, soft, alive. As meteors sliced up the sky and let fire bleed through, Alekhai lifted the blade. Again, and again, and again.

And again.

And again.

And again.

When it was all over, Alekhai crawled into his skiff. He refused to let Kacper carry him. The man followed anyway, just long enough to crush Alekhai into an embrace. Alekhai forced himself to return it. Then Kacper let him go, and Alekhai turned on the engine. Sand billowed out around him, and the desert swallowed him whole.

☾

The crowning glory of the imperial temple in Eira was its first set of doors. Nearly as massive as the palace's, they had been cut from the mountainside itself. Plated in purest silver, they shone brighter than the sun.

Alekhai paused before the temple's entrance, but only just long enough to gather himself. He forced his fists to unfurl, his back to straighten. He took in a long, deep breath. Despite their immense weight, the doors swung open with a push. The temple, of course, had no barriers beyond the trip here. It served as a shrine to the Eternal Mother, and was therefore open to the entire empire. Never mind the Senmavari stationed at the foot of the great stairs.

Alekhai marched into a vast chamber. A wave of heat rolled over him as he made his way toward the entrance hall. He scanned his surroundings, shrugging off his cloak and tucking it under his arm. He'd been here once a year for every year of his life, and absolutely nothing had changed since the first visit.

The new cleric-chieftain and his retainers lived in an underground system of hot springs said to be as old as Newearth itself. Alekhai had always been fairly certain they were human-made. The temple looked less like a natural habitat and more like the gaudy imitation of one, a too-neat stream winding through the complex, illuminated by dozens of floating bronze globelanterns. Reeds poked up through the crystal-clear water in whimsical patterns. Rows of silver statues stood against the tapestried stone walls, gleaming feet planted upon plinths of solid blue goldstone. The air susurrated with the hum of idle gossip and somewhat less idle prayer. Clerics of all ranks milled about, tending to the temple, running errands for their seniors, and preparing for the evening service. Everything reeked of flowers, just on the edge of rot. Alekhai registered none of it.

High Cleric Tákan materialized at his side, bowing low. "My prince, it is an honor to have you visit us."

"Where is he?" Alekhai asked. His voice was still hoarse from screaming.

"Forgive me. The Sovereign is currently in a period of meditation. He is not to be disturbed—"

"Where. Is. He?"

Tákan lifted his arms in entreaty. His elbows and wrists shimmered in the flickering candlelight, silver leaf pressed to his skin in a wave of curling designs. The metal would be peeled off, melted down, and cut into new shapes just before midnight—all in accordance with the liturgical significance of the coming day. Assuming he kept his arms. Alekhai's hand was already on the hilt of his knife. It had slid there without his knowing, but now he was thinking about it, about Tákan facedown in a steaming pool of red. The fury of fifty murdered souls was in his marrow now, and it would not seep from his bones anytime soon. His eyes narrowed.

"Just through there," Tákan said at last, pointing to an intricately carved door.

Alekhai shoved past him.

Inside was a great slab of quartz, and on that slab sat Akrysanth. He cracked open one eye. "Little brother. How good to see you."

"Bakrai," Alekhai said.

"Oh." Akrysanth's lip curled. "So that's where you went." He sighed, taking in Alekhai's face. "Can't we be familial for at least a half minute?"

"I stepped right into it, Akrysanth," Alekhai spat out. "I—"

"Oh, please." A gentle scoff. "The smell would've warned you."

"There was none," Alekhai bit out.

"Hm," said Akrysanth, frowning now. "I'll have to ask my Accuser to let the meat rot next time, then. Won't seem authentic otherwise."

"Authentic?" Alekhai whispered. "You're going to do this again? I—"

"Of course I am," said Akrysanth. "Many times, in fact. And I need it to look like bandits did it."

Alekhai stared at his brother agape, the knife-sharp pieces falling together in his mind. "Please," he said. "Please tell me you aren't going to massacre your own people to—to save food."

Akrysanth's gaze flicked away for a second, and for a single heartbeat, Alekhai saw something that looked like remorse. "There is no other way."

"Oh?" A bubble of hysterical laughter rose up Alekhai's throat. He forced it back down—barely. "Or are you too much of a monster to see otherwise?"

"Take care." Akrysanth smiled now, bright as the sun. "You are speaking to your Sovereign."

"My Sovereign," Alekhai echoed softly. "And you think that gives you the right to butcher the innocent?"

"It gives me the right to do whatever I please," said the Sovereign, "and that includes cutting out my brother's tongue if he fails to control it." He closed his eyes again. "You're dismissed."

Alekhai's fingers had been tingling since Bakrai, as if there were a slight electrical current running through them. He'd been unable to stop the shaking. Now he wondered what it would be like to wrap these trembling hands around his brother's pale throat. After another long moment, he twisted on his heel. But he did not leave the temple altogether. He headed toward a small, nondescript stone door. It ground open at his command.

Alekhai knelt, head bowed in rage. His hands fell atop his knees, fingernails biting bloody crescents into his palms.

"YOU DID NOT HANDLE THAT VERY WELL," said a voice.

"He killed my friend. The whole family. The children."

"AND HE WILL BE WATCHING YOU MORE CAREFULLY FROM NOW OWN."

"I don't care. I want him dead," Alekhai snarled. "So Enkaiia might live."

"AND WHAT ARE YOU WILLING TO SACRIFICE TO MAKE IT HAPPEN?"

Alekhai did not respond. The answer was obvious.

Everything.

# BOOK TWO

Four months passed without much excitement. There was a particularly raucous party after another of the Sovereign's last two siblings met their untimely death, but royals murdering royals was hardly news. The Masks were still licking their wounds after the carnufex attack.

Fen could see her life falling into a pattern, marked by the cold gaze of the stars at night and the scorching glare of the sun by day. The rebels took what little they could from their enemies, but first-years like Fen and Mettan were never permitted to join the raiding squads. With so few opportunities, there was no margin for error. Especially after the last large expedition.

After the empty lieutenant slots were filled, training commenced under Ruiha's hollow gaze. Fen went out of her way to watch Sijara fight. If the other young rebels were water, Sijara was oil. She was separate in every sense of the word, above them all. No one could touch her.

At some point, Fen started winning as many matches as she lost, but fighting was far from the only skill she honed during those months. She experimented in the kitchen with Zepha whenever Ruiha's right hand had spare time. And Ying made Fen finally think about seriously taking care of herself. One day, after training, the medic caught her by the arm and dragged her up to one of the mostly empty tiers of the base.

"What are your coping mechanisms?" she asked, once Fen had given up complaining.

Fen sat down in front of her. "I'm sorry, what?"

Ying's eyes crinkled up, like she was trying to hold in a laugh. "What do you do when you start to panic? When things start spinning out of control, or the world just feels like it's too much?"

"Oh." Fen planted her elbow on her thigh, leaned forward, and dropped her chin atop her fist. "I tell myself that it's only temporary and try to focus on my breathing."

"That's a great start."

Fen shot her a flat, unimpressed look. "Eternal Mother, don't patronize me."

"Sorry." Ying laughed, pulling in her legs and crossing them. She placed her hands palm side up on her knees. "What do you know about meditation?"

After fifteen minutes of griping and fidgeting, Fen gave in and closed her eyes. She tried to appreciate the distinctive dry scent of the woods. She tried to find the inner peace Ying spoke of. She tried to let herself be open, vulnerable.

She found varying success, struggling especially with that last goal, but it was enough. By the time she opened her eyes again, it was dark and Ying had fallen asleep. Fen was about to prod her awake—the uneven floor couldn't be comfortable—when Mettan joined them. He looked up at the thin branches above, where enesi were singing themselves to sleep. Their song sounded eerily human.

"Sometimes I forget we're not the only animals here," he murmured, leaning against Fen. "Besides the insects, of course."

Someone cleared their throat by the ladder. They turned around. Sijara stood by the edge of the platform, arms crossed. Fen felt Mettan poke her side and valiantly resisted the urge to jam an elbow into his ribs.

Sijara began, "Can we—"

"I *can't* believe you didn't invite us." Ihazan clambered over the side and pushed past her, closely followed by the twins. They looked from Fen to Sijara as they sprawled out on the platform. "Mother, you two are always so *intense*."

"I'd say we have good reason to be," Sijara said flatly. "After all, the imperialists—"

Ihazan lifted both hands. "I'm not judging you or anything! The imperialists never touched my family. Well, not directly. I'm an outlier here."

"So why'd you join?" Fen asked.

"Too many mouths to feed. No one pushed me to go, but . . ." Ihazan's easy smile faltered. "I didn't say goodbye. Thought it would make leaving easier." They blinked rapidly, possibly forcing away tears, and looked over at Mettan. "What about you?"

"I . . . " He went silent.

"Oh, sorry. If you don't want to say, then that's perfectly fine. Just if you wanted."

"It's all right. Bad marriage." Mettan's face was a calm, collected mask, but the slight tremor of his hands betrayed him. Fen placed a gentle, steadying hand on his back as he spoke. "My father-in-law murdered my sister. He was going to come for me, too, so my family sent me where he'd never think to look."

"Oof." Ihazan grimaced in sympathy. "I'm sorry."

"It's—" Mettan's chest rose and fell. "Well, it's not *fine*, but I am."

He looked over at Naijima. The others followed his gaze. The twin was rapping his fingers against the wooden floor, mouth tightening. It wasn't that he seemed reluctant to speak, but rather that he appeared unsure how to say what he wanted.

But after some time, he spoke. "On the edge of Eira, by the coast, there's a mining town called Maridon." He threw an unreadable glance at his brother. "That's where we're from. After my tribe surrendered without a fight, the old emperor elevated half of our government to aristocrats. Our cleric-chieftains went from leading us to ruling us to owning us. Everyone works for the same extraction company now: Irin."

Ihazan made a face at the name.

"It's owned by the regional lord. Deep in the mines, there are at least five different species of venomous arthropod. Every two weeks, Irin was supposed to hire specialists to clear out the animals and double-check that the tunnels were safe. It was even written into law. But the examinations put everything on hold for days at a time, and since the CEO's also a noble, he had the law tweaked so that the checks only had to happen once a month. And then four months. And then every *year*."

His voice wavered. "Two months before we were supposed to get married, my partner got stung. They told us our insurance didn't cover the treatment needed to save them, so we had to pay for it out of pocket. But the company that manufactures the antivenom has a monopoly on the formula, and we couldn't afford the necessary second dose. Even after Hahru and I took on triple shifts. Even after we sold the house. So I signed away my life. Every wage I would ever earn, handed from one corporation to the next." His hands curled into fists. "But by the time payment was approved, my partner was dead. The drug company wouldn't return the payment, and the aristocrat wouldn't release me from the indentured servitude I'd promised, so I ran." He pulled the companionship pin from his hair and pressed his thumb hard into the enameled head. There was a hopeless, haunted look on his face that squeezed Fen's heart. "I came here because I had nowhere else to go."

As much as Naijima clearly despised the imperialists, Fen had assumed idealistic, honorable Hahru had dragged his twin off to join the rebels. She opened her mouth to comfort Naijima, but what could she say? She could understand working yourself to the bone to save someone, only to have them slip through your fingers anyway. But unlike Naijima, unlike Sijara and Mettan, she'd barely known the people she'd lost. She had no idea how they felt.

Hahru slung an arm around his twin's shoulders and gave a limp half shrug. "Where my brother goes, I go." His fingers fidgeted in his lap. "But also, I broke the nose of one of the company agents and there's a hefty price on my head, along with the bounty for breaking my contract."

"So this is where you all ran off to."

The rebels twisted around to face Ruiha. Her eyes were red, her expression shattered. One hand absently toyed with the pommel of a sword, neither threatening nor chiding, but nervous. Fen could feel the discomfort rolling off their commander in thick waves.

But then, wonder of wonders, she sat down between Ihazan and Naijima. Fen's chest filled with a heavy ache as she and the others watched Ruiha's face. The captain looked as though someone was dragging a hot, jagged blade through her insides.

"He wanted to see us win," was all she said.

That was it: the final stroke. Those five words were a mallet against a gong. Determination sliced through the ache behind Fen's ribs.

They'd pay for this. Everyone responsible for the execution of Sijara's family, for the broken systems that had killed Mettan's sister and Naijima's partner, for Barra's end in the jaws of a creature driven to starvation by the ravaging of its habitat. She knew exactly whom to blame—the same people who'd destroyed her family. It went beyond the city imperialists hoarding food and water. It went beyond the corporate nobles wringing labor and blood from the people, celebrating their riches as the gap between those who owned and those who were owned grew vastly larger. None of their evil would be possible without the Sovereigns, presiding over all that pain and suffering.

It was so easy, in that moment, to forget that she'd joined the Broken Masks for herself: to save her own skin, to secure personal vengeance. Her desire for retribution remained as sharp as ever, but she didn't want revenge if it meant chaos. Everything came with a price, and she'd be no worse than the Sovereign if the innocents suffered for her sake. Still, there had to be a way.

The squad sat there until midnight, or what seemed like it, filling the silence with nothing but their breathing. Fen found it oddly comforting. What glorious insanity it was to have spent her whole life under an emperor's boot and still refuse to accept his authority, even as his hold on the people tightened. And what a strange and terrifying joy, to have company in her madness—to stand with others in wretched defiance. When they left, they left almost all at once: Ihazan convinced Naijima and Hahru to get a drink with them, Sijara went off to bed, and Ying took Ruiha to the medical tent for some kind of sleeping draught.

That left only Fen and Mettan, leaning against each other in the dark.

"What are you thinking about?" he asked.

"The future," she said. "And how to get there."

On the twenty-second day of the Month of Brass, Ruiha received an encoded message from the border patrol. She'd ordered them to keep an eye on the land between the woods and the nearest stone cities, a job as thankless as it was dull. Or at least it *had* been dull. The rebels had come across a band of Senmavari terrorizing a caravan of peasants. A fight had broken out. Only when the dust had settled did the rebels realize that the soldiers had been protecting a high-ranking postwoman.

The skirmish had left the patrol in bad shape. While the injured patched themselves up, the remaining Masks worked on obtaining the letter the imperialists had been tasked with delivering. The message was stored in a datachip, which was itself stored in a case that could only be opened with a fourteen-character key. The rebels "questioned" the messenger until they got the code, and then, since the datachip was programmed to self-destruct if an attempt to transfer its contents beyond a limited radius was made, dispatched a courier of their own.

The week between securing the datachip and the arrival of the messenger was a fraught one. The whole base seemed to vibrate with anxiety. Even Mettan, who'd told Fen she was going out of her way to find things to fret about, couldn't keep still. Sometimes Fen would catch him walking around in circles, chewing his nails so far down they bled. And she was no better; even sitting down between sparring sessions made her feel vulnerable, as if the imperialists would pounce as soon as she dropped her guard.

The pair were having lunch when the courier reached Kanoh. They were both carrying bowls of stew as they paced back and forth, trying to talk of anything but the datachip.

"Ying's late. Again," remarked Mettan, fishing for one of the dumplings in his bowl. They were Fen's latest creation: plump, juicy balls of dough filled with root vegetables and bits of a ten-legged insect no one knew the name of. "I wonder where she runs off to."

Fen laughed at his dry tone. Ying, of course, was with Ruiha. Whenever either the medic or captain could not be found, chances were that the other would vanish as well. "When do you think she's going to admit they're, ah, involved?"

Mettan smirked. "I bet—"

"The captain! Where is she?" A person draped in the bloodied uniform of an imperial courier stomped across the nearby bridge and barged onto the platform. There was a jagged slash across the middle of their tunic; it was a wonder the stolen disguise had worked. The messenger was flanked by two rebels in battered imperialist armor. "I need to see her. *Now.*"

Fen pointed up to Ruiha's sleeping tent. "There, I imagine."

"What happened?" Ying appeared out of nowhere, pushing through the throng forming on the platform. Strands of hair were sweat-plastered to her face. "That's the messenger?"

Mettan shot Fen a look and snorted. "You look out of breath," he said pleasantly.

Fen grinned. "Must've been an intense workout."

Ying's cheeks pinked adorably as she ripped aside the stray hairs.

Fen was about to needle the poor medic further when her omnichip chimed. She activated it. Her heart skipped a beat. "Ruiha's summoned us," she said, patting Mettan on the shoulder. "She wants the whole squad in the command tent now."

"See you later, then," said Ying. "Tell me what happens!"

Fen and Mettan turned to go, but not before the former quipped, "Only if you tell us about you and Ruiha!"

Ying cursed under her breath and scampered off.

The second they were inside the command tent, Ruiha slapped a datachip into Fen's hand. "You said you had a hobby of reading the magistrate's mail, yes?"

"It was more a matter of life and death than a pastime." Fen looked around. Besides Ruiha and the messenger, Ihazan, Hahru, Naijima, and Sijara were the only people there. "Where are the other officers?"

Ruiha's eyes narrowed dangerously for a moment before she heaved a sigh. "I cannot control what's in the letter, only who finds out what's in it first. I need to formulate a response before anyone else. The key the imperial postwoman gave up, along with her biometrics, unlocked the case. But the letter's still encoded. Get to it."

Fen dove in without another word. Unlike the dispatch that the emperor had sent Onath, which had been a personal order of vengeance, this was clearly a letter of importance to the state. Its contents weren't protected by straightforward character replacement, but a polyalphabetic cipher that consisted, in turn, of a series of interwoven shift ciphers based on the letters of a keyword. A keyword she did not have.

Fen sat down on the floor. She needed to concentrate. "What was the code the courier gave you?"

"'All hail the Sovereign.' No spaces or capitalization." The rebel messenger pulled a stray lock of dark-blond hair from their face and crossed their arms. "I can't believe we wasted *five* days getting that out of her."

Fen fed the key through her omnichip, in which she'd written a program that would prevent her from being locked out if she exceeded the permitted number of attempts. Nothing happened, as expected. She wasn't nearly so lucky. "Did you get the courier's name?"

The messenger's face scrunched up for a moment as they thought. They had a long, thin nose that looked like it had been broken and reset a dozen times. "It was Tema Laedev."

Fen tried the first name, the last name, both, and then thirty different combinations involving varying capitalization, letter order, and spacing before she gave up. She slumped back against the wall, pinching the bridge of her nose.

A keyword unique to each imperial courier would be the smart option. But the imperialists prioritized tradition and flattery above common sense half the time, and the messenger's biometrics were personal enough. Given the code that had unlocked the datachip in the first place, Fen wondered if the keyword for the cipher would be equally foolish. She typed Akrysanth into her omnichip, berating herself as she did so.

Nothing, as expected. To humor herself, she input his middle name, Kanem. The imperialists couldn't possibly be *that* simple, but it was worth a try—

It worked.

Fen brought the omnichip's holographic screen closer to her face as her squadmates squeezed close. She read the words as her omnichip decoded them. By the time she was finished, a lump of ice had formed in her gut. Cold incredulity froze her solid, and the datachip slipped between her numb fingers to clatter onto the floor. She couldn't believe what she'd just read. But . . .

But of course they would do this.

"What does it say?" demanded Ruiha. She stood apart from the group, a stylus spinning in her hand.

Fen forced herself to her feet. She handed the datachip back to the messenger with slick, clumsy hands. "The imperialists are running out of food and water far faster than they can get it. The emperor has decided that the riots must be stopped before they even begin. He's . . . he's ordered the army to ensure that the existing food stores will suffice."

Everyone went very, very still as understanding dawned on them.

"Eternal Mother." Naijima's voice was raw. "He's going to cull his own people."

"So he's going to just slaughter tens of thousands?" Ihazan asked in disbelief, hands balled into fists.

"*Hundreds* of thousands," Fen whispered.

"But *everyone* would revolt—"

"They're going to make the executions look like bandit attacks. Or rebel offensives." Fen felt as if someone had a hand around her throat as she spoke.

The stylus in Ruiha's hand broke in two.

"This makes no *sense*," said Sijara, her lips twisted into a snarl. "Covert mass murder on that level isn't logistically possible, unless they're planning on using some sort of bioweapon. But that's forbidden by the Makers' Benevolent Directives."

"It's possible," Fen said quietly. She flicked a hand, sending the fully decoded letter to everyone in the room. "And they *will* do it. Someone spent a lot of time finding the right loopholes to escape Accuser punishment. They're going to take out a few villages at a time, no more than twenty a year, over the next decade. And they're hoping the resulting chaos will see even more dead. They'll blame us."

Hahru's nostrils flared. "Monsters."

When Ruiha finally spoke again, her voice reminded Fen of the glaciers she'd seen in images of Oldearth—impossibly cold, impossibly even. "I will paint this planet red with imperialist blood before I let that happen."

"We can't stop them," the messenger said, their voice low.

"We've fallen short of our recruitment goals every year since Moru's murder. And even with the other bases, the imperialists outnumber us a hundred to one. It's suicide."

Fen's brows lifted at the mention of other rebel forces. The commanders had been extremely tight-lipped about the state of the Broken Masks.

"We have to," Ruiha snapped. As she looked around the room, her gaze paused on Fen. "Barra made too many sacrifices for us to give up now without even trying. What are we fighting for, if not the common people? We exist so that the villagers sentenced to death by the emperor might survive."

Mettan swallowed. "Some of them, at least."

"There's hope," Fen forced out.

The messenger turned on her. "What?"

"There's hope." Fen straightened her spine, looking back over the message before she spoke. "Look at the end. The imperialists will be transporting a prototype of the weapon they'll use to destroy the villages. The descriptions here are incredibly vague, but it's mechanical in nature and can be set to target only people rather than buildings, making the lie of a bandit attack easy to sell. If we can steal it, we can use it."

"Good. We'll form a plan around that." Ruiha opened the letter on her own omnichip and skimmed through the pertinent section. "I'm going to summon the officers now. We're going to figure out how to stop this before it starts."

The odds were far from in their favor. There were just over two hundred rebels in Kanoh, with about a hundred and seventy of them able to fight at present. There were other, larger bases that had spies within the imperial fortresses, but communications between groups had frayed after Moru's death, with the survivors breaking off into their own factions. The only assurance the Kanoh rebels had that the emperor hadn't already crushed the other bases and exterminated the spies was because he hadn't bragged about it publicly yet. Even if they were able to send this news and convince the others to join them, the total number of rebels that could be assembled into a military force was barely twenty thousand. In an open field, the imperialists would slaughter them. The only way they'd save the villagers was by taking the imperialists' secret weapon.

"We need to be careful about this," Ruiha said, once her lieutenants had assembled in the command tent. Her voice cut through the space like an expertly wielded knife. "Based on the letter we seized, the convoy responsible for transporting the weapon will be going through Umut Pass, one of only four ways to reach the first testing site. They're planning to rendezvous with one of their generals, who will oversee the operation from there."

Lowering a hand to the large map before her, she traced a route painstakingly painted in black and crimson ink. Sketched on realpaper, Makhan resembled a massive hand cupping the rebel forest and the wilds. Umut Pass linked the middle of the palm to the base of the thumb, a shortcut that would allow the imperialists to pounce on the settlement with ease. The villagers would have no way of knowing their doom was upon them until it was too late.

"To maintain as much secrecy as possible, there will be no more than twenty or so Senmavari protecting the convoy. We may have lost the last fight, but the imperialists are still recovering, too. Their military is stretched thin, and their main weapon is one of five prototypes. My squad of seven, as well as the platoon of forty-five soldiers under my command, will put down the enemy and take the weapon. If we position ourselves on either side of the road cutting through the pass, we can take advantage of the higher ground and ambush them before they can use the weapon against us." Ruiha tapped two points on the map before placing her hands on the shoulders of the two nearest lieutenants. "Any questions?"

"Yes." A tall man with ruddy skin nearly as red as his hair stepped forward. Lieutenant Karstek, one of the sergeants promoted in the wake of the training exercise disaster. "An enemy convoy cutting right through our territory, carrying a secret weapon of untold power? It's like an eryx that brought its own pot and seasoning. What if this is all a plot to draw us out?"

"You don't think I've considered that?" Ruiha crossed her arms. "That possibility is the only reason I'm not taking *everyone* there to intercept that convoy. But if this is real, we can't just stand by and let the emperor wipe out countless innocents." Though her voice didn't rise, she might as well have been yelling. "And once they're done testing out their new toy on the common people, who do you think they're going to come after next? If the weapon really can do what they suggest it can, we're done for. Even if we were heartless assholes who didn't give a damn about the targeted villages, we need to get our hands on a prototype." She looked around the tent. "Anything else? No?"

Silence answered her.

"Then we leave at sundown tomorrow," the captain said. "Zepha, you're in charge. Send word to the targeted villages. Increase our recruitment, I don't care how you do it. We're going to need all the help we can get in the coming months. Everyone else is dismissed."

The next morning and afternoon were consumed by packing and preparation, counting rations and sharpening weapons. By the time the sun began to sink, there was nothing left to do. They were as ready as they'd ever be. Ruiha gave the order to descend to the forest floor.

Fen and Mettan grabbed their knapsacks and walked past the lines meandering toward the lifts. He knew a shortcut, so they went down through a series of platforms that had been abandoned as the Masks' numbers had withered. As they clambered down a ladder, they heard Ying's voice, hushed and urgent.

"Ruiha, *please*. Let me come with you."

Mettan and Fen looked at each other. Though the medic had complained long and hard about how Ruiha had refused to bring her along, she'd seemed to accept her orders by morning. They'd already said their goodbyes. The new recruits ducked down so the women wouldn't see them at the edge of the platform.

"My word is final," the captain said coolly.

Ying grabbed Ruiha by the arm. "I'm not some porcelain vase that shatters at the slightest touch. You know I can fight."

The captain twisted and seized Ying's wrist. "You *will* remain in Kanoh. Do I make myself clear?" Then she sighed, eyes dropping to the planks at her feet. Her grip loosened. "Zepha is a good lieutenant, and he leads his soldiers well, but I don't trust him with the cause, not entirely. I . . . " She let go of Ying, but only to twine their fingers together. "If something happens to me, I need to know that someone like you is here to guide our people."

"That won't be necessary," Ying said quietly. She bent down and pulled a mask from the discarded satchel at her feet, the very mask she'd been working on when Fen first met her. "I'm not finished yet, but take this with you."

"Give it to me when it's done," Ruiha said, managing a smile. "When I return."

"Promise?" Ying cupped her cheek. Without waiting for an answer, she lifted herself on her toes and gently pressed her lips to Ruiha's.

Ruiha laid her fingers over Ying's, melting into the touch. Her eyes fluttered closed. "I promise."

The moment was so intimate, so *close*. Fen felt indecent for having witnessed it. She grabbed Mettan by the collar and tugged him down the rest of the way, making sure to keep out of sight. They stepped onto the lift alongside ten rebels from Ruiha's platoon and descended in silence.

"I thought this mission was supposed to be easy," Fen whispered, looking around for the rest of their squad on the forest floor. "If *Ruiha* thinks she might not make it . . . "

Mettan shrugged. "She's just acknowledging the possibility that we might not be coming back."

"I suppose." Fen crossed her arms. "I'm still nervous."

Mettan snorted, giving her a look that clearly said, *You're always nervous*. "If you weren't, I'd say something was seriously wrong with you."

"Hey, over here!" Hahru waved at them. He clapped them on the shoulders when they reached him and the others. "I hope you two got a good night's rest. You won't have another for the next two weeks."

Mettan groaned.

"Attention!" Mkarkara, one of Ruiha's sergeants, called.

The captain descended from the canopy, hands clasped behind her back. She gave a short whistle, and the lift stopped three-quarters down.

"Our mission is simple," Ruiha declared. "It's a seventeen-day march to our target. All reports from our contacts in the border villages agree that the convoy is lightly guarded. Given their trajectory and current speed, we will arrive at Umut Pass two days before the imperialists, giving us just enough time to set up an ambush. We'll crush the convoy and take the weapon it's carrying before it reaches the general on the other side. The hard part will be avoiding the patrols the imperialists have sent to keep an eye out for us. Preserving the element of surprise until we attack is obviously of the utmost importance. The enemy cannot be permitted time to prepare, or, Mother forbid, use their weapon on us. We'll keep to the hidden paths in the wilds, and we'll avoid traveling in broad daylight as we get closer to our target." She grinned. "This should be good practice for when we finally crush the imperialists. But for now, our goal is to protect the people of Enkaiia."

The rebels cheered uproariously as the lift lowered her the rest of the way. Though the forest swallowed the shouts and laughter, the sound filled Fen's heart until she felt it would burst.

They stuck to the tree line wherever possible, but there was no way to avoid crossing vast stretches of steppe during the last half of the journey. The grass was more dust than foliage here, and it crackled like fire beneath the rebels' boots. The force trekked through the wilds, not in the crisp, clean lines of stomping Senmavari but in an uneven, undefined mass of half-jogging rebels. And they talked quite a bit. Scouts were sent in several directions to ensure that they'd never encounter the imperial patrols prowling about, but Fen was still agitated by the lack of effort her comrades were putting into stealth. She jumped when Ihazan slung an arm around her shoulders with no warning whatsoever.

"Did you hear?" they asked, brows vanishing into their hairline. "The imperial general is none other than Alekhai." He waited.

"Alekhai *who?*" Fen looked to Mettan, who was staring at her, aghast. "Was I supposed to give some sort of reaction?"

Ihazan sighed heavily, shaking their head as if in supreme disappointment. Even so, they didn't seem surprised by Fen's ignorance. "Alekhai, the prince."

Fen shrugged. "So? Aren't there a thousand of them?"

Ihazan's right eye gave a slight twitch. Their lips pressed into a thin, bloodless line.

"He's not a *minor* prince," Mettan said gently. "He's the emperor's brother, a direct descendant of the first king of Makhan, which is why he doesn't have a last name. It's just Alekhai."

"Again," said Fen, "aren't there a thousand of those?"

"Eternal Mother, what did they teach you in Talishminn?" demanded Ihazan.

"How to hit people with a stick," Fen said. "And I certainly didn't need to know about the intricacies of the imperial family tree to do that." She huffed. The correspondence she'd hacked into over the years had never bothered to mention this particular Alekhai, and anyway, it was a waste of time to memorize the names of royals unless they sat on the throne, given their mortality rate. "Why should I care about this prince? If all goes well, we'll have nothing to do with him."

"Because he's next in line." Ihazan's voice went low, forcing Fen and Mettan to lean in to catch their words. "Akrysanth's already made it clear he's not having kids, and Alekhai has always been the favorite sibling, despite the fact that he's been repeatedly banished from the royal court—"

"Again, I don't really care," said Fen.

Ihazan either didn't hear her or chose to ignore her. "To further secure his claim to the throne, almost all his siblings plotted each other's deaths. Or were killed by the late emperor when he decided they were more trouble than they were worth. And with Sona's recent assassination—"

"Ihazan!" Fen grabbed their right shoulder and shook. Nothing they'd said was a surprise, and now that she thought of it, perhaps the name Alekhai did sound familiar. Nevertheless: "I truly could not give less of a damn. Why do you care so much about the minutiae of his life, anyway?"

They gave her a long, flat look. "Because knowing what makes the next emperor tick, what drives him and what he believes in, is how we figure out his weaknesses and bring him down. And unfortunately, I inherited an obsession with royal drama from my parents. Except in my case, it's actually useful."

"Is it?" Fen asked. "*If* this princeling of yours ever becomes the emperor, we can worry about him then. We all have enough to stress about as it is, including this Motherforsaken so-called march."

As it turned out, however, Fen was practically alone in that sentiment. Much to her annoyance, the matter of Alekhai rapidly became all anyone wanted to talk about. Ihazan started on a story about how Sona had pushed him into their then-eldest sister's funeral pyre. It had taken months to regenerate the charred bits. Fen could not find a kernel of entertainment in the tale.

That night, once everyone had gathered around solar-powered heaters for a dinner of rehydrated vegetables and soggy insect-flour pasta, Fen finally found a real reason to pay attention.

As she slurped up her last noodle, Sijara set down her bowl and said, gravely, "Some call Alekhai the Executioner. The Butcher of Bakrai."

"Bakrai?" Ihazan tilted their head. "I've never heard of such a place."

"There's a reason for that," Sijara said, her gaze falling on the softly glowing heater at the center of the circle.

Fen had heard of Bakrai, but she couldn't place where, when, or in what context. From the hard look of Sijara's face, however, the reason for its obscurity couldn't be good. Well, that and the fact that the prince was called the *Butcher* of Bakrai.

"I heard this from Jurek. Bakrai was a tiny hamlet rooted in the ruins of a once-great city, only a few days' travel from my hometown in Makhan. Mostly weavers and artisans, a few merchants, and only one market." Sijara's hands twisted together. "Then someone invented a new automated loom. They offered the idea to Qaro Maheka, their magistrate and the chieftain of the Mikan-Talo clan, which controls practically all the textile trade along what used to be the Ejo River. Without delay, she implemented it across her settlements, including mine. But when the emperor's tax collectors arrived later this year, she handed over the same amount of revenue as the previous cycle, hoping to keep the new wealth her people had generated all for herself."

Ihazan leaned forward. "And then what?"

Sijara swallowed thickly. "Well, the Sovereign might be a fool, but it's hardly as if everyone in his service is. The master of finance quickly figured out that about four million credits were missing, though she had no idea where the money had gone. It took Alekhai less than a week to discover that the magistrate had stolen the profit. But she was highborn, heir to three noble corporations with even better relations, so the prince punished her through the commoners. Bakrai was her scapegoat." Her fingers curled into fists. "To make the taxes sent from Mikan-Talo match the population, Alekhai had half the hamlet executed and forced the rest into indentured labor for the crown."

The food in Fen's stomach turned to cold stone. "How many people?"

"I don't know. But they say the killing wasn't indiscriminate; it was calculated. He murdered the citizens deemed least productive by the annual work records. Even the children were not spared." Sijara looked up without warning and caught Fen staring at her. Her eyes burned in the darkness; her gaze bit into Fen's bones. "Alekhai earned his nickname twice over. If we fail, he's going to visit every injustice and insult his family's meted out to him upon innocents—but a thousandfold."

Fen looked away, ashamed by her earlier nonchalance.

A harsh laugh broke through the silence. "That's just a myth."

They all whirled around. It was the mustached man Fen had dueled so long ago. He gave Sijara a pointed smirk. "I've read that story and a thousand others like it across the hidden channels of the omninet. If such a thing were true, more of us would've heard of it by now."

Sijara smiled. It was not kind, and it was not amused. "A masked stranger passed through the slaughtered village some days later. An Executor."

A hush fell over the rebels.

Once, Executors had been all but worshipped alongside their otherworldly creators. But now, only the Eternal Mother was truly divine. Now, the Benevolent Directives were viewed not as holy commandments, but alien shackles. Now, the few Executors who walked the world were seen as nothing more than the chambermaids of the Makers' brutal enforcers. Accusers destroyed. Executors cleaned up the mess—and only part of it. The stories said they had little control over whom they could restore to life, and that the Accusers had grown increasingly ungenerous over the centuries.

"The stranger promised to raise the slain if the people of Bakrai left the city and held their tongues," Sijara continued. "They agreed, and he did as he'd sworn to do. An oath made to an Executor is an oath made to the Accusers, ensured by their powers, and the memory of the slaughter vanished from the villagers' minds as they stepped through the gates."

Mustache lifted his eyes to the night sky. "And how, pray tell, did Jurek come to hear this miraculous tale if everyone else forgot?"

Sijara's smile widened. "Accusers' manipulations are imperfect. Some villagers remembered fragments of what had come to pass. Their new neighbors called them mad. And what is madness but the truth no one wants to hear?" She looked around at her audience. "Jurek passed through Mikan-Talo territory on the way back from his last solo mission. He saw and heard enough to weave together what had happened, but realized that without proof, spreading the news would only make us look desperate. He only told me because he knew I have distant relatives in the region."

Mustache still looked unconvinced. "And no one noticed the massacre? What stopped the Butcher from repeating his punishment?"

Sijara shrugged and sighed. "I've told you what I know. Ask Jurek for the rest."

Mustache's mouth shut with a snap. He returned to his dinner, and the squad's attention returned to Sijara.

That night, sleep eluded Fen. All she could think of were the dead of Bakrai, how their ends had been even more unjust than her fathers'. And she thought of how they'd been brought back to life.

Fen's existence quickly became nothing but long days and short nights and the sap-slow trudge toward Umut Pass. Each and every day followed the same painful pattern. The Masks woke up, they ate, they walked, they ate, they slept. Again and again. And, of course, there were the steppe winds. They were ravenous, sinking their claws right through the rebels' mismatched clothes. After all those months in the silent woods surrounding Kanoh, Fen had all but forgotten the sound of wind.

After sixteen days of hard travel, they came to Umut Pass a whole day early. The rocky valley opened below them, framed by stark, sharp-sloped cliffs. The twenty-kilometer path itself stretched just above a long-dead river, twisting and turning all the way to the horizon. The narrowest section, in the middle, would force the imperial convoy into lines no more than five across. With the high ground, it would be child's play to pick them off.

The Masks made camp above the choke point and settled down for the night, but by then, Fen had stopped grasping for sleep, though her eyes burned red and fatigue pressed against the inside of her skull like a fist. She'd been trying the meditation tricks Ying had shown her, but it was all for naught. Fear had curled around her, and it would not let go. She couldn't fend off the terror of knowing that she and her friends could get hurt, no matter how airtight Ruiha's plan was. It was likely they'd all bleed and possible they'd all die. The thought was a vise around her throat. She didn't know if she'd survive losing them.

Two nights before the convoy caught up to the rebels, Fen went off in search of peace she knew she wouldn't find. She sat near the edge of the gorge—though not so close she had any chance of plunging in—crossed her legs, and placed her hands palm side up on her knees in imitation of the pose Ying had demonstrated. She struggled to take long, deep breaths as her nerve-wracked body fought to suck in breath after shallow, panicked breath. After a while she gave up and flopped onto her back. She glared reproachfully up at the stars, but they were distant and cold as ever, and they had no comfort to give her.

☾

The next day, the rebel force was a flurry of movement back and forth across the pass. A third of them were busy building up piles of grass and rock to conceal the warriors who'd lie in wait on both sides of the road below. The next group, to which Fen had been assigned, were finishing up the spiked defensive obstacles they'd hide on the sides of the pass to prevent the imperialists from stealing the high ground. The rest were sharpening weapons and preparing medical supplies so that any wounded could be treated as soon as the dust settled.

That night, Ruiha's squad squeezed in around a cluster of heaters, tighter than they ever had before. Fen ended up with her head in the hollow of Mettan's arm, her ear against the gentle pattern of his heart. She closed her eyes, but even now—even surrounded by her friends and comrades, with the reassuring lullaby of Mettan's pulse—sleep evaded her.

After an hour, when nearly all the others had fallen dead asleep, Fen heard Sijara whisper, "Why are you still up? You need your rest."

Fen wriggled out from under Mettan's arm and turned to face her. "I could say the same."

"I'm awake because you're awake." Sijara's tone was soft, without a drop of irritation.

"I'm sorry."

"Don't be. What's keeping you up? Besides the obvious."

After a very long pause, Fen said, honestly, "I can't stop seeing Barra—what he looked like, just before the end." She swallowed, closing her eyes. She wished she'd gotten to know him better. "He didn't deserve to die like that."

"No one does," Sijara agreed. "But if it makes you feel any better, perhaps his death balanced the scales, after what he did to your parents." She bit her lip. "I'm sorry—that was horrible. Forget I said anything."

Despite the heat, a chill crept between Fen's bones. "What do you mean?"

Sijara propped herself up on an elbow, her widening eyes searching Fen's. "You don't know?"

"No," Fen said lowly, lifting herself too. "I don't."

Sijara's lips pressed together. "Well. We won't be getting any rest now." She clambered to her feet and left the warmth of the heaters. Fen scrambled after her.

"What happened?" she demanded, as soon as they were out of earshot. "What did Barra do to my fathers?"

"He betrayed them."

"If this is a joke, it's far from funny." Fen ground her teeth together. "Barra believed in the rebellion more than he believed in himself."

Sijara shook her head, her expression pained. "That's why he did it. The Synedria, with the emperor's permission, promised to spare Moru when the treaty turned out to be a lie and she was captured, in exchange for the identities of any spies in the royal court. When Barra betrayed your parents, the ambassadors were already suspected to be rebel agents, and the imperialists were closing in anyway."

A cold comfort. Fen's fingers curled inward. Ruiha's words came to her in a flash: *Barra made too many sacrifices for us to give up now.* "And it was all for nothing. Moru is dead."

"Yes." Sijara's voice was so, so quiet. "Omiko Gatasan had already murdered Moru when the imperialists asked for spies."

Fen's nails cut into her palms. "Who else knows?"

"Only Ruiha and I." Sijara finally met Fen's eyes. She looked shattered. "She didn't tell you? She said—"

"Of course not," Fen spat. She could feel her heartbeat in her clenched fists. Rage coiled like a noboa in her gut, tight and venomous. She leapt to her feet.

Sijara grabbed her arm. "Fen, *no*. Talk to her later, after the ambush. You're both grieving right now."

"I don't care." Fen struggled against Sijara. "Let *go*!"

Sijara released her. "Please, Fen. Don't do this."

But she was already headed for Ruiha.

Fen cut her way through the camp. There was a fire in her churning gut, a conflagration in her chest. The words she would scream in Ruiha's face—consequences be damned—raced through her mind. First, she'd demand to know why the captain had *dared* to hide Barra's treachery from her—

A rustle.

She spun, her muscles already coiling for attack. Her eyes scanned the brush to her right. Her empty hands flexed, and a shard of panic speared her gut. In her haste to confront Ruiha, she'd forgotten her quarterstaff.

There.

A hunched silhouette, staring from the shadows. But when Fen blinked, it vanished. She rubbed furiously at her eyes and cursed. Then cursed again. Her options were simple: She could be a good soldier and investigate, even though she was certain she'd been mistaken, or she could pretend her mind hadn't played a trick on her and face Ruiha now. She stood there for a moment, palms pressed into her face and fuming.

The enemy would not arrive till morning. The rebels had taken great care to avoid the scouts, and she had only seen—only *imagined* she'd seen—a single pair of eyes. Imperialist patrols were never fewer than five people. No one besides the rebels was out here. It had to have been a wild animal, if it'd been anything at all.

Fen sucked in a sharp breath and moved on. The scare had jolted much of the hot rage out of her. What was left was mostly cooling ash. She wasn't going to roar at Ruiha. All that would earn her was banishment, and probably a broken spine for her insolence. Ruiha was still her commander.

She found Ruiha seated in a circle of her sergeants, going over the plan—simple as it was—for the thousandth time. As Fen approached, the captain looked up with bloodshot eyes. Seeing the look on Fen's face, she dismissed her officers with a small, swift wave of her left hand. With the same hand, she beckoned Fen closer.

After a few tense seconds, Fen sat. "I know Barra sold out my parents to the imperialists." Her gaze dropped to her hands. "They're dead because of him."

Ruiha didn't even bother feigning surprise. "And you've decided that now, the eve of the battle that will decide the fate of hundreds of thousands, is the best time to confront me about this." Her tone was mild, but Fen still heard the warning in her words.

Fen didn't much care. She could die tomorrow. "I deserve answers," she said, meeting Ruiha's hard stare.

"*Deserve?* What have you done for this rebellion?" Ruiha asked, cold as ice. Her eyes were narrowed into slits.

Fen wanted to argue that she'd saved Sijara's life and decoded the letter that had led them here, but knew whatever graceless words were forming on her tongue were useless. Ruiha's fingers were drumming on the pommel of her left sword.

"You want to do this now? Fine." Ruiha lowered her voice, a frozen monotone that chilled the air. "You're selfish. Shortsighted. When you came to us, you had no drive but a paper-thin sense of duty to the ghosts of your parents."

In a rush, all of Fen's anger returned. It blazed through her veins. "And I was a fool, too, for believing you cared about me. About any of us. We're just tools to you, aren't we?" She struggled to speak as coolly as Ruiha had, but her voice was jagged, the words scraping the inside of her throat. "Forgive me for the *distraction*, sir." She stood.

Ruiha snapped, "You're not dismissed, Fenyyang. People we loved are dead. We have lost enough." In that moment, she looked decades older. Her mouth shifted into something between a smile and a grimace. "Sit. Please."

Fen slowly unfurled her clenched fists. Each of her palms now sported a row of red crescents. She reluctantly returned to her spot on the crushed grass.

"Barra did what he thought was best for the rebellion, but he was deluding himself." Ruiha dragged in a breath. "He was simply trying to do what was best for his wife. For their child."

Fen's jaw fell. "Barra and Kira were married?" She sputtered for a moment. "They had a *child*? Why would they keep that a secret?"

"*Think*," Ruiha said. "If the imperialists knew, they would've targeted Barra and defeated Kira through him." She lifted her chin, staring up at the unfeeling stars as if in defiance. "Barra was a great friend and a better husband, but often failed as a leader without Kira to guide him. He hoped the merciless would show mercy if given the chance. And then . . . well. He lost his family forever. Their son Kharakh died trying to avenge his mother. He was so young." To Fen's shock and horror, a tear rolled down Ruiha's cheek. "I try to spare those under my command from pain when I can, but I see I've failed here. I am sorry."

Stunned, Fen blinked away the sting swelling in her eyes. She dragged in a rattling gulp of air and held it, afraid that it would return as a sob.

Ruiha swept away her single tear with the back of her hand.

"That said, this is an army first, and I'm your captain before I'm your friend. *Everyone* in the empire has lost someone, and more than a few by the orders of their own leaders, imperialist or rebel or other. A different commander would have you flogged half to death for the insubordination you've exhibited tonight, especially before a critical operation."

Fen looked away. "Forgive me, sir."

"Assuming you survive the morning," Ruiha continued sharply, "if you ever try something like this again, I'll send you back to Talishminn to see how the imperialists tolerate disrespect. Am I clear?"

Fen nodded. "Yes, sir."

"Then you're dismissed." Ruiha crossed her arms. "Go get some sleep."

Night slowly gave way to morning. The meager light of the steadily approaching sun cast strange and swirling shadows, tugging and twisting the shape of the world. The sky above was streaked with campfire orange and pearly blue, so soft and so at odds with the brutality to come.

Fen crouched between Mettan and Sijara, right behind a lifeless clump of grass the exact color of tea-stained teeth. Anxiety burrowed under her skin like a ravenous swarm of myrma. She struggled against the itching need to drag her nails down her arms and neck and face. The traditional rebel paint slathered over her skin in flaking, crumbly layers didn't help.

That awful feeling ballooned as the imperialists came around the bend in the path. Senmavari in gray-lacquered armor marched out in the first few pairs, tramping forward in perfect lockstep. It occurred to her then that the thought of desertion hadn't crossed her mind once since the fateful day Ruiha had let her in. Part of her wanted to run now, but it was a small part. If her destiny was to die with her friends, to die fighting to save the world, then so be it. It was not so terrible a fate.

Fen shifted, grip tightening around her quarterstaff.

*Hold.*

*Hold.*

*Hold . . .*

*Now.*

With a battle cry, the rebels poured down the sides of the pass. Half took up position behind their barricades, while the first wave pounced on the soldiers to draw them in. The Senmavari's shield-vests would negate the effects of a stun blast, but the only protection they had against more traditional weapons was their armor. And there were gaps in the plates, gaps the rebels had trained night and day to target.

As Fen raced down toward her fate, anxiety finally broke the dam holding back her terror. She had never been a true warrior, only the tawdry imitation of one. She had trained and sparred, yes, but nothing more. How easy it had been to be brave when her life was never truly in danger. The fear she'd felt when she'd woken up in that temple to find imperialists at the doorstep was nothing in comparison to what she felt now.

Dread consumed her, twining its fingers through hers and shaking her hands so badly she could barely grip her quarterstaff. Her lungs forgot how to work as wave after wave of nausea threatened to pull her under. Shaking, Fen froze and forced her eyes shut. Counted to five. Opened them again. She reached the bottom of the pass and joined the battle.

All around, people were dying. She glanced around, searching for Mettan and Sijara, hoping they could fight side by side. But the second the bloodshed had begun, they'd been torn from each other. Fen couldn't find either, but up ahead, Ruiha danced between a cluster of Senmavari, felling one with each strike and slash of her dual blades.

A battle cry sounded behind her. Enough observation. Fen spun around, blocking the sword flying toward her through instinct alone. There was no time to think, no time to consider the best parry or thrust for every enemy action. She dodged the soldier's next blow and caught him with the end of her staff between two plates of chest armor. He went down, wheezing for breath.

She faltered as she closed the distance between them. He was already incapacitated—should she kill him? *Could* she? Of course, she'd thought long and hard about what it might be like to end a life, but nothing could've prepared her for this. Not her training with the Broken Masks, not her time protecting Onath's clients.

She sensed movement from the very edge of her peripheral vision. There was no more time to debate. She left the first Senmavar choking for air and faced the next. Even then, she found herself hitting only as hard as she needed to, striking to wound rather than kill.

As the third soldier hit the dirt, Fen took a split second to take in the layout of the enemy. Far too many Senmavari were already here, caught up in the melee. Most of the imperialists she saw locked in combat should've only just reached them. All the convoy's protection would've had to be concentrated in the front to match these numbers, leaving the rear vulnerable. A jagged knot of sick anticipation formed in Fen's gut, chilly dread snaking through her. All the soldiers they'd expected were at the front because . . .

Because the real force was at the back.

They must've joined the convoy after the last batch of scouts had returned last night, but there was no way Ruiha's spies could've missed the movement of such a large force across the empire. They'd been set up. Lieutenant Karstek had been right.

The convoy was a trap.

"For the Sovereign! For the Chosen Son of Oldearth!" a woman roared.

Senmavari who shouldn't have been there flowed toward the battle in a gleaming wave of armor. Fen couldn't breathe under the weight of her horror. But she had to keep fighting, or they'd cut her down like nothing.

Dodging a crackling energy axe, Fen caught another glimpse of Ruiha. She slammed her quarterstaff into the wielder's head and found the captain again. As Ruiha pulled herself up from delivering a death blow, Fen saw realization dawn on the older woman's face.

"Retreat!" the captain yelled. "Retreat!"

But it was too late.

The Senmavari didn't try to follow the rebels back up the sides of the pass. They didn't fall into the traps hidden in the rock and brush with such painstaking care. No, the moment the rebels turned their backs and started scrambling up, the soldiers unholstered their stingers and started shooting. Bodies lay still where they fell, easy pickings for the rows of imperialists that advanced to finish the job.

Ruiha spun around, blasts zipping by. She stood frozen for a moment, staring down at her people as they died. Her expression—she was already mourning them. Then the look vanished and she screamed at the top of her lungs.

"Fight! Stand and fucking fight!"

It was chaos.

Some rebels ignored Ruiha and tried to make it to the top of the pass, only for a stun blast to find their backs. They tumbled, bloody and broken, down the stone and dirt like rag dolls. The ones who turned and lifted their weapons fought well, but they were outnumbered. By what factor, Fen couldn't determine. But it was the factor of defeat, a factor so high no amount of skill or honor or righteousness could scale it.

Her knees trembled as she rushed back down with her comrades. Eternal Mother, where was Mettan? Where was Sijara? Her empty stomach felt like it was full of writhing Oldearth eels. Sweat broke out over her skin as it never had before, running down her face and arms in stinging rivulets.

There, to her left, was Hahru with his war fan. Its unfolded blades cut through the tumult like a scythe through grass. He twisted and turned, jabbing and slashing at any enemy within reach. Senmavari fell around him as he whirled, his feet barely touching the bone-dry ground. But then, without warning, he came to a sharp, jerking stop. The fan hit the ground in a puff of dust. Hahru collapsed to his knees, and the soldier behind him yanked out the spear tip shoved between his shoulder blades.

Shock sent Fen stumbling backward, gasping in pain.

"*No!*" came Naijima's wretched scream.

Fen beat a soldier into the dirt with what remained of her rapidly draining strength and whirled around to look. Beside Hahru stood Ihazan, their mouth unhinged. Fen couldn't hear the sound coming out. Naijima ran toward his brother. A Senmavar leapt at him with a swing of her sword. He parried, his blade dazzlingly fast. Ihazan repaid her first attack with a downward slash of their own weapon. She blocked, slipped around them, struck out with the side of her weapon. The edge sank into Naijima's flesh. With a strangled cry, he twisted and jabbed. Blood burst from between the plates of her armor, and she went down. But she was replaced by more Senmavari than Fen could count. A trap within a trap. Or perhaps the Eternal Mother just despised them all. Naijima and Ihazan were brought down by stinger fire, and their lives were stolen by steel.

Fen let out a moan as she saw the light fade from her friends' eyes.

"I was worried you fools wouldn't come," drawled a voice like two rusted blades crashing together.

From the dust clouds emerged a hulking brute of a man. He wore a severely cut tunic over spidersilk trousers trimmed in gold. Silver chains dangled from his ears and circled a wide, veined neck. At his hip hung a pair of broadswords with elaborate jeweled hilts. His face was concealed with a smooth mask of sky blue. A prince-general. No doubt the commander and orchestrator of this operation.

There wasn't a speck of armor on him, and Fen feared the reason was that he didn't need it. She was proven right as a rebel dashed toward him, short swords angled for an upward slice at his neck. The prince-general unsheathed a sword and, with impossible ease, beheaded the rebel.

"It's a good thing death spared Moru from seeing *this*." His low, rumbling laugh echoed like thunder in Fen's ears. "This is all that remains of her rebels? The *Broken* Masks. What a fitting name."

As if in answer, Ruiha stepped out of the fracas. She moved like a ghost.

"Drusus!" she roared.

"I know that voice." The prince-general smirked when he laid eyes on her. "I thought you were dead."

"You prayed I was." She charged.

The prince-general didn't move. He merely jerked his chin at the captain as the space between them vanished. Three imperialists dove between Ruiha and their commander. She'd lost one of her swords somewhere, but she was still a force of nature. The first slipped inside her guard, but she grabbed his collar and rammed the fist of her free hand into his gut.

As he doubled over from the blow, wheeling back, she sliced across his neck. The second attacker, wielding an energy axe, rushed her. Or attempted to. She sidestepped the blade without even looking at it. As the soldier slid past her, carried by her own momentum, Ruiha caught her in the back with a sharp, quick jab between the ribs. The last soldier flinched, carving their own fate. Ruiha got them in the belly.

The prince-general lunged. He crashed into Ruiha, his sword clashing against hers. He matched her blow for blow. Though her skill was greater, he was stronger. A strike from the captain would wound him, a strike from the prince-general would end her. Fen would've stood there and watched them fight but for the spear that nearly pierced her heart.

*Fool!* she screamed at herself, launching backward. The skin below her collarbone roared in razor-sharp agony. The imperialist had grazed her.

Fen managed to parry the next blow but just missed the one after that. The Senmavar used her spear like a quarterstaff, spinning and slashing rather than thrusting and jabbing. It threw Fen off, and the blunt end of the spear found her cheek. The coppery tang of blood flooded her mouth. Panicked bursts of adrenaline tried and failed to force her worn body to move faster, hit harder.

Her eyes stung. Through the tears, she swung her quarterstaff in untamed, desperate arcs. She was only delaying the inevitable. Even if she'd been fighting at full strength, the imperialist was clearly the superior warrior.

The Senmavar switched tactics, shoving her spear toward Fen for the killing blow. But unlike Fen, she hadn't spared a glance at the terrain. The rocky ground was slick with blood. The soldier slipped, and Fen smashed the side of her quarterstaff into her opponent's head. Despite her helmet, the soldier was unconscious before she hit the dirt.

Gasping for breath, Fen looked up just in time to see the prince-general slam both of his swords into Sijara's blade. As talented as she was, no perfection of form could hold off such strength head-on. Her wrist snapped. Her sword clattered to the dirt. The prince-general planted his foot on the hilt and kicked it away. He spun just in time to block the strike Ruiha aimed at his throat.

They traded blows as Sijara scrambled for her sword, but Fen could see that Ruiha's attacks grew farther and farther away from landing. Finally the prince-general tossed aside one of his weapons. He clenched the remaining sword in both hands, lifted it, and swung down. It was clear Ruiha wasn't going to get her blade up in time.

Fen couldn't bring herself to watch.

But she couldn't stop herself from watching.

The blade went past the captain's head and arm. It went down through her shoulder and across her torso. The prince-general had struck so hard, his broadsword almost sliced the left side of Ruiha's body clean off.

Then he twisted on one foot and drove his blade through Sijara's chest, just as she picked up her sword.

And just like that, they lost the battle.

The look on Sijara's face as she died hit Fen like a stone mace to the head, leaving her shattered and empty. The utter anguish of it. A fire sparked in Fen's lungs and spread through her veins. She burned. She was the worst fighter in her squad. There was no reason she should still be alive, when Hahru and Naijima and Ihazan and Ruiha and Sijara were dead.

Mettan.

She had to find Mettan.

But as quickly as the fire began, it was smothered. She'd worried that she might get hurt, or—Mother forbid—lose her life. But now it finally dawned on her that her last moments would be at the bottom of a remote mountain pass, on the bones of a long-dead river. The Senmavari would not take prisoners here.

*I'm going to die.*

Fen felt horribly hollow, as if she were observing her final minutes from a great distance. The whole world hung in suspension. Time lost all meaning. She would never avenge her parents. She would never have a family. This was it. Had her life meant anything? Had it been *worth* anything? Oh, she knew the answer. And now there was nothing in the world she wanted to do more than curl up in the dust and the blood of everyone she cared about. Panic devoured her, the same thought ringing over and over again in her head.

*I'm going to die.*

She couldn't breathe.

*I'm going to die.*

It had all been for nothing. For less than nothing.

*I'm going to die.*

She found herself thrown back onto the training mats in the magisterial estate in Talishminn. She thought of one of her fellow guards who liked to puff his awful breath in her face when they were sparring. She thought of the month that had consisted of nothing but push-ups and pull-ups when she'd broken an ankle after he'd cheated. The times she had to fight while sick. The taste of blood the first time someone well and truly punched her in the face. The slick-smooth slide of a tooth rolling around in her mouth. The greasy feeling of someone sweating beneath her as she finally tackled them down. The first time she'd felt a bone break underneath her hands. How she'd vomited afterward.

*I'm going to die.*

Fen snapped herself out of it.

But not in time to save herself from the brutal blow to the small of her back. For a second she thought she'd been cut, but the pain was the dull screech of blunt force. Someone had crashed into her, perhaps even unintentionally. She slammed flat against the dirt, where she belonged. Her vision burst into hot white sparks and the breath whooshed out of her lungs. She almost made no effort to fill them again.

Then she saw the glint of steel and decided, no, she was not going to die facedown. She was still holding her quarterstaff. She flipped onto her back and swung upward, shoving aside the downward cut of a short sword. For half a breath, her enemy was exposed. She wasted no time. Her abused tendons screamed as she thrust her quarterstaff at the imperialist's neck.

He sidestepped the attack. Fen scrabbled to her feet as he struck again. Air hissed past her ear. She cried out, eyes watering again as blood burst over her cheek. The Senmavar jabbed at her. Fen stumbled backward, trying to put more space between them so she could use her weapon's longer reach. But he was too fast. She couldn't keep up.

Then his whole body flinched and went stiff, his sword hilt slipping through his twitching fingers. Sputtering helplessly, he looked down and regarded the crimson-coated steel sticking from his chest with mild fascination. He took a shaking step forward, as if stepping off the sword would save him, and then toppled to the side.

Mettan stood behind him, his bloodless face streaked with tears and flecked with crimson. His dark eyes were open very wide.

"We're not going to make it," he whispered.

"No," Fen said, just as soft.

Mettan reached out. He squeezed her hand. He made a choked, wet sound that might've originally been intended as a laugh.

"Guess I *do* get to make it up to you," he said. He let go. He spun to face the Senmavari converging on them.

"What—" Fen let out a wordless, enraged noise. "I'm not leaving you!"

"I can hold them off long enough for you to get away. You have to save yourself. You have to run."

"No!"

"What's the point of both of us dying when I can die for you?" Mettan turned just enough that she could see the edge of his half smile. "Please. Let me do this." And then he lunged at the nearest soldier.

Fen took an immediate step toward him, but Mettan howled, "Run! Damn you, Fen, run!"

It was his voice, not his words, that made her pause. He was doing this for himself, she realized, not her. He wanted to die for something more than a failed rebellion.

Fen did as he asked.

She sprinted around the fallen, dodging axe blows and stray slashes as she searched wildly for safety.

There.

A dip in the side of the pass with just enough brush to make her a hard target. If she was very quick, she could get to the top. And from there, she would run and run and run. All she had to do was reach it. Fen wasn't fighting to capture or to kill; she was just fighting to escape, and that made her job much easier than that of the Senmavari who got in her way. She carved out openings with her quarterstaff, knocked aside spears and swords, smashed knees and shoulders and anything in reach of her weapon.

Somehow, someway, she got through. She scrabbled up the rock and dirt, zigzagging as best she could to avoid stinger fire. She flung herself over the edge and immediately keeled over, barely catching herself on her hands. Trying not to throw up, she glanced around. Her heart sank as she heard soldiers below give chase.

She threw herself upright again and ran, sidestepping scattered bodies. Others had made it up here. And they'd all died, rebels and imperialists alike. She headed for the woods, the only real cover in sight. But the trees were too far away. She wouldn't make it. Then it hit her. The imperialists weren't over the edge yet. If they hadn't gotten a good look at her . . .

Fen threw herself flat against the ground beside a cluster of dead Senmavari. She flung a corpse's arm over her middle and shut her eyes as low voices accompanied by footsteps approached. Someone wheezed, far too close. She cracked open an eye to find an imperialist body very much alive, staring wide-eyed and furious at her. He was going to reveal her to his comrades.

*No, no, no.*

*Please, no.*

Her prayer went unheard. The Senmavar convulsed and groaned, blood-pinked spit frothing at his lips. His arm twitched as he tried to lift it.

"Hey, look. Over there!" said a voice.

Fen wrestled with the urge to jump up and flee. The Senmavari would just shoot her down and eviscerate her if she did. The footsteps grew closer and closer. They stopped right by her head. Shadows fell over her. Her heart thrashed against her ribs like a caged animal.

"Poor bastard's still alive," sighed the same voice.

Eternal Mother.

"Well, put him out of his misery," said another. "And then we'll head back."

The half-dead man writhed and spat out more blood, trying and failing to alert his comrades. A stun blast and a quick stab later, he was still and silent.

The shadows slid away, and the footsteps and voices faded. Fen counted down from one hundred. Then she swallowed, steeled herself, and sat up. She was alone, save for the dead. Utterly, completely alone.

She could hold the tears back no longer.

She wept.

When Fen awoke the next morning, curled up at the edge of the woods, she no longer knew who she was. Grief clawed itself out of her body and devoured her. The sunrise was a fitting shade of deep purple, the precise color of a fresh bruise. And as the sky wept blood, for one knife-sharp moment Fen thought of ending it. It would be quick. It might not even hurt much. Finding a good blade among the dead would be easy.

But then a heavy wave of guilt swept over her. Mettan had given his life to save her. She couldn't let his sacrifice be for nothing. Sorrow was a swift-flowing river; she needed to take care or she'd drown.

She had to get up. She had to see if anyone was, however impossibly, alive. But the moment she stood upright, a burst of agony shoved her back down to her knees. She needed antibiotics, bandages, and painkillers, or she'd die whether she wanted to or not.

Fen struggled to her feet and made her way to the rebel camp, fresh spikes of pain stabbing into her with each shaking step. She unearthed one of the hidden medkits and ripped open a restorative wrap with her teeth. With agonizing slowness, she drew out the wet bandages within and set them over her worst wounds. The wraps dripped with a powerful antiseptic blend of analgesics and healing factors, but within minutes, they hardened into flexible casts. She emptied the rest of the supplies into her bag.

Fen limped over to the edge of the pass and looked out over the carnage below. Corpses choked the valley, limbs arranged in unnatural patterns. From the top of the pass, it was impossible to tell which side the dead were from. Pooling blood and stained metal glistened in the crimson light. Stillness and silence reigned supreme. The rebels had lost, but miraculously, so had the imperialists. Fen was the lone survivor.

But when she crawled down the slope to confirm her suspicions, she found that was not quite true. As she dragged herself across the battlefield, bodies began to stir. Rebels and imperialists alike cried out for food, for water, for death, for mercy. Fen had none to offer; she'd been unable to recover supplies beyond the medkits, and even if she had, the near-corpses calling out to her were beyond saving, though she could not bring herself to kill them.

Her heart squeezed each time she looked into a rebel's eyes and saw the exact moment they realized she would not deliver them from their suffering. People she'd cooked for and sparred with and slept beside rasped wetly at her feet now, blood-crusted fingers reaching uselessly toward her tunic.

Then she saw Mettan.

He lay several meters away, collapsed atop a pile of armored bodies. There was a clear slash from his right shoulder to his hip, and another across the base of his throat. He was too still to be alive. Even from a distance, Fen could see that the scarlet smears around the cuts were old. His heart no longer pumped blood.

It was then, meeting his unseeing gaze, that she finally recalled the eyes she'd seen in the grasses the night before the battle. In her rage and in her later exhaustion, she'd forgotten. She was certain now that the hunched figure she'd glimpsed the night before hadn't been an illusion. She'd stumbled upon an imperialist spy. In her petty anger and self-absorption, she'd let them go. And now everyone she'd come to care for was dead. She had killed them all.

Fen could go no farther. Stomach heaving, she doubled over and retched. An agony that had nothing to do with her wounds sliced into her, splitting her apart. Her hacking turned to gasps and then sobs. Scalding tears wove through her fingers when she covered her mouth with her hands.

With a sob, she turned from Mettan's corpse and staggered to her feet. There was nothing for her here but pain. She considered her options, and she made her way back to the side of the pass. She could try to find her own way to Ata, but without the rebels to guide her, the imperialists would cut her down before she ever set foot on the border. She could return to Talishminn, but Onath would have to be suicidal to allow her back in. Assuming he was even still there. Either way, he couldn't protect her; he'd already given her all the help he could, and she wouldn't endanger him by reaching out.

Fen's desire for vengeance engulfed her. This time, she'd lost the people she'd chosen. Ending the Sovereign was her only possible path toward atonement. But she'd still have to live with shards of guilt lodged between her ribs, a shroud of loss over her bowed head, for the rest of her days.

Her dull gaze fell on the body before her. The man lay on his back, a spear sticking out from the center of his chest. But though his mask marked him as unmistakably imperialist, he wore not armor but a fine purple robe. Silver Oldearth animals, embroidered in precious metals along the hem, shone against his pale skin.

His remaining hand—the other had been hacked off—clenched the neck of a duruqin. The instrument had been smashed in half so that its jagged realwood top could be wielded as a makeshift weapon. Blood stained the sharp wood, painted the snapped strings. One thing was clear: This was no warrior. He shouldn't have been here.

Now that she was paying attention, Fen found more retainers scattered about. All sorts of entertainers, servants in shredded livery, ceremonial guards in fancy gilded armor that would've only slowed them down in battle. All in all, an incredibly impractical army from the royal court.

Only one kind of person would've been accompanied by such an entourage. A princex. And not a minor princex, like the one whose squad had surrounded Fen in the abandoned temple, or even the brutal general that had killed—

Fen took in a centering breath, pushing the thought away.

No, a sibling of the emperor had been on the battlefield.

Perhaps they were still here.

She found the royal floatcraft toward the end of the procession. The real soldiers had headed up the traveling party, while the decorative honor guard had pranced around the transport with the entertainers. The cerulean, hut-sized vehicle was festooned with spidersilk banners and flanked by the contorted bodies of musicians and servants.

The cobalt doors, studded with gilded hemispheres, were broken. They hung just barely ajar, as if some desperate bodyguard had tried to conceal their state by shoving them back together. Which meant that whoever that guard had tried to protect was likely still inside. Fen pressed her ear to the gap and listened. Silence. She readied her quarterstaff, wincing as pain cut through the drugs seeping into her system, and drew open the left door. She crept inside.

The entrance area was small, but the blue-tinted mirrors paving the floor and ceiling spun an illusion of vastness. Grip tightening around her weapon, Fen wove between carved realwood furniture and made her way to the beaded curtain on the other side. She took a moment to square her shoulders. If there really was a high princex in there, she couldn't afford to show weakness. She grabbed a handful of heavy brocade and wrenched it aside.

There was a single occupant. A man perched on a lapis lazuli throne, carved to resemble a seated sphinx. He wore a robe of blue samite so dark it was almost black, appliquéd with shimmering silver eels and edged in gold. His hair was dark but flashed like electrum where the light hit it. It was bound up into a ridiculously intricate coiffure, held together by hairpins glinting with jewels—fine gems that Fen had never seen even in holoimages. His mask matched his raiment in hue if not ornateness; a plain piece that concealed even the eyes with tinted glass.

Fen wanted to rip out a hairpin and stab him in the throat. Just one of the stones atop his head would've kept a small village fed for a year.

"I was wondering when one of you would crawl in here." His voice was surprisingly soft, but there was something keen and cruel under the melody.

Fen wondered what his screams would sound like. "I know who you are."

"I'm surprised you know anything at all." His words dripped with the bored, distant condescension of a man who'd rarely had to consider the humanity of other people.

He could only be one person: the hated heir, the Butcher. Alekhai. The convoy had been *led* by him, not on its way to meet him. But it seemed preposterous that he would put himself in such a vulnerable position.

"You didn't know this was a trap for us," Fen said. "You would never have risked yourself if you had."

"How curious," he drawled. "A rebel with at least a few brain cells."

"I wonder why the heir presumptive himself would oversee the transport of one of many prototypes." Fen kept her voice low and measured, even as she stepped toward him, quarterstaff raised. "I imagine you have far more important things to do. Or perhaps you were *forced* to be here? Yet another humiliation meted out by your beloved brother."

Alekhai went very stiff for a moment. Then he snarled, "Not nearly the humiliation you cretins have suffered. There are millions of us, merely a handful of you. You should've given up long ago. You're just a bunch of children playing at war."

Fen glared at him with loathing. Why hadn't he moved? His best bet would've been to get as far from this floatcraft as possible. He had to know any rebel who found him would bash his jeweled skull in. Then she noticed how his right hand was pressed hard against his side, as if holding together his flesh. He was badly hurt.

That gave her pause. He was worth far more alive than dead. But could she really take him prisoner? What if he somehow got the jump on her and killed her before they reached Kanoh? She had nothing and no one to rely on but herself, thanks to her cowardice. She should've told Mettan to run. He should've been the one standing there, still breathing. But instead, there was only Fen with all her sorrow and rage and all-consuming exhaustion. She bit the inside of her cheek until it bled.

As if sensing her thoughts, Alekhai lifted his chin, revealing a slice of brown skin between the high collar of his gown and the blue edge of his mask. "Get it over with," he snapped.

Fen caught the plaintive tremor, faint though it was. She found herself smiling down at him. "No," she said. "I'm taking you prisoner."

With a speed she could not have anticipated, Alekhai leapt up. His ceremonial dress billowed stupidly behind him as he tried to slam her against the wall. He lifted an elbow to shove into her throat, but his garb caught on the arm of a gilded chair.

Fen seized his wrist before the knife found her heart. He'd been clutching a weapon, not a wound. She wrenched the blade from his fingers and slashed across his neck. Alekhai cried out—there was the scream she'd wanted—and toppled onto his back in a flurry of spidersilk. He touched his fingers to his throat, where a single drop of crimson had pearled.

"Do that again and see what happens," Fen said quietly.

Alekhai was shaking slightly. "I should've skinned you and your warmongering friends alive when I had the chance—"

Fen flung aside the knife. "Where is the weapon?"

"What weapon?"

She swung the quarterstaff into his side. He let out a cry, too loud and too pained for the restrained force she'd applied. Perhaps he truly had been wounded. Well, that worked in her favor.

"Try again," she suggested.

Alekhai spread his arms wide. "There is no *weapon*."

Fen pressed her weapon into him; a pathetic whimper escaped from clenched teeth. She stopped only because she was half horrified to discover that the pleading sound only made her want to hurt him more. She pulled away the quarterstaff, breathing hard. She was better than them.

She had to be.

"Why didn't you activate the weapon?" she demanded. "Whatever it is, winning this battle should've been child's play for you."

"I'm telling the truth," Alekhai snarled at her. "This was only a ruse to draw you out. Why would we decimate whole cities? The logistics of clandestinely massacring settlement by settlement would be a living nightmare. All we have to do to conserve food is simply let you all starve. A rebel army cannot subsist on air." He was speaking slowly now, as if to someone young and stupid. "You peasants will be too busy fighting each other for food to rise against us. And those who do amass enough resources will be preyed upon by bandits."

Fen was shaking. Her friends could not have died for nothing. She refused to believe it. "You must have access to schematics, data, *something*. You're going to download everything you have about that weapon onto my omnichip."

"If you're not going to hear what I have to say, just kill me," he hissed. "And make it quick."

Fen exhaled sharply. It did nothing for the hard, tight ball stuck in her throat. "I just said I was taking you prisoner."

"You're pathetic," said Alekhai. "You can't do it, can you?" He let out a humorless bark of laughter. "Or is it that you believe me?"

Fen tried to scoff but only let out a low, broken sound. Everything he'd said did make perfect, agonizing sense. The Sovereigns had been content to let rot fester in their empire for their entire dynasty, to let troublesome people tear each other apart. The only exception was when the previous emperor had crushed Moru's rebellion under his heel, but that was all that was: an exception. No one had expected the rebels to get as far as they had.

"That's right," Alekhai said sweetly, inclining his head. "Your comrades gave their lives for a paper-thin rumor my brother spun after an hour's thought. All it took to defeat you was a little misinformation and a few paltry bribes."

"And yet, here you are, kneeling at my feet," Fen said, her voice suddenly and shockingly cold, even to her. "Our target should've been an overwhelming military force that outnumbered us ten to one, not a handful of soldiers accompanying an army of servants. You were betrayed just as we were." She smiled. "The scheming sycophants of your dead siblings, I suppose? Or your living kin?"

"Does it matter?" Alekhai asked. "When I find them, I'll flay them to the bone." The quick cadence of his voice, the straightening of his posture—he seemed almost excited at the thought.

He really was a monster.

"And now?" the prince said. "I assume you have some sort of master plan to get me all the way to your pathetic excuse of a military base."

Fen frowned. Transporting him to Kanoh *was* her plan, but she hadn't exactly had the chance to think through the details. She turned to the half-silvered mirror at her right, studying the chaos outside in the hope it would offer a solution.

Alekhai laughed mirthlessly again. "Ah, so there's no plan." He threw up his hands. "Wonderful, just wonderful—"

Fen tensed suddenly as she caught a flicker of movement. "Be quiet."

"Oh, so just because you can swing around a stick you think you can—"

"Be. *Quiet.*"

Alekhai made an indignant noise that was comically close to sputtering. "You cannot speak to me like that."

"I just did." She jabbed a finger at the mirror. "We have a bigger problem. Bandits."

Alekhai snorted. "*We?*"

Fen gestured at the ragged, eerily silent figures emerging from the shadows and creeping about the battlefield. They held their weapons at the ready, rusted swords and axes that would still do the trick, and probably far more painfully, too. Not so different from the bioscavengers who dug through harvest piles outside certain hospitals, they circled the corpses like corags, gathering new blades and armor.

"Yes, *we*. They'll kill me, certainly. But they'll hack off little pieces of you to send to your brother for weeks till there's nothing left."

She could hear Alekhai grit his teeth behind the mask. "We'll make a run for it."

"So you can scurry off? No, I don't think so. Besides, I have no idea where all of them are. There could be a whole army out there." Fen scratched at her chin. *Come on,* think. *Protecting people used to be your whole Motherdamn job.* "We need to get them all out of the way. But first: Take off the mask."

"No."

"I wasn't asking," said Fen. "If they see me running, they might just let me go. But they'd never let a high prince slip through their fingers. Take off the mask. The jewels. And some of those layers."

After a moment of hesitation, he did. Fen, morbidly curious, watched as he undid the ties at the back of his head.

It was not a kind face. Very little of Alekhai's visage was adorned with paint beneath the mask, revealing a complexion of dark gold. His features were sharp enough to cut glass. His eyes, outlined in kohl, were a deep brown. He seemed a little too perfect to be human, a marble statue given breath.

Fen turned back to the one-way mirror, tracking the bandits' progress. "It won't be long before they find us, so we need to move quickly," she said. "We're going to set lures."

Alekhai's bloodless mouth bent into something that could've been called a smile on anyone else. The grin faded fast, though, after she tied his wrists in front of him with a makeshift rope formed from one of his robes. She pulled him from the floatcraft and out of sight just as the bandits came upon the vehicle. The brigands' greedy whoops of joy chased them down the pass.

They gathered up great piles of twigs and leaves and grass—or rather, Alekhai did, barely managing with his bound arms while Fen jerked at his rope and sent a frantic message to Ying. The medic's contact was the only working one she had, her last line of communication to Kanoh. For safety reasons, the only other contacts she had belonged to her cohort. Fen felt a fresh wave of tears surging up within her as she fired off the letter, but she shoved it down.

When she judged a heap to be of sufficient size, they moved on. After the fourth pile, Alekhai had exhausted all the popular curses and began muttering all the colorful ways he wanted her to die. She tried to ignore him but found herself yanking on the rope harder than necessary as they worked. She might very well kill him before they reached Kanoh.

Then she tugged Alekhai back the way they'd come. Armed with the lighter all rebels carried, she set the heaps afire. Now there were five false campfires in total; not so many as to frighten the bandits back into the woods, where Fen and Alekhai might run into them, but just enough to be tantalizing and worth the trek. After all, the royal floatcraft wouldn't be going anywhere.

She dragged Alekhai up the side of the pass to wait and watch. After she crawled over the edge, she turned to haul the prince up faster. Her unguarded back faced the vast steppe rolling out endlessly behind her.

Alekhai's only warning when the bandit struck was a tight, pleased smirk. Fen spun away as the man lunged for her, a knife clenched in his left hand. She swore as she dodged his slashing blade. She couldn't fight with her quarterstaff like this; he'd gotten inside her guard. Alekhai leapt into the fray and kicked at the back of her knees. The first of his blows struck true, but the second went wide as Fen twisted and punched him hard in the nose. The cartilage cracked loudly under her fist.

The bandit made the mistake of shifting his attention to Alekhai, even for just a second. Fen threw herself backward. When he struck at her, she swung at the soft hollow of his outstretched arm. She felt the snap of a broken bone through her quarterstaff before she heard it. Before he could reciprocate, she smashed her weapon into his jaw. A scream caught in his throat as he bit clean through his own tongue. By the time he hit the ground in a cloud of dust, he was unconscious.

Fen allowed herself to catch her breath as she scanned the grassland ahead for immediate danger. She listened carefully for the sound of footsteps and the telltale rustle of dry grass, but they were alone. She threw a glance over the edge of the pass to find the bandits fast approaching the lures.

She stalked over to Alekhai. "I warned you," she growled. She lifted her quarterstaff, positioned to stave in his skull.

"I'm sorry," he said.

"Not that sorry. You'd do it again given half a chance."

"Not that sorry," he agreed. "You can't blame me for trying."

"I can and I will."

But that was a lie. Her grip loosened. She wasn't like his barbaric family. Killing him now would bring her only the brief pleasure of swatting an irritating insect, not the rich satisfaction that would come from the imperialists' defeat. If she wanted to help realize that future, she needed him alive. A dead crown prince was just another body at best, a martyr at worst. A living one had a thousand uses. The rebels could keep him as a hostage or use him as a bargaining chip in negotiations. Probably both. Didn't matter; soon he'd be out of her hands. Fen lowered her quarterstaff.

"You've just spent the last of my mercy," she told him. "If you ever attack me again, I'll burn you like your sibling did, and no one's going to fix your pretty face for you at Kanoh." She hoped that sounded threatening enough. She dragged him up with the rope. "Do you understand?"

For a moment, Alekhai's glare faltered. His facade of righteous scorn splintered, betraying a tendril of pain and shame that vanished just as quickly as it had appeared. He stared at her with all the hate in the world, in all the worlds. But then he nodded and lowered his head.

"Good," Fen said shortly. "Let's go."

News of the mutually destructive ambush—and of the royal convoy's unguarded treasure—spread like wildfire. Fen didn't have to hear a single whispered word to know; within days, the woods would be swarming with bandits. With the steppe too bare to provide any shelter or secrecy, she was forced to drag Alekhai along the forest's border. The terrain was rough, and the trees were too low and sparse to provide much shade. It was the worst of both worlds.

And Alekhai would not shut up.

"In my grandmother's reign," he was saying, "this was the route taken by emperexes as they journeyed through Enkaiia, sitting in judgment over regional courts. Or somewhere very near the route." He stumbled as the rope went taut.

"Faster," Fen snapped.

It wasn't only that Alekhai kept running his mouth. Her messages to Ying were still unread, and she was terrified that something had happened to the base.

"It gave the local peasantry the opportunity to beg for justice from the very pinnacle of the law," Alekhai babbled on. "Not all magistrates are honest ones."

Thinking of Onath, Fen felt an absurd bubble of laughter swell in her chest. The man was probably the best magistrate in the whole of Enkaiia, and he had no qualms about lying and cheating—and murdering and maiming—to get whatever he wanted when he wanted it.

"Obviously the current Sovereign rarely steps foot outside Ivytra," Alekhai continued. "But along the way to the next court, emperexes would inspect fringe villages and the border forts." His tone went flat and unimpressed as he said, "Pageantry to remind everyone to whom they owed their allegiance. And obviously, their fear."

Fen stopped and turned around. She scratched at the crown of her head as if that would stop the sun from scorching her scalp. Then she tugged hard on the rope. "Please," she said. "Stop."

The prince's ceaseless chattering was starting to remind her of Ihazan. And she needed to think of anything but her fallen squad. With every step back to Kanoh, grief slammed into her like gusts of wind, nearly knocking her flat. She was exhausted and despondent, and the painkillers were beginning to wear off. She was spacing the doses out more than she needed to, but she'd heard all manner of horror stories from Onath. The last thing she needed was an addiction.

"What I'm trying to say is that I understand." Alekhai took an unwise step closer. "I understand why you all revolted. I really do. Things are getting worse and worse, and my family ignored the suffering of the common people."

*Yes, that's obvious,* Fen thought, but her lips did not move. She was so, so tired. She stared balefully at the slowly darkening landscape ahead. She knew they could, they *should,* travel for at least a few more hours, but she couldn't bring herself to take another step.

"That's enough for today."

Alekhai glared at her. "You're not listening—"

"I meant walking," she said, sighing. "But all your blabbering, too."

She looped the rope once around her fist and tied it in an intricate knot around the lowest branch of a nearby tree. Alekhai would probably be able to break the branch with enough effort, but certainly not without alerting her. And the knot was far too complicated for him to disentangle with bound wrists.

Fen sat down just outside Alekhai's range of motion, nearly collapsing into the dirt. She found him glaring at her. She glowered back, deciding now was as good a time as any to study her captive as she built a little campfire.

Out of his cloak and most of his ridiculous robes, she saw that he was even less physically imposing than she'd thought. Alekhai possessed the same delicate, pampered look of every other noble she'd seen out of their masks and makeup: hair like velvet; high, sculpted cheekbones; some type of aristocratic nose, his being the flat, round kind; a fine brow arching over expressive eyes that would've been alluring with a soul behind them. It was the kind of carefully considered, obnoxious symmetry that could only come from generational genetic tinkering. If his face had not been attached to the person, and the throne awaiting that person, she might have thought him beautiful.

Alekhai pursed his lips. "You're staring," he said with a faint touch of menace.

"A master of deduction," she drawled, though she was furious. "How much of our taxes were spent on your family's faces?" she asked.

Alekhai shrugged, which was only expected. Why would he ever consider how and in what excess the hard-won earnings of the people he trod upon were spent, so long as the credits kept flowing? She'd been right, of course; he was nothing but a finely dressed parasite.

"*What?*" Alekhai widened his eyes before rolling them dramatically. "Are you just going to scowl at me all night, peasant?"

His exaggerated expression revealed what she'd missed before. His eyes weren't brown, but a gold so deep they might as well have been. Fen's dark eyes shone like polished bronze under direct sunlight. It was the same thing here: illuminated by the campfire, Alekhai's irises were the lambent yellow of the purest ingots. It was the sort of color that no artificial iris could replicate.

"Your eyes aren't prosthetics," she said in awe. "They were regrown from scratch."

It would've been much easier to simply replace the eyes with tech, so someone had made the conscious decision to go the longer, significantly more painful route. And there was no doubt at all that that "someone" was kin to him; perhaps the sibling who had shoved him into a fire in the first place. The damage had to go far beyond merely physical—

Eternal Mother.

She could not afford to care about this. She had enough problems, and even if Alekhai weren't the enemy, she had neither the energy nor the power to do anything about his family troubles. Her own difficulties—and calling them that was the understatement of the century—had her wanting to do nothing but curl up into a ball and rock back and forth until the world felt all right.

But she had a strong feeling that showing such weakness in front of the prince would be the last mistake she ever made, so she lay on her back and gazed hopelessly at the sky. The first stars were coming into view.

"I have a name," she said finally.

"I know that, Mekantai." He sounded so very resigned. "The ambassadors' daughter. You know they're dead?"

Fen closed her eyes. She wasn't surprised he recognized her. How long had her parents been rotting in the dungeons beneath his feet? "How do you think I got here?"

☾

When Fen awoke to the rustling of grass, she was shaking. Even when her eyes flew open, she couldn't stop seeing her newfound and newly lost friends dying around her. Gray-clad arms lifting swords. The wide, horrified eyes of her doomed companions. But before the tears even began to coalesce, she felt the cold press of a stinger against her temple.

"Mekantai—" started Alekhai.

"Quiet. Or I'll make it hurt," came a low, hollow rasp of a voice. Then, to Fen, "Don't. Move."

Shock pinned Fen in place as the stinger lifted away. She didn't dare look over. She didn't have to, in the end. Her assailant turned her with a sharp, savage kick across the side. The woman wore a nondescript brown tunic over baggy brown pants. She could've been anyone, but Fen was certain all the same.

"Bandit cur," she wheezed. Her fingers twitched uselessly; there was no point reaching for her staff if the brigand could shoot at point-blank range.

"I am no bandit," the woman snapped. "I serve the will of the great Kira Moru and all that came after. Who are you?"

Fen brightened immediately, despite her aching side. "You're a Broken Mask? So am I." She gestured at Alekhai. "I'm delivering him to . . . " She trailed off, cursing herself. What if the woman was an imperialist spy?

"Where?" the woman demanded.

"To my base." Fen narrowed her eyes. "How do I know you're not one of the emperor's pets?"

"How do I know *you're* not? You could very well have been sent to retrieve the prince."

"No one outside the imperial family has ever seen my face,"

Alekhai said flatly. "Well, except for you two, now. How did you recognize me?"

The woman's head jerked toward him, stinger still trained on Fen. "I knew what to look for." Her expression was between a sneer and a scowl. "Your features were obviously designed. The robe you're wearing is spidersilk; the cut suggests it was meant to be worn under something even finer. And I can tell you're slender because you're spoiled, not because you had to miss six meals out of ten." She turned back to Fen. "Once you drag him to Kanoh, what then?"

Fen forced down surprise at the mention of her base. "I don't know. It's not up to me."

"Well, I'm sorry about this," said the rebel.

Something twisted in Fen's gut. "Sorry about what?"

"My squad was sent out with clear commands. I'm to kill the prince and anyone with him." Her grip tightened around her stinger. "It won't hurt, at least."

"Wait, please," Fen said desperately, "you can't really believe I'm an imperialist."

"I *don't*, and therein lies the problem." The rebel sighed. "My commanders want the prince dead for his crimes in Bakrai, but some of the other Broken Mask camps want him alive and unharmed, to use as bait or leverage. But keeping him prisoner would be like holding a live grenade."

So the wider rebellion was in even greater disarray than Fen had suspected. If they couldn't agree on what to do with Alekhai, then how could they possibly take on the imperialists' united front? The thought was almost more terrifying than her impending demise.

"You don't have to do this," she whispered.

"Actually, I do." The rebel shook her head. "Orders are orders. And unlike Ruiha, I'm not going to let my people get slaughtered."

*Unlike me, then, too.*

"I can help you deliver him," Fen pleaded. "I'm not going to try to steal him away, I swear to the Mother."

The rebel gave a harsh laugh. "Look at it this way: I'm doing you a favor. Even if you survived all the way back to Kanoh, the base is abandoned."

Fen froze. The rebel was so much better informed than she or any of her friends had been. "What? Where'd they go?"

"Enough conversation."

A blur of movement, almost too fast for the eye to track. The stinger fell from the rebel's hand as a small, dense book flew into her wrist. Fen didn't bother throwing a glance at Alekhai, who must've gotten a hand free, instead taking the opening he'd bought her. She launched herself into the woman in a tackle, shoving a knee into her stomach. Mid-fall, the sputtering rebel shoved a hand into one of the many pockets of her tunic. She pulled out a serrated knife as they hit the ground.

Fen flung herself backward, the glinting slash of the blade only just missing her. It stabbed through the precise spot her right eye had been a moment ago. She did not, however, dodge the kick to the gut that followed. She collapsed, wheezing, barely managing to wrench out her quarterstaff and half extend it before the rebel was on her again. Fen slammed it into the side of her attacker's face.

The rebel lost her knife. She hissed in pain, spitting out saliva pinked with blood. Fen scrambled and leapt to her feet. The rebel pulled out another weapon just as her leg struck out in a low sweep. Fen slammed back down to the ground. She stopped the blade just before it sank into a lung. She didn't knock it aside as planned; the woman was faster and had far too strong a grip on the hilt. Now the blade was braced against the half-extended pillar of the quarterstaff, caught by its jagged edge.

The woman pressed mercilessly down, baring her teeth. Lungs afire, Fen sweated and squirmed as the glittering edge tipped toward her collarbone. She couldn't risk even a scratch; the blade gleamed with the telltale sheen of a poison coat. Two drops of bloody spittle fell onto Fen's chin.

Then another. And another. And then the drops became a vermillion stream. The rebel's eyes rolled up back into her head as liquid red petals spread out from the center of her chest like a blossoming flower. Her whole body went slack before she fell to the side, knife still gripped in her hand.

For a terrible, wrenching moment, Fen saw Mettan standing there, hand outstretched. But then her mind returned to her, leaving Alekhai looking down his nose at her.

"Oh good, she lives." He sounded for all the world like he wished it were not so.

"How'd you get free?"

"My eldest sister used to tie the youngest of us to trees in the palace gardens. Then she'd try to knock apples off our heads with her throwing knives." He shrugged. "It was either I learned to untie myself quickly or end up like poor little Ganzaya."

Fen had no idea what an apple was—some remnant from Oldearth?—but she felt an annoying surge of sympathy. She'd heard something about the youngest high princex, years ago. Onath and the other bodyguards had been horrible in their own ways, but next to Alekhai's family they seemed like Eirese clerics. (The good ones.) Alekhai knew exactly what he was doing when he casually dropped venomous personal morsels like these. Already he'd had taken the measure of her. The fact that she knew she was being shamelessly manipulated did little to dampen her pity, reluctant as it was.

"How could your father have allowed that?" she asked. "Even if he didn't care for you as a parent should, you're his *heirs*. His legacy."

"He could always make more of us, as he was fond of reminding me," replied Alekhai. "And we have dozens of obsequious cousins, all of whom knew full well that if my father ever gave up on his own progeny, they'd be next in line."

"Well, I'm sorry," she managed. "And thank you. For throwing the book." She couldn't bring herself to admit aloud that he'd saved her life.

Alekhai shrugged again. He didn't offer her a hand, which was good. She wouldn't have taken it. He merely stepped back, picked up the little book, and sat down. There was a measured agility to his movements, probably the half-erased mark of the formal combat training she imagined all royal scions had to undertake.

"So what now?" he asked. "Your base is abandoned, apparently. Do you know where any of the others are?"

"No." Fen's shoulders sank inward. "She could've been lying, but she had no reason to."

She'd failed before her mission had even begun. She'd hoped a new purpose would give her the strength to go on, but with nowhere to take Alekhai, she had nothing.

"You know," she said, "I knew it was only a dream." With all the infighting and lack of unified command within the Broken Masks, there was no way they'd ever defeat the Sovereign. She'd leapt onto a sinking ship in the hope it would save her from the whirlpool behind her. And she'd made friends with its doomed crew, now mostly gone. "I worked so hard to earn a place. Their respect. And I was happy for the longest I've ever been in my life."

She met his hard, half-gold eyes. *Just go.* It was on the tip of her tongue.

But no.

A dead prince was better than a breathing one. What few rebels remained would tear each other to shreds over him. She had to kill him. Fen reached for her quarterstaff. But before her fingers touched the cool graphene, her mouth opened of its own accord.

"I can't let you return to the palace," she said. "I can't let you do it again."

"And what exactly would I do again?"

"Slaughter an innocent village. I know about Bakrai."

He actually had the grace to flinch, though he recovered quickly enough. "You should know better than to put stock in rumors."

"I know better than to ignore a rumor that rings true."

"Well, then." Alekhai was very, very still. "Go ahead, take your revenge."

"Do you know the people you condemned to death still live?"

The prince narrowed his eyes at her. "I saw them die."

It was a convincing act. But Fen knew better. "And you saw them rise."

Alekhai gave her a look of incredulity. "You speak nonsense."

"Don't play the fool," Fen said. "It doesn't suit you. You know, 'Executor' and 'Executioner' sound quite similar."

He scoffed. "If you hadn't noticed, I specialize in taking lives, not returning them."

"That's not completely true," Fen said slowly. "Is it?"

"What happened in Bakrai was regrettable, but it's just one village. Why would I give a single flying fuck about it?"

"It sounds like you care quite a bit," said Fen.

"Why would I have half the village killed just to bring them back myself?"

"Guilt? I don't know," Fen said, though she was surer every second. "But it's you. It has to be you. You're the only person connected to the hamlet who also has the means to conceal the repopulation from your brother."

Alekhai shook his head. "Grief has driven you mad."

"Of course it has," Fen snapped. "But that doesn't change the fact that I'm right."

"What an extraordinary leap your addled mind has taken," Alekhai said, half wonderingly. "Truly, I'm impressed—"

"If you resurrected the people of Bakrai, it would be the one good thing you've ever done," Fen said. "I don't believe that you could ever understand what it's like to live under your family's rule. I certainly don't believe that any part of you can or will sympathize with the Masks. But bringing Bakrai back would mean you're not entirely a monster."

"Do you think the opinion of a failed terrorist matters to a chosen grandson of Oldearth?"

"Yes. When she holds his life in her hands."

She stared at him. Alekhai, Butcher and savior both. A man chosen by the Accusers at birth to balance their power. But instead of denying it again or running off or attacking her, as she'd anticipated, he bent forward, elbows planted on his knees.

"Well, then?" he said after a long silence. He sounded almost hoarse.

She tried to conceal her sigh of relief. She'd been right. "It's safer to take your life."

"Will you?" He did not taunt or goad her this time.

Fen took in a breath and held it. When she spoke, she did so carefully, knowing the words were precious. "I will spare you if you resurrect my people."

"I have no control over who I can resurrect, or when."

"You know, we were always told that the Accusers saw your kind as an experiment, an increasingly unnecessary one." She folded her hands together. "It was a good lie. It would explain why your numbers dwindled over the decades. Few would question it; why would a human touched with what was once thought of as divinity diminish themselves? Why not live a life of glory? But you've been hiding yourselves. I have to wonder if your brother even knows."

"Of course not," snapped Alekhai. Fen heard the unspoken: *And he never will.* "My Accuser never revealed itself to my family."

"So I have to wonder, what other fabrications did your kind feed us?" Fen tilted her head. "We were told that the Accusers were parsimonious with returned lives these days. And you claim you have no say in the matter. But half a village, all at once, seems like quite a lot to me."

Alekhai's gaze swept over her like a blade on a whetstone. "All your friends are dead," he said, after a moment of study. "You couldn't protect them then, and you wouldn't be able to protect them now."

"They could protect themselves better than I ever could," Fen said. She swallowed thickly, her gaze dropping to her hands. "The last sacrificed himself for me."

Alekhai lifted a brow. It was a movement so precise she bet he'd practiced it. "You ask out of a sense of obligation?"

"I ask you out of selfishness." She met his eyes again. It was so much harder this time. "You're right. Everyone I loved is dead. I'm alone."

"That doesn't make you special," said Alekhai. "The whole empire is on the brink of collapse. You can find new people to suffer your presence in the time we have left."

Fen placed a hand deliberately upon her quarterstaff. "This is not a negotiation."

"Yes, it is." Alekhai's smile could only be described as predatory. "Everything is a negotiation. You said 'people.'" He shook his head. "I'll give you a life for a life. And then we'll part ways forever."

"No."

"No?"

A memory flared up in her head—Onath showing her an old image of the traditional pose of supplication commoners were meant to assume when begging highborn for aid. The petitioner would kneel at the noble's side, place one hand on the patrician's knee and another on their chin. These days, aristocrats were just as likely to gut the poor petitioners for daring to touch them, so it had lost its popularity. Either way, Fen would take out her own eye before showing Alekhai such respect, and she doubted he'd react very well to it anyway.

So she just said outright what she wanted. "Nine lives."

Barra. Ruiha. Naijima. Hahru. Ihazan. Mettan. Sijara. Her fathers.

"That's ludicrous." But he tilted his head in consideration. "What will you give me if I bring them all back for you?"

Fen's hands curled into fists. "What do you want?"

"Your protection."

She gaped at him. Of all the requests he could've given her, it was the last she'd expected. "Why? Can't you just resurrect yourself if you're killed?"

Alekhai stared back at her, not in surprise but in pitying condescension. She might've asked if one needed air to live, such was his expression. "When I die, I come back with and *for* someone else, or not at all. Outside of my duties as an Executor, I'm as mortal as any. Given that, you and I both know I won't make it very far alone, and I can't return to Ivytra just yet. There are certain goals I must achieve, in a certain order, and my attempted assassination makes it clear that the time is now. You and the one—only *one*—soul I return to life are mine until those aims are met."

"What aims?"

"Do not concern yourself with my objectives, only the execution of them."

Fen glared at him. "How many goals, then?"

"Three."

"Then you'll give me three lives," she said, "plus another to match your own."

Alekhai waved a tired hand. "Fine."

*Mettan. Sijara. My fathers.* She could live with that, and with the guilt of how quickly her mind supplied those names, subtracting the others. She would have to.

"But I will not bring back your fathers."

A hand gripped Fen's heart, sharpened fingernails digging into the muscle. "Why not?"

"I cannot."

"Because your Accuser conveniently refuses to allow you?"

"I cannot."

The hand squeezed harder. She nearly gasped at the pain of it. "That's no answer."

"Then I have no answer for you."

"You brought back a whole village not so long ago. Are you being miserly for the sake of it, or are there limits to your power?"

Alekhai clasped his hands together. "This isn't a favor between friends. Four lives, and not your fathers': two now, and two at the end. For insurance."

Fen gritted her teeth together, but she made herself nod. So be it. She would get the reason from him eventually. She would choose Mettan and Sijara now, decide on the others later, and then force him to bring back the rest, no matter what it took. "Four lives. Two now," she echoed in agreement.

The smile he gave her did not meet his eyes.

"I can't trust you either," she said. "Once you're back in your palace, what will stop you from shoving my head on a stake?"

"Look, despite everything, I actually like you," Alekhai said, in a voice that told her just how much he'd like to shove her head on a stake. "You know, I never really took issue with you rebels," he added, "since you were never much of a threat to begin with."

"Eternal Mother," Fen muttered.

"One more thing. Your friends. When I return them, you should know that they'll be different," said Alekhai. "They might—"

"I don't care."

"No, *listen*. They won't be the people you remember. They'll be the exact people they were when they died. Whatever convictions and emotions, whatever regrets and relief they felt in their final moments—these things will define them for the rest of their new lives."

"I understand."

"I don't think you do. But you will." The seconds ticked by as Alekhai's jaw tightened. Finally: "May the Accusers bind me to this oath: No lasting mortal harm will come to you or your friends after I achieve my goals." His voice was surprisingly soft. "And hear this: I will do everything in my power to right my family's wrongs."

The last words echoed in her like a shout in a canyon.

This princeling was her only chance. The only way forward. Before them were half-starved peasants and desperate bandits with little more than a threadbare banner to bind them. The rebellion would never win; the massacre at Umut Pass was proof enough of that. Their only hope was through Alekhai, the Butcher of Bakrai. She pinched the bridge of her nose and swore loudly.

Fen had only an old quarterstaff and a satchel with a handful of medical supplies, five days' worth of emergency rations, and the gloves Onath had given her. Besides that, she had more grief and rage than she could bear, a dangerously high resting level of anxiety, and what felt like an oncoming tidal wave of depression. She was laughably unprepared for whatever mission Alekhai had in mind, let alone protecting a prince wanted dead by most of the empire. But her only alternative was lying down in the dust to await death.

"Fine," she said.

Alekhai grinned. It seemed almost genuine this time, but his face appeared far more dangerous than it did when he was just glaring at her.

He held out his wrist expectantly.

Fen sighed a long-suffering sigh, even as she rolled up her own sleeve. "If you give me even a quarter of a reason to think you might go back on your word, I'll make you wish I was as merciful as your family."

"Fair enough." Alekhai flashed another shallow smile before tipping his head down to kiss her wrist.

Fen cursed again, and did the same. And as she straightened, she saw a shadow against the stars, vast and shifting and somehow ancient. She knew what it was, just as she knew her own name.

An Accuser.

Then, in the blink of an eye, the construct was gone, and all she saw was Alekhai smirking at her.

"Come on," he said cheerfully. "We have much to do."

The bottom of the pass was brittle and broken, as if some angry giant had smashed a fist into a sheet of rusted metal. The ground was a dark, stinking red, for the dirt had soaked up the blood of the fallen like a sponge. Whenever possible, Fen kept her eyes on her feet or on the sky.

A century ago, when Accusers and their pet Executors had openly roamed the land, corpses had been honored as the vessels of the precious souls that had once animated them—souls that could very well be returned. In battle, comrades had fought to protect the body for sacred funeral rights, over which an Executor would always preside. If the fallen warrior was deemed sufficiently good and just, they would be raised from the dead. Meanwhile, enemies would seek to steal the body as a war trophy, or at least ransom it back. Now, for the most part, death became just that: death. Final, eternal, inescapable. All that remained of the ceremonial struggle over bodies was the scramble for their treasure.

After only a day, almost all the valuables had been plucked off by bandits. Only stragglers remained now, picking at the scraps left behind by faster scavengers. Still, they were dangerous, and made more so by their desperation. And even though the prince had saved Fen's life yesterday, he truly was no warrior.

"You really can't fight?" she'd demanded that morning. "I find it hard to believe that your family would've spent a ludicrous amount of time and credits designing the minutiae of your faces, then turn miserly when it came to anything remotely more useful than perfectly straight teeth."

"Well, yes. I'm a little stronger and faster than average, but *useful* modifications are for aristocrats or commoners who need them—the ones who can afford them, anyway. Purely aesthetic ones are the prerogative of royalty, the Children of Earth." He shrugged. "That's not to say my more martially minded siblings didn't order extensive changes made later."

They crept carefully along the edges of the valley, slowly making their way toward the corpses of Fen's friends. She tried to buttress herself against a flood of guilt, fixating on inane thoughts of how she should've taken some of the scattered gems she'd seen among Alekhai's entourage. She remembered how the jewels had shone, how they'd glittered under light like pure water. But then thinking of water reminded her of the cenote, and the carnufex, and Barra, and all the other friends she couldn't save.

The friends she'd *agreed* not to save.

They found Mettan first. He was closest to where Fen had fled the valley. He looked almost the same as when she'd last seen him, except for the slight sag of his graying skin, the stench of rotting flesh, and the buzzing insects swarming his face. She fell to her knees and threw up what little she'd eaten.

Alekhai, on the other hand, looked pleased. "Oh, good," he said. "He's all in one piece."

"What?" Fen coughed out.

"To bring someone back, I need a part of their body, or something that was once their body. Resurrecting from a handful of ash is excruciating, but a fresh corpse like this, with relatively simple wounds? Child's play." Alekhai held out a hand. "Hand me that knife right there."

Fen looked around and found the engraved blade he was pointing at. "What are you going to do?"

"Slit my throat," he said.

Fen gaped at him.

"Oh, are you worried about me?" Alekhai asked sweetly.

When Fen only glowered at him, he rolled his eyes. "I must die in a fashion as close to their death as possible. You can imagine why I'd be reluctant to do this *nine* times. And why I'm glad he wasn't burned alive." He waved a hand at Mettan, but Fen kept her eyes down. She couldn't bear to look again. The prince sighed but continued. "That cut across the torso took him down, but it's the one across his throat that ended him."

"And then?" she rasped.

"The death is akin to a code word, I suppose. It lets me access what you might call a soul."

Fen's brows drew together. "A soul," she repeated skeptically. "Really?"

"Yes," said Alekhai. "Our minds, our consciousness, all the things that make us what and who we are. It's all just data."

"And how do you access this . . . data?"

Fen watched Alekhai's boots shift. "Very early on in every person's life, an Accuser visits them in their sleep and implants an undetectable neural chip that records their memories, their emotions, their very being. Souls are constantly being uploaded to the Accusers' database—yours included—and if anyone dies, they can be brought back in a process not dissimilar to rebooting a computer. Among the initiated, this power is known as katabasology, the final science. I call it technomancy." He looked inordinately proud of himself.

Fen drew out the syllables. *Tech-no-man-cy.* "Sounds like magic."

Alekhai huffed. "Our abilities come from alien technology, not magic," he snapped. A reluctant pause. "Though, at a certain level of sophistication, the distinction hardly matters." He lifted the knife to his neck.

"Wait!" Fen held out a hand, her head still bowed. "What of the wounds?"

"My Accuser takes care of the rest," said Alekhai, impatience coloring his words. "While I search for the right soul, It summons the nanites."

"Nanites?"

"Yes, the invisible cloud of nanites that permeate everything on Newearth," Alekhai said. "Frankly, they're the only thing preventing complete environmental collapse."

Fen just stared at him hopelessly.

"I can't really explain how I do what I do," he said, a little more gently now, "beyond what I've already said. This power, it's not human. I can't describe it with any words our language has. I'll be back momentarily."

Then he drew in a breath. There was a flicker of hesitation, barely noticeable, and then he cut his own throat. He took one step forward before collapsing to his knees. It was not the blood of mortals that poured from the gash and down the front of his robe—it was gleaming ichor, molten gold that spurted, steaming, from his neck. The dagger, now gilded, slipped from his fingers. It fell to the dirt in a whisper of dust. And then Alekhai died, crashing down at Mettan's side. Droplets of gold hardened to glittering nuggets as they cooled around him.

Fen stared into the prince's eyes as they went dull and hard. She reached toward him with a shaking hand. But before her fingers made contact, his pupils began to glow as golden as his blood.

The unnatural light spread to his irises, setting them aflame, before seeping into his sclera. Fen gasped and scrambled back as he rolled to his feet in a single smooth motion. It was like he'd been pulled by a giant invisible hand on his neck. His lips moved soundlessly, and then he was on the tips of his boots, and then he was floating a few handspans above the ground. The gold beads at his feet, on his clothes, at the tip of the dagger, melted and began to rise upward. They coalesced around his wound before flowing back in, sealing the jagged cut shut.

The light in his eyes vanished in a flash, his irises returning to their strange shifting gold-brown, so very normal now by comparison. He dropped to the ground with scarcely a stumble.

"Oh, thank the Mother," he whispered, trembling a little.

Fen's gaze snapped to Mettan. She saw now that her friend's wounds had sealed shut as seamlessly as Alekhai's had. Some color had returned to his now-smooth cheeks, and the insects that'd been burrowing into his skin leapt from him as if in confusion. But he lay utterly still. His fingers remained crooked in rigor mortis. His chest did not fill with breath.

"What about him?" Fen choked out.

Alekhai nodded tiredly. He staggered over to Mettan.

"Get up," he said.

Mettan did not get up.

Alekhai lurched forward and slapped Mettan hard across the face. Fen surged to her feet in fury. But then her friend was flinging himself upright with a strangled scream. She rushed to him, dragging him into a hug. He thrashed for a moment, eyes wild, and then he went still as stone. His arms went around her shoulders. Gentle at first, and then crushing.

"Fen—what—I . . . "

She pulled back just far enough to look him in the eye. "Mettan, I'm sorry. I'm so sorry." And then, suddenly, it was impossible to meet his gaze. "The rest—they're dead. But I've made a deal to save you. Sijara, too. I'll . . . I'll explain after he brings her back."

Mettan looked to the prince. "You're him," he said.

"And you're mine," said Alekhai.

Fen sputtered, outraged, but Mettan only nodded. To Fen, he said, "There was nothing, and then there was . . . Well, I don't know how to explain it . . . But he was there, and he told me what you offered for my life."

She bit the inside of her cheek. "You're angry."

In truth, she'd had no idea how Mettan would react. Alekhai *had* warned that her friends would come back different. What if Mettan had found peace in death alongside his sister? And now she'd dragged him back into the world of the living.

But he shook his head, lifting his gaze to the sky. "Fen. Of course not." He gave her a small sympathetic smile. "Now, ideally, I would've had some say, but . . . I'm glad to be alive, even though I don't regret dying to save you."

Fen drew herself to her full height, dragging in a breath. It did nothing to steady her. "I'm happy to hear that," she managed. "How do you feel?"

She studied his face as emotions surfaced across his features. Alekhai's power—this *technomancy* or whatever it was—had stitched Mettan back together, but there were dark half circles under his eyes where they hadn't been before. Or maybe she'd never noticed because Mettan had always smiled so much. There was a subtle hardness to his face now, a tightness around his mouth and jaw she'd glimpsed only twice before.

Mettan looked down at his left hand, flexing the fingers, turning the palm this way and that. He was studying the flesh like it wasn't his. "I . . . I don't know. Maybe relieved? And determined to do something, but I'm not sure what."

"Tell me when you do." Fen let out a grateful sigh. He was still *her* Mettan, even if there was an edge to him where there'd been softness before. "Let's bring back Sijara."

It was all so simple—as simple as resurrecting rotting corpses could be expected to be. Fen couldn't help but feel there would be a price to pay for the ease of this later.

Mettan nodded, glancing around. He found his sword a few steps away, and his sheath a few paces next to that. Then his gaze flicked meaningfully to a spot just above Fen's shoulder. "I suppose that's an Accuser?"

Fen whirled around. She saw only a not-quite-shadow, shimmering darkly in the far distance, but Mettan gazed upon it as if it were as solid as the ground under their feet.

Alekhai snorted at Fen's reaction. "That one's mine. It's been following us since we came down here. Now, where is this Sijara?"

Given the steep shrubby walls of the pass on either side, there was only one way forward.

"This way," she said.

The corpses grew clustered as they neared where the fighting had been thickest. Fen did her best to keep her eyes from falling onto faces, lest she find another member of her cohort staring back. She was making a choice right now: Mettan and Sijara over Ruiha, Ihazan, Hahru, and Naijima. And while she'd accepted that she'd spend the rest of her life bearing the weight of that decision, she did not want to look it in the eye.

"Why is the Accuser here? To lend you its power?" she asked, mostly to distract herself from the festering bodies heaped around them.

Mettan made a low, irritated sound as his boot sank into something wet and brownish-red.

"My power is my own, bestowed upon me at birth and taken only on my deathbed," said Alekhai. "It's merely overseeing my work, ensuring that I'm not abusing my powers."

"And what would abusing your powers entail?" Mettan asked, shaking his foot violently before giving up and tramping forward.

Alekhai shrugged. "A thousand things. If you were paying me. If I truly believed, in the hidden depths of my soul, that what I was doing was wrong. If I was breaking an Accuser-overseen oath by reviving someone."

So, the promise he'd given her *had* meant something. Given the glaring holes in the Directives and the prince's general slipperiness, Fen didn't doubt that he could still somehow find a way around, between, or through his words and escape the Accuser's wrath. But he'd have a hard time doing it. Assuming he was telling the truth.

When they found Sijara, Alekhai groaned. She lay on her back, a gaping hole torn straight through her middle.

Somehow, Mettan seemed to understand what had to happen. "I can do it for you," he offered helpfully, a hand on the hilt of his sword.

"You're very kind," Alekhai said tartly, "but no. I must do it myself. I need to die as she did, and only I can achieve a sufficient level of mimicry. Intuitive knowledge of how any death occurred is one of my Accuser-given gifts." His eyes landed on a broadsword, half hidden under another body.

Fen recognized the weapon immediately. It was the prince-general's, though his massive body was conspicuously absent.

Alekhai picked up the weapon, spat out a curse, and speared himself on the blade. Everything happened just as before, though now Fen was prepared. She knelt at Sijara's side, grabbing Mettan's fingers with one hand and reaching for Sijara's with the other. The skin was loose and oddly warm, heated by the sun rather than by life.

Sijara did not require slapping to revive. And the look on her face, confusion and pain and fear giving way to warm recognition, was worth any discomfort. But the familiarity soon evaporated. Because, unlike Mettan, Sijara was furious. Not with being resurrected, but with what the princeling had revealed to her when he was returning her soul to her body.

"So you would have us all desert?" she said. The words were quiet, but she ripped her hand away as if Fen had burned her.

This anger was different from Sijara's usual sort; it had to be the feeling Mettan had spoken of. There was a depth to it Fen had never seen before. It didn't seem mortal.

"No, of course not. We'll rejoin the Masks. But we need to help him first," she said, eyes downcast. "It's the bargain I had to make."

She told them about the rebel assassin who'd almost killed her on the steppe, and of what she'd gleaned from the encounter. The Broken Masks were far from the polished force of Kira Moru's day. The bases were in disarray; their chances of overthrowing the Sovereign, let alone banding together under centralized leadership, were as slim as a strand of spidersilk. But Sijara's displeasure only grew.

She whirled on Mettan. "And you're fine with this? You don't mind that she whored us out to the Butcher?"

"In exchange for your lives," Alekhai reminded her.

Fen was almost grateful for the support.

Sijara shoved a finger out at him. "*You*. Don't talk."

Alekhai's mouth popped open, but Mettan cut the princeling off before he could speak.

"My loyalty was—is—to the people of Kanoh," he said, squeezing Fen's hand, "not some commander I've never met who sees us as little more than a few nameless tallies on a roster."

Sijara gaped at him for a moment. Then she snorted, her eyes narrowing. "I shouldn't be surprised," she said lowly. "After all, you ran to the Broken Masks like a child dashing behind his parents' legs. Not even your own family would protect you."

Mettan's whole body flinched. He let Fen go, taking a step toward Sijara. Things were turning ugly. Fen had never known Mettan to start a fight, but he looked just as he had when he'd nearly beaten her to a pulp in the training ring. It hadn't scared her much then. It scared her now.

"Sijara," Fen said sharply. "Listen to me. Infighting is the reason our people will *never* destroy this empire. Quarreling amongst ourselves will hardly amend that."

Impossibly, Sijara's scowl deepened further. "But—"

"No." Fen swept out an arm. "The future doesn't lie with the mass slaughter of any side. If we can fix things with minimal casualties, then we must try. And if the princeling's Accuser somehow allows him to break his oath to right his family's wrongs—"

"Trust me, it won't," Alekhai cut in.

"I *don't* trust you," growled Sijara.

"*Nevertheless,*" Fen said tightly, "if he reneges on his promise, we can always kill him and look for a new base. The Masks would take us back."

Sijara looked as convinced by her words as Fen herself was, which wasn't very. After a long moment, she sighed. "I *do* trust *you*. I'm willing to try. Thank you for bringing me back." She looked up at Mettan. "And I'm sorry I called you a spineless, cowardly worm."

"That's actually worse than what you *did* say," Mettan said flatly, but he was almost smiling again.

"In any case, I regret it. Forgive me?"

With a sigh, Mettan pulled Sijara to him. Fen leaned forward, and then her arms were around them both. They held each other for a long time before she heard the princeling clear his throat meaningfully. She twisted and met his eye through a gap in the tangle of limbs.

"When you brought back Mettan, you seemed almost relieved," she said slowly. "As if you didn't expect it to work."

Alekhai shrugged. "Resurrection never gets easier."

She wondered if he was physically capable of ever telling the whole truth at once. "But that's not all, is it?"

Mettan and Sijara unwound themselves from Fen and sat back, all facing the prince as he sat heavily on a large rock.

"No." Alekhai clasped his hands behind his back. "The ritual isn't always guaranteed to work. Each time an Executor revives someone, there's always the chance that it might be the last thing they ever do. At some point, when we die, we stay dead, and there's nothing we can do to prevent the end when it comes."

"What if you die bringing back the others at the end of this?" Fen asked. "I *will* have every life I was promised."

"The depth of your concern for my well-being touches me," said Alekhai, as if there were a universe in which she could ever care for him. "You'll have to settle for whatever I can give you, even if it's one life less. But I doubt it. The Accusers like making sure we uphold our oaths, as I said."

"*Fine.* So what is this master plan of yours?" asked Fen. "You have to tell us *something*."

"I don't *have* to do anything," retorted Alekhai. "I swore to resurrect your friends, not divulge every detail of my personal affairs. All you need to know," he said softly, "is that I will finish what I began."

"We don't need every detail," Sijara said, eyes narrowed. "Just tell us what we're risking our newly returned lives for."

"Do not forget that it was I who returned them," said Alekhai.

"Trust me," said Sijara, jaw tightening, "when I say I won't."

They glowered at each other, and Fen was reminded of the time she'd seen two alpha diruses tear each other to shreds over a bone. By the time they were done, their fur was more red than white. Hopefully this would end without Sijara and the princeling bleeding out on the ground.

"Just share what you can," said Mettan, his voice firmer than Fen had ever heard it. "Please."

Alekhai broke his standoff with Sijara to look at Mettan. After a moment, he huffed and leaned back against a huge chunk of rock. "I suppose you'd piece it together eventually. I'm on a mission to resurrect a select few allies of mine. Three in total, their bodies scattered across the conquered tribes. My family killed them, one way or another, but they shouldn't have."

"So you're bringing back your own dead friends?" asked Fen. She found it hard to imagine Alekhai ever growing close with another person. Crown princexes probably couldn't, if only for the safety of everyone involved.

"Yes." He crossed his arms. "Look, all you have to do is watch my back and stay out of the way. My plan is foolproof; I have accounted for all possibilities and then some."

Sijara and Mettan both looked like they were debating beating Alekhai to a pulp, but Fen couldn't have cared less in that moment. So long as the princeling upheld his end of the deal, nothing else mattered. She'd promised to protect him, not ensure his plots unfolded exactly as planned. The finer workings of the prince's machinations were hardly her problem, and she would take pains to keep them that way.

She cared what happened to the empire, but not very much. She'd already tried to fight it, and she'd lost. Now she was doing this for her friends. That was all.

Alekhai yawned. "That's enough questions for today. I'm taking a nap. If you try to wake me, I'll kill all of you, and you'll stay dead this time."

"What about bandits?" Fen asked.

"What did I say about questions?" replied Alekhai, settling down on a relatively dry patch of dirt. "You should find those other people you want resurrected and cut off, oh, at least a thumb."

"What did you say?" barked Sijara. She looked like she had half a mind to strangle the man.

"A head would be better," said Alekhai venomously, "but I'm not going to ask you to decapitate your friends." He flopped onto the ground and closed his eyes.

Fen put a hand on Sijara's shoulder before she really could throttle him. "He needs part of them to bring them back later. He agreed to resurrect two more of us. Three targets, four lives."

"But there were seven of us," said Mettan. "Not counting Barra." He touched Fen's elbow. "And what of your parents?"

"I . . . " Fen's mind went blank for a moment. She shuddered and shook herself a little. "For now, we should just . . . take a little of everyone we can. Bury the rest."

There must've been something in her voice or in her face, because Mettan and Sijara exchanged a long glance and said no more. Something passed between them, something Fen couldn't begin to untangle. Unfortunately, the prince took it upon himself to fill the silence.

"I suggest you hurry up and get to it," he said, cracking open an eye. "As you mentioned, bandits abound here." Then he was unconscious.

Sijara glared at him but nodded. "He's right. I'll find Ruiha. She should be close." Her mouth quirked. "We died together."

"Ihazan, Hahru, and Naijima will be near each other." Fen forced herself to her feet, only for Mettan to draw her down again.

"Stay with the Butcher," he said. "We'll be right back."

"But—"

"You need rest." Sijara gestured at Mettan and herself. "We've gotten more than enough, trust me." She grimaced. "And as much as I want to disembowel the prince, we need him alive. We can't have some brigand sneaking up and killing him. Permanently, anyhow."

Fen didn't have the energy to fight. "All right." She sat heavily by Alekhai's side.

Mettan patted her shoulder, then he and Sijara marched off.

Fen watched them until she could see them no longer. She turned to the princeling. Slumber had turned his face as smooth as a mask. She knew full well there was more at stake than a handful of murdered companions. But his sleeping visage divulged no more secrets than his conscious one.

"Are you certain this is the fastest way?" Sijara asked for what was quite literally the twentieth time that day.

"Yes, I'm certain," Alekhai snapped. He held out the holographic map hovering over his arm for her to inspect. "This route is known to few. It'll get us to Emikoteth a week early."

Sijara reached over, pinching the fingers of her right hand together to zoom out on the map. "I'm assuming that's where the first of your dead friends is."

Alekhai yanked back his arm, glancing over it for a second more before dismissing the screen. He pointed to the winding path at his left. "This way."

He set off down a barely trodden stretch of grass, making sure to stay within the tree line. Fen stomped after him, trying and failing to ignore the swelling ache of her feet. Things would be easier, of course, if they had some sort of a transport. But hovercraft were owned exclusively by the wealthy or very well-connected, and even a simple Oldearth-style wheeled vehicle would stand out in the woods. And that was assuming they'd be able to find one thin and maneuverable enough to make it over the rough, slender trails they were forced to take.

A few moments later, the princeling sniffed. And sniffed again, louder.

The third time, Fen snapped. "What is it?"

"Do you smell that?"

"Smell what?" asked Mettan.

Alertness flashed in Alekhai's eyes. "Smoke."

Fen sucked in a deep gulp of air, a sick feeling pooling at the bottom of her stomach, but she couldn't smell anything but dead plants and baking dust. "For your own sake, I hope you're not jesting."

"My senses are far better than average." A fine, dark wisp of hair escaped what remained of Alekhai's intricate braids. He blew it away when the wind swept it into his eyes. "You'll catch it yourself soon enough."

He was right. In half an hour, the stench of ash began to replace the scent of desiccated dirt and grass. And just below the smoke were hints of something oily and rotten and *wrong*. It hit Fen like a punch to the nose. She recognized it; she'd smelled the beginnings of it at the bottom of Umut Pass.

As they neared the source, the sky darkened with smoke-smothered clouds. Greasy flakes of ash drifted in the air, spiraling along hot wind currents like snowflakes. Another hour brought them to the gate of a village.

No—the remains of one.

The wooden arch had been reduced to a pair of scorched posts guarding little more than charred, unrecognizable wrecks: houses and inns and merchant stalls. They stepped through the gate, their footsteps loud as drumbeats in the utter silence. A coldness passed over Fen as they walked between the collapsed, still-smoking husks of homes, of places of rest and refuge.

Burn marks paved the streets, hinting at the paths the flames took. The attackers had lit each structure afire as they cut their way through the settlement. But as far as Fen could see, there were no witnesses left to tell the tale. Nothing moved, not even vermin or scavengers. It was unnatural.

It was some time before they found the first body. A peddler lay in the middle of the main path through the village, a hand still clutching his tray. Perhaps he'd tried to use it as a weapon; the roasted insects he'd had for sale lay scattered around him. His head lay a few meters away, red hair still tucked neatly into his cap.

The wind changed, and the reek of the entire village hit Fen in full force. She doubled over, choking. She heard Mettan and Sijara cough beside her, but that was all. Alekhai, despite his heightened senses, merely tilted his head. He seemed perfectly, impossibly normal.

Sijara was glaring at him. Her body's reaction to the stench had barely been more pronounced, but her face was still carved with horror. "Something is deeply wrong with you."

"You need not be so formal with me," Alekhai said mockingly, even as he offered Fen a hand. She scrambled up on her own.

"We're nearly out of supplies," Alekhai went on. "Perhaps there's something salvageable here."

Fen nearly failed to wrangle down the anger that reared in her. She dragged in a breath.

"Show some respect," she snarled, pushing past the prince.

They found more bodies first, their burned and bloody forms scattered haphazardly across the soot-smeared dirt. Some were clustered together, clutching each other's arms. Fen knelt by the nearest corpse. She pulled on the gloves Onath had snuck into her satchel and turned the body over.

She flinched as the face came into view. The nose and ears had been burned off, and the eyes were liquid, bloody holes. Flashes of raw flesh shone wetly where hardened patches of charred skin had fallen off, like the sapwood of a tree with the bark chipped away.

She could still make out the strike that had ended the villager's life, a jagged slice through his belly. It was the sort of cut made to inflict maximum suffering before death. But other bodies had cleaner, quicker wounds. This was no usual bandit raid.

It was a culling.

Fen could see it all in her mind's eye. The bandits marching into town, demanding that all the food and water be handed over. The villagers refusing. Then dying, one by one, until the survivors did as ordered. And the bandits slaughtering them all anyway for their trouble. The villagers hadn't even had a chance to fight back.

Here before Fen was the bloody, broken consequence of the rebels' defeat. They'd lost before they'd even crossed blades with the imperialists. The people were tearing each other apart for whatever bloody scraps remained. And the Sovereign remained seated on his throne, feasting day and night with his favorite technocrats.

Her fathers had died for nothing.

Her friends had died for nothing.

Fen's vision shrank rapidly into a pinprick before bursting outward again. Her mouth filled with salt from the tears running down her cheeks. Her head sank between her elbows.

"Eternal Mother. Look at this."

She dragged her head up and looked where Mettan, kneeling beside her, was pointing. There, written in blood on one of the few intact walls, was a message: *DEATH TO THE CHOSEN SON OF OLDEARTH!*

"How dare they," Sijara growled. "How *dare* they."

"We don't even call him that," Mettan ground out.

Of course the bandits would align themselves with the rebel cause. They would proclaim their actions were just, that the massacre of whole villages was a strike against the emperor. And all the while, they were doing the imperialists' work for them: cutting down the swollen population, sparking infighting. And they did it all in the name of the Broken Masks, an all-too-convenient target for the rage of an empire.

The raw, brutal insult of it. It was just as Alekhai had said.

Fen felt feverish. Breathing hurt; she felt like her ribs were being crushed into her lungs.

The only crimes of the people burned at her feet had been the safekeeping of a few handfuls of grain, a few sips of water.

Alekhai was looking at the three of them, his expression eerily serene. "You can't honestly tell me you're surprised." By his tone, he might as well have been discussing the weather.

Fen's fingernails bit into her palms, nearly drawing blood. His own family's misrule was ultimately at fault for this atrocity. But why should a prince care for the plight of peasants?

"This," she said softly. "This is what forces us to fight, Alekhai. You call the Broken Masks warmongers, but the emperexes began it. For most of your empire, it's fight or starve. Fight or watch your loved ones die as the world crumbles around us. This is your family's fault."

Alekhai only raised an eyebrow. "Better to starve than turn to banditry," he said. "At least they got quick deaths."

The cool indifference in his voice made the words strike all the harder. How had she tolerated his presence this long? He was a princex, descended from a murderous tyrant and brother to the reigning one. And even if he died, the only thing that would be lost would be his life. Everyone he cared about, everything his family stood for—it would all survive.

But Fen didn't drive her fist into his stomach as he deserved, because Sijara stepped right into Alekhai's face, her nose a mere handspan from his. She jabbed a finger toward a nearby plank of burnt wood, her eyes never leaving his. Its splintered edge was wickedly sharp.

When she spoke, her enraged voice was not her old rough bark, but a whisper that burned like dry ice. "If I told you to shove that down your own throat, would you? Would you let me do the honors?"

Alekhai's jaw gave a twitch. "Under an Accuser's gaze, your

friend swore you'd help me finish my mission. If you lay a single finger upon me, you will die a thousand deaths."

"Did you specify that *you* had to be alive for the completion of that mission? Or with all your limbs attached?" Sijara asked quietly. When Alekhai didn't answer, her lips twisted into a frightening smile. "But the answer to my question is that no, you wouldn't willingly die with a throat full of splinters." Her outstretched arm shook. "You'd defend yourself. Or try to. You'd fail. But then, at least you'd get a quick death."

"That is not the same as—"

"You're right. It isn't. Your brother essentially commanded people to starve their own children in the hope their emergency stores would last until the end of the drought. I'm not defending the raiders. They should rot for this. But your kind's not much better, and unlike us peasants, you all *deserve* to die." She lifted her other arm, gesturing expansively. "But you're already comfortable with dead villages, aren't you?"

Alekhai went very still. "Bakrai wasn't like this," he said.

Fen could've spoken up then. But she waited.

Alekhai said, "Look, I didn't—I didn't have a—"

This time, Sijara did strike him. She did it just before Fen hit him herself. The idea that the man who'd executed half a village over missing taxes hadn't had a *choice,* while the peasants who took up arms so they could stop smothering their kin to save food had, was so ludicrous that Fen didn't even have time to feel wrath. She didn't even remember standing up and leaping over. But before she could raise a hand, Sijara punched the princeling in the eye so hard Fen heard a knuckle pop. Alekhai collapsed at Sijara's feet.

Once he was done writhing in pain, he wheezed, "I suppose I deserved that."

"I don't care what your orders were," Sijara said lowly. "You're right, princeling. There is always a choice, and you chose wrong. The people of Bakrai were innocents, just like the ones here."

Alekhai let out a harsh sound, a crude mockery of a laugh. "Look around. Innocents are always the ones who suffer," he said, getting to his feet, "because they're the easiest to harm."

Sijara's lips curled in disgust. "If it weren't for your damn Accuser, I would slit your throat. You're all monsters."

"You're not the first to call us that." Alekhai lifted a shoulder in a half shrug. "And you won't be the last."

Mettan stepped forward, staring down Alekhai with pure, staggering hatred. He said nothing, just stood there and shook with rage.

"Mekantai," said Alekhai. His eyes met hers. The one Sijara had struck was already starting to bruise. "Don't you have anything to add?"

The wind changed again, and Fen caught the light, tinkling sound of a wind chime. It was such a gentle sound. She shivered again.

"No," she said. If he wanted to share that he'd resurrected the fallen, then he'd do so on his own.

There was a long silence, and then Alekhai shoved to his feet and stomped away. "We need supplies."

It was hard to find water, harder still to find a source that wasn't tainted with blood and ash. But they did manage to find a sip-peddler. The drink vendor must've fled from the carnage. She'd nearly made it; she was halfway over the town border. The stab wound in her back was crusted with black blood. The bandits had taken most of the ersatz hydration spheres she'd been selling, but the group found a few satchels' worth scattered under buildings and benches. They'd spilled from her bags as she'd fallen. The spheres they collected lacked the added electrolytes of the real deal but altogether contained enough potable water to last them a week or two if they were careful.

They had very little luck finding food at first. Going by the lack of destruction near their locations, both the village grocery and outdoor marketplace had closed long ago. The emergency stores were bare, as expected. They'd been the bandits' obvious first target.

Then Alekhai broke into one of the few remaining houses and uncovered a hidden storage unit underneath the bloodstained floorboards. There were at least three weeks' worth of dehydrated food kits, which included water packets for easy reconstitution.

"Look at what they were hoarding, all while their neighbors starved!" Alekhai muttered.

Mettan fixed him with a wide, unblinking stare. "Yes, and what were you eating before you left the palace?"

Thankfully, the prince went silent after that. As Fen, Mettan, and Sijara packed up the last of the kits, the prince disappeared up to the second floor. When he returned, he'd swapped his blood-soaked undertunic for a new set of robes. He held a few spare changes for them under his arm. A truce of sorts, even if it was a paltry one.

They discovered a few packets of allergy medicine that would no doubt come in handy. With temperatures rising, the pollen season began earlier and ended later each year, and a severe reaction could be worse than falling ill. Nothing else they found was worth the trouble of carrying. Though Alekhai seemed to be perfectly fine with the notion, the others had no desire to spend the night in the village, even in the relatively untouched homes. They headed back to the woods.

As they passed the sip-peddler's body, a tight, nauseating feeling came over Fen. What if she'd been wrong to place her trust in Alekhai? There was so much more than her own life—or even the lives of her dearest friends—at stake now. If the princeling betrayed them or died, Enkaiia would fall with them, too. Or was it hubris to even think she had the power to change things?

She wanted to scour Newearth until she found everyone responsible for all that she'd seen, from the lowliest bandit to the emperor himself. She wanted to beat them into the dirt and tear them to shreds. She wanted to throw their ashes to the four winds. But she was not the deified soul of lost Oldearth, nor had she been the best fighter in even her minuscule segment of the rebellion. What could she do alone?

Nothing.

Fen slumped against the rough bark of the largest tree they could find. Mettan and Sijara pressed in beside her. But even they couldn't prevent her mind from sinking into familiar spirals of bitter hopelessness as she tried to force herself to sleep.

She didn't worry about Alekhai trying to murder them in their slumber. His oath to spare them only applied to the time *after* they completed this mission of his, so there was probably a loophole somewhere in there. But even if any of them managed to lose consciousness for a few blissful moments, the prince knew better than to attack three skilled fighters with tempers honed to a hair-thin edge. He needed them, anyway.

## ALEKHAI

Keeping his distance after the day's events probably would've been wise, but there was a difference between cleverness and wisdom, and Alekhai rarely possessed both. He strode right up to the three rebels, holding out an armful of twigs and leaves as—even he had to admit—another shoddy peace offering. Mettan cracked open an eye, and Sijara turned fully to face the princeling.

"I'd be more than happy to make your other eye match," Sijara said, by way of greeting.

Alekhai had hazarded a glance in his omnichip's mirror function minutes before; despite his advanced healing factor, the bright-purple bruise around his eye looked like it was well on its way to consuming the whole left half of his face. Mettan snorted and curled up closer to Fen.

"May I sit with you?" Alekhai asked. He kept his tone as polite as he could manage. "I have something to tell you."

Fen flicked a hand at him in irritation. "Fine."

Alekhai crouched in front of them and crossed his legs, resting his elbows on his knees.

"So?" Mettan prompted.

Before uttering a single word, Alekhai started a fire with Fen's lighter. She'd never bothered to get it back from him after making him put together the bandit lures in Umut Pass. He pulled out a food kit and began heating the water packet.

"You can eat?" Sijara asked, incredulous. "After all that?"

"No, I'm preparing dinner for the rodents of the forest." He rolled his eyes, or tried to. Mostly he just winced in pain. "Yes, I can eat. And you three will have to, too." He looked at Mettan and Sijara. "I know you don't feel hunger as you used to. Your appetite will probably never come back as it was. Still."

When Alekhai added the boiling water, Fen recoiled, like the smell of vegetables, spices, and roasted insect had slapped her across the face. Her friends looked even more repelled. But when Alekhai offered each of them some stew, they took it. They knew he was right, and Fen especially would be no use to anyone half starved. As they slurped up their last slippery mouthfuls of insect-flour noodles, Alekhai put down the stick he'd been poking at the fire with. He stared blankly at the small flames.

"I didn't get there in time," he said.

Death had not blessed Sijara with patience. "Either speak your piece or leave us in silence," she snapped.

Alekhai's lips twitched. "No one remembers this, or cares to, but when my brother first took the throne, he really did want to make things better. All anyone *does* recall is what he did to our uncle when he tried to usurp the crown." He let his eyes close for a moment, remembering. "He changed, after that. Affairs of state and business tire him. Governance exhausts him. All he wants now is to ensure the dynasty before he abdicates or dies, whichever comes first."

He could feel his expression start to shift and stopped it, maintaining a mask of disinterested blankness. The same one he'd worn during his earlier display. "The Akrysanth I know now always chooses the most economical solution. The swiftest punishment with the longest-lasting-lesson. And when everything is replaceable to you, even people, you tend not to be very careful with them. A sentiment shared by the rest of my siblings." He gestured flippantly at his regrown eyes.

Sijara stared at his face in silence.

Mettan was sitting up now. "But—"

"Yes, yes, I know what you and your anarchist friends tell each other." Alekhai paused. "But my brother didn't send me to Bakrai. He didn't even tell me he'd ordered the massacre. And after . . . afterward, he was more than happy to hand me the credit. The Sovereign and his mad dog of an enforcer."

"You went to stop the slaughter," whispered Fen.

"No." The fire flickered, devouring and dying all in the same breath. "No, I only found out because I stumbled upon the carnage. I was paying a visit to an acquaintance, and by the time I got there, everyone was . . . If I'd gotten there a day earlier, ordered my brother's butchers to stand down, perhaps things would've been different." He had to stop for a moment, jaw twitching before he went on. "But as things were, the village had already been executed."

Alekhai tore his eyes from the flames and turned to pin the three with his stare.

"I died fifty times, thinking each would be my last, but I brought them all back." He let his not-quite-smile resurface, flicking his gaze from Mettan to Sijara. "Neither of you seem surprised to hear of this."

"It was obvious from the moment you brought us back," Mettan said flatly. His face had softened, though not by much. "Executors are few and far between. Those with connections to Bakrai, I imagine, even more so."

"I wasn't angry just because I believed you'd ordered the executions," said Sijara. "It's *you*. You act like lives are your own personal playthings. We're not human to you." Her hands gripped her knees.

Her brows were drawn together, her mouth twisted into a tight knot. *I don't know what to think of you,* her eyes said. *I don't know how to trust you.* The same look was on Fen's and Mettan's faces. That was all right. Alekhai could work with that.

He didn't need the rebels to like him. He just needed them to do as they were told.

"Oh, I'm the monster you think I am. Worse, probably." He shrugged. "But though I might be my brother's last surviving sibling, I want him dead more than any of you ever could."

He stood and found another tree to rest against.

When Fen jerked awake the next morning, she was still exhausted. She couldn't sleep without the screams of her family and friends haunting her. She couldn't close her eyes without seeing Mettan and Sijara torn apart in front of her.

Groaning with fatigue and all the little monstrous aches and pains of hard travel, she rubbed the rheum from her eyes and looked around. It had become a habit to check if Alekhai was still there. Yes, there was the oath, and the shared practical need to remain together. But the trust between them remained paper thin, and every passing moment was another tiny weight upon it, threatening to tear the whole thing apart.

But, as with every other morning, Alekhai hadn't fled.

Fen, stretching out the tender spots of tightness in her back, found him staring openly at her from across their small camp. His face was perfectly blank, but his fingers toyed with the embroidered edge of his purloined robe.

It was hard to hold his gaze, knowing he'd suffered to resurrect the people of Bakrai. Knowing he'd brought back two of her friends and sworn to fix the empire. His strange face was still the face of the emperexes: a pair of cold eyes, a too-neat nose, an expressionless mouth.

Fen had to look away. "You're staring, princeling."

She'd whispered, but Sijara, sleeping beside her, grumbled something incoherent and rolled unhappily onto her other side.

"I'm . . . unused to you," he said simply, voice toneless.

Fen almost laughed at that. She sat up. "You mean you're unused to people not licking at the dust between your toes."

"It's not that." Alekhai yawned politely behind his hand, got to his feet, and started kicking dirt over the smoldering campfire. "You're just strange."

Sijara seemed to have given up on catching a few more minutes of sleep. With a heavy sigh, she rolled upright and prodded Mettan awake. As the others began packing up, Fen opened the map on her omnichip. Her eyes widened when she spotted the emergency public notification sign floating in the upper-right corner of the screen. "Oh no."

Sijara turned toward her. "What is it now?"

"We have a tattletale."

Mettan stilled. "What?"

When the drought had first hit Talishminn, and wildfires raged a stone's throw from the city gates, a month had passed before the capital sent back a flippant response to Onath's twenty-five requests for aid. But in less than a day, Fen's, Mettan's, and Sijara's faces had been sent to every single registered omnichip in the region. A concerned someone had witnessed a suspicious group of travelers lurking around and had described them in detail to the authorities, probably for a handful of rations. It didn't take a master detective to figure out what had happened from there.

They hadn't seen anyone themselves, but it was entirely possible that a traveler had seen them scavenging in the slaughtered village from the hills above. Alekhai's visage was absent. Perhaps he hadn't been spotted, but it was more likely that the emperor wasn't about to embarrass himself by revealing that rebels had taken his brother captive.

Their faces were three among a broader spate. The throne was cracking down, and evidently the number of notable enemies of the state had risen. This sent an unintentional message: Though the Broken Masks had been massacred after the ambush, so had the Senmavari. Fen saw for the first time that the rebels of Kanoh *had* achieved something that day: They'd given the other tribes hope.

Alekhai bent over, narrowing his eyes at the holoimages Fen's omnichip was spitting out. "That's *you*?"

"Just ten years ago," she said dryly. "This was taken during my declaration of self."

Alekhai gave the image a thoughtful look.

Thank the Mother that the only picture they had of her was this one. She was wearing full formal facial paint, and her hair hadn't yet grayed. Onath had never been a sentimental man; he'd never saved recordings of his staff and charges.

She cocked her head. "I suppose I should dye my hair when I get the chance, though."

It wouldn't take long for the imperialists to pull together a more accurate rendering of her appearance from the lictors and Onath's clients, though for now, she doubted any regular person would be able to identify her with what was out there.

Mettan and Sijara, on the other hand, were not so fortunate. The images the imperial agents had of them were more recent, especially Mettan's. Sijara hadn't had a picture taken of herself since she'd joined the rebels, but her face hadn't changed much since her late teenage years. Their anonymous friend had gotten a good enough look at Mettan to recognize him from the records of his family's scandal. They'd have to make some changes immediately.

Altering their hair was the easiest; all rebels from Kanoh had their locks cut short or tied up. Sijara undid her braid, letting her black waves tumble down the slope of her neck. She trimmed her bangs so they fell above her brows in a fringe, but she let the rest fall untouched to her shoulders. Mettan let his own hair hang free from the tiny ponytail he'd been gathering at the base of his neck.

Fen caught Alekhai looking at them as they did this. She glanced away, but not before raising two expectant brows at him.

"At your declaration ceremony, how did you all know who you were?" he asked quietly.

Of all the things Fen had imagined coming out of his mouth, the question did not come close. Declaration of self meant whatever you wanted it to. There were the basics, of course: people chose new names; they selected specific gender designations or kept the neutral labels of childhood; they announced the vocations they wanted to pursue if they had the freedom to; and before the empire, they'd reaffirmed their loyalty to their home tribe.

After a moment Fen said, "I spent four years agonizing about it, but I figured it out eventually." She cocked her head. "Are you saying you didn't know?"

"Oh no, I knew. My name and duty were decided long before I came into this world, but I've known who I was since before I was even able to grasp the concept of identity."

"Same here," Sijara added, brushing stray bits of hair from her shoulders. She glanced at Mettan, still fussing with a lock of hair that refused to lie flat. "What about you?"

He just shrugged. "Not much to tell," he said. "I just used the first randomizer I found on the omninet for pretty much everything except my name and job."

A fair few were like Mettan, and Fen knew most were like Alekhai and Sijara. They just *knew*. But others, herself included, had spent the months leading up to their ceremony tugging their hair out and biting their nails off. It wasn't uncommon to push back the date. Fen had once guarded a sixty-year-old ally of Onath's who still hadn't declared.

"If I hadn't known, I probably would've done the same,"

Alekhai said to Mettan, a wry look on his face. "My father strongly encouraged all of us to have our ceremonies young."

Ah. Of course.

Fen knew that the higher your rank, the more complicated your declaration got, and that an early ceremony was thought of as the telltale sign of a sagacious child. But she'd never considered that a late declaration might be seen by a Sovereign as a sign of immaturity. Was the thinking that an uncertain person couldn't govern a kingdom?

She shook the thought from her head. Alekhai's family wasn't her problem. *He* was.

They all swapped clothes, pulled their collars high, and yanked hoods over their heads before continuing on their way. They took greater care going forward, and by unspoken agreement forced themselves to travel at an even more punishing pace. They kept to paths so faint they were indistinguishable from the wilds, resting only during the deep of the night when they could no longer make out the terrain ahead.

Over the course of two days, Fen scrounged up enough herbs to concoct a foul-smelling potion of black hair dye. It would suffice so long as she touched up her roots every so often. Alekhai, meanwhile, scrunched up his fine nose and made underhanded comments about the stench, only for Sijara to turn on him and demand he make a few changes of his own. After much prodding, he undid the last of his old coiffure. His hair poured over his shoulders in a dark, electrum-threaded tumble that went halfway down his back.

"I'm surprised even your inflated skull can support all of that." Fen laughed harshly, scratching at her scalp with one hand and combing the dye through her tangled curls with the other.

Alekhai pulled a knife from his robes.

Mettan and Sijara barely tensed, but Fen jerked back. It was the same blade he'd tried to stab her with in the royal floatcraft.

Alekhai rolled his eyes dramatically. "I'm just going to cut my hair. May I?"

Fen gestured her assent with a flick of her hand, deciding—probably unwisely—to let him keep the blade. Now that she and her friends had been identified together, they were probably more trouble for Alekhai than they were worth. But the oath remained, and the princeling was still vulnerable on his own.

Alekhai got to hacking. When he was done, his hair hung a little past his shoulders.

"It should be slightly shorter than that," said Fen.

Alekhai gave her the tired, almost mournful look of a person who thought everyone around them was a fool. "Why, pray tell?"

Fen finally let her anger—at Alekhai refusing to share any of his plans, to explain his powers, to resurrect her parents—take over. "Because of *this*." She reached over and yanked hard on a fistful of hair.

Alekhai yelped. He rubbed at his skull as Sijara cackled and Mettan grinned unsympathetically. "I wonder sometimes whether the whole purpose of your existence is to vex me."

"You think too highly of yourself, princeling. Your looks aren't worth your life." She shoved past him as she walked off. He could keep the knife, but that didn't mean she had to be nice.

## ALEKHAI

Another week of travel, another culled village. Alekhai had seen the plans; he'd known Akrysanth would continue his reign of fire and blood. That did little to assuage his outrage.

This massacre had been swifter than the first; the villagers hadn't even had a chance to run. Corpses were littered throughout the settlement, their charred shells frozen in wretched, writhing positions. The air vibrated with the buzzing of feasting insects, the greedy caws of corags and other carrion birds.

The group picked through the scorched, smoking ruins of what had once been homes, scavenging what little they could: new changes of clothes; a few parcels of unbloodied, nonperishable food; antibiotics; a couple of precious water bottles; a month's worth of the compostable cleansing wipes all but the wealthiest used. Though Alekhai's barge had been outfitted with all the comforts a spoiled royal might desire, including a full bath, his less official trips had required him to adjust to the demands of harsher travel. But stealing from the slain, stepping around their corpses and creeping through their scorched homes, was new.

As they left the village behind, Mettan said bitterly, "They didn't deserve this."

The statement was obvious enough on its own, but they all understood what he really meant.

"No one ever gets what they deserve," was Alekhai's quiet reply.

From the looks on their faces, the rebels understood what he meant by that, too.

The next settlements they came across were the same. A smoking slash of wanton destruction cut through the woods, broken only by quiet, abandoned towns. As news of the attacks spread, people fled their villages before what they believed to be brigands could pounce. And with the emergency food stores dwindling, many forsook their homes simply in search of something to put in their mouths. Crumbling hovels and fine mansions alike were left to the elements.

Enkaiia was returning to its origins as a land of fabric foundations. Commoners began to take their villages with them once again, trading stone huts for the great round tents of yore, the sturdy cloth dyed with all the hues of the heavens. The people of the northern tribe had lived as nomads long before anyone else. But the first Sovereign had looked upon the lifestyle of her people with scorn and shame and called for the widespread establishment of permanent cities. A hundred or so years later, by the end of Alekhai's grandmother's reign, to remain in a tent settlement had become a symbol of resistance against the new government, and dissenters had been punished with impunity.

In the days that dragged by, the only life the four encountered were scavengers of the air and dirt, their stomachs swollen with blood and fat. But once, as they made their way through another city of corpses, they glimpsed a group of merchants unexpectedly returning to their desecrated home. One man collapsed onto his knees and screamed, high and wailing, while a woman crawled over to what must've been her house. Even as she cut her hands clawing through the wreckage, she made no sound. The others merely stood and wept, their faces pinched with confusion and horror. None of them so much as glanced at the four as they hurried by. Later, they saw the smoke of a massive funeral pyre rise through the treetops.

The horrible truth was that both the rebels' and Akrysanth's plans to address the famine were perfectly viable in isolation. The Broken Masks would've disemboweled the noble masters and redistributed their resources; the Sovereign would've whittled down the population to a more manageable number. So very simple. Both solutions would've worked if the other side hadn't ruined it all.

If neither the insurgents nor Alekhai's family were fit to govern, that only left everyone else. The four tribes themselves, independent enough to defend against tyranny but united in a single purpose: survival.

After the fifth settlement, Alekhai simply stopped feeling anything. Or almost anything: The hatred in his heart solidified and sharpened like the tip of a wooden spear hardened over the fire. He awaited the day his old oaths were finally fulfilled, the day he'd have Akrysanth bleeding at his feet.

Until then, he would force himself on.

A fortnight later—many nights of writhing on uneven ground only to wake up shivering and soaked with sweat, of gritty rations and raw grubs, of scrubbing down with cleansing wipes that removed the worst of the dirt but barely half the smell—the group arrived at the border of the first living town they'd seen since setting off.

The rebels' faces were still floating around on every omnichip in the area, but they had no choice but to venture into Lyvera. They needed to make ready for their first mission, the particulars of which Alekhai explained that morning.

"Right now, we're on the border of Makhan and Eira," he said, flipping a map on his omnichip with a flick of his wrist. He pointed at a gray speck before swiping a finger onto a large blue dot. "My first target is here, in Emikoteth."

"The old capital of Eira," Mettan said, a strange hunger in his voice. "It'll be crawling with Senmavari."

Alekhai narrowed his eyes. "If we're lucky, we won't run into any. My late ally's family laid her to rest deep within the catacombs of the city, and no one else knows she's there. Not even my brother."

"Who was she?" Sijara asked.

"It matters little. To you three, anyway." When Sijara glared at him, he added with a sigh, "The less you know, the better."

Sijara's jaw tightened, but she uncrossed her arms. "Fine. Go on."

Alekhai expanded the blue dot, dropping down through a flickering three-dimensional rendering of the city. A complicated subterranean maze came into view. He swiped up, and a glowing silver line raced through the winding passageways.

"The plan is simple," he said. "We get in, I bring her back to life, we get out."

Fen arched a brow. "The plan sounds *too* simple."

"Oh, would you prefer a convoluted one?" Alekhai snapped. "I've been planning this little project for years, and I can tell you that the hard part is over. You couldn't even begin to imagine the things I had to do to obtain this map without my siblings finding out." He deactivated his omnichip.

"If the hard part's over, then what do you need us for?" Sijara asked, tilting her head.

"As unlikely as it is, I could be wrong about no one guarding her tomb," Alekhai said. "And before we infiltrate Emikoteth, we need to ensure we won't be spotted in a major city. We've been lucky in the weeks since the calls for your heads were put up, but we can't count on that good fortune remaining fresh."

Thus, their current objective: better disguises. Their biggest concern was Alekhai's own face. Though no one outside the imperial family had gazed upon his visage, the artificial perfection of his features was a dead giveaway of his aristocratic birth.

Lyvera was in nearly as bad shape as the abandoned settlements. That it was inhabited made it worse; the people had neither the funds nor the strength to repair their town, even without "bandits" lurking. The four strode through the rampant weeds growing in the unpaved streets, passing half-collapsed huts with shredded oil-paper windows. The architecture was a disorganized maze of traditional tents, mud-daub hovels, and sheet-metal shacks, all layered on top of each other like strata. Once, the Eirese village must've been a place of rabid, ramshackle expansion. Now it was breathing its last as scavengers arrived to feast on the bones. One day soon, real bandits would come to suck out the marrow—if Akrysanth didn't send his Accuser to wipe out the settlement here first.

A cluster of lopsided smoking dens squatted near the gate. Even twenty paces away, Alekhai could smell the bitter, burnt aroma of cheap pav—a thick paste made from the ground pods of the pavera plant, which could then be heated in specialized pipes that vaporized the morphine within. The eyes of countless shadowy figures rested heavily upon the group, tracking them as if they were prey. Alekhai grappled with the urge to adjust his hood as they made their way to the bustling center of the village.

Scrap vendors scrubbed grime from rusted handfuls of scavenged tech, crouched beside grandparents sipping pungent medicinal brews on their front steps. Pop-up carts choked the streets, crammed against each other like children jostling for treats. Hawkers and shoppers traded gossip, their words only just audible over the low hum of machinery coming from the noble-owned refinery at the edge of town. According to Alekhai's reports, the factory had already successfully shackled most of the villagers with labor contracts.

And the graffiti—there were the normal rude lines, the typical bawdy poetry and filthy drunken sketches. But at the center of one crumbling wall was a moss-green dragon ripping into what could only be the Sovereign. The disemboweled emperor didn't look anything like Akrysanth, but the dragon's scales had been painstakingly painted, and the shattered imperial mask was flawless. Alekhai had to admit he was impressed. The sheer bravery of it was astounding—the artist would be begging for death if Akrysanth ever got his hands on them. The fact that no one had gotten around to painting over the piece spoke volumes, too.

Alekhai guided the rebels onward, barely stopping to glance at his extensive maps as he wove through the crowds of Lyvera. Up ahead was a multistoried stone building, capped with a thatched roof. It was the largest inn in the village, which wasn't saying much. Although the tallest building in sight, the establishment was almost impossible to pick out from the tumult of people, cloth, and wood crammed around its stained walls.

Sijara stomped over to Alekhai's side. "If the goal is to get caught, the inn's the perfect place to do it," she hissed.

"I have an associate," Alekhai said. "A live one. We have an arrangement; they're going to help us. Come on."

Scrawny, giggling children dashed between their legs, chasing after a worn rubber ball. One girl crashed right into Fen, and she nearly careened into a pile of partially liquified produce.

"Watch where you're going!" the girl yelled, laughing.

Alekhai froze for a moment. After so much death and destruction, being around living people who mostly weren't battered and bruised like himself and his reluctant allies was enough to infect him with something like relief. He led the group through a short-cut, stepping around a tattered cloth screen and into an alleyway of sun-warmed stone. Three people sat cross-legged on threadbare rugs, cooking breakfast. One worked a cylindrical stone over a flat board to grind wrinkled red tubers. The second snatched up bits of the oily paste before his fingers could get crushed, rolling the mush into balls. The third lobbed the spheres into a copper pot sizzling with thin broth. They scuttled through, Alekhai narrowly avoiding overturning the vessel, while Fen tiptoed around a heavily bandaged boy dozing on a woven mat nearby.

The interior of the inn, when they finally found it, was just as noisy as the hubbub outside. Rowdy patrons sprawled on the dirty wooden floor or on splintering benches shoved against the walls, calling loudly for food. Servers in aprons so stained they were more brown than white scurried to refill communal bowls. And there, of course, was Taras. They hadn't changed a day. Clean-shaven face, wiry hair, twiglike frame. They still looked far too young to be the proprietor, but they had the pinched mouth of a miser and surveyed all before them with too-sharp eyes. Eyes that glared at Fen, Mettan, and Sijara before finally falling on Alekhai. Then their expression melted. Alekhai smothered his answering grin.

With a subtle tilt of their head, Taras gestured at a shadowed door at the far corner of the room, half obscured by threadbare tapestry. Its haphazard positioning was just so; it would seem unintentional to the untrained eye.

Alekhai caught Fen exchanging an indecipherable look with her friends, shrugging before she turned to follow him through the door.

Once the door was shut firmly behind them, the innkeeper dragged Alekhai into a bone-crushing embrace. Fen was shocked that he let it happen, and even more so when he wrapped his arms around this stranger in turn. The princeling was still a mystery to her, but she would've bet every credit to her name that he wasn't a hugger.

"I never thought you'd come back, not after what happened at Juliset," the innkeeper whispered.

"Trust me, it's not that I *want* to be back," Alekhai said, his mouth forming something disturbingly close to a genuine smile. "There's absolutely nothing for me here in Lyvera."

The innkeeper burst out in unrestrained laughter. They finally let Alekhai free, but only to slam a hand repeatedly into his back as they cackled. "That's my Wren, all right! Sharp as a thorn!"

*Wren?*

Fen tried to keep her face blank of both surprise and satisfaction—she was oddly pleased that she hadn't been wrong about the princeling at all. "Wren" might be the most physically affectionate man in all the tribes, but he was nothing but a fabrication of Alekhai's.

Alekhai gestured to the innkeeper. "This is my dear friend Taras," he said, giving the innkeeper's arm a light shove when they snorted at the word "friend."

"Ah, your 'associate'?" Sijara asked, smirking.

"Associate! That's more like it." Taras chuckled. "So what is it you want from me now?"

Alekhai folded his hands together. "Oh, the usual. Disguises. Food, if you can spare any."

"Will you at least compensate me for your supper?" Taras asked.

The right edge of Alekhai's mouth slanted upward. "Perhaps we could come to . . . an arrangement."

Fen nearly choked on her spit.

"There must be something I can do for you," Alekhai continued, his voice lowering to a rumble. "Perhaps *to* you?"

Taras rolled their eyes so dramatically it was a wonder they didn't pop from their sockets. "All I want from you are credits, as always."

Alekhai leaned forward, smile widening. Before anything horrible could slip from between those too-white teeth, Fen activated her omnichip—fake identity still intact—and paid Taras enough to reasonably cover four dinners. There was only so much atrocious propositioning she could withstand hearing.

Taras shot her a grateful look and snapped twice. With a low click, a door-shaped section of wall sank in a few centimeters before sliding away. In the newly revealed space was a clothes printer. In essence, it functioned much like a food printer: It took in raw ingredients and spat out a product. But distribution of these was strictly regulated, and only the wealthiest could afford private machines. Yet here one stood, in the back room of a hamlet halfway in the wilderness. It had even been heavily modded.

Fen waved a hand at all the unwieldy additions, a colorful assortment of labeled nodules and cranks and receptacles. "What's all this?"

"It's downright criminal what those nobles charge for raw materials, and it's not even the good stuff." Taras patted a nodule proudly. "So I make everything from scratch. These are all growing chambers. Come closer so it can scan you."

One by one, Fen, Mettan, Sijara, and Alekhai stepped forward to have their measurements taken by the printer.

"I know better than to ask what you four are getting up to, but what sort of disguises are you looking for?"

"We could be mid-level bureaucrats," Fen suggested. She paused, glancing briefly at Taras. Alekhai caught the look and gave her an imperceptible nod. "My omnichip registers me as an official anyway," she said, "so we might as well."

"That works for me," said Mettan. Then he waved at Alekhai. "But what about *him*?"

"His face needs to be covered, that's for certain," Sijara said, looking inordinately happy with the prospect.

Taras tapped a finger against their jaw. "Where are you headed?"

There was a half-second pause, almost unnoticeable, before Alekhai answered. "Emikoteth."

"They say that if you throw a stone in that city, you'll hit a vowed religious," murmured Taras. "You could be a junior cleric. The veil, the robes, all that."

Alekhai grinned. "As an added benefit, people will steer clear of me to avoid the expected proselytizing."

Mettan nodded. "It's a good idea."

"Of course it is," Taras quipped.

Fen was beginning to see why the innkeeper and the princeling were friends.

Taras nodded sagely and turned to the printer, their fingers flying over a holographic screen. Within seconds, the machine began pulling from the nodules, sucking up spidersilk, algae fiber, and microbial leather. There were smaller containers for pigments, scarlet dye from ubiace roots and deep yellow from the stigma of iridac flowers.

As they waited for their clothes, Taras ran out to grab their promised supper. They added a jug of warmed cider, free of charge.

"I have to head out before one of my employees sets the whole inn on fire," they said, a hand on the door. "You should probably all slip out the back when you go—Wren knows the way. And if you're planning on dropping in unannounced again, my dear 'associate,' don't bother saying farewell."

Alekhai had the grace to look a tad embarrassed. "Then I won't. But I will do this."

He pulled Taras in for a hug as tight as the one the innkeeper had given him. "If I survive this, I'll see you soon."

"Dramatic as always, I see. I'll be waiting with bated breath." Taras snorted as Alekhai planted a kiss on their cheek. "But do take care. My own 'associates' in Emikoteth say the whole region's about to blow. Thrice as many Senmavari prowling the streets these days, plus a new curfew. And there are whispers of rebels having infiltrated the magistrate's own compound."

Alekhai looked strangely touched, as if Taras had shared words of affection instead of intel. "Thank you, friend."

With a small wave, Taras pushed through the door and vanished. Alekhai sank gracefully onto a bench beside Mettan, with Fen and Sijara plopping down to face them.

"So." Sijara picked up a spoon and surveyed her options. There was only one: a two-handled bowl of painted pottery at the center of the table, brimming with brown stew. "Wren, hm?"

"Don't start." Alekhai plucked a spoon from the basket before him and wiped the end on the inside of his tunic. "I chose an alias as a small additional measure to protect them. I doubt Taras is even *their* real name, anyway."

Fen picked up a utensil and helped herself, giving her friends meaningful looks until they started eating. Ground inner tree bark and mashed worms were far from the food she herself had eaten in better times, but at least it was hot and filled her stomach.

"Personally," Fen said, "I'd feel safer knowing what we're getting into."

To her surprise, Alekhai munched thoughtfully, seeming to seriously consider her words. He took a slow sip of cider, holding the mug by the cup rather than the handle. "I understand that. But trust me, you wouldn't be, regardless of how you might feel."

Fen drew in a deep, centering breath, wishing again that she could be certain of what she'd bound herself and her friends to. But she let the subject drop for the time being.

The printer gave a happy series of chirps, and Fen turned around to see three sets of official casualwear hanging beside the flowing storm-cloud-gray robes of a cleric. The four quickly scraped their bowls and stood to don their disguises.

By the time Alekhai had finished tying the last of the nine symbolic knots on his sash, he looked like any one of the few remaining devout servants of the Eternal Mother. The rest were all but invisible in their drab uniforms.

"I suppose that's as good as it's going to get." Alekhai gave them a despairing look before whipping the final layer of his robes around his shoulders. The sleeves were lightly embroidered with a faint scattering of bright yellow spidersilk.

"Not all of us can—or should—be wearing fancy costumes. It's bad enough that you are. We're trying to blend in, not stand out, remember?" Fen rolled her eyes at the smudged mirror before her, which she was using to help touch up the rebellious gray roots of her hair. She'd need to make fresh dye, and soon.

"I'm well aware," Alekhai said. "The problem is that you don't carry yourself like a loyal minion of the emperor."

"Oh, you mean like this?" Fen pulled herself to her full height and curled her lip, staring down her nose at the princeling despite his greater height.

"Tone it down a little. But yes, exactly. Now follow me."

Fen tried to ignore the ache in her chest as they snuck out of the inn and left Lyvera for the woods. She was already missing the sights and sounds of other people. The villagers were barely managing, but at least they were all *alive*. And if Alekhai kept his word to make things right, they'd stay that way.

But would he keep that promise? Or would he kill her friends once he'd finished bringing back his own, then run back to his brother and the safety of the palace?

That night, Alekhai agreed to take the first watch. Fen curled up on the ground, expecting another useless night of attempted sleep. But she sank into darkness moments later. When she dreamt, she dreamt of gold—fire and blood and spidersilk.

Between the unchanging scenery and the slow acclimation to traveling together, the journey got very boring very fast. And there was, of course, the dense, oppressive gray fog that swirled around Fen. She missed the rest of her friends and dreaded the decision she'd have to make if she survived this. Some of the rebels would remain . . . as they were, and though they hadn't fallen by her hand, the difference between ending a friend's life and choosing not to bring them back felt small. Who was she to make such a decision? It seemed as if Mettan and Sijara were asking themselves the same question.

Summer was slipping away, and a chill began to settle in the air. Fen hated traveling after sundown with a growing passion, when the forest murmured and hissed and the shadows cloaked danger. Her mood worsened, but Alekhai's remained much the same: bitter, sarcastic, aloof, and, when she expected it least, heartbreakingly open. When he spoke of his past, it no longer felt like manipulation. It felt like a man sharing a story he'd never been able to before. Fen and her friends were growing closer to the princeling than any of them were comfortable acknowledging.

When they finally reached their destination, even the boisterous, oddly celebratory shades of life coloring the city couldn't pierce her stormy mood. Emikoteth's brightness was a sharp slap of realism to the face, reminding her how useless her efforts with the rebels had been. Even if she got Ruiha, Ihazan, and the twins back, the rebellion had died twice. First as a raging fire, and then as a weak hiss of smoke, no greater than what they warmed their scraps of dinner over.

The walled city paid the sour-faced four no mind as they crossed one of the three bridges leading into town. The stone arches had once spanned a great river, but now the bridges and the vast, dry ditches beneath them were home to two-tiered markets. Honest business took place on top, among the stalls with yellow awnings, while decidedly less honest trades carried on below within mismatched tents. Emikoteth was a tapestry of sound, the air ringing with the laughter of pedestrians and the cutthroat haggling of merchants, all overlaid with the heavy shuffle of foot traffic.

Peddlers sold Accuser talismans and Maker statues painstakingly carved from realwood, strips of decorative paper, tiny glass bottles of fragrant oil, and minuscule cones of incense. A pair of peripatetic bards meandered through the swelling throng of townspeople. One spun sonnets. The other beat a rapid, recursive number out on an octagonal drum. Above wafted the smell of oversweet tea and bitter smoke, sweat and stale beer, roasting vegetables and baking clay.

To Alekhai's left, a woman in the half-assed guise of a cleric carefully swung a hanging thurible, begging for alms and resolutely ignoring the hungrily meowing lema at her feet. When she saw Alekhai, she scampered off guiltily, likely expecting to be publicly shamed.

Fen groaned inwardly. From the preening lift of Alekhai's shoulders as he observed the accuracy of his costume in action, she knew he was going to be insufferable for the rest of the day. He was so pleased with himself, he nearly crashed into the farmer screaming at his clucking abachens, which were busy helping themselves to the spoils of an overturned grain barrel.

On their way to the city center, where the shops would be selling rations for slightly less extortionate prices, they passed musicians in borrowed spidersilk calling out to passersby, their bruised fingers plucking away on duruqins. The only thing Fen did not see were the usual paupers who wandered every city in a hopeless search for sympathy. The closest thing they'd laid eyes on had been the fake cleric, but she'd been more charlatan than true beggar.

"What's going on?" Fen whispered. Nothing in their immediate vicinity did anything to explain the festive commotion.

They scanned the people, products, and produce around them. Alekhai's eyes narrowed when they fell on a merchant waving painted jars in the faces of anyone who strayed close.

"Someone in my family died," he said, his voice only mildly curious. "See how she's only selling two colors? Blue for the dynasty, white for death. Based on the level of effort these people are wasting, it's probably someone close."

"I'm sorry," Mettan said simply.

Alekhai stared at him for a long moment. "I'm not. The only thing I'll miss is the banquet. If there were any justice in the world, this would all be for my brother."

"Were you two ever on good terms?" Fen asked.

Alekhai sighed. "We were, once. But in the years since he took power, he's spent more and more days drinking, smoking pav, or haranguing servants who displease him. Occasionally all three simultaneously. We don't see each other much outside of formal occasions now." He looked around. "The death must only have been announced this morning, or we would've heard about it on the omninet before."

Sijara scowled. "I would expect the death of a princex to be treated in a more somber fashion."

"It normally is," Alekhai said. "For the first six days, at least. On the seventh, it's customary to celebrate whoever replaced the deceased. Feasting and all that." He gave a wry smile. "It seems this city skipped to the festivities."

Fen suppressed a wry chuckle. Somehow Onath must've consistently forgotten the last part of the ritual. But as she took in the festivities of Emikoteth, any mirth evaporated into a sour cloud of anger. The irresponsibility of whichever noble or lickspittle magistrate governed this place could not be understated. With the drought showing no signs of abating, the city should've been storing every grain and crumb rather than burning through them in a flagrant exhibition of imperialist support.

"Why can't you lot just institute a day of mindful rest like everyone else?" Mettan asked.

Alekhai sniffed. "I wouldn't expect peasant boors like you to understand."

Fen knew he was joking but wished she could hit him nonetheless.

"Oh, fuck you," Mettan said.

Fen and Sijara exchanged a look. They'd never heard him utter a single profanity before.

"Hm, I'll pass." Before Mettan could spit out a retort, Alekhai added, "I don't do charity work."

Despite the insult, Mettan laughed aloud. Sijara chuckled, too, but her gaze was shifting thoughtfully from Alekhai to Mettan and then back again.

"Look," said Alekhai, his veil fluttering as he gestured grandly. "This is why my family still rules. Don't underestimate the power of pomp and pageantry. We remind the people of their heritage. Their history."

Fen's brows lifted. He couldn't really believe that. And yet, his tone was as serious and sure as she'd ever heard it.

"And you remind us of the mistakes of our ancestors," Sijara replied flatly. "You must know that 'heritage' and 'history' are merely justifications for the revival of the same systems that allowed people like you to trample over everyone else on Oldearth."

Alekhai waved a dismissive hand. "The future is paved by the past. The greatest empires were always that: empires."

"Greatest for whom, princeling?" Fen asked. She shook her head with a sigh. "Just because you argue well doesn't mean you're right."

And Alekhai's acknowledgment of his family's most grievous wrongdoings didn't mean he hadn't benefited, once way or another, from their misdeeds.

She was so deep in her thoughts that she didn't realize Alekhai had stopped walking until she was five paces in front of him. She turned to find him frozen and staring at a statue of the previous Sovereign. Judging by the aggressive gleam of the blue enamel on the mask, it was a recent installation. Fen lifted her eyes to the sky. Was there no end to the ass-kissing of whatever obsequious worm ruled this city? The cost of the sculpture had to have been ridiculous; it must've taken a whole team of artisans to craft the thousands of glazed beads in the flowing cape.

Fen walked over, Mettan and Sijara following with varying levels of hesitation in their gaits. Fen briefly considered setting a hand on Alekhai's shoulder but decided instead on a nudge with her elbow.

"All right, princeling?" she murmured.

He flinched but spun to face her, the veil swinging aside for a moment to reveal his face. "I'm—I'm fine."

"If this is how you react to an effigy of your dead kin," she whispered, low and sharp, "how will you face the living in person?"

"That isn't my father," he said stiffly. "He bequeathed his mask."

"What?" Sijara drew back, incredulous. "Then who is it? Akrysanth?"

"It's me," said Alekhai. His fingers were clenched so tightly.

Fen's heart began to race. Her breath shortened as understanding came upon her. "Are you saying . . . "

"This festival . . . It's my funeral." Alekhai looked up at his own likeness. "I've been proclaimed dead."

"Dead?" Fen whispered. How could they have missed this?

She activated her omnichip and searched frantically for any mention of the prince's death. Hundreds of results from the last few hours popped up immediately, with thousands more loading up one by one in what seemed to be an infinite queue.

She berated herself as she scanned the first few articles, but the answer to her question was clear as cut glass. They simply hadn't been checking their omnichips very often, relying on only the barest functions out of fear of being monitored. It seemed impossible that the four of them could've missed such a critical announcement, but they'd simply kept themselves a little too isolated from the rest of the world.

They scrambled into the shadow of a narrow alleyway before they could call attention to themselves.

"What are they saying?" Alekhai demanded. He stood apart from them, as usual, arms crossed over his chest.

Mettan said, "Your brother tasked a quarter of his army with tracking you down—"

Alekhai cut him off with a sharp, joyless bark of laughter. The sounds of revelry faded into gray nothingness. Silence poured into the space between the four, swelling into an uncrossable ocean.

After a very long moment, Fen stepped toward him and asked in a low voice, "What does it mean for us?"

She realized then that she was standing very close. Close enough to see the minute tightening of Alekhai's features. He stared at the three former rebels with cold, luminous eyes.

"That my brother wants me dead." The words were soft. "Will you be the ones to fulfill his wish, then?"

At once, Fen understood. He wasn't wounded by the declaration of his death. He was worried that they'd turn on him. That his plans would go unfinished.

Mettan sighed through his nose. "Of course not. We're still going to protect you."

Sijara crossed her arms. "Speak for yourself. If I ever suspect there's more than a chance you'll betray us or renege on your oath, I *will* end you."

Alekhai huffed. "Like I said, I can't break an Accuser-enforced vow. No one can. But there *is* a vague gray area where I could fulfill my promises without doing as any of us intended."

A dull anger flickered through Fen at Alekhai for not admitting this earlier, but she wasn't shocked. She'd suspected there was some way to squeeze past an Executor's vow. Loopholes were the whole reason the Makers' laws had failed to completely curb humanity's capacity for violence.

"Heir presumptive or not, Akrysanth certainly won't just step aside and let you take the throne," she said. She had to ask: "Are you prepared to kill him?"

"Of course I am," Alekhai spat. "But this isn't about my feelings on fratricide."

Fen cocked her head at him. "No?"

"No. It's not a question of whether I'll kill him, but how. I *must*. My ancestors got us into this mess, and there's only one way to fix it."

Sijara's expression was pinched. "Then how exactly do you plan to end him?"

"Carefully. Arranging an accident will be difficult, but—"

Fen wrestled with the urge to smack him on the back of the head. She knew it wasn't his fault; he'd just never had a teacher as ruthlessly efficient as Onath. "You people always seem to forget that all you need to destroy someone is a decent knife. For some, it's even less than that. Let your so-called bloodright get you through the door and a blade do the rest."

"You want me to run into the palace and shank him?" Alekhai growled. "That's not a plan. A thousand things could go wrong before I ever got close enough to—to the Sovereign."

"Do you have something better in mind? Faster, more direct?" she asked.

Alekhai glared at Fen. She stared back. After a moment, his shoulders fell in grim acquiescence. "No."

Fen felt a momentary pang of guilt, knowing she had no intention of sticking around after he fulfilled his oaths to her. How terrible it was to care again. Getting her people back—some of them, at least—should've been enough.

Fen clasped her hands behind her back. "Then for now, that's our plan. Let's find our target, get her undead, and leave this Mother-forsaken city."

☾

Whatever Alekhai had done to obtain his map, it had been worth it. Getting into the catacombs was the hardest bit—most of the entrances sat in broad daylight, with endless townsfolk milling around. But once they were in, the map took them through a labyrinthine nest of tunnels, smooth as a needle through cloth.

The twisting, interlocking passageways were narrow, forcing the Masks to walk in single file behind the princeling. Every few dozen meters, the tunnel would expand like a balloon, swelling to accommodate the sepulcher of one cleric or another. In other places the dusty stone around them shrank, forcing them to crawl on hands and feet. The catacombs must've been designed as a web of escape routes, in addition to the final resting place of the tribe's vowed religious—a glance at the map showed that many of the paths branching from theirs led to dead ends and, almost certainly, fatal traps.

In some sections, light and dust filtered in through the slats of storm drains, which Fen could only assume had once been useful. Most of the catacombs, however, were long stretches of complete, disorienting darkness. But Alekhai led the way with confidence, guiding them with hushed directions to watch out for a sudden step here or turn a sharp corner there. Part of Fen was terrified they'd end up stuck in the darkness for all eternity, but a larger part somehow trusted the princeling to get them out whole and hale. At the very least, he'd save himself, and they'd be able to follow him out.

Finally, they reached the tomb of Alekhai's so-called friend. It was even smaller and plainer than the others, nothing more than an uneven hole carved in the wall. It was barely large enough to fit a coffin of incredibly shoddy craftsmanship.

Alekhai interlaced his hands and pushed them out in front of his chest in a graceful stretch. "Well, I certainly don't need any of you for this part," he drawled. "Why don't you find some nook or cranny to hunker down in for a while? Once I bring her back, we'll have much to discuss, and none of it is for your ears."

Fen hardly heard him. She was staring at the coffin, which bore the mark of Eira. Four tribes. Four allies, all bound by a sacred promise. All unjustly killed by Alekhai's family. And this one here, laid to rest in an unmarked grave deep within the bowels of the city. Fen could count on a single hand the number of reasons why Alekhai might want her group gone for the next part of this mission, and only one aligned with the theory she'd been nursing since she'd sworn her own oath to him.

"You're resurrecting rulers, one for each tribe," she said. "The last generation of native leaders before your father and brother stopped letting their subjects elect locals, and started appointing their favorite sycophants instead."

Alekhai said nothing as he met her gaze. Fen saw Sijara's eyes narrow at the corner of her vision, heard Mettan's subtle intake of air.

"Tell me I'm wrong," Fen said. "Tell me you're not plotting your own rebellion."

"If you're waiting for me to congratulate you on arriving at that fairly obvious first conclusion, then I advise you not to hold your breath," Alekhai said slowly. "And as for your second theory—yes, I *will* tell you that you're wrong."

"Am I?" Fen snapped. "The nobility might accept fratricide, but they would see half of Enkaiia dead before they let the tribes regain their independence. There will be rivers of blood running across this land, the whole nation set ablaze. Is that what you want? To be lord of ash and bone?"

"I don't want to be lord of anything," Alekhai said flatly. "The rulers of crumbling nations don't stay rulers for long. Or alive, for that matter."

"Enough," said Sijara. "Enough with the secrecy. Tell us what your intentions are. *Now.*"

"Now's not the time for this." Alekhai's glare sank its talons into her. "My *intentions* are all in service of the people. You must trust in that. You *will* trust in that—you all owe me your lives. I've paid for your service in full."

He radiated authority in a way even Ruiha never had. But he was not Ruiha, and the sense of command he wore as a cloak did not make up for the lack. Every word he said grated against Fen's nerves like a rusty sword against a whetstone.

But before she could say or do anything, Alekhai was up against a wall, a knife at his throat.

"The game is over," Mettan whispered. His free arm was pressed up against the princeling's chest.

Sijara rushed forward. "Mettan—"

"I am tired," Mettan said, "of being a pawn in the schemes of others." He smiled then, and it was a horrible thing, mirthless and sharper than the blade at Alekhai's neck.

Fen stretched out a hesitant hand, terrified that she had no idea how this new Mettan would react.

Alekhai, meanwhile . . . Mettan's rage seemed to slide off him like oil on water. He lifted a hand and wrapped his fingers around Mettan's arm, though he made no motion to move it. He merely pressed his thumb to the inside of the wrist.

And then he spoke. "Do you know what this empire is?"

"I do not have the patience for riddles," Mettan growled. "Tire me, and my hand may slip."

"It's not a riddle," Alekhai said. "This empire is a megacorporation that ranks its people not only by wealth, but by blood. It's the greatest dream of the economies that destroyed the civilizations of Oldearth. The taxes you pay are payment for the services the crown provides, the protection of the law and the assurance of a full stomach. But when was the last time you saw justice, or weren't just a little bit starving?"

Mettan's grip tightened on the hilt of his blade.

"My earliest memory is of a family trip to Ophthia during the dry season," Alekhai began, as if there wasn't a knife pressing into his throat. "There was a great duststorm, and we were forced to travel through the smallest hamlet I've ever seen. Lirivka, it was named. One of our retainers called for a feast. To refuse was to die.

The villagers had little, but they gave us all of it. Afterward, as we left . . . I recall seeing a woman by the roadside. She was eating fistfuls of dirt, because we'd taken everything else." The smirking arrogance Fen had grown used to seeing in his eyes was gone. All that remained was a steely glint of determination. "I have seen much of our world. And it is wretched."

Fen thought back to the people she'd seen eating grass on her way to Kanoh.

"Perhaps we weren't clear. We're not asking for another of your sob stories, or some pathetic attempt at a rousing speech," Mettan said. He angled the knife so that Alekhai was forced to tilt his chin up. "We're asking what you plan to do with the lives you return, including ours."

"The empire was doomed to fall as soon as it spread out of Makhan," Alekhai said, "because the farther it grew, the harder it became to govern. My family's imperialism sowed the seeds of its own destruction. The tribes must be governed by their own people, even if they're all bound together under the name Enkaiia." He remained against the wall, but his thumb dug harder into Mettan's wrist. "I'm not planning a revolution. My allies and I are just going to give the empire a strong push forward in the right direction. And in the end, the four tribes will have the power to decide not only which path the world takes, but which routes exist at all."

"A fine goal spun in pretty words, but what happens once you resurrect the murdered tribe leaders?" Sijara demanded. "Do you think the puppets your father installed will simply bend the knee once your brother's gone?"

"Haven't we already settled this? They'll die," Alekhai said, as if it were the simplest thing in the world.

"You can't just kill everyone who dissents," snarled Sijara.

"I may not be a warrior," said Alekhai. "But eventually, yes, I can and I will."

"You *shouldn't* just kill everyone who dissents," Fen said.

Alekhai gave her a flat look. "And you'd prefer things remain on their current course? You and I both know that doing the right thing rarely means doing a good thing."

"I'm sure it comforts you to think so," Fen snapped.

"So your great plan is to rule through terror, then?" asked Mettan.

"Fear is necessary. And I won't rule at all. For this land to escape slow, agonizing obliteration, all kings must die. There is no other way."

"How does killing your brother and his cronies solve anything?" asked Sijara. "Taking them out just clears the throne for another tyrant."

Fen had been turning over the same question in her mind. Assassinating a single man would hardly change much when the system that had bestowed him power was broken to begin with.

Alekhai's answer was immediate: "It doesn't. Akrysanth's death only opens the door for my allies to restore their tribes' freedom." He cocked his head at Mettan. "There. Is that enough for you?"

"No, of course it isn't." But Mettan wrenched the knife away from Alekhai's throat, releasing a heavy breath.

"You have such fine hands." Alekhai rubbed absently at his throat. His gaze wandered over Mettan freely. "There are better things to do with them than threaten me."

Mettan's eyes narrowed. "It sounds like you're shoving the empire off a ledge. And why are you only resurrecting dead leaders? There are no doubt new ones who'd serve just as well guiding Enkaiia out of chaos."

"Nobles understand the system we're dismantling," said Alekhai. "And they'll know how to piece it back together into something new. Fixing things will be their penance. Unless you want to put the burden of shoveling aristocratic shit upon peasants?"

"Let me remind you that your old friends *failed,*" said Sijara.

"So did yours," Alekhai shot back. "You think I haven't considered working with new, common-born leaders? That I've never *tried?* At the end of the day, my allies have intel, support networks, access to hidden supplies, *power* at their disposal that the rest of the empire does not and cannot wield." He shook his head. "Ultimately, it is not your place—*any* of your places—to question my plans. Let this be the last time you interrogate me."

Sijara's lips thinned. "And if it's not?"

Alekhai sucked at his teeth, a spark of excitement in his eyes that chilled Fen to the core. "I suppose I'll improvise."

The threat was not an idle one, but at least Fen and her friends knew what they'd been recruited for.

"Fine," she said.

With a nod, Alekhai spun and pushed away the lid of the coffin. It was realwood, and it fell with a solid thump. Fen choked on the putrid, sulfurous stench that emanated from within. Alekhai looked utterly unperturbed, even as the reek of an open, festering wound filled the tunnel. He gave the embalmed corpse a quick once-over and lifted the knife that had pressed against his trachea just moments ago. Quick-fingered as ever.

"You little—" Fen cut herself off with a gag and slapped her hands over her mouth and nose.

"You'll return it when you're done," Mettan said, not a question.

Alekhai nodded and turned back to his work, letting out a long-suffering sigh. He brought the blade to his own left eye. Gritting his teeth, he lifted his other hand to the end of the pommel and flattened his palm against it. Then he pulled back the hand and slammed it into the back of the knife, driving it into the socket. He slumped halfway over the edge of the coffin with scarcely a sound, save for the patter of hissing golden droplets on the dusty ground.

Moments later, he rose from the bloodied box, ichor flowing back into the ruin of his eye. Throughout it all, Mettan and Sijara remained utterly unmoved. In fact, Sijara even began scrolling through the news on her omnichip. Fen was as amazed by this as she was by Alekhai's power. Perhaps the act of resurrection was mundane to those who'd undergone the rite themselves.

Sijara only glanced up from her omnichip when the former cleric-chieftain of Eira sat up in her coffin. Her complexion reminded Fen of carbon-free ash, of undyed spidersilk, of recordings she'd seen of falling snow. Surrounding that extraordinarily pale face was a cloud of faintly golden hair. Her eyes were violet, tinged with scarlet, and framed by fine laughter lines.

Mettan handed her a mostly clean pair of clothes.

"Chinonso," Alekhai said, one arm braced against the splintered edge of the coffin. "Welcome back."

# BOOK THREE

## ALEKHAI

"... AND that, my dear friend," said Alekhai, swiping a hand across the projected screen of his omnichip, "is everything that you need to know about what's happened in the years since Akrysanth killed you." He flicked a glance at Fen and her friends. "As well as the state of our shared mission."

Chinonso gave the files she'd received a quick once-over and smiled. "I don't recall us ever being friends. Certainly not dear ones."

"You wound me," Alekhai drawled, a hand over his heart.

"Well, I've obviously missed quite a bit." Her eyes took in his robes. "Such as you deciding to take the holy vows."

He laughed. "Friend or not, I'm glad to have you back."

"Friend or not, I'm glad to *be* back."

Alekhai clasped the cleric-chieftain's arm. "We'd better make ourselves scarce. I still have the others to return."

Fen, unsubtle as always, was gaping at the both of them from the edge of his vision. Between Taras and Chinonso, she was obviously having a hard time coming to believe that Alekhai was capable of companionship. He couldn't exactly blame her—he'd done nothing to counter the stories of him butchering innocent villagers, unlike the great pains he'd taken to conceal the connections he'd forged in exile.

"Then you'd best get on your way," said Chinonso, gripping Alekhai's elbow in turn. "I will see you when the time comes."

Alekhai nodded and pulled up his map again. Without another word, Chinonso sank into the darkness of the catacombs. Alekhai gave the shadows his ally had slipped into a long, fond look before turning on his heel and leading the rebels back the way they had come. Their egress was silent, dusty, and overall uneventful, and Alekhai took the time to reflect on what had just happened.

One ally resurrected, two to go. He would see this through. Stronger than any Accuser-enforced oath was his promise to himself—that his brother would pay for Bakrai and every other slaughtered village. Once the ashes cooled and the blood stopped running, a better Enkaiia would rise.

These thoughts consumed him as the group turned to leave the alleyway. He was so distracted, in fact, that he didn't notice the three city guards blocking their path until he nearly stumbled into them. The others froze behind him. Rather than the imposing armor and helmets of their elite Senmavaris brethren, the maskless officers wore casual cloth uniforms reinforced only with gray-painted panels of alumina ceramic. But they were as heavily armed as the imperialists who had slaughtered the Broken Masks at Umut.

"Stop right there." The closest already had a hand on her stinger. "You four are coming with us."

Alekhai's heart pounded. Then he saw Fen slip a hand into her satchel. He bent toward her before she got them all killed.

"Wait," he hissed into her ear.

Fen hesitated, but she withdrew her hand.

"There seems to be a misunderstanding," Alekhai said amiably, hands raised. "I'm a cleric. And these are my companions, all servants of the emperor."

As if on cue, Fen strode over and activated her omnichip. She waved her hand, sending over the identification her magistrate had fabricated for her. The enforcer dismissed the file without a glance.

"I don't care who you are," she snapped. Her gloved fingers drummed on the grip of her stinger. "Do I need to repeat myself?"

Alekhai drew in a breath, the perfect words on the tip of his tongue—

And then Fen wrenched out her quarterstaff, extended it in a sharp swing, and leapt forward.

Well, fuck.

The first enforcer flung herself backward as she struggled to free and aim her weapon. Fen jabbed the second in the gut and wrenched the other end of the quarterstaff around to strike the third's head. Alekhai dashed into the fray behind Fen's friends, all their weapons at the ready.

But before Mettan and Sijara could draw blood, Fen grabbed Alekhai's arm. "Let's go!"

They took off before the enforcers had a chance to fully recover. Alekhai swore at Fen as she tugged him through the crush of bodies ahead, the officers roaring behind them.

"What the fuck was that? Where are we going?" Alekhai snarled.

Fen's only response was to speed up.

"Stop! That's an order!" screamed an enforcer.

His voice was uncomfortably close. Adrenaline shot through Alekhai's legs as they darted around flimsy tents and stalls, overturning piles of fragile goods and dodging enraged proprietors.

"I could've gotten us out of that!" Alekhai snapped.

"Hah! You were about to get us shot and imprisoned," Sijara said.

Alekhai injected deep offense into his glare. "I was not—"

"Shut up and run faster," Mettan yelled.

They shouldered their way down a congested throughway, shoving aside townspeople as the enforcers' commotion faded into the distance. The four burst from the crowd onto a nearly empty backstreet. Alekhai glanced around wildly, but all he saw were shoppers giving them startled looks.

"Thank the Mother," gasped Fen, hands on her knees.

Sijara leaned against the uneven wall beside her, head thrown back.

Mettan grinned. "I didn't think we'd actually get away—"

"I can assure you that you didn't," hissed a voice. "This is our city, remember?"

They all spun around.

Oh.

Oh no.

They'd stumbled right into another pack of enforcers, five in all. Four of them carried stingers, along with the curved blades the others wielded. The three who'd first caught the group slid in from behind, blocking the path they'd scrambled down.

One enforcer unsheathed her sword. "Hand over your weapons or we'll shoot," she barked.

They had no choice. With a bit of luck, one of the stinger-armed officers would miss. But all of them, together? Alekhai and the others would be shot into unfeeling mush. And even if he'd been at his best, he'd sapped his strength bringing back Chinonso. The hunched forms of Fen and her friends told him that they weren't much better off. Alekhai lifted his arms, Mettan and Sijara following suit. Fen was the last to relinquish her weapon, throwing down her quarterstaff and kicking it over to the nearest officer.

The very first enforcer jerked her pointed chin. Five strode forward, four grabbing Alekhai, Fen, Mettan, and Sijara by the shoulders. Alekhai grimaced as his captor twisted his arms behind his back. The fifth officer bound his wrists together before moving on to Fen and then the others. Alekhai flexed his wrists to test the give as they were all shoved through the city. The ropes were nothing but thin plant fiber, meant to give an unruly commoner a hard time rather than restrain a dangerous criminal. It made sense; these people were just the street patrol, not elite Senmavari.

The magistrate of Emikoteth was not a subtle man. This was evidenced by the massive gate of the compound he'd set up shop in. Its carved surface had been freshly painted, its corners retouched in silver leaf. The gate doors swung open with a crisp screech even Alekhai could only describe as pretentious, revealing five long buildings arranged in a half decagon around a sprawling garden. Construction workers scuttled around, sawing hefty planks of newly synthesized wood. So this was what the people of Emikoteth were working for: empty, exorbitant gestures for imperial favor and the refurbishment of the magisterial estate.

The enforcers marched them through the nearest door and then a series of winding corridors framed by ornate stonework. The interior of the magistrate's mansion was a web of paneled walls, filigreed globelanterns that flickered to simulate firelight, and pale hanging scrolls in black ink.

The enforcer behind Alekhai gave one final push between his shoulder blades, shoving him into an immaculate sunken courtyard. The rebels soon followed. Oily braziers chased away the swirling shadows of dusk, splashing light over lacquered pillars, delicate spidersilk rugs, and a chattering dinner party of high-ranking bureaucrats and minor nobles. A masked guard stood at attention between each column, twenty in total. Each was decked out in charcoal-dyed formalwear, complete with a black sash that flowed diagonally across their chests from shoulder to hip.

Seated cross-legged upon a dais at the opposite end of the space was the magistrate himself, observing the drunken proceedings below with an indolent grin. He had the unnatural beauty of any high-ranked noble, with perfect olive skin and a scattering of freckles so arresting Alekhai was certain the man's parents had hired a specialist. He wore a fine gold-embroidered vest over black trousers. At his right hip hung a bejeweled dagger, secured with a samite sash. The animal-headed hilt glared with ruby eyes at the boisterously laughing woman beside its master. Behind the dais hung the magistrate's mask, painted the exact shade of gray to indicate a junior functionary who'd recently ascended to a high rank. No doubt through the nepotistic efforts of his highborn relatives.

When Redya's flat gray gaze fell on them, his smile tipped into a wide smirk. He beckoned at the enforcers with a crooked finger before popping a slice of pan-fried fruit into his mouth.

"Could he recognize you?" Fen whispered.

"I don't know. We only met once." His nose scrunched. "Stop fidgeting."

A hush fell over the guests as the soldiers pushed the four across the courtyard. Alekhai couldn't help but notice the overabundance of food: sliced roots soaked in sugar syrup, grain simmered with nuts and what smelled like realmeat. Of course, he'd harbored no delusions that his fellow aristocrats were starving alongside peasants, but seeing the naked truth still sent a spark of anger up his spine. He'd stopped dining so richly a decade ago—partly because simpler fare was harder to hide poison in—and *he* was a chosen grandson of Oldearth. Even when things had been half as bad as they were now, he'd heard tell of desperate parents smothering their babies when they could no longer bear their cries for sustenance.

The officers forced the group to their knees and ripped away Alekhai's veil. The magistrate's lips pulled back to reveal even more of his perfect white teeth. For a long moment he simply regarded the four of them. His thin, graceful fingers toyed with the jade around his neck, a glittering torc carved from a single piece of stone.

Alekhai waited, tensed, for the silence to finally break. He wondered if Redya had glimpsed his face back at the palace, despite all the ridiculous imperial protocols in place to prevent unworthy eyes from doing so. Perhaps the magistrate had heard a rumor about the color of Alekhai's regrown eyes. All he knew was that if Redya identified him, they'd never leave Emikoteth alive.

"Do you know why you're here?" The magistrate's tone had the eager edge of someone who liked lording their power over others and little else. There was no recognition in his voice.

Alekhai swallowed the bitterness pooling beneath his tongue, lowered his eyes, and said with marked deference, "No, my lord."

"All newcomers to this city must pay obeisance to me," Redya drawled. "You and several others failed to do so, but in my infinite mercy, I have decided to let you right your wrongs instead of flogging you all through the streets. It is, after all, a day of celebration." He lifted an expectant brow.

If Alekhai had been a lesser man, he would've sighed in relief. "Thank you, my lord," he murmured.

Without delay, Fen, Mettan, and Sijara bent to touch their heads to the stone floor between their hands. With unsteady movements, Alekhai shifted to follow them. They repeated the motion six more times, as the magistrate's station demanded. But when they raised their heads after the last bow, the functionary did not bid them to rise.

"Now, I want to let you go, as I did the others," drawled Redya, and now there was a keen glint of awareness in his eyes. "I really do. But alas, I cannot. Duty compels me."

Alekhai's gut twisted. He shot to his feet before panic froze him. When enforcers flew forward to shove him back down, the magistrate lifted a hand. Alekhai forced himself to stay still. To Fen and the others, he whispered, "Stay back." They complied.

"So is this your revenge?" he asked the magistrate.

Terror didn't lessen the embarrassment Alekhai felt to have been caught by Redya, of all people. He hadn't ordered anything done to the man that he hadn't deserved for his stupidity. Redya had bad-mouthed the late Sovereign to the wrong aristocrat, and Alekhai had been asked to punish him. Fen might've been right about it only taking a knife to destroy someone, but picking apart the tapestry of someone's life thread by thread and watching the whole thing unravel could be an unrivaled pleasure. Still, things had turned out all right for Redya: though disowned and destitute for a short period, he'd been brought back and made magistrate during one of Akrysanth's rare magnanimous moods. But he had not forgotten his long fall from grace, evidently.

Redya's eyes narrowed, though his smile remained in place. "I told you you'd regret crossing me."

"And I'll tell you now what I told you then," Alekhai said, hammering his voice into the icy, flat inflection of a scholar-official. "I have no regrets."

Redya snorted. "I look forward to seeing your head grace a spike." He folded his hands together over the table and addressed the guards. "Lock him in our most secure cell and await further orders."

Fear, that old, familiar friend, wound around Alekhai's throat like a noose. When two guards grabbed him by the arms and began to haul him back, his lungs filled with a sudden rush of hot air.

"No!"

Redya cocked his head at Fen, motioning for his guards to pause. He'd probably forgotten the others existed. "No?" he echoed.

Fen froze. "I—I'm sorry, my lord. Forgive me, I only—"

"Who are these people?" Redya looked back at Alekhai, his eyes gleaming with interest.

"No one," Alekhai spat. "Just some minor officials I met on the road."

"Hm," was all Redya said.

Alekhai forced out a regally irritated huff. "Just let them go, Redya. Don't bring anyone else into this."

The magistrate scratched his chin in contemplation, pretending to mull it over. "No," he said. "I don't think I shall." He pulled his dagger from its golden sheath and traced a fingertip to its wicked point. "After all, I promised my guests entertainment, and this doesn't quite yet meet my standards." He chuckled. "It's hard to enjoy the play without knowing the cast, is it not?"

Alekhai went very still. Fen was still right beside him; he refused to meet her gaze.

"Redya," Alekhai said, and there was a warning there. "There is a better way."

The magistrate rolled his eyes. He opened his mouth, but before he could utter a single word, an enforcer rushed in. He shoved his way between Alekhai and Mettan and threw himself at Redya's feet.

"The armory, my lord," he choked out, panting. Beads of sweat fell between his trembling hands.

"Yes, what of it?" Redya demanded, irritation sharpening his words.

"My lord." The soldier knocked his head so hard against the stone Fen heard it. "A thousand apologies, but—"

"Out with it!"

"Half the armory is missing," the officer spat out in a desperate rush. "Including the—the prototypes. Forgive me, my lord."

Redya's eyes went wide. And then he laughed, though it was painfully forced. "Who came up with this jest?"

"It's no jest, my lord."

The change that came over the man was immediate. "Those Motherdamn Masks. I want those responsible," he growled. "Find them! Now!" he roared, his hands slamming into the table. A porcelain cup rolled off the gleaming realwood and shattered upon the floor.

"Yes, my lord!" the man squeaked. He jerked to his feet and scuttled backward as Redya stood.

"Guards, to me!" he yelled.

The two behind the magistrate stepped forward. But when they unsheathed their swords, it was only to place their blades at Redya's throat.

A heavy wave of silence flooded the chamber.

Redya's handsome face slowly turned an ugly shade of purple. "How dare you!" he said, and Alekhai had to admire the steel that remained in his voice.

One of the guards wrenched off her mask, revealing a lined face further creased in rage. "How dare *you*," she demanded. "Did you not think anyone would notice the poor you sold off to the factories? Did you not think those people had loved ones?"

So that explained the lack of beggars in Emikoteth.

The woman pressed the edge of her blade into Redya's neck. A single bead of scarlet bloomed. "Did you not think there would be consequences?" she hissed.

Twenty arms lifted in unison to tear off twenty sashes, revealing twenty cloth badges. All of them depicted a green dragon mask with a jagged crack down the middle. It could only be one thing: the new crest of the Broken Masks. A single note echoed throughout the room: the sharp whine of a dozen stingers being activated. The rest of the rebels unsheathed an array of curved blades.

Redya and the rebel leader stared at each other as if caught within a mutual trance.

Fen whispered something under her breath—a prayer?

Alekhai finally turned to her, eyes wide, as the enforcer behind him let go in favor of freeing their own weapon.

"Protect the magistrate!" they cried, rushing forward.

It was a foolish, useless effort. The rebel leader swung. Redya crumpled to the floor, dead. But then the Mask let out a broken hiss of air, and Fen saw that her blade was unbloodied. Redya's throat was as smooth as the rest of him—except for the very center of his forehead.

Just above his brows was a small, dark hole, gushing blood down both sides of his nose.

Alekhai's gaze sliced through the frozen crowd beneath the dais until it landed upon a young rebel. She was shaking, just as he was shaking. In her hands was a slingshot. A projectile weapon. Technically.

*No, no, no . . .*

"What have you done?" the leader roared.

"I—I . . . " She gulped. "I just—I didn't realize . . . "

The woman who'd sat at the magistrate's right hand let out a furious screech, reaching for her own weapon. The leader slit her throat in a single downward slice. Then she reached into her gray tunic and hurled a knife. Its blade sank into the young rebel's throat. She fell.

Someone cried out, "Iriram, why?"

The rebel leader's eyes squeezed shut for a moment. "It was a mercy."

No sooner had she uttered that last word than the air began to shimmer. All at once, the stench of iron was too sharp; the steaming crimson across the courtyard was too bright. Alekhai could hear the creeping steps of a line of dark-shelled myrma winding between the ties at his feet. He could feel every stitch in his robes.

The room finally erupted into chaos as the assembled guests realized what was happening. An Accuser had arrived.

*His* Accuser.

It was a pale shadow, a dark mirror, a smooth and knotted form that never remained one shape for long. It was a thing of sweet nightmares and terrible daydreams. Suddenly it made perfect sense why no two villages agreed on what the Accusers looked like.

Fen, halfway out of her bindings—thank the Mother for the countless tricks Onath had drilled into her—froze in horror as the Accuser extended an appendage into the center of the courtyard. A thousand glinting specks coalesced around the construct, glittering like silver dust—were those the nanites Alekhai had spoken of? In half a second, the Accuser's limb was scaled with carbon steel. In another, it was a hundred melting glass swords. Whatever its shape, when it struck out, heads rolled. Corpses fell, rebel and imperialist alike. Blood and wine ran in rivers over the tiled ground.

And then the real carnage began. The killing was overzealous. But Fen knew the rules. The Makers had been explicit: The moment a projectile weapon was used, anyone even tangentially involved would suffer the same punishment as whoever fired it. The Accuser set about dismembering anyone who'd played a role in the slingshot's deployment, no matter how unwillingly or unwittingly.

Not all those gathered had been judged guilty by the Accuser, but that didn't mean they would escape unscathed. Fen's friends were still trussed up. As for Alekhai, there was no way he'd make it out alive without help. She had to move.

The rope scraped Fen's wrists as she maneuvered the rest of the way free. The enforcer beside her had just turned to protect the nearest noble. She spun and dove left, driving her shoulder into his gut. He grunted as she tackled him to the ground, making a grab for her quarterstaff. Though she'd knocked the air out of him, he was up again just as her fingers clenched around the weapon.

She threw a glance back to check her companions' positions. "Get behind me!" she ordered.

The Masks ignored them, but the real officers were another matter entirely. They attacked anyone who wasn't an aristocrat or official, stun blasts bursting deafeningly all over the enclosed space. Wretched screams echoed as the Accuser half swam, half flew about the courtyard, slicing off limbs or pulling whole bodies into the air to shred them apart.

Fen gave no quarter. She spun and slashed, her quarterstaff whistling through air and striking between plates of armor. She beat and bludgeoned through a full line of enforcers, but others rushed forward to take their place. She was driving the end of her weapon into a man's chest when Sijara's voice cut through the tumult.

"Behind you!"

Fen whirled. An enforcer slid over the table and dashed toward her, sword held high. She swept her quarterstaff upward and they blocked. Their weapons scraped together as they pushed against each other. The officer managed to outdistance her jab to the ribs, but she grabbed their wrist when they followed through on their own attack. She slammed the side of her quarterstaff into their chin so hard they flew backward, hit the floor, and skidded several paces away.

Another officer leapt before her. His weapons were only open hands, and that—along with the copious blood on his uniform and the fact he was still standing—told Fen he was more dangerous than all the other enemies she'd faced that night. With a fearsome battle cry, he began a whirlwind sequence of complicated kicks and flying jumps. Fen had no idea of where or how to strike. If she missed or he managed to parry, he'd snap her neck. The enforcer twirled and launched himself at her.

Alekhai was suddenly in front of Fen, a stinger in his left hand. He'd broken free; the enforcers' knots were evidently no match for his eldest sister's. He took aim and fired. The officer dropped to the ground like a stone from the sky.

Mettan yelled, "Over here!"

Alekhai whirled and fired off two shots in quick succession, covering Fen as she dove to fend off Mettan's attacker, an enforcer wielding an energy flail. Then Alekhai snatched up a fallen sickle sword and ran to aid Sijara. The princeling wasn't graceful in combat. His blows were slower than she'd expected, and they fell less heavily than they could've. But he fought well enough to keep himself alive.

The enforcer swung, the chain of his flail wrapping around her quarterstaff. He tried to yank it away, but she was too quick. She gripped her weapon with both hands and twisted on the balls of her feet, wrestling it back toward her. She swung the other end of the quarterstaff into his lower leg. He cried out in pain, his hold on the flail slackening for a second, just long enough for Fen to knock the hilt from his hands. With a mighty swing, she beat the side of his ribs. He dropped.

She turned in a circle to scan the courtyard. The Accuser had vanished, as silently and as swiftly as it had come. Mettan had cut himself free and now held a bloodied short sword of a much finer make than the one he'd previously carried. Sijara and Alekhai stood back to back, each armed to the teeth with scavenged weapons of their own. The battle had been reduced to sparse knots of struggle, with only a few enforcers remaining. Now was their chance. Fen looked to her friends and Alekhai. They looked back and took off with her.

But they'd barely fled the courtyard when a hand shot out from the shadows and latched onto the princeling. Fen yelped in surprise. Alekhai made no sound, but his free arm was a blur as he touched the tip of a blade to his attacker's chin.

"Oh, calm down, it's just me." The figure stepped out fully from the darkness.

"Chinonso!" Alekhai immediately sheathed the dagger. "What are you doing? You shouldn't have come back!"

"*You* shouldn't have landed yourself in such trouble," said Chinonso. She gripped Alekhai's shoulder. "Every enforcer in the city is headed this way. Follow me, I know the safest way out."

Chinonso took them through a narrow splintered wooden door, then a series of empty, interconnected back rooms. Some sat in abandoned apartments, others were hidden behind the walls of bustling homes. Soon enough, they were outside Emikoteth's walls.

Sijara sucked in a deep breath, as if the city had been suffocating her. Fen could sympathize. The sooner they were out of here, the better. But she wasn't quite done with the supposedly rightful leader of Eira. The attack in the magistrate's estate had made one thing clear: The Broken Masks were far from finished.

"The rebels need you," she said.

Alekhai made a long-suffering sound deep in his throat. "The whole point of having secret allies is that they *remain secret*," he said, slow and lethal. "I need them for what happens after we kill Akrysanth. And even if we fail, and the Masks fail after us, there must be someone left to pick up the pieces."

"I'm not talking to you," Fen snapped. She stared into Chinonso's eyes. They were like shards of glass; the chieftain's face might as well have been a mask. "The rebellion *will* fail," she said, "if they don't have whatever made your cabal so dangerous that his family had to kill you."

"Don't listen to her," said Alekhai. "We've already discussed—"

Chinonso's mouth quirked. "She makes a good point, though. If the old guard and the new worked together, we might actually stand a chance."

"The Broken Masks are disorganized, petty, and weak," Alekhai said. "They're led by squabbling fools who would rather my brother win than the rival faction."

Fen glared at him. She'd known he was trying to restore the old tribes to their power, but had he really thought so little of her side all this time?

She'd barely escaped one skirmish with her life. And part of her wanted so badly to sit back and let the empire implode as soon as she had more of her friends back. But the world could not be rebuilt by noble hands alone.

She reached over, grabbed Alekhai's wrist. "Four people cannot be the only ones to decide the fate of Enkaiia."

Alekhai looked down at where her fingers gripped him. "We shouldn't rely on what *feels* right, but what simply is."

"What simply is, is that when Talishminn burns or starves or both, it survives not through the mercy of benevolent nobles, but the stubborn efforts of its own people." Fen tightened her hold. "Your kind is slowly killing this world. We've already seen the consequences, and they're only getting worse. Whatever tragedies befall humanity on this planet befall peasants first. And the worst part is, we don't know what those terrible things will be, or when, or why."

Forget bandit attacks or work injuries; there wasn't a settlement outside Makhan where heart and brain diseases weren't serious problems. Chemicals and radiation from technocratic plants relocated from the northern tribe had not only gnawed down the lifespan of the empire's poorest, but had made their shortened lives harder. Fen had heard of villages where headless babies had been born, of children whose skin sloughed off under the faintest sunlight.

"The Masks are doomed," Alekhai said, softer now.

Chinonso turned to face the city. After a long moment, she murmured, "We'll see, princeling."

Alekhai yanked his arm from Fen, narrowing his eyes at Chinonso. "Fine! The decision is with you and the others. But I'm not sending you to your second deaths just because Mekantai here can't accept reality." He sighed. "One last thing."

The chieftain turned her head to the side. "Hm?"

"Why did you really come back?"

Chinonso smiled. "I realized I hadn't gotten a proper goodbye."

"Ah. That's easily remedied," said Alekhai. He stepped forward, pulled her into a hug, and kissed her cheek. "Farewell, my friend."

Chinonso pulled Alekhai in tighter before letting go. "I trust you'll do the same."

Later, much later, when they were safe—or at least as safe as they could be—under the cover of darkness and foliage outside the city, Fen shifted around on the spot of dry dirt she'd chosen for her bed. But no matter what position she wriggled into, sleep evaded her.

What if Chinonso went to find the Broken Masks and they didn't trust her? What if they executed her? What if she got tangled up in the rebels' power struggles and carved out her own faction? But Fen knew the alternatives were worse. What if the only thing keeping the rebels from victory was the expertise and intel of Alekhai's companions? What if the rebellion died once more because Chinonso and the others *weren't* there to help?

With a bitten-off curse, she turned to face where Alekhai was keeping watch. But she couldn't make herself voice any of the questions bouncing around her head once she set eyes on him.

Alekhai sighed. "Yes?"

"You fought well today."

Alekhai gave an unprincely grunt. Fen should've known he could defend himself—she'd touched his hands before. Royalty who didn't fight didn't have palms and fingers like his, roughened as they were. She wondered why no one at the palace had grown suspicious, but then it came to her: No one at the palace had ever dared to touch him.

"I'll take over," she said, sitting up. "How's your wound?"

"What?"

Fen lifted her brows, though she knew he wouldn't be able to see them in the darkness. Or perhaps he could. "You were injured when we met. Or do you not remember?"

"Oh, that." But he said no more as he settled down for the night.

Beside her, the moonlit line of Alekhai's right shoulder and hip was as still as a mountain range. Figuring he was making good use of her turn to keep watch and had already fallen fast asleep, she sighed and shifted into a more comfortable position. It was going to be a long night.

"It's fine." And then, almost as an afterthought, "Thank you for asking."

Fen sat at the grassy edge of a massive lake, Mettan and Ying on one side and Sijara on the other. Ruiha, Ihazan, Hahru, and Naijima sat before her.

Sijara yawned and stretched, tilting her head this way and that. "When this is all over," she murmured, "we should go to the coast. Build a house. Be a family."

Fen combed a hand through her hair. It was long, floating around her head and down her back in a dense gray cloud. That was odd—she'd never had time to manage so much volume, nor the credits to afford a machine that could do it for her. And there was something else, lurking at the back of her mind.

Her brow creased, but she found herself responding anyway. "It should have a courtyard."

Ruiha turned. Eyes as dark as black jade met Fen's. "And a fountain in the center."

Fen could almost see it. A big hunk of simply carved stone, sweet-smelling water misting the air. But something felt wrong, like a loose tooth on the edge of falling out. She couldn't figure out what.

Fen swallowed, the spit sticking to the sides of her throat like glue. This world wasn't hers.

"Are you all right?" Mettan asked.

Ying's brow furrowed. She hooked a finger under Fen's chin, turning her face.

"When *what* is over?" Fen whispered.

Naijima cocked his head. "What?"

"Sijara. You said, 'When this is all over.' What are we waiting for?"

Sijara's mouth fell open.

Ihazan cut in. "Even your memory isn't that bad, Mekantai." Their voice was concerned under its taunting armor.

"Don't you remember?" Hahru asked. His eyes searched Fen's, something like hurt snaking across his features.

"No, I . . . " Fen pulled herself back. "I just . . . "

Ruiha's face went perfectly, terrifyingly blank. She stared out across the lake as its surface went eerily still. In the space of a single second, the shimmering ripples flattened like a rumpled sheet pulled taut. "Don't you remember?" she echoed.

She should've. Fen knew she should've. These were the people she loved most in the world; the least she could do was recall . . .

*Had* loved. These were the people she *had* loved.

Oh.

Ruiha, Ihazan, Hahru, and Naijima. They were all dead, weren't they? And Ying likely wasn't better off. After Alekhai had brought back Mettan and Sijara, they'd sent message after message to the medic. And each time, the only response had been silence.

Mettan and Sijara vanished, slipping away into Fen's periphery like smoke in the wind.

"You could've stopped this, you know," murmured Ruiha. Her eyes were still trained on the water.

"Stopped what?" Fen choked out. But she knew.

"You saw the spy," said Ihazan, their trademark smirk colder than usual. "The night before the ambush."

Naijima strode away through the lush grass. It was emerald

and turquoise, as the native turf of Newearth had once been. "You knew," he called over his shoulder.

"I think you wanted this," said Hahru, following his brother. "I think you wanted to be the last one standing."

"No—" Fen reached for them. "No! If I could've died then so you'd still live, I would've done it." Her face felt hot, almost as hot as the scalding tears running down it. "I'm so sorry."

"All I want to know," said Ruiha, "is which of us you're going to choose, when the time comes."

Fen went still. She felt the answer on the tip of her tongue. But before she could respond, the rest turned to her as one.

"Don't you remember?"

☾

Fen jerked upward, folding in on herself before she was even fully awake. Her head dropped atop shaking knees, her hands curled into fists. She was a leaf caught in a storm, spiraling out of control. Her gut heaved, trying to empty the meager contents of her stomach, but all that escaped was a sick mouthful of acid. Distantly, she registered someone crawling to her side.

It was Alekhai. Of course it was. His hearing was leagues better than anyone else's, after all. His hand drifted toward her, but eventually he let it drop into his lap. Tears, hot as those in her dream, ran down her face and dripped onto the skirt of her tunic. She tried to pretend she wasn't sobbing. Weeping was embarrassing enough; doing it in front of the prince mortified her to her core. But the indignity of it all only made her cry harder, her shoulders jerking with the force of her sorrow and anger and humiliation.

The great sages of Eira were charlatans; time hadn't closed the wounds carved open by her fathers' and friends' deaths. Time had only forced her to learn to live with the pain of their loss. She'd been trying to bind her grief, to lock it away in the farthest, deepest recess of herself. Now, when she shut her eyes against the tears, bloodied and broken images flashed through her mind as they did in her nightmares, too fast for her to shove away. Hahru. Naijima. Ihazan. Ruiha. Sijara. Mettan. Their last moments cut into her like blades.

"It's all right—" Alekhai cut himself off. "No, it isn't. Is it?" He sighed. "But you're going to asphyxiate if you keep this up."

He was lucky her limbs weren't responding; she would've hit him if she could.

"Leave me . . . leave me be." Fen couldn't go on. Her teeth were chattering so violently she feared she'd bite her own tongue off.

"Breathe, Fen. Nothing more. Just breathe."

She hardly heard him over the roar of her pulse in her ears. Her heart thundered like a desperate fist against the door of her rib cage. She tried to count her breaths the way Ying had shown her, but she could barely draw in enough oxygen to keep herself conscious.

"Breathe for them. You owe it to them to live." Alekhai poured words into her silence, his voice as sweet and warm as wine heated over fire.

The change was so shocking, so unnatural and unexpected, that Fen's lungs filled with a sharp intake of air.

"Good, good," Alekhai murmured. "That's it."

"Don't patronize me," she gasped before failing to retch again.

"I'm not," he said, and for some reason she believed him. "I know loss. How deeply it cuts."

"Do you?" Fen pulled her head from her clenched fingers and met his eyes. She tried to scrounge up a response that would hurt him as much as she was hurting, but nothing came to her.

Alekhai reached for her again, even slower this time. He placed a cool, gentle hand between her shoulder blades. She stiffened instinctually, shame flaring briefly in her chest. The touch didn't make her feel better, but it didn't make her feel worse. And after weeks of slipping down toward utter despair, it was almost an improvement.

"Do you want me to wake the others?"

Anything but that.

Anything but Mettan's and Sijara's concerned faces. Anything but their worried questions. Anything but them comforting her, when they'd probably strangle her if they found out what she'd done. What she *hadn't* done the night before the ambush. She'd almost be glad if they did. She deserved it, and worse. But she couldn't die until she'd done everything she could to right some minuscule fraction of that terrible wrong.

"No. I'm fine," she announced, despite the wetness still trailing down her cheeks.

"Are you?"

"If I'm not," Fen said slowly, "it's not like there's anything you could do about it."

"Do you want me to hold you?"

She flinched. "Do I want you to *what*?"

If Alekhai was offended, he didn't show it. "Your hearing isn't half as good as mine, but it's decent enough."

"*No*, princeling. You're a fool if you think I would ever . . . " Fen had gone very still, expecting another bout of ire and indignation, but none came. She pressed her lips together and shifted, turning her back to him.

"Well, go on. Ever *what*?"

Fen considered her options. She could either curl up and fail to sleep in a pool of her own tears, or she could let her friend—*no*, traveling companion and sworn but slippery ally—attempt to help her through this. After a moment, she leaned against Alekhai, though she was sure she'd come to regret it.

She closed her eyes. "I'm so fucking tired," she said.

"I know. I know." His voice was very soft. When he reached around her and took her hands in his, she let him. She told herself that she was too tired to do otherwise.

"Thank you," she said. The words came out as a low whisper. She grimaced when she looked down at their hands and found she'd twined their fingers together.

Despite this, and though the tears kept flowing, the tightness behind Fen's ribs began to loosen, like a knot under deft fingers. By the time she was done weeping, her whole body ached and her throat was a rasping tunnel. But she felt just a little better than she had before.

"You know," said Alekhai, ruining the moment as he was wont to do, "nobles used to have to pay to go within ten meters of me and my siblings."

"I despise you." Fen considered elbowing him away but remained as she was.

After another few minutes in silence, she extricated herself and stood.

Alekhai remained on the ground. "You don't have to—"

"I know." She forced her eyes toward the sky. "But I'm all right now, really. Do I look like I've been sobbing my guts out?"

He searched her face. "No," he said. "Not really."

With a sharp nod of thanks, Fen picked up her satchel and adjusted the strap. Her fingers were barely shaking now. "We can wake the others. Let's get going."

The morning had already begun to sweep away the pale curve of the first moon, its white visage washing away into thin wisps of cloud.

Alekhai's gaze was heavy, smothering. "Are you sure? We can wait—"

She waved off his concern. "We still have two more of your allies to bring back and not much time to do it in."

Alekhai paused as if an argument was taking form behind his lips, but he swallowed it in the end. "Fine. But you're eating first."

Fen sat down again with a huff and reached over to shake Sijara. But Alekhai held out a hand, halting her.

"On second thought," he whispered, looking over her features again, "your eyes are still a bit puffy. Perhaps you should let them awaken on their own."

*Eternal Mother.* She sighed. "All right."

As usual, they'd let their tiny fire die overnight. Fen watched as he resurrected a flicker of flame from the charred twigs.

"I know I'm not the best at consolation. You should probably talk to a professional. When my brother is dead," Alekhai said, pausing to rip open a few packets of dehydrated porridge with his teeth, "I'll see to it that the people get every kind of support they need, and at no personal cost."

Fen laughed without humor. "Don't make promises you can't keep."

Alekhai shot her a look that seemed almost hurt. He waited until the fire withered, leaving red-hot charcoal. He added a few meager teaspoons of water to each packet, resealed them, and laid them on the smoking fire pit. "It'll take time, but—"

"It'll take a hundred lifetimes," Fen said, crossing her arms over her bent knees and dropping her head back into them. "You're talking about free care for everyone when right now, if you're a peasant, hospitals will throw you, still *breathing,* onto harvest piles if you can't pay up front. They don't care if you're bleeding out, or even if you're conscious. They even do it to children."

"Harvest . . . ?" he whispered.

Fen looked up to find Alekhai staring at her blankly. "Harvest piles. For organs, princeling. Blood. Bone. Any usable biomaterial."

His mouth opened and closed without a sound escaping before

he managed to get out, "I'd heard of something like that, but I hadn't thought it could be true."

"Whatever we can imagine, we can create," Fen said. It was one of Onath's favorite sayings.

"But we have tissue vats," Alekhai sputtered.

"Do you have any idea how much lab-grown organs cost?"

He didn't have an answer for that. Eventually he returned to the matter of breakfast, but Fen had lost what little appetite she'd had. For a while, there was silence, save for the sad creak of shriveled branches and the rustle of dead leaves across the forest floor. Unlike the eerie giants of the rebel forest, the trees here didn't swallow sound. A few drab-feathered eryxes crept out of the shadows, beady eyes trained on the porridge packets Alekhai gingerly reopened.

Sijara rolled over with a groan as the smell wafted over. "Breakfast? Thank the Mother."

She blinked blearily up at Fen, who gave Alekhai a panicked look. But the princeling gave a tiny nod that told her she looked sufficiently normal. Mettan smacked his lips, and Alekhai's attention turned to him. Mettan's nose twitched adorably, and Alekhai's eyes softened a little.

The princeling pushed at Mettan's shoulder with none of the hesitation he'd shown Fen. With a little grumble, Mettan sat up. He brightened visibly when Alekhai handed him a packet and gratefully slurped up a mouthful of porridge.

They ate in companionable, sleepy silence before packing up their little camp. Alekhai balled up the biodegradable wrappers when they were done and buried them in a shallow hole.

Later, when they were well on their way, Fen strode to Alekhai's side. Mettan and Sijara walked ahead, arms hooked together.

"You're wrong, by the way. You're good at it," she said quietly, "when you want to be."

Alekhai shot her a narrowed look. "At what?"

"At—" Fen gestured helplessly. "At comforting people. At being nice when they need it."

He shrugged, his expression both shy and self-possessed. "I'm not. I just do my best." He met her gaze and held it. "I'm not going to apologize for who I had to become to survive. But . . . I'm sorry for any part I may have played in your suffering."

For some reason, his apology took her aback more than anything else he'd said to her. Fen might not have been the most deferential of bodyguards, but she'd always shown Onath's clients a modicum of respect. If anyone had apologized during one of those useless jobs, it was her. And now that she thought of it, she could count the number of heartfelt beg-pardons she'd received on one hand. She bit the inside of her cheek.

"A chosen grandson of Oldearth shouldn't apologize to a peasant," was all she said, not quite managing a grin. "To do so is to tarnish the sanctity of Newearth."

"As you say." Alekhai's sharp eyes probably noticed that her smile didn't touch her own, but he said nothing of it.

Newearth's seasons rarely followed a regular pattern, but it was clear the planet's summer was readying for a long departure. Daylight hours shrank, and the breeze carried a stinging chill. Yet still there was no rain. Even during the worst years, at least a few handfuls of water had been tossed from the sky by now. But clouds coalesced and darkened, only to dissipate hours later.

The drought and dropping temperatures brought on further rationing. If food had been scarce before, now it seemed nonexistent. Posts across the omninet spoke with reverence of the half-kilogram measures of grain that had once been distributed in village squares. Riots broke out when stores ran dry and the imperialists began distributing nutrient powder. The Sovereign dispatched Senmavari to quell the fighting, but that only stirred more unrest. Gore choked the gutters of streets as tales of whole cities resorting to cannibalism spread through the omninet and by word of mouth. The rumor that the emperor plotted to wipe out a sizable chunk of the population, once dismissed as rebel nonsense, began to recirculate.

The four trekked along the edge of the woods, remaining under the forest's cover. They kept to the quickest routes where they could, but Akrysanth's sentries were posted along both the main highways and half-forgotten wilderness paths. Patrolling Senmavari apprehended any commoner who breathed incorrectly. It was a wonder the bandits still ravaging the land managed to evade the imperialists at all. But perhaps not. The emperor's soldiers left much of Enkaiia to rot, focusing their efforts on the nation's largest and richest cities.

Everyone—from the smallest of children to the most learned of scholars—knew the tribes were on the brink of collapse. Enterprising bandits who'd been too weak to take the imperialists head-on dove in to feed on weakened prey. Anything physical that could be moved was easy prey for brigands, and the imperialists certainly helped themselves to commandeered food and supplies. Fen suspected the Broken Masks' hands were not entirely clean of robbery and worse. It was sometimes hard to differentiate her comrades from the bandits in the few news sources she could trust.

The Masks' leadership remained in obvious disarray, even as its numbers swelled. Two dominant factions fought for control of the movement: the one that preferred peaceful protest and political maneuvering, and the one that did not. The latter called for villagers to fight off or kill the soldiers the emperor sent to oppress them and to leave for the nearest rebel base. The latter declared that any aristocrats that fell into its grasp would be hanged. And it was the latter that seemed to be winning over the pacifists, because the peacemongers achieved so little in comparison. They were also dying off in droves, since they were the ones baring their bellies to imperialists as they attempted diplomacy. And whenever Senmavari got their gauntleted hands on rebels, it was the pacificists the emperor carved his ire into.

Every once in a while, the group stumbled across a quiet outpost with silent streets and creaking doors. They'd see wagons and carts sat parked before empty stalls. And dozens of Senmavari, sometimes entire platoons, sprawled around the settlements, left for the scavengers.

Typically, during times of unrest, nobles would simply retreat behind gilded walls and feast until the peasants got tired of stabbing each other. No longer. The Broken Masks had learned from their many past mistakes. As in Emikoteth, rebels had already infiltrated the highest ranks of servants and guards by the time the revolution reached a target city. Locals were finally allowed to lead the charge in their hometowns, wielding their intimate knowledge to fend off imperialists who'd never bothered to learn the lands they ruled. If nobles weren't beheaded in their beds, they were dragged out into the streets and left to the mercy of the workers they'd abused.

The emperor commanded the posting of identical bulletins across all major omninet forums and on every door in every major city. It read:

> **TO DOUBT THE CHOSEN SON OF OLDEARTH IS TO DOUBT THE WORLD ITSELF. TO RISE UP AGAINST HIM IS TO RISE UP AGAINST THE WORLD. TO DEFY THE WORLD IS TO DIE. TRAITORS TO THE CROWN OF ENKAIIA SHALL BE EXECUTED. ALL THOSE ASSOCIATED**

WITH SUCH TRAITORS SHALL BE EXECUTED. DO NOT FALL PREY TO THE LIES OF THE TERRORISTS WHO CALL THEMSELVES THE BROKEN MASKS. LOYALISTS SHALL BE RICHLY REWARDED AT THE SOVEREIGN'S GENEROUS HAND. INSURGENTS SHALL BE SHOWN NO MERCY, FOR IMPERIAL JUSTICE IS ABSOLUTE.

Below was a new list of the twelve familial groups that would pay the price of one person's rebellion.

As far as any starving commoner was concerned, this was an endorsement of the highest order. It showed that the imperialists finally considered the Broken Masks a threat. That this time, they might actually win. People flocked to the cause like never before in the empire's history. The less everyday Enkaiians had, the more they were afraid to lose it, and the worse the wrongs they'd permit to keep what little they owned. But now people from across the four tribes had nothing left to lose. Akrysanth had underestimated the will of the commonfolk but—more importantly—their desperation.

Though Mettan and Sijara were optimistic, Fen was not. So far, only minor outposts and a few small cities had been won by the Masks. These were barely victories, given that much of the populace had already abandoned permanent houses in favor of tents that could be rolled up and carried away before danger arrived. And if one was counting by settlements controlled, the bandits were beating the rebels soundly.

Abandoning, bartering, or killing Alekhai and running off in search of the Masks was still a bigger risk than what Fen and her friends faced by sticking to his plan.

At least, that was what she told herself.

Fen soon realized she wasn't alone in warming to Alekhai. She caught Mettan smothering a smile when the princeling struggled to mend a tear in his robes, Sijara rolling her eyes instead of grimacing when he cracked a terrible joke. If Fen was being honest with herself, it was inevitable. Their journey was an unending stream of long days and nights with no one else to look at, let alone talk to.

One afternoon, they stumbled off the right path, and Fen was left alone with Alekhai while Mettan and Sijara went off to retrace their footsteps.

"Hopefully this doesn't take all day," Fen grumbled, pretending to sort the handful of objects in her satchel. Weeks had passed since she'd wept in front of him, and she was still embarrassed.

"Mhmrm," said Alekhai.

Fen turned to find him hunched over, a wad of fabric pressed against his nose. From the look of things, he'd ripped it from the hem of his robes.

"Nosebleed?"

"Yes," he said, tilting his head up, though it came out more like, "Yrrmph."

Fen offered him a spare bandage from her bag. "Not used to hard travel and hard weather, are you? I suppose all the palaces are climate controlled." She sighed, gazing up at the cloudless sky. "Eternal Mother, I miss humidity."

Fen stiffened when Alekhai pulled away the ball of cloth—there was more blood there than she'd expected.

He said, "No, it's only that I'm dying a little."

Fen's guts twisted into a knot. "What? What do you mean?"

Alekhai waved a far-too-casual hand at her. "Don't worry, I'll last long enough to hold up my end of our deal. I've got a few more years, at least, before I'll need a fresh batch of organs."

Fen couldn't return his smile. "Are you in pain?"

Alekhai's brows lifted fractionally. "No," he said. "Not much."

"You were engineered for perfection," Fen said, ignoring the anxiety trickling into her gut. "Why didn't they fix this?"

Alekhai lowered his head and swiped a thumb under his nose. When it came away mostly dry, he looked back at Fen. "The palace gene technicians tried and failed. This is simply the price I pay for strength and speed and better senses." He gestured at his face. "And don't forget, this overabundance of beauty."

Fen crossed her arms. "I hate your family."

Alekhai laughed, pinching his nose. "I know. So do I." He dug a shallow hole in the dirt with the toe of his boot and dropped in the bloodied cloth. "Just so you know, I did try. To change things the proper way."

Fen didn't want to have this conversation; they were already too close. "Is that a fact?"

"Yes," replied Alekhai. He adjusted his new woven sun hat. He'd picked it up in an abandoned village to replace his cleric's veil, which had been damaged beyond repair during the attack in Emikoteth. The hat was supremely impractical, so of course he insisted it suited him. "I tried to win my siblings' support against our father. I entertained dreams of us banding together and dethroning him. Killing him, too, perhaps. He wasn't . . . good to any of us." For a moment, he almost looked wistful. "But when I suggested that there might be a better way to do things, they told me I was too young to know anything. Which is what they said whenever I was right, and they couldn't argue. By the time I *was* old enough, though, all the reasonable ones were dead. My father had been building a dynasty for some time. During the uprising, he'd made the eldest of us his generals. After Moru's death, Senmavaris officers. It was the same. We were all just kids. He ordered us, in more or less the same words, to die for him."

And for maybe the first time, Fen saw raw, unfettered pain on the princeling's face. His vulnerability made her horribly uncomfortable; she hadn't imagined him capable of such an open expression.

"I'm sorry," she said. "For all of it."

"You weren't at fault," Alekhai said. "I always thought their cruelty would make their passings easier. That as they murdered each other, I could care less because of everything they'd done to the world and to each other. To me."

"And did it?"

Alekhai's mouth pulled into a stiff grimace. "No," he said. "Not at all."

She opened her mouth to say something comforting. What came out was: "Today is the Festival of a Thousand Lanterns."

He must've wanted a distraction, because after a moment of surprise, he asked, "What's that?"

Fen was all too happy to oblige him, but that was when Sijara and Mettan came crashing into the tiny clearing.

"We found the trail!" Sijara said.

"After only two hours!" Mettan added. "That's a record for us."

"How impressive." Alekhai plucked a leaf out of Mettan's hair before the rebel could shove him away.

As they headed back to the path, Fen explained, "It's a local celebration in Talishminn. It's about bonds. Between family, friends. Strangers, even."

The corners of Alekhai's lips twitched, as if he were suppressing a smile. He seemed to be standing quite close to Mettan. "What would we be doing, if we were in your city?"

Fen's half-empty stomach seized as she recalled the crunch of candied myrma. She'd eat so many at once her stomach would ache for days. But it had always been worth it, even when she'd had to sit through Onath's scolding.

In this patch of the woods, waist-high clumps of native blue grass had dried to a pale gray. Fen plucked a tall, thin blade and twirled it between her thumb and forefinger as they walked. "We'd honor the Mask Bride."

"The Mask Bride?" Alekhai tilted his head. "Does she have anything to do with your side? Or, Mother forbid, mine?"

"Neither." She pursed her lips. "I think her tale predates imperialist masks, and obviously also rebel ones."

"I'm pretty sure it's all related," said Mettan, jumping in. "But these days, most people call her the Wife of Two Worlds to avoid trouble from either side. We have our own version of the festival in Eira to celebrate the Night of Two Moons, sans any brides."

"Oh," said Alekhai. "I know of that holiday."

"Okay, but I don't," said Sijara. "Someone explain."

Mettan smiled. "It's when two of Newearth's moons align and ghosts can visit the mortal world."

It was a sacred event in Eirese mythology, which Enkaiia had mostly adopted when the last emperor had tried wielding legends and lore as tools of imperialist power. But he'd soon discovered that religion could be used against him, too, when rebellious clerics had gone around the empire quoting old scripture about equality and generosity.

"The Mask Bride's story goes like this." Fen dropped her blade of grass and clasped her hands behind her back. "One Night of Two Moons, a ghost named Ainara found herself lost in the middle of the woods on the way to see her family. She ran into a living woman called Uma, who guided her out of the forest and all the way home. Uma never suspected that her acquaintance was a dead woman walking, and they fell in love that evening. Ainara returned to the afterlife in the morning, but she couldn't forget Uma. So on the next Night of Two Moons, Ainara risked the wrath of the gods—"

"Gods?" Alekhai echoed. "You mean, the Makers? I thought their worship had ended long ago."

Sijara laughed. "Maybe in the largest cities, where your family didn't allow any sort of corporeal power to challenge them." She shrugged. "But the old ways persisted on the fringes."

Alekhai nodded to himself, gesturing at Fen. "Please continue."

"Ainara risked the wrath of the gods and remained in the mortal world. Many years later, after their betrothal ceremony had ended, the pair went through the gifts their guests had brought them. The last present to be opened was an unmarked, unadorned chest of seamless realwood. When Uma peered inside, she found a beautiful mask, carved so intricately that at first, she feared it was a real face."

Alekhai scrunched up his nose.

Fen snorted at his reaction. "When she awoke the next morning, Uma discovered that her betrothed had vanished. She wept for twenty-nine nights, until finally the mask took pity on her—"

"Wait, what? The *mask* took pity on her?" Sijara frowned. "How? Was it magic?"

"How would I know?" Fen said flatly. "You know how these stories go. They're incomprehensible unless they're imperial propaganda, and then they make *too* much sense. But I guess so. Anyway, the mask told Uma that the gods had dragged her wife-to-be down into the land of the dead. If she wanted Ainara back, she'd have to find a way to descend to the depths of the underworld and rescue her intended herself."

"And then what?" asked Alekhai.

Fen shrugged. "I forget the middle of the story. But Ainara's family decided that Uma had destroyed their daughter's peaceful rest. They did everything they could to make her life a constant torment, and eventually her own family abandoned her."

Mettan's face did a complicated thing. Fen, apologetic, pulled him to her side.

"With the help of the mask," she said, "Uma built a stairway from ten thousand enchanted globelanterns and brought Ainara back to the mortal realm, where they lived happily ever after. Or maybe the mask was really Ainara all along, but with her memories erased, and the whole thing was just a test from the gods. Either way, we celebrate their bravery and honor their love with food and music. There's even a poetry contest."

Alekhai drew in a breath. "Why are you telling me this?"

"I recall my audience being three people," Fen said. "But the point of the story, I suppose, is that family is complicated. Maybe they want to use you for their own ends, at least until you're more trouble than you're worth." That had been Onath, or so she'd thought. "Or maybe they're dead, killed in battle or murdered by cowards." Her friends. Her fathers.

Alekhai was giving her a strange, pinched look.

Sijara arched a brow at him. "What?"

He looked at the three of them. "I can't be your family, if that's what you're asking."

When Fen let out a startled laugh, Alekhai and Sijara joined her. Mettan just gave a wry smile.

"I'm just saying that family can sometimes be more of a curse than a blessing," Fen said.

"And?" Alekhai pressed.

"What were you expecting, princeling?" Sijara cocked her head at him. "Some pithy moral? A happy ending outside the myth?"

"Of course I was!" he exclaimed, throwing up his hands. "I thought you were trying to make me feel better!"

"Obviously you're unfamiliar with Eirese-Enkaiian folktales," said Mettan.

"I *was* trying, to be fair," Fen said. She wanted to add that not everyone was as skilled at the art of consolation as him, but then the others would ask what she meant.

Nevertheless, that pained expression had vanished, and Alekhai was almost, *almost*, smiling. Fen was internally congratulating herself when the princeling sucked in a short, sharp gulp of air.

A spark of fear shot through Fen's veins. "What is it? Smoke?"

Sijara grabbed his arm. "Another culled village?"

Alekhai's eyes were glazed and wide with glee. "*Food.*" He didn't wait for a response before pulling down his hat and heading off to the right.

Fen froze, staring at Mettan and Sijara. Had Alekhai hit his head without their noticing? It was wildly uncharacteristic for him to be so impulsive. Cursing, they rushed after him. He was faster than any of them; they had to run to catch up.

"What are you doing?" Sijara hissed out.

Fen panted, "We can't risk exposing ourselves like this—"

A heavenly smell filled her nose and mouth, carrying hints of burnt sugar and savory spices she couldn't name.

"Oh," she said softly.

"Yes, *oh*," Alekhai said, grinning.

They ducked low in the foliage as a man came around the bend in the path, tugging a curtained cart behind him. He was roughly Fen's height, with ears full of bronze and copper rings. He wore a rough-hewn jerkin edged in magenta and rouge-shaded ribbon. The colors suited his complexion well. He was a different type of pale than Chinonso; where the cleric-chieftain's complexion was that of porcelain and paper, the vendor's was faintly pink, like a layer or two of white cloth set over red.

"Aren't you tired of rations?" Alekhai asked.

"What if it's a trap?" Mettan asked.

"What if it isn't?" Fen countered, salivating. Her stomach was already cramping with desperation.

Alekhai's eyes narrowed at the vendor. "The likelihood of an assassin finding us in the middle of the woods—impossible. If we were in a settlement, then I'd be worried. Akrysanth might be sharper than I ever gave him credit for, but not even I could plan for a chance encounter like this."

"That almost sounded like humility. You must be starving," Sijara said dryly.

"But even if you aren't underestimating your brother, the list of people who want you dead is very long," Mettan argued.

"He could be a bandit," said Sijara. "One who lures hungry travelers with his wares before slitting their throats and stealing their supplies. How else could he afford the ingredients for all that?"

Fen licked her lips, fear and hunger battling in her gut. Her friends might've lost their appetite in the afterlife, but she definitely still had hers.

"That's a stretch," Alekhai said.

Mettan rubbed tiredly at his eyes. "Do you really want to die for your dinner, princeling?"

"Stop calling me that," Alekhai said, but the anger in his voice was outweighed by the mirth underlying it. He tucked the stinger he'd gotten during the Emikoteth bloodbath into the back of his belt. "I'll shoot him if he attacks."

Fen sighed. "We can't waste a shot on him."

"Okay," Alekhai said amicably. "Let's kill him and eat, then."

Mettan gasped.

"I'm obviously joking," Alekhai said.

But Fen knew better. She hated herself for considering it, too, even for a fraction of a second. But she'd never smelled anything so wonderful in her life.

"Only if he attacks us first," she said.

Sijara made a grab for Alekhai but missed as he stood. "Wait, no—"

Alekhai strode into the path. Fen gave her friends an apologetic look before heading after him. Grumbling, Mettan and Sijara followed. The vendor's eyes widened before he shoved a hand into his sleeve.

"Friend or foe?" he demanded.

"Friend," said Fen, before Alekhai could say anything. "What are you selling?"

The man smiled as he slid out his empty hand. "As if you can't smell it." He turned and pulled aside the curtain on his cart. Alekhai looked on the verge of tears when the vendor slid open the lid.

Fen found herself jerking forward like a puppet on yanked strings. There were protein cakes swimming in broth, root vegetables with kaleidoscopic pigmentation, fruit dried and pressed into balls. There were thick, hand-shredded noodles glistening with spicy oil and sprinkled with wild greens, salt-crusted bread that looked like it had been made from a mix of grain flours instead of insects. There was a pitcher of wine with floating slices of some sort of citrus, tucked beside a shallow bowl of peeled abachen eggs—*realeggs*—boiled in tea. Even with the eggs, it was simple food, the sort a well-to-do peasant or low-ranked official might've had for supper before the drought had truly set in. But times had changed.

"How does a traveling street vendor have all this?" Fen whispered. She'd probably eaten better food with Onath at some point, but she couldn't remember.

"He doesn't," said the man. "He works as a cook for a noble

until the loyal citizens in his city decide loyalty isn't going to fill their stomachs. He steals a month's worth of ingredients from the kitchens when they finally come for his employer and runs for his life." He crossed his arms over his chest, as if daring them to judge him. "The name's Gemarra, by the way. Who're you?"

"I'm Brother Wren, and these are my traveling companions," Alekhai replied.

"Strange hat, Brother," said Gemarra.

"I'm afraid I've lost my veil," said Alekhai. Even without glancing, Fen could see the affronted face he was making. "I had to make do to protect my modesty."

"Cost?" Fen asked, gritting her teeth. No doubt Gemarra was going to rob them blind.

"A hundred credits each."

Fen's brows shot up. "You're out of your mind."

"Can't blame me for trying." Gemarra sighed. "Fifty, but that's my final offer. Most of the empire would murder for this."

*You have no idea,* Fen thought. She exchanged a look with Alekhai. She'd rather pay a mildly ludicrous amount than kill in cold blood. The vendor seemed nice enough.

"Fine." Fen transferred the credits.

"You should know I was willing to haggle more," the vendor said, chuckling. "Not like I'll have many customers. Ones who won't just gut me and take what they want, anyway." Fen felt foolish for underestimating the man. "Tea?"

Sijara huffed but gave in. "Please. For all of us."

Gemarra went to the back of the cart. He produced a finely enameled pot, from which he poured four steaming servings. Mettan took a cup with a grateful nod. He'd always had a remarkable tolerance for heat; as Fen and Sijara blew on their drinks, he lifted his own to his lips.

Alekhai grabbed Mettan's wrist before he could take the first sip. "No," he said, plucking the cup from his fingers and holding it out to the vendor. "You drink it."

Gemarra's eyes went as round as Oldearth coins. "It's just tea!"

"Drink it," Alekhai repeated. His voice was a riptide, calm on the surface, lethal just beneath.

Gemarra took a step back, both hands lifted.

Fen's skin went cold. Her heartbeat filled her throat.

"Poison?" Mettan hissed.

"The smell is faint, but it's there." Alekhai kept his eyes on Gemarra.

They could've all died, right then and there. Fen's mouth went dry. They could still die—

She'd barely grabbed her quarterstaff when the vendor—no, *assassin*, of course he was an assassin—pulled a knife from his sleeve and slashed at Sijara, who hadn't yet unsheathed her weapon.

Fen blocked the attack with the side of her half-extended quarterstaff, knocking the blade away. Sijara tried to ram her fist into the assassin's exposed gut, but Gemarra slipped around and drove his shin into the backs of Sijara's knees. As she fell, he tried to kick her in the gut with his other leg. Fen and Mettan rushed forward before the blow landed.

Gemarra twisted, dodged Mettan's attack, and tripped Fen. This time the assassin's kick landed true. She slammed onto her back with a shout, the air knocked from her lungs. Her head struck the ground. Her vision flickered and her ears rang from the force of impact. Her eyes watered from the pain as she clutched at her stomach. Alekhai stood off to the side, frozen. Or was he choosing not to move? Was this some way around his deal with them—

No.

She knew better. Something else was going on here. She saw it in Alekhai's eyes—he was in shock. She had to get up. She had to fight. But her body wouldn't listen, and as Gemarra wove to avoid Mettan's sword, he pulled out another knife, one designed to throw. He angled it at Fen's head and pulled his arm back.

A sob wedged itself in Fen's chest. Eternal Mother, after everything, she'd hoped she wouldn't have to die in the dirt. But suddenly, Alekhai broke himself out of whatever trance had ensnared him and threw himself between them.

"Stop," he commanded.

Miraculously, Gemarra went still, though his blade was still held high.

"I know that poison—I know only the imperial chemists can synthesize it," Alekhai continued. "My brother sent you to find me, or else you would've attacked me first. I'm still your prince, and I command you. Do not touch them."

Gemarra drew in a deep breath. Then he lunged. Fen heard the sharp whistle of metal through air before she even saw the assassin move his arm. Alekhai shoved himself into Gemarra, wrestling for the new knife he'd unsheathed as Mettan and Sijara tried to hold the man down. The assassin cut the princeling across his outstretched arm. Alekhai didn't make a sound, nor did he relent. But Gemarra used Alekhai's weight against him, knocking him to the ground and wrenching himself out of Sijara and Mettan's hold. He rounded on Fen a second too late.

Fen launched herself forward and jammed the assassin in the eye with the end of her fully extended quarterstaff. Gemarra screamed, blood gushing from his crushed eye socket. Sijara scrambled forward, grabbed the knife, and brought it down in a sweeping arc into Gemarra's shoulder. Mettan rammed the hilt of his sword into the back of the assassin's head so hard Fen thought she heard a crack. Gemarra slumped over with a moan, his remaining eye fluttering shut.

"Well," said Alekhai.

"What were you thinking, jumping in like that?" Fen yelled at him.

Something like contrition flashed across his features, almost too quickly for her to catch. "To be completely honest," he said slowly, "I wasn't." He looked around at the three of them. "I—"

"You could've died!" Fen snapped.

Alekhai's smile never truly met his eyes, but this time the distance seemed a little shorter than usual. "It was a risk I was willing to take. This was all my fault." Alekhai faced Mettan and Sijara. "I should've listened."

"I'm as much to blame," said Fen. "I'm sorry, too."

Sijara waved a flippant hand. "Forgiven and forgotten. But . . ." She exchanged a meaningful look with Mettan.

Mettan looked into Alekhai's eyes. Gently, he asked, "What happened back there?"

Alekhai seemed to look anywhere but at the three of them. His response was a whisper. "I didn't realize I cared."

Mettan's brows drew together. "What?"

The princeling coughed. "I didn't realize I cared about you all until now."

Sijara blinked. "Oh."

Alekhai looked down. "After losing my siblings, I didn't know that I still *could* care. I've shut that part of myself out for so long. I mean, I still have my oaths and my ideals, and of course my allies, but even the ones I'm fond of, we're not exactly . . . " Each word sounded like it cost him a few years to voice.

Fen took mercy on him. "Friends?"

"Yes." Alekhai looked like she'd just pulled him out of a cenote. "That."

"You sure?" Fen tried hard not to laugh at his struggle. "You seemed pretty affectionate with Chinonso."

Alekhai considered this seriously. "Did I?"

"And Taras," said Mettan, who evidently had no qualms about finding humor in the princeling's plight. "I think you have a greater capacity for friendship than you give yourself credit for."

"Now, this is all very touching," Sijara cut in, "but I suggest we focus on the problem at hand. Namely, him." She pointed at Gemarra, still unconscious and slumped on the ground. "I'm sure there's some useful information we could get out of him, so we should tie him up and ask."

Alekhai picked up the bloodied knife Sijara had stabbed Gemarra with and waved it like a paintbrush. "And after that, we kill him."

Fen swallowed thickly. "Is that really necessary? I . . ."

"You what?" Alekhai looked confused for a moment. "Of course it's necessary. He tried to kill us. He has to die."

"But I've never killed anyone before," Fen said quietly, averting her eyes. "Let alone tortured them."

"That's all right," Alekhai said, like she was admitting a fault. "I'll do it."

"But we should try speaking with him before resorting to anything else," said Mettan. "Maybe he'll cooperate if we promise him an easy death."

"Maybe." Alekhai looked far from convinced.

They bound Gemarra's wrists and ankles together before propping him up against a tree. Fen suggested eating while they waited for the assassin to come to, mostly because she figured she'd lose her appetite when this was over. But even after sniffing each dish thoroughly, Alekhai announced it was better to be safe than sorry. He knew of at least four poisons that even those with enhanced senses couldn't detect, and it wasn't worth the risk.

So Fen stood, stomach grumbling and twisting, and helped dig through the various compartments of the assassin's cart. There was nothing useful besides a simple handheld whetstone, which made perfect sense given their luck. The drawers and boxes were filled with nothing but worthless trinkets—dozens of them, neatly bound with eight different colors of string. Chipped glass earrings and frayed bits of silk and tarnished copper rings.

"Second hell," whispered Mettan. "Are these—"

"Mementos," said Alekhai. "From his victims."

All that was left to do was wait for Gemarra to regain consciousness. Alekhai grabbed the assassin's teapot and plopped down beside Sijara, where she was sharpening her blade with the whetstone. He took off his hat so he could get a better look as he turned the teapot this way and that.

"Eternal Mother, are you really that bored?" Fen asked.

"Only you three were given poison, you know," he said. "And yes."

Sijara paused, her gaze lifting to the canopy in exasperation. "So he snuck something into ours when we weren't looking."

"But *I* was looking." Alekhai placed two empty cups on the ground and rearranged his fingers on the back of the teapot before pouring. "Look at that!"

Mettan crouched beside him. "Look at what?"

Alekhai flipped the teapot around. "There are two separate compartments, controlled by holes on the back and on the bottom of the handle. One sits atop the untainted tea, while the other sits above the poisoned brew, the bottom layer of the vessel. Depending on which hole you cover, you get a nice drink or death. It comes down to air pressure. How clever!"

It was hard not to find his excitement endearing, despite everything. But the moment didn't last long. The assassin let out a low, agonized groan before jerking fully awake. He struggled with his bindings for a few seconds before giving up with a long-suffering sigh. Fen, Mettan, and Sijara looked blankly at each other. Fen felt as if Ruiha had just asked her to go a couple rounds in the sparring ring.

"I suppose I'll start," Sijara muttered under her breath. She strode over to Gemarra. "Did you rest well?" she drawled.

"Excellently," spat Gemarra, as if he bore no injury. "Thank you for asking."

"How did you find us?" Sijara demanded.

"No idea."

Mettan stalked over. "Tell us you don't know again, and I'll have to resort to violence."

The assassin bared his teeth in a mocking grin. "I believe we're past that."

"You're right," murmured Mettan. "Try again."

Fen drew near. "Who sent you?"

Gemarra gave her a deeply unimpressed look. "Pray tell, what happens if I give yet another answer you don't like?"

"Then I'll slit you from nose to navel," Fen said lowly. It was a threat she'd once heard Onath use on an upstart minor noble.

Behind her, Alekhai gave a startled laugh. She whipped around with a glare, and his mouth snapped shut. She turned back to Gemarra, rolling her shoulders.

"Look, you three obviously don't have what this takes," the assassin drawled. "Stop wasting my time and let the prince try."

"You're going to regret that." Alekhai got to his feet with an exasperated huff. "But thank you." His smile became poisoned honey.

He moved like someone used to drawing blood. Every step as he strode toward Gemarra was natural, smooth, and utterly focused. Alekhai never shied away from violence. He didn't seem to derive pleasure from it, but he was accustomed to it, even drawn to it. He was going to kill this man, and probably make him want to die before he did.

"So." Alekhai lowered himself to a crouch before the assassin, slinging an arm casually over his knee. "How did you find us?"

Gemarra said nothing. His mouth thinned into a sharp line as he glared into Alekhai's eyes. Despite the stretching shadows of the woods, the gold of his irises seemed to shine brighter. Something in his face frightened Fen. Perhaps it was the stillness with which he held himself, or the joviality of his tone.

"I'm not going to repeat myself," Alekhai said pleasantly.

"I won't give you anything," said Gemarra.

"Oh?" The pitch of Alekhai's voice dropped, vicious and spider-silk soft. "We'll see."

Fen expected him to cajole the assassin. She'd experienced the princeling's tactics firsthand—he could be quite persuasive when the situation called for it. But no. He pulled out the assassin's own knife and worked the blade around the inside of the man's right thumbnail. He ripped the whole thing off, Gemarra screaming the whole time.

"What are you doing?" Fen choked out.

"Relax. It's just a fingernail."

Mettan touched his shoulder. "Be reasonable. You've barely tried to make him cooperate."

"But I'm not reasonable. And this *is* making him cooperate. Fingernails grow back." Alekhai arched a brow at Gemarra. "Well?"

The assassin shook his head weakly. Alekhai let the knife slip between his fingers and took hold of Gemarra's arm. Then he snapped it. The assassin screamed and screamed, bucking against his restraints so hard it seemed for a moment that he might really free himself. Fen gaped at the bloody wreck of a wound. She could see the bone. It was a perfect break, the sort that would take less than a week to heal if he got a meshbrace and a restorative wrap around it. The strength it must've taken to snap the bone like that . . . And Alekhai had done it effortlessly.

It made sense that he'd concealed the extent of his strength until now. Fen supposed much of being royalty was convincing others to overestimate one's abilities. But it would pay to let your enemies think you weaker than you were every once in a while, to see which of them were brave enough to strike. She reviewed every moment she'd had her back to him since the day she'd found him in that hovercraft. He'd been holding back during the melee in Emikoteth. The prince could've killed her at any time in that hovercraft.

And he'd tried only once. Or . . . pretended to try.

"If you go on like this, you're no better than them," Mettan said. He was rubbing at the spot where Alekhai had held him in the catacombs, so close to where he'd broken Gemarra's arm.

Alekhai's mouth quirked as he held back a laugh. "I'm not better than them. I *am* them. You'd think we hadn't traveled together for months." His eyes never left the assassin. Gemarra was shaking, sweat running down his face in rivulets. "I'm not going to lie to you and tell you I'll let you go. You're going to die. But you get to decide how painfully. I have all day."

"I—"

"Careful, now," Alekhai warned, touching the glistening point of the knife to Gemarra's cheek. "Consider that you owe my brother nothing. That no one is going to save you from me." He pressed in, and a glistening pearl of blood welled up over the point of the blade.

Gemarra set his jaw and met Alekhai's gaze with a strength Fen couldn't help but respect.

"I didn't expect you to protect them," the assassin ground out. "My orders were to kill any captors or companions of yours and rescue you."

"Rescue?" Alekhai asked gently. He dragged the blade down, just a little.

Fen wanted him to stop. She wanted the almost-friend who'd comforted her in the woods to return to his body and oust whatever monster had taken up residence behind his skin. This was much worse than when Mettan lost himself to his death-sealed rage, because this was still the same Alekhai, just as much a part of him as the smirking and sarcasm. She bit down hard on her tongue.

Gemarra groaned. "No—I . . . I was to take you to a secure location just outside the palace, where the emperor would meet you. He trusted no one. He wanted to see you die himself."

"Your own brother . . ." Fen shook her head, not in disbelief but in disgust. "How many of your kin have died at each other's hands?"

Alekhai shrugged. "Most."

And this was the family that reigned over them all. Eternal Mother, how had the tribes fallen so far?

"How did you find us?" Alekhai asked.

Gemarra rushed to speak before Alekhai drew further blood. "The Sovereign founded an experimental order of traveling spies and assassins. We're meant to wander through the empire on the off chance we encounter an enemy of the throne."

"The Rovers?" Alekhai let out a harsh little laugh. "Akrysanth didn't create you. I did."

Gemarra sucked in a sharp breath. "What?"

"I presented the whole idea in jest to our father," Alekhai continued. "A complete and utter waste of taxpayer credits. Perhaps my brother really is a fool."

"Perhaps not," Gemarra growled, "considering that I did find you."

Alekhai chuckled. "True enough. So, you're saying you just stumbled upon us?"

"Everyone in the order saw the unabridged report of a strange quartet of travelers, one of whom seemed to fit your general description. Most of us tried to follow your trail, but I suspected you weren't merely fleeing. All I had to do was lie in wait along the routes to rebel-sympathetic settlements and hope our paths would cross."

"And how did you know I wasn't just on the run?"

For a moment, a little of Gemarra's terror and pain drained away. His mouth stretched into an unnatural grin. "I know what really happened in Bakrai."

Alekhai was no longer half smiling. "Thank you," he said. "Was that so hard? Did you tell anyone else?"

"Why would I? I wanted to bring you in myself."

Alekhai narrowed his eyes before nodding once. "All right. I believe you."

Gemarra tried to speak again but couldn't get his words past the knife Alekhai had shoved into his throat. His eyes bulged, lips trembling as blood dribbled from one side of his mouth. It was over in a handful of seconds.

For a long time, Fen couldn't speak. For a long time, Alekhai merely stared at Gemarra, peering into the assassin's eyes as if searching for further answers. The wind picked up again, whipping the prince's hair angrily about his face.

"You three didn't have to watch that," he said finally. He picked up a corner of Gemarra's tunic, wiping the blood from his hands.

Fen stepped forward. "I'm going to hack into his omnichip and tell Akrysanth he killed you, but that he's badly wounded himself."

Sijara clapped her on the back in approval. Fen shot her a weak smile before she faced Gemarra's corpse. The smell of blood flooded her lungs. Trying not to gag, she took the assassin's limp wrist in hers and flipped it over. Thankfully, Alekhai hadn't snapped the arm containing the implant. Fiddling with the tech would've still been possible, but she was having a hard enough time keeping her porridge down as it was. The whole process took mere minutes; hacking into high-security conversations was her forte, after all.

"Can I keep the teapot?" Alekhai asked when she was done.

Sijara answered at once. "Absolutely not."

☾

He kept the teapot.

The rebellion formally announced itself the next day. If the common people starved any more than they already were, they'd be dead. Bandits ruled the outlying towns as much as they did the woods. And after weeks of trying and failing to regain control, the imperialists had pulled most of their forces in around the capitals of the four tribes. There was no better time for the Broken Masks to declare the new revolution had arrived.

Agents of the insurgency plastered propaganda all over the cities, flooded the omninet with notices, and posted calls to arms along every forest route. It was on one of these paths that Fen, Mettan, Sijara, and Alekhai learned the rebel factions had finally consolidated into a single force. Led by a trio of seasoned leaders called the Sworn, the Broken Masks had built a new base of operations in a secret location. They were flush with allies now; the Masks claimed to be supplied by a reformed bandit lord, apparently the same one who'd been forcefully absorbing his rivals in Makhan. There were no instructions on how to locate the base, of course, but the placard promised that those truly willing to fight for a better world would be sought out by the revolutionaries.

The Senmavaris had always had everything: an overabundance of funding, greater numbers, better weapons, more equipment, supplies that hadn't been scrounged up from dumpster heaps or outright stolen. The Broken Masks had been struggling just to exist before the battle at Umut Pass, ambushing scattered regiments and cutting off minor supply lines. The rebels had already lost—that was textbook history—and when Fen had bound herself to them, the Masks of Kanoh had been little more than the dregs of a failed effort, waiting for the suicidal blade of a cause to throw their lives on.

But their sacrifice had been an inspiration, and what so many of them had died for that terrible day was finally coming to pass.

The rebel contingents across tribes had finally banded together under one banner. Now they had good numbers and strategic positions and a robust spy network, with agents placed in key roles. Now they had Chinonso, with all her resources and expertise. At long last, the playing field was leveling. Especially in Eira, where Chinonso no doubt orchestrated local liberation efforts from the shadows. The group hadn't heard from the chieftain since they'd resurrected her, but her fingerprints were all over the rebels' new strategies, according to Alekhai.

A week after the Masks declared war once more, the insurgents launched an attack on the imperialist stronghold of Elzvia, right on the border of Eira and Ophthia. Two days after that, they took the city. There'd been no warning. The plains surrounding Elzvia had been still and silent the night before the bloodshed began, and the next morning the yellow grasses were trampled under the force of ten thousand Broken Masks.

That the imperialists had been caught completely unawares spoke to either great incompetence or great mismanagement. Most of the empire was empty steppe and wood and desert, with much of the land left abandoned after it had been sucked dry of resources. There were endless towns and villages, but they were scattered and small. Cities, which oversaw nearby settlements, were what mattered strategically. The rebels' obvious aim was to work their way up to larger targets. The imperialists should've been prepared. Heads would roll for the shameful defeat, that was certain.

Even the first rebellion, led by Kira Moru, hadn't had such an auspicious start. Fen tried not to let hope devour her, but it seemed that the Broken Masks might really, actually win this time. A handful of prominent aristocrats had even begun to quietly side with the rebels. Perhaps they'd discovered some morals. More likely, they didn't want to be on the losing side.

But even if she hadn't been bound by oath, the rebels' incredible recent successes wouldn't have changed her plans. While Alekhai's ultimate goals lay parallel to the Masks', he was no rebel. Fen and her friends' job—their *only* job—was to resurrect the fallen leaders who'd allied with the princeling. The other chieftains would join the Sworn, and they'd share the intel and resources they'd gathered with the rebellion. It was the only way forward, the path to victory. A final alliance would form, the old and the new working together.

Fen believed it.

She had to.

☾

In the shifting darkness of early morning, Alekhai squinted at Fen. It was shaping up to be a particularly smoggy day. The sun floated like a scarlet buoy in a sea of ozone, dust, and chemicals.

Fen squinted back, her whole body tensed for attack. Alekhai looked as immaculate as a fugitive could. He kept his stolen clothes tidy, if not entirely clean, while his hair was twisted up into a mercilessly tight topknot.

"I'm confused. Is this a duel or a staring contest?" Alekhai asked, hands tightening on the long, straight stick he'd selected as a weapon.

"You think you're hilarious, huh?" said Fen.

Then she lunged. She'd swapped her quarterstaff for a stick, but she was no less lethal. She smacked Alekhai's makeshift weapon right out of his hands.

"Ouch, fuck! Are you punishing me?" Alekhai asked. "I'm sorry, all right? You were right about sending Chinonso to the Masks. I'm. Sorry."

She gave an exasperated sigh as he retrieved his stick, though she was pleased down to her bones. "What is that?"

"A stick."

"Yes." She drew herself to her full height and said, "But it's also an extension of your body, so use it like one. The moment you let me get close is the moment you lose."

Alekhai rolled his eyes. "Eternal Mother, shut up."

Fen laughed. "C'mon, I've seen you move much faster than that." She twirled her own stick and pointed it at him. "Let's give it another go. Watch your footwork this time, too."

Alekhai scowled. He looked shiftier than usual, sweat beading at his temple. "Remind me again why we have to do this."

"I've told you fifty times already."

"No, you woke me up by poking me in the ribs. Then you said to find a stick before you started smacking *me* with one." The expression on his face couldn't be called a pout, but it was near one. "Mettan and Sijara got to sleep in."

Oh. Right.

"Because the next assassin might use steel rather than poison. I've seen you fight. Your technique is admirable, clearly fine-tuned by some of the best instructors on the planet, but you only get by because of your modifications. Not that you use them very often, or even as effectively as you could." She held his gaze. Not long ago, he would've been able to dodge her strike with ease. "What happens as you get weaker?"

Alekhai's eyes narrowed. "I seem to recall saving you from your rebel friend back on the steppe. And again when—"

Fen cut him off. "I need you to be able to defend yourself with something besides good fortune and surprise."

Alekhai huffed. "What do you honestly think you can teach me that my teachers couldn't?"

"Not much," Fen said easily. "But at least it won't be the same lesson your instructors taught your family, the Senmavaris, and any other imperialist who might try to kill you."

"Fair. But if all I have at my disposal is a twig, I'm already dead. Why not let me practice with your quarterstaff?"

"I will." Fen grinned, dropping into a low crouch. "Once you disarm me."

After a moment, Alekhai mimicked her stance.

"Ready?"

"Oh, so *now* I get a warning—"

Fen leapt forward again. Alekhai rushed to meet her. He took four steps before he collapsed. He fell on his hands and knees, wheezing.

"Alekhai! What's wrong?" Fen crouched beside him, grabbing his shoulder. She could feel the tension coiled under her hand. "The degeneration?"

"No. It's—" He let out an agonized moan, fingers clenching around his abdomen. He curled in on himself like he was trying to disappear. "It's nothing, just . . . "

Fen dug her fingers into his shoulder. "Tell me!" She stilled. "Is it the wound you sustained at Umut?"

Had he been suffering for that long?

Alekhai hissed in pain, and guilt sank into Fen's gut. "No. That healed long ago," he said. "I was . . . stabbed during the fight in Emikoteth."

*Shit.* So that was why he'd answered so oddly that night, when she'd asked after his old injury.

Fen started undoing the ties fastening his collar. Despite being a master strategist, Alekhai occasionally showed fascinating moments of complete stupidity. But this was another level. By the time Fen got his tunic off, she was furious.

The smell of blood and rot hit her like a slap across the face. The cloth Alekhai had wrapped around his middle was already soaked dark red.

"What in the world were you thinking, princeling?" she snarled.

"I wasn't," he wheezed. "Normally I'd be fine, but my body's under more stress than normal. I was hoping we'd reach Melodaris in time for me to get professional help."

Fen heard the lie; he'd kept the wound secret so they wouldn't know of his weakness. Fine. But by letting it fester, he'd endangered everything she and her friends were risking their lives and the fate of Enkaiia for. Once she saved his life, she was going to yell at him until his ears bled. She shot a message to Mettan and Sijara, who were away foraging, before taking Alekhai's knife from his shaking hands. She sucked in a breath and started sawing through the bandages. A strangled scream clawed its way between his clenched teeth as she peeled away the stinking cloth.

"Oh, you fool," Fen breathed out.

It was much, much worse than she'd thought. Alekhai had tried closing the gash with a couple lengths of thread, but it was shoddy work. The stitches were too wide and too deep; the only thing he'd succeeded in doing was making the wound larger. Infection had set in long ago. The surrounding skin was a swollen, angry red, burning hot to the touch, and shiny with cloudy pus. The stench was almost too much to bear, so sickly sweet and putrid she nearly fell backward. If he hadn't been royal, if his body hadn't been designed to withstand twice what others could . . .

Panic overtook Fen for a moment, coherent thoughts swept away by the fear flooding her skull.

Then Alekhai spoke, dragging her from her horror. "Well?" he said, mostly a groan. "Am I going to die?"

She had no idea. At least the cut hadn't reached his stomach or intestines. She'd absorbed enough from Ying to know he'd be dead already if that were the case. As it was, he must've been in agonizing pain.

"Fen," said Alekhai, eyes wide. "Am I going to die?"

"I won't let that happen, you fool," she managed. "But I can't treat this here. I need supplies and medicine and—"

"Fuck. Okay," said Alekhai. "Okay."

Fen couldn't tear her eyes from the seeping wound. Eternal Mother, where were Mettan and Sijara?

As if on cue, her friends stormed out of the underbrush. Mettan gasped when he saw Alekhai.

Sijara pulled herself together the fastest. "Where's the nearest abandoned village? We can't be seen by—"

Mettan was already checking his omnichip. The Broken Masks posted constantly updating lists of the allegiance and condition of every settlement on their secret forums. "Close, thank the Mother. There's one only two hours away." He met Alekhai's gaze. "Can you make it?"

"Do I have a choice?" the princeling wheezed.

Fen ripped away the bottom of his tunic and fashioned it into a tight makeshift bandage around his middle. At least it would staunch the flow of blood.

She stuck out a hand. "No, you don't."

Alekhai reached out to grasp her elbow. His grip was surprisingly firm. "So be it."

Without another word, she pulled him to his feet. She threw one arm over her shoulders and Mettan took the other.

☾

Mettan hadn't been lying when he'd said the trek to the village was two hours. But it was two hours for relatively unstabbed people. They reached the settlement just after sunset, stumbling from the tree line and toward the main gate as night fell. Barren paddy fields flanked the cluster of huts and cracked-open storage units, empty layers folded one atop the others like an elaborate paper sculpture. The broken brown mosaic of a dead riverbed snaked around the right side of the lopsided walls.

Just as the rebels' list reported, the village was forsaken. The winding streets were devoid of life and sound. No stray animals ran between the ramshackle huts alongside laughing children. No merchants screamed at the group to purchase their wares.

Mettan, the tallest, caught sight of a sloped roof up ahead, crowning the largest building in town. Half dragging, half steering Alekhai, they navigated their way to what had once been an inn. The two-story building took up much of a large cobbled compound. The bottom floor jutted out like a prominent jaw, housing a bar and three rows of empty benches. Dusty globelamps were strung along posts, half of them broken. If they'd been on, they would've illuminated looming apotropaic statues, peeling shutters, and a slightly ajar door.

Solartiles were built to last, even the cheap new ones, so there was a chance the inn still had electricity. But functioning air filters and globelamps weren't worth the chance of alerting a scout. They made do with what little sunlight remained as they settled Alekhai on the ground with his knife—not that he was in much of a state to fight anyone off—and crept inside. The entire building was constructed from fabricated dark-brown wood that hid stains and brewed shadows. Fen and Mettan crept around the bar and then upstairs, throwing open cabinets as they went. All bare. They looked around the second floor. They pushed open doors, Mettan with his sheathed sword and Fen with her quarterstaff, before rushing inside empty chamber after empty chamber. The rooms all smelled faintly of incense, probably burned nightly to keep away unsavory smells when something more than dust had lived here. As it was, the rancid matting soured the air.

In the end, an exhaustive search of the premises—and a dozen cleverly hidden receptacles—turned up no hidden enemies but most of what they needed: clean bandages, a bundle of spare thread speared by a needle, and a medkit. The seal on the single antibiotic pill bottle was broken, but it would have to do. They'd also unearthed three whole jugs of liquor from behind a tiny false wall. It tasted only a little off.

They returned downstairs to collect Alekhai and lug him up into the cleanest room Sijara had found. Fen stumbled at the last second, her strength giving out just as they dropped Alekhai onto one of the two wide bedrolls Sijara had set up. On the low eating table were the results of their scavenging efforts. Alekhai looked them over with baleful eyes.

"Who's had the most experience with this?" Sijara asked.

Mettan swallowed hard. "I do, I suppose. I picked up a few things from Ying." He handed Alekhai a jug and started untangling the thread Fen had collected.

Alekhai sniffed and grimaced. "Alcohol is a blood thinner."

"I know that better than you, princeling," Mettan replied. "But we don't have painkillers."

"How much is this going to hurt?" Alekhai asked quietly. His fingers twitched.

Mettan reached out and took Alekhai's hand in his. "Quite a lot." He squeezed once before returning to the thread.

Alekhai took a deep gulp from the jug. The alcohol flowed over his chin and down the front of his clothes. He lifted a hand to wipe it away, but after a moment, let it fall. His tunic was already dark and stiff with drying blood. He took another swig, coughed, drank again.

Fen dragged the table over and sat beside him. "Do you need help undressing him?" she asked Mettan.

Alekhai narrowed his eyes at her. "I'm still conscious. I can manage it myself." He undid the ties on his tunic and tried to pull his right arm from its sleeve. The sound he made was as if they'd all taken turns kicking him. "Help. Please."

He gritted his teeth and clenched his hands and made more of those awful noises, but eventually they got the tunic and the soiled bandages off. He looked down at the wound, eyes swimming with something between frozen resolve and dripping horror.

"I'm ready." He slid down on the bedroll and stared up at the ceiling. He offered Mettan a weak smile. "Are you?"

Mettan nodded, dragged in a breath, and got to work. The wound was a jagged mess; the initial stab hadn't been a clean one, and Alekhai's efforts had made the whole thing much worse. They had precious little water to spare, so Sijara dampened a piece of cloth with a bit of what they did have. Together they wiped away blood and pus and unnamable reeking fluid, Fen trying not to gag as she did so. Whatever disgust Mettan had once felt at the sight of blood had clearly died with him, and the same went for Sijara. Alekhai's chest rose and fell in a spasming, uneven pattern, every muscle in his face twitching with pain.

Mettan threaded the needle with faintly shaking hands. "Open your mouth," he ordered.

Alekhai did so without hesitation. Mettan wiped his hands on the princeling's ruined tunic and helped him gulp down more alcohol. They all took a few sips before Mettan stuffed a roll of fabric between Alekhai's teeth.

Alekhai screamed as Mettan knit skin and muscle back together, hot breath puffing around the cloth. The skin around his eyes grew wet with tears. But whether through sheer force of will or agony-included paralysis, he remained still long enough for Mettan to stitch him up. Finally, Mettan cleaned away the blood and wrapped Alekhai in cloth.

"Done. It's done." Mettan shoved the antibiotics into Alekhai's hands and lay back beside him, panting, as his patient choked down a dose.

The back of Alekhai's hand pressed into Mettan's. "Thank you," he gasped out.

"You're welcome." Then Mettan sighed. "Can't let you sleep in a pool of your own fluids. I should've done this on the bare floor. Get on the other bedroll."

Alekhai did so, more through the effort of the others than his own, and sprawled out.

Sijara scowled. "Move over, princeling. These were the only clean pallets we found."

"To the end," Fen added, giving him a gentle push. "It's only just big enough for all of us."

Alekhai stared at them, wide-eyed.

Mettan raised a brow. "Did you think after all that, we were going to sleep on the floor?"

"No, I—" said Alekhai. He stared up at the ceiling.

"What, you've never shared a bed? Or—" Mettan coughed, averted his eyes.

"It's not really a bed, so calm down," Fen said dryly, gesturing impatiently for Alekhai to scoot over before he finally did.

The former rebels settled in around the former heir, shoulder to shoulder. Despite his apparent unfamiliarity with sleeping accompanied, Alekhai gave a great yawn and was instantly asleep. Fen did her best to follow suit.

But the night was doomed to be a restless one. Alekhai could be dead before sunrise. He could be dying right now, and she'd be helpless to stop it. She could only hope for the best and distract herself.

She sat up, watching him carefully. If she focused a little, she could hear his breathing. With his engineered senses, she knew he could hear hers too without even trying. But he was drunk and passed out. Perhaps she could finally get around to doing what she'd been planning for weeks without waking him.

Fen slipped from his side, clambered over Sijara, and crept over to Alekhai's abandoned satchel, eyes trained on him all the way. He remained perfectly still, deep in slumber. Making sure to put her back to her sleeping companions, she flicked open the bag's latch and pulled out the items one by one. There wasn't much besides the expected rations and food they'd stolen and scavenged together. Just the compact little book she'd glimpsed in his hands a few times and a thick realpaper letter. The seal was already broken. It was plain and unadorned, but blue. A blue so deep it might be black, but Fen knew better. She swallowed thickly, pulse throbbing in her ears.

The Sovereign had sent Onath missives over the omninet for official business. He'd sent datachips by courier when the business was less than official; unsavory matters he wanted under wraps but imperial orders nonetheless. For example: murdering the daughter of political enemies. When featureless letters sealed with blue-black arrived, Onath had always gone away. He'd return a week or so later with just as much warning and shut himself in his chambers for days.

Fen spread the letter open over her knee, hands shaking even worse than when they'd been while helping Mettan stitch Alekhai up. It was in code, of course, a series of numbers arrayed into neat lines. She scanned the letter and dove in on her omnichip. And was promptly spat back out. She shot technique after technique at the wall of encryption before her, but each tried-and-true strategy bounced back off like a ball. She tossed aside the letter in frustration. Then her gaze caught something, and her head turned back so hard she nearly pulled something in her neck.

The book.

Her eyes narrowed. She snatched up the compact volume, flipped to a random page, and scanned the first few lines. There was nothing glaringly unusual, save for the words themselves. The book had been printed not in Standard but in Oldearth English, a language with an infamously difficult and occasionally nonsensical set of grammatical rules. But Fen had forced herself to gain basic literacy in it years ago, along with the other seven ancient languages that formed the basis of Standard. She'd had to pass the time on particularly boring missions somehow.

> A weak kingdom has no walls. Its people are at the mercy of its enemies. A strong kingdom has walls. Its people are protected. A stronger kingdom has high walls, strong walls—walls so great no enemy within or without can scale them. Its people are pure.

And on and on it went. But by now Fen was smiling. She knew Alekhai well enough to know he'd never carry around such a boring text. The letter was a cipher.

There were numerous options to explore now, far too many to try alone and by hand in a single evening. There were no spaces in the letter to indicate which digits were page numbers and which were line or word numbers. One sort could be followed directly by the other, or all the page numbers could be listed in the first half and the line numbers in the latter. So on and so forth.

Thank the Mother for omnichips. Fen unlocked the letter in minutes. Her throat was in a vise as she read.

Burn after reading.

Those who would see my family cast down have bred like the vermin they are. My spies inform me that they have begun to gather. I shall crush them before they even begin to dream of becoming a true threat. I shall wipe them from the face of this world.

Sona was right about one thing. Our brother is weak. I cannot allow him to destroy all that our forebears have built. You know that war has its costs, as does battle. As does putting down even a few paltry handfuls of rebels.

Sometimes that cost includes imperial blood.

There's no need to make it quick.

Fen tucked Alekhai's belongings back in his bag. A complicated tangle of emotions formed within her. Hatred for the Sovereign; a spark of hurt at Alekhai hiding the letter, as logical as it had been; something soft and tender for . . . for her friend.

She snuck back over to Alekhai. He still looked terrible, eyes screwed shut as if against the too-bright sun, fingers twisted up in the pallet's thin covering. At least he was still breathing. His breaths were unsteady and thin, but they sounded a little deeper than they had when he'd first slipped into sleep.

Alekhai would live, and when he awoke, she'd be there beside him.

The next few days were hard. Alekhai's complexion settled into a corpse-like shade of gray. His tunic soaked through with so much sweat, they had to take it off for fear of reinfection. He writhed in fever during the day and thrashed violently at night. They often had to restrain him with spare cloth or their own hands.

They'd been taking turns watching over him. Fen discovered eventually that burning incense helped a little. Holding him very tightly helped more. When Alekhai started whimpering about masks and lakes of blood, she'd take his head in her hands and run her fingers through his hair. The princeling quieted each time.

Then, after three long days, he woke up. He caught Fen at a bad time; she was in the middle of combing his sweat-dampened curls. She launched herself to her feet, but it was too late.

"Don't say anything," she snapped, her face already growing hot.

"Good morning to you, too." Alekhai's grin was something feral as he sat up. Under a wide ray of morning light, his eyes glittered pure gold.

Fen put as much space between them as possible. Then she shot off a message to her friends. Mettan and Sijara came bounding up the stairs seconds later.

"Well," said Alekhai. "Thanks again for stitching me back up."

"I hate you," said Fen. "I hope you fall into a cenote and get eaten by a carnufex."

"After all the effort you three put into saving me? I doubt that." Alekhai's grin smoothed into his usual not-quite-there smile. "You're fond of me, don't deny it."

"Don't flatter yourself," Sijara snapped. But then she said, "You should've told us you were hurt!"

"I know," Alekhai relented, falling back onto the pallet as they loomed over him. "I know just how witless that was, and I'm sorry I scared you and jeopardized everything. I'm grateful for you all."

"Good," said Mettan, crossing his arms. "Now: the letter. You were never going to be Sovereign."

Fen, of course, had told them everything.

The princeling groaned.

"In my defense," he said, "even if Akrysanth wanted me dead at times, I was formally the heir *apparent*—not presumptive. I never thought my brother would actually follow through with assassinating me and finding a cousin to take over next. Well, until I stole that letter."

He gave Fen a pointed look but didn't seem overly irritated she'd gone through his things. He'd probably known it was inevitable. Perhaps some part of him had *wanted* her to find the missive; he could've gotten rid of it at any time.

"But the main reason I lied," Alekhai went on, "is that I thought you'd kill me if you knew the truth."

"Even if we were that merciless," Mettan said dryly, "we're bound by an Accuser-overseen oath to aid you. In case you'd forgotten, *Executor*."

For a time, Alekhai was silent. Then, as if weighing each word, he said, "Technically, you could still complete my mission without me." He offered his second half smile of the day, this time tinged with an apology. "Or you could hurt me."

"For all you speak of trust," Fen said, "you certainly struggle with it."

"I'm working on it," replied Alekhai. He winced as he sat back up and looked around the room. "Now, if you're done, can you pass me the booze? I'm in agony."

☾

Mettan and Sijara had stepped out for the evening. They still needed to forage for half of their daily meals, and after days of being cooped up, they all wanted to stretch their legs. Fen stayed behind to keep an eye on the princeling, even though he seemed mostly fine. Bandits, fresh peasant militias that hadn't yet been absorbed into the Broken Masks, and imperialist deserters still roamed the land in droves—leaving Alekhai alone in an abandoned inn wasn't worth the risk.

Fen's original intention had been to take a short nap. Alekhai had other plans.

"The sages were wrong. The truth doesn't free you," he mumbled from his spot beside her on the bedroll. "It binds you and bleeds you out."

He was very, very drunk.

"No one likes a philosopher, even when they're sober."

"If you'd never found out what happened to your parents, you'd have happily lived out your whole life in Talishminn serving that magistrate—"

Fen froze. She cracked open an eye but did not move. "Watch it."

"—at least until he killed you or someone else did," Alekhai finished. His tone was light, absent-minded. He spoke as she had never seen him do before, his words sliding straight from his mind to his mouth.

"I wasn't happy there," she ground out.

"Oh, and you're happy now?"

"I'm alive."

"Barely. You're a woman consumed, though I don't know what it is that consumes you."

*Eternal Mother.* How much had they let him drink? She should've kept a better eye on him.

"I just want to know," he went on. "Do you mourn your parents' deaths? Or do you simply feel bound to avenge them?"

The words were uncomfortably close to Ruiha's.

Fen turned around. To her vexation, she found herself face-to-face with Alekhai. There was a delirious slackness to his features, but his eyes were sharp as ever as they searched hers.

He bent closer, so close that their noses almost touched. "I know you, Fenyyang Mekantai."

"Is that so? I'm not even sure I know myself."

They lay there in silence for a moment, holding each other's gaze.

Fen sat up. "Enough," she whispered. "The only thing I want to hear from you is why you refuse to resurrect my parents."

"I want to protect you."

"Alekhai." It was a warning.

He straightened beside her, wincing only a little at the movement. "Because," he said, dragging out the vowels, "there are some limits to the sorts of people I can return."

"Like what?" she demanded. "Is it only lowborn peasants who attain their positions by hard work alone? Who gave their lives for the cause?"

Alekhai gave her a flat look that was somewhat undercut by his wine-loosened features. *Come now,* he seemed to be saying. *If that were true, Mettan, and certainly Sijara, would still be dead.*

Fen let out a breath. "Who can't you revive?" she said again, quieter now.

"Traitors."

She stared into those gleaming gold eyes. "What did you say?"

But she'd heard him perfectly, and he knew it.

"Traitors," Alekhai repeated anyway, very calmly.

"To whom?" she demanded. "To *what*?"

Her mind was a whirlpool with the answer at the center. Down, down, down she spiraled, until she hit the eye of the storm. And then she knew. Only one thing made sense. It made horrible, perfect sense.

She'd never understood why the late emperor hadn't just murdered her fathers the moment he'd gotten his hands on them.

"The rebellion?" she whispered.

Alekhai gave a single nod. "Kira Moru's revolution was a trap, though she didn't lay the snare. Your parents did."

He spoke without emotion, and perhaps that was a kindness—he offered no pity, no sweetened words. The cleanest wounds were made with the sharpest weapons.

Fen let out a small, strangled laugh. "No." Her heart thrashed against the cage of her ribs. "No. You're—that's wrong."

"I wish I were," he said. "Our parents were great friends, once. Together they founded a false rebellion to weed out potential insurgents. The irony, of course, is that Juma and Kagiso Mekantai ended up laying the foundations of the very real insurgency that now threatens my brother's rule."

And that, along with so many others, their daughter had fallen prey to their trap.

"But they were captured," Fen forced out. It was a fragile, paper-thin sliver of hope. "Handed over to your father by one of our captains in a gamble to save Moru's life."

"Barra Jin Sherida? Another ruse." He said it in a tone that brooked no argument. "Some of the true rebels had begun to suspect that something was amiss, and your parents had to be extracted somehow."

Fen crumpled like she'd taken a knife to the gut. "But your brother murdered my parents." She sucked in a breath. "Unless—"

"No. I'm sorry. They really are gone." Alekhai looked down at his hands. "I believe my father's original plan was to fake their deaths and set them up in comfortable exile somewhere far from the capital. But instead, he decided to keep them close to advise him, and as 'leverage' over the rebels. Akrysanth always resented our father's reliance upon them."

"What proof do you have of this?" she asked helplessly.

"I have none. But think about it: Why would my father keep the architects behind an uprising alive for even a minute after he got his hands on them?"

"To keep them from becoming martyrs."

"Come now. He was never that clever." A grain of empathy slipped into the cold stream of Alekhai's voice. "I'm sorry. The truth hurts."

"Pain doesn't make something true," she insisted, though she knew it did here.

*Traitors.*

The word echoed in Fen's skull over and over again. Her tunic was suddenly too tight around her lungs. She pulled uselessly at the cloth. Her parents had left her to rot.

"I didn't find out until my brother received confirmation of their passing," she heard Alekhai say. "My Accuser frowns upon their actions. I know it would forbid me from bringing back my father, too, if there were some reason I'd ever want to. But perhaps . . . perhaps I could convince it otherwise for you."

"How?" Fen choked out.

"Like their creators, Accusers are ancient, eternal, unchanging beings. They love novelty, and I've never asked it to reconsider its decisions before. I never dared."

Fen tilted her head back. She sucked in a sharp breath. And

then another. After she pulled in a third gulp of air, "Leave them," rose out of her mouth like steam from hot tea.

Alekhai stared but said nothing.

Fen shook herself, swept a thumb under her eyes to check for tears. "If you're right"—and she knew he was—"then there's no need to bring them back." She swallowed hard and thought of her friends. The ones who were still alive, still fighting at her side. Mettan and Sijara—and Alekhai. She had a family. "Our parents . . ." She dropped her head into her hands. "I suppose we're more alike than I thought."

"You're not anything like me," Alekhai said, placing a warm hand on her elbow.

Fen met his cool gaze.

He was a prince, the once-heir to the throne of a planet, an Executor chosen by the Accusers at birth. But it sounded like a compliment.

# ALEKHAI

Alekhai took a long swig from the last jug of liquor before passing it to Sijara. The alcohol burned as it went down, melting some of the chill inside. After Fen had shared the secret of her parents' true allegiance with Mettan and Sijara, they'd all decided to spend the rest of the evening drinking away, sprawled over the floor of another, less bloodstained room.

Sijara gulped, then wiped her mouth with the back of a hand. "What I don't understand is *why* they'd do it. Ata never got better treatment than any of the other tribes, so it wasn't to protect their own people. They lived in squalor until they were captured. And their only reward at the end of it all would've been exile at the edge of the empire, so it certainly wasn't power."

Fen shrugged limply. "I don't know. I . . . didn't know them." She took the jug from Sijara and emptied it. "I never will."

Sijara pulled her close. Alekhai didn't miss the concerned look she exchanged with Mettan over Fen's head.

"We should get some rest," Alekhai said. He hoped his yawn didn't sound forced. "We have a long day of travel tomorrow. And the day after that."

Fen mumbled her assent into Sijara's shoulder. She was already halfway asleep, and with good reason—she'd had the most to drink by far. They tucked her into bed, scoured the inn one last time for anything of use, and packed up their meager belongings for their journey deeper into Ophthia territory.

Mettan curled up beside Fen soon after, but Sijara vanished into the hallway outside their new room. Alekhai heard her footfalls, almost silent, fade away. In the dark, the undead always moved quietly. If not for his enhanced hearing, he wouldn't have noticed her leaving at all. After a moment, he followed her.

He found her at the end of a balcony in one of the inn's finer rooms—or at least, formerly finer. They'd passed it over in their survey of the establishment because of the gaping holes in the wooden floor and the nest of togau everyone could hear scratching faintly at the peeling walls. Going by the long-dead petals on the floor, the balustrade had been wrapped in thickly flowering kameen vines, infamous for the painstaking care they demanded. A luxury among luxuries, descended from a tropical Oldearth species; the water alone would've been exorbitant, even years ago. The palace gardens were festooned in kameen, last he saw them.

Once, this town had flourished. It might've been a great city, even. But long before the inhabitants had abandoned their homes and shops, shifting trade routes had drained its wealth. Not unlike Bakrai. These wrinkled gray petals were the last vestiges of the settlement's good fortune.

Sijara's shoulder bumped Alekhai's as he leaned against the railing beside her. He nearly froze at the contact. Before they'd all piled onto the pallet, she'd never touched him without a good reason to, and he'd been the same with her.

She'd coaxed a little stub of incense to life, and now she trailed her fingers through the dark tendrils of smoke.

Alekhai broke the silence. "Did you have to leave anyone behind when you joined the rebels?"

Sijara shook her head. "My friends were all too happy to see me go, even if they didn't know where I was disappearing off to. I was angry and unpleasant. Even more so than I am now, if you can believe it. And my family was laid to rest some time ago."

He shot her a sideways glance.

Sijara put up a hand. "No—I won't ask you to bring them back, though for different reasons than Fen. I've made my peace with their loss. I couldn't bear to see them die all over again when the time came. Is that selfish of me?"

"Maybe a little," Alekhai said honestly. And then, "Aren't you going to ask if *I* had to leave anyone when I ran off with you three?"

Sijara arched a brow. "They say you can speak to the closest thing we have to gods, that you're connected to this world in ways the rest of us can't even imagine. Yet when we met you, you were the loneliest soul I'd ever come across. So no, I'm not going to ask a question I already know the answer to."

Alekhai snorted. "And Taras says *I'm* sharp as a thorn."

Sijara laughed. Alekhai liked that he could trade barbs with her without inflicting injury. He liked that she was honest, even when she knew it might hurt.

As the incense stung his eyes—what else could it be?—understanding trickled slowly over him. He mattered to these people. Alekhai, the Butcher of Bakrai, the Executor, and, if all went according to plan, the last of his bloodline.

*He* mattered to them.

Sijara's hand set down gently atop his. "Alekhai. Thank you for taking care of her."

She didn't elaborate, and he didn't feign ignorance. She'd been awake that night, when Fen had wept in his arms. Sijara wasn't nearly as light a sleeper as he was, even with the changes, but she must've awoken when Fen had refused his comfort the first time. She'd surely been about to scramble over and grab onto Fen herself when Alekhai had asked if he should wake the others. He'd heard the change in Sijara's breathing, in her heart rate; the question had been as much for her as it had been for Fen.

Sijara smiled. "I'm glad she has you. That we all do. So thank you."

After an eternity, Alekhai squeezed his friend's hand. "It was nothing."

# BOOK FOUR

# A BEGINNING

ABOUT TWENTY YEARS AGO

## *KIRA*

The revolution was over, and it ended with Kira sitting before her captor's tent, knees folded under her and teeth chattering furiously. Her hands were balled into tight fists over her knees, though she kept her head down. The guards standing watch outside looked upon her with wary eyes. She shivered. Though no snow had fallen on the planet since her youth, the nipping wind still remembered the taste and sting of hail and sleet. Kira tugged her cloak tighter around herself. How long had it been since she'd lowered herself before the tent? An hour? Hours?

Most imperialists had long ago abandoned the windswept grasslands and sunbaked deserts for cities of stone and metal, but they'd agreed to meet on open land for this. The tent was a monstrosity of damask and diamonds, a bitingly intentional mockery of the old ways. Kira's lip curled with disgust every time she looked up at the solid gold spire perched atop the structure. The woman who'd helped destroy her life, her purpose, and her home was inside. She heard shuffling from within, even though the princess had sent her retainers away an hour or so ago. She ought to have been alone.

First, Kira had agreed to a temporary armistice. Then she'd

agreed to travel from the nearest rebel base to meet with representatives of the so-called realm on their so-called territory. And she'd agreed to the sham of a peace treaty the Sovereign's favorite niece had shoved in her face. Kira had sworn to Barra long ago that she'd rather cut out her own heart than give up the fight. And in the end she'd done just that, in a way. Twice. The first time had been when she'd sacrificed their child for the cause, abandoning Kharakh in the palace to serve as her eyes and ears. The second time, when she'd slipped out of Barra's arms and driven here. Her heart pounded painfully as she remembered her husband's last words to her: *The greater good is never good for everyone.* Oh, how true that was. But Juma and Kagiso's wisdom had prevailed. The Broken Masks were losing. They had to fall back for now, if only to save the tribes from decades of bloodshed and strife.

And now, Kira and her soldiers had laid down their arms and bent their knees in reluctant obeisance. In return, the Sovereign had promised to wrest power from the voracious new corporations of Enkaiia and return it to the people. He'd promised mercy to all rebels, free and captured. And he'd offered up his own blood. In a better world, the princess would've been Kira's equal, a partner for peace. And yet, here Kira was, on her knees, her patience wearing as thin as a dancer's slippers. How long would she be made to sit here in the cold, awaiting the princess's permission to enter and sign the damn marriage papers? She was a leader and a warrior, the commander of the revolution that had threatened to tear down the empire and rebuild it into something new. Something better.

If this day was to set the precedent for days ahead . . . Kira gritted her teeth.

"Let her in," ordered a voice as rich as nectar, as smooth as spidersilk. The princess. Next to her, Kira knew she must sound like a braying beast.

Kira stumbled as she stood; her feet had gone numb from both the dry chill of winter and from kneeling for so long. As the guards pulled open the painted blue door of the tent, the beat of her heart echoed in her chest. She stepped inside.

It took a moment for her eyes to acclimate to the darkness within, but once they did, she sucked in a sharp breath. When she knelt before the princess, it was mostly because she would've collapsed anyway.

"Oh, don't look so dour." The princess sank into a gilded chair, rolling her slender shoulders. "I've heard the rumors. We all take comfort where and when we can."

Kira shook her head, words dying on her tongue. She'd barely looked at the princess. Her attention was pinned on the woman perched on the edge of the satin-smothered bed. Her features were agonizingly familiar; her skin was the pale brown of desert sand, her head and neck framed by a waterfall of hair.

"Omiko," the rebel gasped.

"Kira," Omiko replied. Her tone was bored. But her dark-brown eyes glittered.

"Oh, you're acquainted?" Yaryun inquired, as if she weren't already aware. As if this weren't a punishment the princess had manufactured.

Kira's gaze broke away from Omiko and slid to Yaryun. The royal possessed deep-brown skin and perfectly arched brows, an aristocratic broad nose and a generous mouth. Jewel-threaded hair poured over her shoulders and back, darker and sleeker than an oil spill. Her beauty was that of cut glass: gleaming, polished, and sharp enough to draw blood. That allure was in no way lessened by the cruel smirk on her bloodred lips.

"No more than you and the insurgent, Your Highness," said Omiko.

Kira glowered. "She's a war criminal," she snarled, her fingers twitching toward her belt, though she knew full well that her scabbard and holster were empty. She'd relinquished her sword and stinger to imperial guards as soon as she'd crossed the informal border between the claimed lands of the loyal imperialists and her people. "She staked thousands of innocents—"

Omiko raised a sculpted brow. "*Executioners* staked thousands of innocents."

"On the orders of the emperor," Kira said lowly, "who took counsel from your father, who took counsel from *you*. I was promised that there would be consequences for you and your lackeys."

The princess sighed loudly. "And you believed that?"

"I believed that somewhere in that nest of serpents you call a court, there might be a kernel of honor."

The princess laughed. "Do you know why you're here, Kira Moru?"

"I'm here because I want to save the tribes."

"There are no tribes," Omiko said. "There is only Enkaiia. Several of your most trusted allies understood that."

Yet again, Kira found herself wondering how this world had come to be. She knew academically, of course—she'd been a good little schoolgirl. Alliances between the tribes had become suzerainty, suzerainty had become hegemony, and hegemony had become empire. But she couldn't understand the sheer naïveté of her ancestors, how they'd failed to stop the tragedy that was the current world from happening.

Well. Perhaps she could.

"You were betrayed," the princess said flatly, as if that weren't clear. "The thing about serpents is that they hide well."

Kira held her tongue. There was no point in responding; she knew what would happen next. If the Eternal Mother looked upon her with favor, then perhaps she would be made a martyr. She could accept her death if it inspired others to take up her sword. She consoled herself with the knowledge that her people would survive to fight another day. Barra would lead them when the right time came. And until then, their son would be safe in hiding.

"You have to die, you understand. The dead rivers of Enkaiia would've run red with blood if you'd gotten your way," the princess said, as if the rivers weren't already scarlet. "The treaty is signed. You and the other rebels in our custody will be buried by morning, but those not yet in our grasp will keep their lives. Be content with that in the time you have left. The revolution is over."

It was precisely what Kira had told herself when she'd first knelt. What she'd heard and thought a thousand times before then. She looked down at the inside of her left forearm, at the brown scar where her omnichip had once been. There hadn't been enough time to disable the tracking or data-harvesting programs the day she'd decided to start a war against the Sovereign. She'd used a kitchen knife to dig out the implant. It had been her second-proudest moment.

"No," said Kira. A peace woven with lies was not peace at all. Though her joints were still stiffened by the cold, she rose smoothly to her feet. Her sword was not her only weapon. "The revolution," she said, "is not over."

Halfway to Melodaris, the supposed final resting place of Alekhai's Ophthek ally, they stopped by a small town. Necessity drove them more than anything else; they were running dangerously low on food and water. Quekden was a visual melting pot. Most of the buildings were built in the traditional local style, boxlike and topped with gravel-layered concrete, perfect for the especially dry climate. But some shops and houses were angular and impractically ornate, clearly built to imitate Makhanish designs. The roads were unpaved in Ataa fashion but were bordered by clusters of native Ophthek succulents. The flowers were night-blooming and white, their petals arranged in delicate crowns. And unlike kameen vines, these plants thrived with minimal water and even less attention. They were doing almost *too* well under Newearth's shifting climate, spreading out of Ophthia and choking the life out of rival foliage in Eira and Makhan. The chill air hung heavy with the scent of sunbaked yellow dirt and flowery perfume.

Fen and Mettan kept an eye out for anyone paying a little too much attention to their group while Sijara and Alekhai haggled with street vendors for rations. It took hours. Food prices had been on the rise for a long time. Now they were skyrocketing.

"All right!" Sijara set a hand on Fen's shoulder. "Let's head out."

"So," said Fen, crooking a finger into the one of the bags Sijara and Alekhai were carrying. "What's for dinner?"

"Our weight in salted biscuits. Best we could find without hazarding the high chance of being spotted in the grocery," Alekhai said apologetically, pausing to offer Fen and Mettan a handful. "But local legend tells that if you eat them when the moons are full, the ghosts of your ancestors from the time of planetfall will appear, bearing water and wisdom."

Fen crunched down on a biscuit. It tasted like someone had plucked beetles from the town trash dump, pickled them, and then mixed them into insect-flour dough—which was, upon reflection, probably exactly what they were eating.

"Local legend, or the vendor trying to peddle off her wares to unsuspecting travelers?" she asked.

Alekhai managed to make it through two biscuits without making a face. "The latter, definitely. Could be worse, though."

Fen bit into another. The fact that she found the biscuits palatable was a testament to the depths of her hunger. She worked to wiggle out a bit of carapace wedged between two teeth, lifted a shoulder in a half-hearted shrug—

And then she saw it. The biscuit turned to dust in her mouth. She made herself swallow before she choked.

Between two crinkled posters of a bandit lord masked in red, white, and black stood a fully holographic wanted sign. It was life-sized, with a slowly rotating three-dimensional torso and half-cloaked head on display. The bounty was enormous, enough to keep a family well-fed and watered for a generation. The target was an assassin, according to the glowing description floating around the waist. A masked murderer of the south's beloved highborn, a bloodthirsty anonymous cutthroat targeting the regional rich and powerful and looting their storehouses. Fen glanced around;

Mettan and Sijara were frozen beside her. Alekhai was making a thoughtful noise from beneath his new veiled hat.

The people of Quekden looked a little less starved than everyone else they'd come by, despite the fact that flour and vegetables here were just as expensive as in any other settlement. Fen could hazard a few guesses as to where the nobles' stolen goods were going. But however badly the rich and entitled of Ophthia wanted the assassin, it was not nearly so much as she did.

She knew that mask.

"Is that—" Mettan started.

"Yes," Sijara breathed out. "Yes. It is."

"Who?" asked Alekhai.

"But *where*?" Fen demanded. "We can't scour the whole town."

Mettan grabbed her by the shoulders. "The clinic!"

Fen latched onto his wrists, holding him fast. "What clinic?"

Sijara let out a laugh, high and wild. "The vendor—she said we could visit the local clinic if we needed to. There's a medic who treats anyone who comes to her for free. It has to be her."

"Will someone *please* tell me what's going on?" Alekhai butted in. He pointed at the wanted sign. "Who is that?"

"A friend," Fen said. "She might be here."

That seemed to be a sufficient answer for him. His finger lifted from the masked assassin to a pale-green dome, just visible over the top of the last market stall. "Well, that's the clinic. I saw a few people carrying a man on a stretcher over there—"

Fen, Mettan, and Sijara took off at full sprint. Alekhai ran quickly and silently behind them. They dashed down one of the town's few paved roads, recently repaired to ease the way of those too poor to afford floatcraft—these days, essentially everyone who didn't work directly for the imperials. It made running easier, too; they reached the clinic in mere minutes.

From top to bottom, the building was painted entirely, scandal-ously green. The engraved dome betrayed it as a remnant of the ancient Maker-inspired architecture that had fallen far out of fashion in the last decade—not that any of them paused long enough to notice. Sijara shoved open the steel sliding door and they rushed through.

The clinic was crammed with moaning patients, tended to by a handful of harried aides in filthy aprons. At the center of the tumult stood the woman they were looking for. She wore an unadorned tunic the color of dried blood, which must've suited her purpose, given the nature of her work.

She turned around as the door slammed shut behind the four. As soon as her eyes landed on them, the color evaporated from her cheeks like spilled water in the desert. She looked like she'd seen ghosts. In a way, she had.

They flew forward, and Ying fell into their arms.

☾

"So," Sijara drawled, "doctor by day, cutthroat by night, is that it?"

The group was walking down one of Quekden's quietest backstreets, trod upon only by nguru and the odd unsavory figure. Alekhai trailed behind, pretending not to eavesdrop and glancing away every time Ying shot him a murderous look.

"You missed your true calling as a poet," Ying replied, drier than a salt flat. "But yes, that summarizes my current situation."

"You know, I can't really say I'm surprised," said Mettan. "We all have our hidden edges."

"Eternal Mother, you two." Ying rolled her eyes, but her smile was soft. "What did you do in the afterlife, scribble stanzas and contemplate the nature of existence?"

"Can't remember," Mettan said, a finger on his chin. He grinned. "But probably."

Fen extended both arms in a gesture that encompassed the

town. "You know, you could've chosen a single way to help the people here, and it still would've been more than enough."

When Ying didn't immediately reply, Fen turned to look at her. She watched as sadness seeped into the woman's large brown eyes. At once, Fen felt like a fool. Nothing would ever be enough. Not when the rest of their friends were gone. While Ruiha was gone.

Ying stopped walking. Made herself straighten. Her fingers flexed at her hands. "I followed you all to battle," she said. "I missed the massacre by *three days*."

They must've slipped just past each other. Sijara placed a gentle hand on Ying's back. Fen and Mettan took Ying's hands into their own. Her grip tightened.

"I saw Ihazan. I saw Hahru and Naijima. I—I saw Ruiha. I saw where you buried them, in their shallow graves. Scavengers had already dug them up." Anger dripped from her voice like venom. "Do you even remember them?"

Fen felt like she was being drawn into an old dance, familiar but half forgotten. "Of course we do," she said, gently as she could.

But the shadow of her grief eclipsed the memories of her squad—she missed them that much. The edges of their faces were starting to soften in her mind, their precious idiosyncrasies blurring together.

"You're not alone in your loss," Sijara said.

"Do not speak to me of loss, when you stand here breathing." Ying wrenched her hands back from Mettan and Fen, shaking Sijara off in the process. "When you left them—when you left *her* to rot with nothing to mark her but her own swords."

"We had no choice," Fen whispered.

Ying jabbed a finger toward where Alekhai stood several paces back, leaning against a cart and innocently inspecting his fingernails. "You should've forced him to resurrect them, right then and there."

"We couldn't," Mettan snapped.

Ying jerked back. He'd so rarely shown any hint of anger during his first life. Or perhaps it was the admission that shocked her.

Mettan said, "The princeling swore an oath to grant us more lives at the end of this. And I trust that he'll fulfill it."

Ying's nostrils flared. "You could've—"

"What, tortured him until he did as we demanded?" Mettan shook his head, frowning. "No, I think not."

Fen thought she saw Alekhai relax a bit, but perhaps that was just her imagination.

Ying's hands were still curled into fists, but the fight had begun to evaporate from her tensed shoulders. "How many lives did he promise you?"

"Two more," said Sijara. Plain, simple, and unsugared.

Ying let out a harsh bark of laughter. "Two? You should've bargained better."

"I might've, if anyone had been there to help me," Fen said lowly, a trace of ire leaking through. She knew she was being unfair, but the medic's criticism still stung. "Why didn't you message me back?"

Ying deflated. "There's another reason I was late to the battle," she said. "I left just after you, but I crossed a band of travelers on my way to Umut. Bandits, imperialist deserters, I don't know. I knew even less than that when I agreed to spend the night with them. One of them hacked my omnichip as I slept, discovered my identity, and put a tracker on my signal. They took me prisoner, hoping to sell me to the nearest imperialist they could find." She swallowed thickly. "I escaped, but I had to cut out my omnichip." She rubbed at the spot just above her wrist. For the first time, Fen noticed the pale brown scar there. "After that, I couldn't bring myself to get another one, and I couldn't risk accessing a rebel channel on a public computer."

*And she wanted to be alone,* Fen thought.

Sijara squeezed Ying's shoulder. "And where are your captors now?"

"In their own shallow graves," she said, something broken in her eyes. "After I returned from Umut, I hunted them down. Discovered I'm even better at ending lives than saving them."

"That's not true," said Fen.

"I've changed," Ying said. "You don't know what's true about me anymore."

A gust of wind rattled down the alley. Fen shivered, rubbing at her arms alongside Ying. She couldn't help but notice that Mettan and Sijara were as unbothered by the cold as Alekhai.

"Let's get inside," Ying said, pulling her thin jacket tighter around herself. "Warm food and drink would do us all some good."

## ALEKHAI

As the four rebels caught each other up on everything that had happened since Umut Pass, Alekhai inspected his surroundings. They were in some sort of combined storeroom-office, just a millimeter of fabric separating them from the hubbub of the clinic. He dragged a finger along the edge of a table weighted down with bandages. It came away perfectly clean.

Hm.

Expensive tile covered the floor, though several pieces were stained or cracked, and the mossy pigment was fading. Lights inlaid into the ceiling sputtered out every few minutes before flashing back to life. Cracks along the wall were plastered over with peeling bits of paper. Once, this place had served as the town hall, long before rule of the tribe had been handed to favored technocrats and palace-approved magistrates. He let out a little sigh. How far the tribes had fallen. How great the work would be to restore them.

"Any constructive criticism?"

Alekhai met the medic-assassin's eyes. Ying, was it? Those were the first words she'd spoken to him directly. He supposed she'd meant to catch him unawares. But he'd always been good at multitasking, especially when it came to listening to conversations that didn't strictly include him. He considered matching the sharpness of her words but thought better of it. Ying had nearly attacked him when Fen had told her who he really was, and though Alekhai was still much faster than the medic-assassin, nothing good would come of provoking her.

"No," he said honestly, striding over. "The work you're doing here is admirable." Including what she did at night under the guise of her mask.

"I swore that if you lived, I would kill you," Ying said.

Alekhai felt Mettan stiffen beside him.

"But it seems that I was wrong about you, princeling, and here I am, owing you a debt I can never repay." Ying leaned forward. "What would it take to even the scales?"

"You owe me nothing," he said after a moment. "The oaths your friends have made more than cover the cost of their resurrections. But . . . " He paused and made eye contact with Mettan, Sijara, and Fen. He received an imperceptible nod from the last before he continued. "You could—if you are amenable—join us for our next mission. We're going to bring back a clan leader. A minor one, but no less necessary than the others on the list."

Ying pressed her fingertips together. "Will there be imperialists? Senmavari?"

"Only if something goes terribly wrong," Alekhai replied.

"Bandits?"

"If the Eternal Mother hates us."

"Good enough for me." Ying rose, dusted off her dark tunic. "Let me pack a bag."

"Will the clinic be all right?" Fen asked. "You won't be missed?"

Ying waved a hand. "The other medics are more than capable. And it's a good time for me to disappear for a bit. They're putting up wanted signs practically on my doorstep."

Sijara rose to meet her. "Are you certain?"

Ying's not-quite-smile was lethal. "I was too late, once," she said. "Never again."

☾

Melodaris was framed with formations of rock salt, the ghosts of a great and ancient sea. The ocean had evaporated millions of years ago, long before even the Makers arrived onworld, leaving vast quantities of halite to rise upward through the underlying rock. The jagged bluffs hugging the city's side were alabaster-white, layered with blossom-pink, bloodred, sunset-orange, ocean-blue, and night-black minerals. The group passed by the city, creeping around its edges toward the tomb of the former leader of Clan Pellgai. On the way, they saw only a single figure, a boy scraping coprin mushrooms from under the shadow of a pale ledge.

He'd lost fat and muscle too quickly for the rest of his body to catch up, the bloodless skin of his face hanging off his skull like a sodden curtain. A charcoal tunic hung limply over the skeletal frame of his body. He was young. The creases framing his mouth and the rough calluses on his hands had made Alekhai think him a man at first glance, but his eyes—they were wide and innocent and *new*. He was fifteen, maybe. Certainly younger than any of them. The boy licked the chapped, bleeding ruin that had once been his mouth before he turned back to his work plucking mushrooms. The dense gills beneath the caps deliquesced the moment they reached maturity, bleeding inky sludge over the boy's fingers as he gathered.

The coprins were barely edible when correctly prepared and certain death otherwise. They were intensely halophilic, evolved to withstand the brutal conditions out here, and in easier times, the salty expanse would've been blanketed in them. But things had not been easy for a long while, and the residents of Melodaris were starving.

The tomb was little more than a stone coffin atop an altar, watched over only by the glittering cliffs. Without delay, Alekhai got to work. He shoved open the coffin and peered at the withered corpse curled up within.

*Oh, Hetarian.*

His killers had been mildly creative.

Alekhai turned to face his companions. "We don't have any liquor still stashed away, do we?"

"Don't tell me this one died of alcohol poisoning," said Mettan.

"Oh, no, he died of regular poisoning." Alekhai rolled up his sleeves and started ripping up a nearby ring of coprins. "A few dozen of these raw will kill you slowly, but if you add a strong drink to the mix, you'll be dead in seconds." He looked up at them expectantly. "You know my death has to align with his as closely as possible for this to work."

Sijara stared back at him before lifting her eyes to the sky. Finally she growled "*Fine*" and pulled a meager watertight pouch from her satchel. She tossed it to him.

Waiting would make this harder. Alekhai stuffed the coprins into his mouth, chewed, swallowed, and knocked back the alcohol. It was a homemade brew, and not even a very good one. It was simultaneously bitter and sour, but it had been gifted to the medic, Ying, by a grateful patient so they'd all accepted portions with gratitude when she'd offered to share.

He sat down among the group. Their faces were a tableau of unnecessary concern. All except for Ying's; she was peering at him with laser-focused curiosity.

"Your nose is bleeding," she said.

Alekhai touched two coprin-stained fingers to his upper lip. They came away as glaringly red as the crimson salt layers around them. Somewhere in the far distance, he saw the hulking pearlescent form of his Accuser. Watching, waiting. It wouldn't be long now.

The salt-blood fizz of technomancy filled him, washed over him, like seafoam under his fingertips, like hydrogen peroxide in a fresh wound.

And then Alekhai flopped over, his back thudding dully against the ground before Fen could catch him.

# 38

Hetarian of Pellgai sat up in his coffin, hacking violently, but Fen saw only Alekhai, a cold, unmoving statue beside him. The blood that had dripped from his nose had flowed back in, golden and glittering, and his eyes glowed underneath their lids, but he was no more alive than the clan leader had been mere minutes ago. A cold coil of fear twisted in Fen's gut.

Mettan offered Hetarian an extra cloak, a threadbare length of cheap cloth. After a moment of hesitation, Hetarian took it stiffly and wrapped it silently around his rag-strewn form. He had a light, fine-featured visage, with heavy-lidded eyes that made him look perpetually sleepy or bored. He'd either come from some money, or gained it after rising to prominence—his eyes were an impossible neon blue, and his restored fingers were laden with burial rings of beaten silver.

Fen stared at the man, pulse pounding at her temples. She didn't know what to do without Alekhai here, and he still wasn't breathing. Hetarian surveyed them all blankly, clambering from the coffin on unsteady legs. Sijara moved to help him.

Mettan turned around. "Princeling, your friend is—" His eyes landed on Alekhai's body. He flew to the other side. "What happened?"

"I—I don't know," said Fen.

Ying nudged them aside to press her hands to Alekhai's neck, then the inside of his wrist. "This has never happened before?"

"No! What's wrong with him?" Fen demanded.

"You tell me." Ying pulled open his eyes. His irises were shining brighter than the sun, but the rest of him was steadily turning dull and gray. "He's dead, Fen. It's up to the Accuser now."

Fen dragged in a breath. She lifted her hand and struck Alekhai, hard, across the face.

"Fen!" Ying shouted. "What do you think you're doing?"

"I don't know! I saw him do it to Mettan, and it worked then!"

Another breath. She raised her arm higher, preparing for a heavier blow—

Alekhai shot upward, grabbing her wrist with a hand. "You're doing it wrong. There's a specific nerve you have to hit," he rasped. "Fuck. That's never happened before."

He looked up at Hetarian, who'd scrambled behind his coffin, his unnatural eyes wide with fear.

"How—how could you?"

The princeling arched a brow. "How could I *what*?"

"You led them right here," Hetarian said. "You've killed me twice."

It was then that Fen heard the hushed, slithering rasp of steel being pulled from its sheath. The group whirled. Just ten paces away there were suddenly, impossibly, thirty warriors. Alekhai should have heard them coming. Or he would have, not so long ago. His heightened senses were fading with his health.

A masked woman stepped forward, her hand on the shoulder of the starving boy they'd seen earlier. "Good job, kid," she said pleasantly. Her eyes flicked to the group and landed on Alekhai. "Well? Hand over the noble."

"No," Sijara said.

"Who are you?" Mettan demanded.

But it didn't matter, and they all knew it.

The woman laughed. "Surrender him peacefully, and I swear that none of you will come to harm. Otherwise . . . Well, I have no need for you." Her voice hardened. "Lay down your arms, all of you. *Now.*"

Fen's gaze met Alekhai's. "Never."

"As you wish." The woman shrugged. "Kill them."

Alekhai might've been slowly dying, but he still moved like a fabled storm cloud over the sun, nearly floating over the salt-crusted rock to engage the nearest warrior. The rest of them followed. Fen extended her quarterstaff mid-swing at a fighter, but he caught the weapon between a pair of gleaming daggers.

She fought as best she could, but he was bigger, heavier, stronger. Her breath grew ragged, and her muscles burned. When she knocked one blade from his grip and then the other, he dove under her next blow, snuck in, and kicked her in the middle. Fen hit the rock wall behind her and slid down the stone with a hiss of pain. Her weapon rolled from her grasp. The soldier kicked her onto her back. He reached down, wrenched her head upward, and slammed it back down. Fen's teeth sank into her own tongue; blood gushed into her mouth.

He loomed over her, grinning viciously. He found a dagger and aimed. Fen's hands scrabbled furiously at her sides, searching for something, *anything*—there. A hilt. She rolled, just missing the gleaming point of his blade. For a fraction of a second, their eyes met. Then she drove his own knife into his side. He went down with a furious scream.

Fen scrambled away. His hands grasped the hilt, already slippery with his blood.

"Don't," she rasped. "You'll bleed out."

He jerked his head up to look at her. His eyes were wide with shock. "Why?" he gasped.

Fen didn't have time to answer. A blade whistled toward her. She grabbed the dagger he'd just dropped and shot to her feet, whirled to face the next enemy. The new warrior facing her wielded a double-bladed spear, the blades glittering in the sun. The quarterstaff was just behind them.

A thin trail of blood speckled the dirt as Fen dove forward, dagger held high. They spun away, giving Fen just enough time to throw aside the knife and kick her quarterstaff up into her hands. The warrior rushed forward. They crossed weapons, once, twice, and then—

Fen faltered, only for a moment. But it was enough. As she twisted away from a strike, one tip of the fighter's spear sank into her right shoulder. Then it dragged down across her back. Fen felt her flesh split open at the seams. For a second, everything went blistering white.

Agony shattering what vision she retained, Fen lashed out wildly, a stray blow cracking against the warrior's chin. She threw herself forward, driving the end of her weapon into their jaw again. Their head snapped back with a wet crunch of bone, and the spear slipped from slack fingers.

Fen crumpled to the ground just after they did. She looked up. She'd defeated two guards, and her friends, better fighters than she, had taken down far more. But they were still outnumbered. Ying, Mettan, Sijara, and Alekhai were still fighting, but they were losing. Fen felt as if a togau had chewed its way into her skull, steadily clawing her brain into neat gray ribbons.

Her breaths came out in rapid gasps, even shallower than before. Reality began to slip away from her.

"Fen!"

*Where am I?*

"Fen!"

She pressed her head against a column of salt.

*Cold.* She was so cold.

"Get up!"

Right—she had to . . . she had to . . .

She blinked away the drifting black spots dancing along her vision and forced herself upward. She fell to her knees. Got up again. Collapsed.

Someone screamed, a cry louder than all the other sounds of battle. And then, suddenly, everything went silent and still. Fen's eyes rolled up into her head, and her body went slack.

## ALEKHAI

The warrior was on the run.

He'd woken up bloody and alone beside the corpses of his companions, and now he was fleeing for his life, because footsteps were coming fast behind him. Alekhai knew, because he was deliberately stepping very hard. He was, after all, trying to chase the man into Ying.

Which was exactly what he did—the warrior let out a tiny shriek when the medic swung herself around a vast slab of salt, daggers at the ready. The man stumbled right back into Alekhai, who grabbed him by the arm and twisted, sending him crashing into the slab. The warrior slid down and fell onto his hands and knees, freezing when he hit the ground. He was clever enough to know when he was caught.

"Where did your friends take them?" Alekhai asked, very nicely. "We already found out you're bandits, so you must have a base."

"I—"

"Now. We don't have much time, and I'll be blunt, I'm very good at getting the information I want." Alekhai dropped down into the bandit's space, lifted his chin with a sharp-edged nail. He made himself smile. "A decent face. I'd hate to ruin it."

"I don't believe you, somehow."

A little edge. Admirable, but a spine would make this all so much harder. Alekhai turned his head and met Ying's stare over the man's shoulder. "Will you keep him alive if I go too far?"

"Whatever it takes," was her grim reply.

Alekhai smiled at the man. "Tell me where your base is, and we won't lay another finger on you. It's that simple."

The man said nothing.

Alekhai sighed. "We already have your leader. Nadja, right?"

The bandit's eyes widened. "No."

"Unfortunately for you, yes. She's in a bad way. Your people thought she was dead, so they left her for us. But Ying here can fix her up, if you help us out."

The man narrowed his eyes. "Why do you need me if you have Nadja?"

"You both get the same questions," said Ying. "You give the same answers, you live. You give different answers, you suffer."

"We just want our friends back. Tell us where they are, and you can go back to looting whatever the imperials aren't." Alekhai grabbed his shoulder and shook, hard. "Quickly now."

"They're in Liyorum."

Alekhai held back a sigh of relief. "There, was that so hard? Numbers."

"What?"

"How many of you are there? In what arrangements?"

The bandit drew in a breath, jaw hardening. "I . . . I can't."

"But you will," said Alekhai. "You'll help us before your compatriots do something they *will* suffer long enough to regret. Because if Fenyyang dies, if *any* of my friends die, I will flay your people alive. I will stake their raw, bleeding corpses along the great roads, so no one dares to so much as breathe your names. And everything you have ever done, except *fuck with us,* will be forgotten. This I swear." He leaned in. "Now, how many of you are there?"

Fen came to on a lumpy cot beneath a dark-green tent. Outside, machinery hummed, people chattered, and boots stomped over dirt. She tried to lift herself. A terrible, nerve-wringing pain tore through her back. She let out a dry croak, unable to draw breath. Warm hands helped her lay down again.

"Oh, thank the Mother. This would've been even more of a clusterfuck if you'd died," Fen heard someone say, as if through water. She'd heard that voice before, low and strangely soft.

"Who are you?" Fen croaked. Her head felt horribly light, and her senses were one great churning vat of sludge. She vaguely recalled someone plying her with painkillers.

"An old friend."

The words prickled at something at the back of her mind. A face appeared before her then. It was angular, sandstone brown, and cuttingly familiar. And then it came to her.

The man in the temple, when she'd first fled Onath's estate. The stranger who'd promised her his life.

"Fenyyang Mekantai," he said. "I never thought I'd see you again." He perched at the foot of the cot. "Your friends are quite angry with me."

"Should they be?" she whispered. The analgesics flowing

through her veins couldn't sweep up every shard of pain; a few slipped through and stabbed into her flesh.

"Well, yes. My people attacked you."

"*What?*" She swung herself upright, her entire torso screaming in protest. She hissed in pain.

"Yes, well, we'd been following rumors of a high-ranking noble and a few Senmavari traveling in disguise. If we captured and ransomed him, we'd be set for life. My scout spotted you, reported to an officer, one thing led to another; lo and behold, we are reunited. Obviously, if I'd known it was you, things would've gone down differently. Your small force killed a fair few of my better fighters."

"Only in self-defense," Fen said.

"I know," he replied. "That's why you're still breathing. But still, they were someone's siblings, friends, lovers."

"I'm sorry." She meant it. "But where are my—"

"Sijara and Mettan are safe and sound. You'll see them soon. Your aristocratic companion—Wren, they said?—is gone, and so are the medic and Hetarian."

"You're lying," Fen said, rage bubbling up within her. "They wouldn't have left us."

He arched a brow. "Did you really expect that a technocrat wouldn't abandon you to die?"

Fen turned her head away, gnawing at the inside of her cheek. "You said you had scouts and an officer, so you're no regular outlaw, are you?" she guessed. "You're a bandit lord."

He shrugged. "We don't have lords. And we don't like being called bandits."

The semantics didn't matter. "Are you going to let us go?"

"Honestly, I haven't decided."

Fen swallowed hard. "And why is that?"

"Because," he drawled, "I know his name isn't Wren. You haven't been traveling with just any noble. You've somehow, impossibly, befriended the Butcher of Bakrai. I really thought he was dead, you know. *And* he's an Executor?"

Fen's blood turned to ice. "That's ridiculous."

His brows lifted. "Denying it will waste my time and yours, Fen. And people who waste my time have a way of ending up dead."

Fen looked into his eyes. She could tell he meant every word. "How—" She gritted her teeth. "How did you know it was him?"

"I didn't torture the others, if that's what you're asking." The bandit lord grinned. "But some of my surviving compatriots caught a good-enough look at his face to describe it in detail. And it's a face I'll remember for the rest of my life."

"That's impossible," Fen said. "No one outside his family has seen what he looks like."

"You're forgetting the people who work for them." The man's voice was as bitter as tea dregs. "My mother placed me in the palace when I was very young. I worked and blackmailed and killed my way up until I was promoted to serve the inner court. I remember all their faces, but Alekhai's is one I'll go to the grave with."

"Who are you?" she whispered.

He gazed down at her. "Kharakh Moru. Son of Kira Moru."

Fen gaped at him. The resemblance was obvious, now that she was looking for it. He had Barra's high cheekbones and broad frame, but everything else was his mother's, from the gentle brown eyes to the wavy dark hair. No wonder he'd had his face fully slathered with paint when she'd met him.

Shock and grief shoved her down, and she collapsed against the bed. "I was told you were dead—"

"Because my father commanded it." Kharakh snorted. "My survival was his greatest secret. But the world will know the truth soon enough."

"Why aren't you with the Masks?"

"I *am* with the Masks," he snapped. "The true ones. The imperials and the ignorant call us bandits, but we're the ones who never stopped fighting." He crossed his arms over his wide chest. "But now we're also helping the self-proclaimed rebels."

So this was the bandit lord who'd been directing resources toward the Broken Masks. Though he clearly wasn't completely reformed, as the news proclaimed.

"Ruiha was a true Mask," Fen countered, sitting back up against her body's protests. "So are and were my friends. So am I."

Kharakh's eyes softened incrementally. "I know."

"So let us go," Fen said. "Let us go, and our ledger is balanced. I saved your life, and you swore—"

"That I would save yours. But that does not apply to your prince."

"What do you want with Alekhai?" Fen tried to steady her breathing. "I'm sorry for your loss, truly I am, but if it's to bring back your parents, he cannot."

There was nothing in Kharakh's face to suggest he caught her lie. He waved a tired hand through the dry air. "I know how resurrection works. You need the remains, and my mother's ashes were scattered to the four winds. The dead, today's included, have earned their rest."

"So let us all go, then."

Kharakh shook his head. "The Sovereign has to die. We're still gathering our strength, but the moment we can, we're taking this fight to the imperial core."

Fen drew in a sharp breath, wincing slightly. She'd known the rebellion would eventually escalate into full-blown war, but she hadn't realized it would be so soon. If she and her friends couldn't resurrect the allies and take out Akrysanth quickly enough, the empire would be torn apart.

"And after that . . . we'll see," Kharakh continued. "But I must work on two fronts. I need Alekhai to get close to his brother."

"Akrysanth tried to have Alekhai murdered. He won't grant you an audience in exchange for his brother. He'll slaughter you both, and the rest of your people, too."

"I'm not going to bring Alekhai to the emperor. At least, not all of him." Kharakh flashed a bladelike grin. "The Sovereign would want to meet the one who ended his last sibling."

Fen let out a harsh laugh. "You think he'd let someone who spilled royal blood anywhere near enough to strike? That plan will never work."

"Listen," said Kharakh, brushing past her argument, "I don't want to hurt you. We're on the same side. If the prince returns, I'll let the rest of you go free."

"We're worthless to you, Alekhai included if you aren't after his powers. Please." Fen put a hand on his arm. "He's different from the other imperials, Kharakh, I swear it."

He snorted. "You *swear* it?"

"I swear it. He wants to fix things."

"A puppet of the Sovereign?" His eyes narrowed. "A *prince?*"

"Your people saw Alekhai resurrect Hetarian of Pellgai," Fen said. "Why would a loyal prince bring back a known revolutionary?"

"For all I know, he did it to torture secrets out of the poor man."

Fen shook her head. "The Masks were struggling to get a foothold in Eira, and now, all of a sudden, the whole eastern tribe's turned rebel. You must've heard the whispers that Cleric-Chieftain Chinonso is back among the living." The sudden stiffness in Kharakh's arm was confirmation enough. "Who do you think brought her back?"

"I don't care if he's resurrecting old leaders," he snarled. "He razed an entire city." He tried to rip his arm away, but Fen held on.

"That was Akrysanth's doing," she said. "With Alekhai's help, we're finally winning."

"We're winning because my people risk their lives every day gathering and transporting supplies," Kharakh growled. "Not because Chinonso lives again."

"It's both. Look, I know what it's like to risk everything." She tightened her grip. "My friends died at the bottom of Umut Pass, and Alekhai brought them back. We will need every tool at our disposal to win."

"The prince only wants his brother's throne," Kharakh insisted.

"No. He'll usher in a democracy. A real one. And then he'll step back."

Kharakh looked down at where her hand was still wrapped around his wrist. "The man you stabbed," he said. "He told me you could've shoved that dagger in his heart, but you struck his lower abdomen instead."

Fen let out a breath. "He survived?"

She'd very nearly killed that man. As their eyes had met in combat, she'd felt a little thrill in her chest. She'd *liked* it. The feeling of being capable of permanently removing a threat to her family. And that had scared her.

"Yes. And that is the only reason I'm even considering what you're asking of me." Kharakh sighed. "What if you're wrong about the prince?"

Without hesitating, Fen flipped his wrist over and offered her own. "Then my life is yours."

He shook his head in disbelief. "You would place that much trust in him?"

"Yes."

"And what of the lives of every other Enkaiian on this world? You'd risk those as well?" He leaned forward, invading her space. "I'm letting you go this once, Fenyyang. You have one chance to gamble with what remains of humanity—I won't let Alekhai slip through my fingers again."

Fen didn't back down. "Alekhai swore to me, before his Accuser. He can't renege on his oath to right his family's wrongs."

"But what if he does?" Kharakh demanded.

"Then, as I said, my life is yours," Fen said, drawing away. "But not before I kill him myself."

## ALEKHAI

"How does he look, Ying? He's lost so much blood."

"He's fine." Ying's eyes were on the ground between her boots. Her hands were bloody. "Keep going."

"I've told you all I know, you fucking monsters," the bandit choked out. "You nobles are all the same—"

"Watch your tongue," said Alekhai, "or I'll cut it out. She's not a noble."

"Go fuck yourself—"

Alekhai jammed his blade in the bandit's mouth before he could close it. He jerked the hilt back and forth while the man screamed, his eyes narrowed in concentration. "Be still. This'll hurt less if you don't move."

He gripped the man's chin with his other hand, removing the knife only to shove in his fingers. He dug out the tongue and looked up to find Ying, of all people, gaping at him.

"What? Don't look so surprised, assassin."

"Alekhai, he could've told us more," she said.

"I don't need him to." He turned back to the sobbing man with a sigh, chucking him hard under the chin. "A few good restorative patches, and you'll be fine. I would've liked to avoid all this unpleasantry, but here we are. Now, I'm going to ask Nadja the same questions. And if her answers differ, I'll make you wish I'd just slit your worthless throat right here."

The man's eyes widened.

Alekhai plucked up the tongue and walked off.

"Not that I have any sympathy for the bandit," said Ying as they headed over to where they'd strung up Nadja, "but what was the point of that . . . 'unpleasantry,' as you said?"

"It's a warning."

"A warning?" Ying scoffed. "I believe that man would disagree."

Well, he couldn't. Not verbally, anyway.

Nadja cursed when she saw them. He'd had to empty his stinger's energy stores to take her down.

"Sorry to keep you waiting," Alekhai called brightly. He tossed the tongue into her lap. She yelped out a curse. "I want to make sure we start off on the right foot: The worst thing you can do is waste more of my time. Am I clear?"

"I'm sorry," she said. The regret in her voice rang true enough.

"Not as sorry as I am," said Alekhai, his voice honey laced with poison. He tried not to recoil at the sound of it. "And not as sorry as you will be."

"So he really let us go because you saved his life ages ago?" Sijara asked for perhaps the third time time. Somehow, that fact had surprised her more than the revelation of the bandit lord's parentage.

"Yes," said Fen, again.

She kept her eyes on the path ahead. They'd been searching for Alekhai and Ying for an hour, and now they were heading down a half-forgotten road.

"Well, would be the honorable thing to do." Mettan was rubbing his clean-shaven chin with one hand; he'd pickpocketed a razor from one of Kharakh's bandits at some point. "Honorable, but stupid, and the sort of person who becomes a bandit lord is rarely either. Even if he didn't want Alekhai to resurrect his family, the princeling is literally worth a king's ransom."

Fen shrugged helplessly.

"There's more, isn't there?" Sijara asked softly.

Fen looked up at the burning sky. "If Alekhai breaks his oath, I promised the bandit lord both our lives."

Mettan stared at her for what felt like a very long time.

But Sijara simply nodded. "Well, we'll just make sure he doesn't break his oath, then."

The words did little to dull Fen's anxiety. "Kharakh let us all go, but he could easily change his mind. And if we don't find Alekhai before he does, it's all for nothing," Fen said.

Mettan squeezed Fen's shoulder. "Then let's pick up the pace—"

He and Sijara both froze.

Fen went still, eyes wide. "What is it?" she whispered.

"Footsteps," Mettan hissed.

They rushed into the scrubby foliage at the side of the path and waited. The thud of boots on dirt grew louder, enough for Fen's mortal ears to pick up. She turned to her friends, mouthing, *One?*

Sijara nodded and then shook her head, holding up two fingers. Fen shared her confusion—no normal person could have a step so light Sijara would have trouble hearing. Mettan's brow furrowed, and then cleared. A slow smile touched the corners of his mouth. Without warning, he shot to his feet.

A cry of alarm, and then—

"Mettan!" Ying's voice.

Fen and Sijara leapt upward. There, in the middle of the road, were Ying and Alekhai, looking scuffed up but no worse for wear.

"Thank the Mother." Alekhai dashed over. For a moment, Fen thought he was going in for a hug, but then he swung around her and poked her back. "Are you all right? I saw that asshole swing for you."

"Ow!" She whirled around and smacked away his hands. "It's a long story, but Kira Moru's son is alive and he leads the bandits. I saved his life once, and he didn't know it was us he was sending his people after. He had his medics stitch me up. It was a shallow wound, anyway. I'm fine, I promise—"

Ying yanked up the back of Fen's tunic despite her protestations and looked her over. Sijara handed her the medkit Kharakh had given them.

"So Moru's son still lives . . ." Alekhai frowned. "Hopefully that won't be a problem."

"We'll make sure of it." Fen, feeling very much like a lema

picked up by the scruff, looked from Alekhai to Ying and then back again. "Where's Hetarian?"

Alekhai looked away. "He fled in the melee."

Fen gaped at him. "*What?*"

"He'll figure out where the new base is," Alekhai said. He flicked a tendril of hair from his eyes. "He actually identified the site as a potential strategic position during the first rebellion."

Sijara crossed her arms. "But is he actually on his way to the Masks, or did he just run off to save his own skin?"

When Alekhai didn't immediately answer, Mettan swore softly. "And we definitely can't get his location?"

"No." Like almost everyone else who'd joined or helped the rebellion, Hetarian had borked his omnichip tracker. Any geospatial data coming from it would be nonsense. "He was never *that* useful. Chinonso knows most of what he managed to scrounge up before his death." He glanced over at Ying. "Fen's actually fine?"

"No thanks to you." Ying jabbed a finger at him.

Anger squeezed at Fen's ribs. "So all that work to bring him back was for nothing?" she ground out.

"He'll go to the Masks."

"You can't be certain of that," Sijara growled.

Alekhai exhaled slowly through his teeth. "I know. I'm sorry for leading us into Kharakh's trap." He sounded miserable. "I'm the reason you're injured, the reason you could've . . . you could've died."

In that moment, Fen saw him as clearly as cut glass. Alekhai: the gamemaster, eternally in control. The cynical part of her hissed that she and Mettan and Sijara had only ever been pieces on a board to him. But the softer part told her that wasn't true anymore.

"I didn't, though," said Fen, reaching for his hand. "Kharakh was tracking us; we would've run into him sooner or later. But . . ."

"But?" Alekhai asked.

"We need to know why each of your allies must be resurrected." Fen had a pretty good guess, though she hoped she was wrong.

Alekhai looked down at their intertwined fingers. "I told you, the old leaders have what we need. Intel. Connections. Supply access."

"You just said Hetarian was useless!" Sijara countered.

"He just isn't as useful as the others. This is a matter of honor—"

"Do *not* lecture us about honor," Ying cut in, her eyes narrowing dangerously. "My oldest friends died for honor during the rebellion. And all that was good in the world died with them."

Fen stepped forward to lay her other hand on his shoulder, defusing the tension. "Alekhai," she said gently. "You can trust us with the truth. Even if it's an unpleasant one."

Alekhai's jaw twitched. "I'm bound by oath."

Fen let out a breath. "I was beginning to suspect that," she said. "What did they make you promise?"

"When I found my allies, the rebellion had ended years and years ago, but my father and brother saw even the smallest acts of resistance as the greatest treason. I promised to raise Chinonso and the others if they were killed resisting my family." Alekhai closed his eyes and tilted his head backward. "And they were. I've already put it off for too long. The oath—at first it was a minor itch under my skin. Now it's fire in my blood. I *must* finish this."

Sijara's fingers balled into fists. "Only one more leader. And then we're done."

"Then we're done," he echoed. He looked so very tired.

"Alekhai." Fen crossed her arms over her chest. "Raising Hetarian almost killed you for good. I'm worried—"

"There's no other way," he said with a sad smile. "I'm sorry."

Fen couldn't watch him hurt himself like that again. Her eyes were burning. Oh no. Was she about to start *crying*?

"But—" Fen cut herself off, narrowed her eyes at him. "You promised to *raise* them? Were those your exact words?"

"Yes."

"Are you certain?" Fen insisted.

"I'm sure."

"What are you getting at?" asked Ying.

"There are other ways this could be fulfilled," said Fen. "He could lift them, and he'd still be fulfilling his oath." She grinned at Alekhai. "Right?"

"I . . . I suppose," said Alekhai, blinking. Then he burst into laughter. "Eternal Mother, you're right."

"So that's what we'll do," said Sijara.

"Fine," said Ying. "I only care whether you'll bring back two more of us in return for their help, my friends' help, princeling."

Alekhai nodded. "That's the oath I made, and in far clearer terms."

Ying tilted her head slightly to the side, looking at Alekhai. "You know, on the way here, I was considering shoving one of my knives between your ribs."

Alekhai looked unperturbed. "And that wasn't just an intrusive thought?"

She strode up to him, so close the tips of her boots nearly brushed his. "I only let you live because I knew you'd help me save what remained of my family."

"It was my fault," said Fen.

Ying whirled around. "What?"

Fen stared back, just as shocked. The words had left her mouth without her permission. "Umut was my fault," she whispered.

"Fen." Ying's voice was sharp. "How could you possibly think the ambush was your fault?"

"I saw something the night before," Fen forced out. Eternal Mother, she was pathetic. "Eyes, in the dark, staring at us from the shadows. A spy. I brushed it off as unimportant, maybe my imagination." Each word was a needle pushed through her throat.

"I should've checked, should've called someone. Nothing I do will ever make up for it."

"Fen—" Mettan began.

She shook her head, screwing her eyes shut. As if that would stop the tears. As if that would fix anything. "I was so angry. I'd just learned Barra had sacrificed my parents to save Moru, and I thought only of them." She forced herself to look up, to look at the friends she was about to lose, but all she saw were four sad, sympathetic faces. "Don't," she snapped. "Don't look at me like that."

She didn't want their pity. She didn't deserve it.

"Well?" she cried. "Say something! Aren't you angry?"

"What do you want us to say?" Sijara said, throwing up her hands. "Of course I'm angry."

*Then fight me,* Fen wanted to beg. Sijara's fury was a formidable thing; it had mass to push against, shape to grip. Her sympathy slipped through Fen's fingers like smoke. Without anything to anchor herself, she dropped to her knees.

The truth was, she hadn't been terrified that they might not forgive her. She'd been terrified that they would.

That they'd let her get away with it.

That she'd go unpunished.

That there was no justice in the world at all. Not for her, and not for the friends she'd failed.

"I *am* angry," Sijara said, crouching down beside her, "that you kept this from us for so long. That you carried it on your own."

Fen froze. "I don't—I don't understand."

"How do you know they were an imperialist spy?" Mettan demanded, joining them on the dirt. "That could've been a random traveler for all we know."

"I—I don't. I only saw a silhouette, but—"

"A silhouette," echoed Ying. Her gaze had returned to the

bone-dry expanse beyond, stretched out before them like a glittering blanket. "Are you certain they were even human?"

Fen swallowed. "Well, no—"

"So you're telling us," said Sijara, "that you sat boiling in your own guilt for months because you *think* you saw a pair of eyes, which *could* have been a spy?"

Fen opened her mouth.

"Sweetheart," said Sijara, "if you try arguing that the imperial army massacring our friends was somehow your fault, I'm going to scream."

Fen dropped her head into her hands.

"Eternal Mother," she heard Mettan mutter. "Even if it was a spy you saw, which it wasn't, what's done is done."

"But—"

Ying cut her off. "*Even* if that night was what you thought it was, since Umut, you've done everything you could to make amends. Just keep doing that."

"Now, this is very touching," Alekhai drawled, "but you all need to eat. And rest. We have a long journey ahead."

Wiping tears from her face, Fen let Sijara help her to her feet. They ate some of their rations and, since the day had grown unseasonably hot, slept the afternoon away, resting in all-too-short intervals in the thorny brush. As they prepared their second meal of the day—a quick bite before walking till dawn toward Ata—Ying stood and faced the group.

"I know you stumbled into me, but thank you for coming," she said. Her eyes pinched shut. When they reopened, there was a wet shimmer over them. "I'm so fucking glad you three are alive."

Fen choked at the words.

Mettan dropped their ladle into their small battered pot. "Wait, Ying, you're leaving us?"

"You can't!" Sijara exclaimed.

"I have to." Ying adjusted the strap of her satchel on her shoulder. "Quekden needs me more than you four do right now."

But she wouldn't meet anyone's eyes as she said it. Of course. Seeing them all without Ruiha was a burden too painful to bear.

Ying turned to Fen. "I've done all I can for you. Your back will be fully healed in a day or two. I'm sorry I couldn't do more."

"No one could." Fen forced a smile and stood. "Thank you."

Mettan and Sijara surged forward, dragging them all into one great embrace.

As they pulled apart, Ying's lips thinned into a tight line. "For the last two lives . . . I won't ask, but I trust you'll make the right choice." Without waiting for a response, she turned on Alekhai. "Princeling."

"Medic."

"I don't like you."

"Somehow, I got that—"

"*Quiet.* Let me finish."

Shockingly, Alekhai shut his mouth.

"I also don't respect you," Ying continued.

"Thanks."

"But my friends seem to have placed their trust in your hands. If you betray them, or if any of them die for good, I will fuck you up."

"I understand," said Alekhai. "More than you know."

# 43

The quarterstaff fell into the dirt for the twelfth time in as many minutes.

"That must hurt," said a flat voice.

Fen didn't bother turning around. Dawn would arrive in a few hours, and then they'd set out for Ata's capital. "It's nothing, Mettan. Aren't you supposed to be keeping watch?"

"That's exactly what I'm doing."

Fen picked up her weapon and tried again to make it through the simplest form. She gritted her teeth together as she stumbled through the set. She did her best to pull on her wound as little as possible, but the fact of the matter was that her quarterstaff required full mobility. Every shift and turn was an agony.

"Stop." Mettan came over to her side and placed a hand on her shoulder. "Just stop. You're going to reopen your back, if you haven't already. You're no use to anyone bled out."

"Is that all I am to you? A soldier?" It was half a joke.

"No." Mettan's smile was thin. "You're my friend." He sat down, pulling what remained of Kharakh's medkit from his satchel. "Come, let me see."

"You came prepared." It wasn't a question, and so she wasn't surprised when he didn't answer.

His hands weren't gentle as they slathered ointment over the wound, only quick and merciful.

"Stop punishing yourself," he said, pulling her tunic back down. "The world has done enough of that already."

☾

The sky, even in the evening as they neared the old capital of Ata, was a burning blue bowl turned upside down, its edge smudged with a faint coating of yellow-gray dust. Winter had never touched these lands.

They were in the deep desert now, endless waves of scarlet dunes gilded in amber orange and blossom pink. The city of Olivack was similarly dusted. Swirling yellow and red gradually condensed into blurry shapes, and then into a settlement tucked into a vast outcropping. Knobby hoodoos and dramatic mesas stood watch over the city, monuments no human art could ever hope to match. And all of it set against the endless sands. In the far distance, a mirror-smooth stretch of saltpan shimmered white as the snow Fen had only seen in holofilms.

She felt like her lungs had been rubbed raw with sand, as though her skull were cracking under the heat. When she scratched at the sunburn on her wind-chafed skin, her nails came away red. The planet was bleeding her dry. Her friends with her. How strange it was to live on a world so damaged it hungered for blood. A world that sucked out one's marrow and filled the bones with dust and decay. How strange, how terrible, and somehow still so beautiful.

Their boots went crunching down a mosaic of interlocking pebbles, glittering with shards of rock varnish. And then, suddenly, as the sun sank beneath the sandy waves, they found themselves before the worn, creaking gates of the city. They slipped right in, blending into a winding stream of villagers fleeing bandits far less kind than Kharakh, pilgrims seeking out the famed temple, fugitives and criminals and refugees.

Oshyeva, the former leader of Fen's tribe, of her parents' tribe, was everywhere if one knew where to look. There were miniature murals of her painted in the shadows of sun-bleached walls, tiny figurines of clay and glass tucked away in cracks and crevices. It all made Fen a little uncomfortable. She knew more than most how dangerous it was to put rebels on pedestals. People made disappointing gods.

From the scattered representations, she gathered that Oshyeva had been a tough, wiry old woman. Scars had peppered her chiseled brown face. Her dark hair, which she seemed to have often held back with a ribbon, had been streaked with snowy white. The holoimages Alekhai showed the group as they caught a spare moment of rest in the shade confirmed the picture she'd been piecing together.

It didn't take long to find the leader's resting place. In a quiet back alley, Alekhai sank to one knee, pressing his hand to the sandy ground.

"It was brutal." He shivered. "Dismembered and disemboweled, her screams covered by the morning bells."

Mettan pulled a collapsible shovel from his satchel and extended it. Then, silently, he got to digging. He took turns with Sijara and Alekhai. Fen, keeping watch, signaled whenever someone wandered by the passage's entrance. Olivack clearly had little love for the Sovereign, but if a single person alerted the Senmavaris, they'd be trapped in the city, and their demise would be no prettier than Oshyeva's. But no one tried to step in for a better look, or stopped to ask questions. Whether it was because the four of them seemed a formidable group or because no one came back there, Fen couldn't tell.

Finally, on Sijara's second turn, the shovel clanged against stone.

"Are you sure we're in the right spot?" she asked, slumping against a wall.

Fen, Mettan, and Sijara peered over either side of Alekhai as he stared into the pit. There was nothing. He leaned in, pressing his palm flat against the rock.

"No," he whispered. "No, no, no, no . . . "

"Princeling, what's wrong?" Fen grasped his shoulder. "Someone must've moved her, that's all—"

"She's not dead," whispered Alekhai.

"But you just said she died, right here," said Mettan.

"She did. Someone else brought her back."

Sijara sucked in a breath. "Are you saying—"

"There's another Executor." Alekhai's eyes were as wide as the hidden moons. "And they found her first."

## ALEKHAI

Mettan strode into the abandoned stall they'd taken for themselves, ducking under the canvas flap. He tugged his scarf loose and shook sand from its threadbare folds.

"The market was a complete waste of time," he said with a groan. "Everyone has a different story, each more ridiculous than the last. What did you all find out?"

It had been his turn today to go out and poke around for intel. As the two least hunted members of the group, he and Sijara switched off while Fen and Alekhai scoured the omninet for traces of Oshyeva's presence. Alekhai knew his friends wanted to spare him from the trauma of resurrecting more people than he had to, but he would've brought Oshyeva back in the end no matter what. If any of his former allies were worth reconnecting with, if any were still loyal to the cause, it would be her. And now they had to figure out who might've resurrected her.

"Let's eat first," said Alekhai. "We can fill each other in later tonight."

Sijara propped her chin on her palm. "I'm certain you will," she said sweetly.

Fen looked at Sijara in confusion for a moment, bringing her water pouch to her lips. Then she snorted out the sip and started choking.

"Firstly, that's a terrible joke. Secondly, I meant all of us," Alekhai said flatly, as Fen's coughing subsided.

"Sijara and I will have to decline, but I appreciate the thought," Fen said, cackling.

"I don't get it," said Mettan, which just made the women laugh harder.

Alekhai gave him a disbelieving look before letting out an exaggerated sigh. "It's best that you don't," he said. "Come on."

The sun, yellow and hungry, reclined high in the pale blue expanse above, a golden eye glaring liquid fire down on the planet. Thankfully, they escaped the worst of the heat—and, more importantly, the notice of Senmavari or anyone else—by traveling through the city's underground network. The passage system connected to a cluster of ancient caves on one end and a mine on the other, but the eyeless, skittering insects that had once ruled the dirt had been hunted to extinction, and the mine had long since dried up. The likelihood they'd encounter anyone down here was incredibly—

A low, murmuring voice crept down the rocky corridor ahead. "I swear to the Mother, I'm never listening to you ever again. I cannot believe you convinced me to go off-course."

"It was a mutual decision," said another voice. "We just need to get to a higher elevation, we'll latch on to a better signal, and we'll be back in time for lunch."

"It was *not* a mutual—"

*Shit.*

Two people, confirmed by the rapidly nearing footsteps. Senmavari, criminals, fellow fugitives, or innocent civilians with a taste for spelunking, Alekhai had no idea. He turned back toward his companions, alarm squeezing his gut.

Mettan, standing just behind him, tightened his fists. His face was cloaked in shadow, save for a single brown eye, lit by an errant ray of light from a vent five meters up. It was wide, but not with fear. Alekhai's chest went tight with anticipation as whoever it was drew closer, their murmured words drifting toward the group.

"Get down!" Sijara whispered.

They shuffled together, balling themselves up as small as possible and pulling their assortment of hoods, scarves, and veils over their heads. They waited. Alekhai's heart beat against his rib cage, the same dull panic he'd felt the first time he'd died. The same panic he'd felt ever since then. A dusty glove, closely followed by a lacquered helmet, appeared around the corner.

Senmavari.

The first one's head jerked up, and for one terrible moment she and Alekhai held breathless, frozen eye contact. Then he snatched up a stray rock and launched himself at the soldier. Without enough time to pull her stinger, she threw a fist at him. But he caught the blow with his right hand and struck her head with the stone, ringing the helmet like a temple bell. The sound was still echoing down the tunnel when she pitched over, unconscious. The second guard, however, was nowhere to be found.

"I know you're there." He sighed. His breathing was almost but not completely even. A worrisome sign of his worsening condition. "Come out and we won't hurt you. Much."

After a long moment, the Senmavar crept into the meager light. Their head was bare, but they held a curved dagger. The blade shook so hard it was barely visible. Alekhai saw then that the guards were no more than trainees; they were both young and utterly unprepared. The guard made a single desultory strike at him, which he barely had to dodge. He flicked them in the nose.

"Just let us go," the guard whispered in a thin, reedy voice. "We didn't see your faces, we won't say anything!"

"Not anytime soon, no," said Alekhai. Then he grabbed their collar and punched them in the face. They went down with a pained gasp.

"Nice work," drawled a low voice.

Four pairs of eyes jerked upward, landing on a tall brown-haired woman.

"Any enemy of the empire is a friend of mine," she continued, spinning on her heel. "Follow me."

Sijara ran up to her. "Who are you?"

"What's more important is that, unlike those poor fools, I know who *you* four are—oh, come on, take your hand off your hilt, I'm not threatening you—and who you're looking for." She grinned. "The name's Hyun. I work for Oshyeva."

Three turns later, Alekhai felt a faint puff of air against his scalp. They were close to the surface. The air in the tunnel grew warmer as they continued, until finally the scorching light of day fell upon them like a hammer. Hyun poked her head out into the blazing heat of the desert city, a light breeze tugging gently at her loose clothes. Fen squeezed by Alekhai's side, squinting into the glare.

"Where to next?"

"We have to cross the city," Hyun said. "Don't worry, I know the paths no one walks. But . . . " She reached into her satchel and pulled out four burlap bags. "You'll need to put these on."

Sijara's face scrunched up. "You've got to be kidding me," she huffed, but she did as Hyun bade.

The sack Alekhai shoved over his head was so thick it obscured all light. He sucked in a breath through the rough fabric, struggling to draw in air.

"You and Oshyeva must be close," Fen muttered in his direction.

Alekhai laughed, and then a hand tugged him forward.

"Hold on to each other," Hyun ordered, and Alekhai reached out for a friend. He found Mettan's wrist.

Robbed of sight, he relied on his other senses as best he could. They were much duller than they were at peak health, but still much sharper than those of a regular human. When Hyun dragged them through buildings or shaded streets, he noted the slight changes in temperature. When they were dragged uphill or shoved downhill, he kept track of how long and in what order. Occasionally they'd run into another of Oshyeva's agents, and they'd trade a code word with Hyun. Alekhai committed them all to memory. By the time they reached Oshyeva's base, he had a rough map of Olivack and a list of verbal keys.

Or he would've, if Mettan hadn't interrupted his train of thought every ten steps to hiss out everyone's names, like a father abachen herding his hatchlings. Not that Alekhai minded it. Whenever the rebel was a second late, some awful part of Alekhai's brain feared that his companions had been carried off, even with the death grip they had on each other. He heard a pair of heavy doors grind open before them, and then, once they were shoved over the doorstep, slam shut behind them.

It was quiet within the chamber, mostly. The air was threaded with a current of danger, as if its calm lay on the very edge of a precipice. Fans whirred, globelamps whined, and sloshing cups clinked quietly together. Weapons clanked as they were stored or retrieved. Boots strode lightly over the uneven floor. Alekhai tried and failed to keep track of the new voices he picked up, but they blurred together as the four were forced over another threshold and down a curving corridor. With a screeching hiss, yet another door slid shut behind them. Hands shoved his shoulders down until he lowered his head. Without warning, the sack was ripped off.

"I could've done that myself," Alekhai grumbled, reluctantly letting go of Fen and Mettan.

A tall, wide, empty throne stood before them, behind which hung a faded desert fresco. Alekhai found this inexplicably hilarious. Had Oshyeva seen the art on the street and just decided to steal the entire wall?

Without warning, a section of plaster and stone to the right rolled open. A tall woman in an asymmetrical tunic strode through. She didn't spare a glance at the group, instead stalking over to the only window, a thin, jagged aperture carved into the rock. A pane of glassy material filled the hole; Alekhai guessed it was a one-way mirror. Oshyeva gazed out over the dusty stretch beyond, hands clasped behind her back.

"Do you know what my favorite animal is, prince?" Her voice was dangerously gentle.

"I'm guessing it's not humans," Alekhai said.

"There's a desert rodent called a leitha that digs an escape tunnel into its burrow," Oshyeva said, feet planted into a wide stance. "If a predator appears, the leitha just pops through that last bit of sand and flees to safety. You know what I love about that? The foresight. Which, it seems, you have none of." She whipped around, glaring down at Alekhai.

"Hello, Oshyeva," he said. "How've you been?"

Her gaze narrowed, flicking over the others before returning to him. "I told you the next time you showed your face in Olivack would be the last time you *had* a face."

"I thought you said she was an ally," Fen hissed.

"She is," Alekhai said, straightening. "I remember, Oshyeva. But I don't have a choice. I must fulfill my oath."

"Remind me, what happens if you don't?" she asked.

"I live in unending agony for the rest of my days," Alekhai said.

Not that he had many left, at this rate. Based on the dull ache in, oh, every cell of his body, he had about a few months before he reached critical organ failure. If he didn't get replacements soon, he wouldn't live long enough to either enjoy victory or mourn defeat.

"Well, as it happens, I am no longer, in fact, dead," Oshyeva said. "And I'm not going to let you kill me again just so you can revive me."

"Actually, we were thinking of raising you . . . literally," Fen cut in.

Oshyeva's gaze snapped to her again. And then she grinned, baring two bright rows of teeth. "And who exactly are you?"

Fen squared her shoulders. "My name is Fenyyang Mekantai. Daughter of Juma and Kagiso Mek—"

"Goodness, fine." Oshyeva rolled her eyes. "You're an orphan, and your poor papas were honorable rebels, born and raised in this city. Except they weren't honorable, nor were they true rebels."

Fen's jaw snapped shut. "I know," she said indignantly.

Oshyeva laughed as she stepped over to her throne. She stretched, reclining like a large lema over the stone. She swung a gloved hand out, gesturing at the four of them. "There's a good story about how you all came to be in each other's company. I want to hear it, along with the rest. I've received some *fascinating* reports from across the tribes. But first . . . "

She set a single finger over a wide black commandisk in the carved arm. Lights flashed down a braid of wires, disappearing into the web of multicolored cables hanging from the walls. For a moment, Alekhai half feared the floor would open from under them, sending them onto a forest of spikes.

But then a handful of people in colorful robes came in, carrying cushions and blankets. They were led by a man in tawdry glass jewelry, his ringed fingers gripping a tray stacked with handled bowls and small spoons. One of his compatriots shoved Alekhai down and stuffed a cushion under him. A woman placed a bowl in his hands before moving on to his companions.

He looked down at the flaky yellow powder within. "What's this?"

"It's shentalé."

She spun away without further elaboration, just before someone new poured hot water into their vessels. The powder dissolved into a thick, sweet-smelling drink.

Alekhai reminded himself that he was among allies and friends, not his family, and that no one here was going to poison him, before he took a long sip. And then he began to speak, his tale interspersed with frequent interjections from Fen and Mettan and Sijara. Oshyeva listened to it all, her expression supremely serene.

" . . . And so we spent two days in your fine city attempting to locate you." He set down his bowl. "I have to ask: Who resurrected you?"

"I had a backup plan," Oshyeva said, winking. "Or, shall I say, a backup Executor."

"And where are they now?" Mettan asked.

"Dead." Oshyeva's smile melted off her face like hot wax. Her eyes bored into Alekhai's. "They spent the last life they had to give on me, not that either of us knew it then. I must make the best of their sacrifice with who and what are available to me."

Sijara looked around at the leader's assembled agents. "Where did you find them all?"

"Most of them came to me, one way or the other. But many are old friends and warriors-in-arms who now assist my successor." Oshyeva grinned. "Mother knows how she got appointed in the first place. She cares too much for her people and too little for her own status."

"You're connected with the reigning leader, then?" asked Alekhai, trying not to think about another Executor dead without warning. Without any time to prepare or say goodbye.

"I'm her primary counselor," Oshyeva said proudly. She lifted her bowl and drank deep. "She makes no moves without my guidance. In this way, we've remained on your brother's narrow good side whilst best serving our people." She licked her lips. "But at the end of the day, I'd prefer him gone. It's clear his time's finally running out. What's the plan once you fulfill your vow to me?"

"I'm going to kill him," Alekhai said, standing. "But first, can I pick you up?"

Alekhai lifted Oshyeva up for a few seconds before letting her down. He didn't levitate, and his eyes didn't glow gold. But the moment Oshyeva's feet hit the floor, he let out a great sigh and rolled his neck as if a great weight had been lifted from his back—one far beyond the former Ataa leader's.

"I'm still wondering," Alekhai said, "who the other Executor was."

"You can keep wondering," said Oshyeva. "But know that they were precious to me."

"I'm sorry for your loss, then," he said. His boots shifted, a rare obvious sign of nerves from him. "May I ask how you found them?"

"It's not so hard, once you know what to look for," she said. "Where others leave dead in their wake, yours leave the living." She shook her head suddenly, as if throwing off a memory. "By the way, you should all stay the night." Before any of them could open their mouths, she added, "I won't take no for an answer. You're all frayed thin. Eat, sleep, be merry for a moment. You've done so much."

Oshyeva put together a feast for them in the audience chamber, which her people filled with battered low tables and nearly a hundred cushions. Cooks placed round copper trays on each table, piling them high with steaming dishes. There were two kinds of freshly baked insect-flour bread, noodles drenched in an oily crimson peppercorn sauce that made the mouth go numb, and sautéed coprins tossed with red and yellow root vegetables. (None of the four sampled the last dish.) For dessert—what a concept!—there were shallow bowls of tender rehydrated berries, afloat in a sea of sweet broth. Fen discovered that she loved sugar. Most people, she thought, liked sweets. She *loved* them. For the first time in her life, she ate until she was sick, and then spent the rest of the evening trying to keep it all down.

It was commoner fare, crafted from simple, everyday ingredients like the ones the rebels had subsisted on in Kanoh. But the quantity and variety of dishes was astounding. Even during the drought, Olivack was practically thriving with good leadership. It bolstered Fen's hope that the rest of Enkaiia could, too.

Eventually, the festivities started to overwhelm. The drunken laughter of people falling over themselves chased Fen up the staircase just outside the hall and toward her awaiting bed. The room Oshyeva had set aside for her was comfortably, if sparsely, appointed, with two deep, wide chairs and a colorful wall hanging. The small table at the center was a piece of art; its surface glittered with inlaid mosaics. The fragments were bits of shattered dishware and cracked marbles, but the humble materials made the finished piece all the more beautiful.

Just before she retired for the night, she sat on the sill of her window. With the gauzy curtains drawn tight, her borrowed chamber was sketched in shadow, but there was ample light to see by when she peeked out over the desert. Newearth's rings hung cool and grayish blue alongside the jewel-bright moons, layered like necklaces of alien silver. Below, rock arches rose and fell in waves.

Fen drew in a shuddering breath. She missed her parents, despite everything they'd done, and she wanted to go home, but there was no home to go back to. The desert blurred into a smear of dark gold and umber as tears coalesced over her eyes. She blinked them away and sucked in another gulp of air. She couldn't afford to waste water on crying. She dragged herself over to the bed and crawled under the covers, even as she heard the door quietly open and shut behind her. She knew his footsteps well by now.

There had been times, in Talishminn, when the simple act of getting out of bed had been impossible. Times when all Fen could do was lie on her back and look up at the ceiling, wondering how long it'd take to pass out if only she held her breath long enough. And that was exactly what she did now.

"What can I do?"

She let out a little laugh. She couldn't help it. "Everyone's told me how sorry they are my fathers are dead. You're the first person who's asked if they could do anything for me." The laughter slipped into a sob. "Then again, your family is the one that killed them."

She didn't know what Alekhai would say to that. But all he did, in the end, was curl up beside her and hum her to sleep. And in the morning, he was still there.

The time had come to fulfill the final part of their bargain with Alekhai. In the end, they simply knew what they'd ask of him—*who* they'd ask of him. There was a horrible irony in it, that they all agreed upon exactly whom to bring back. Fen had been expecting a heated argument, but there wasn't.

Sijara looked to Fen and Mettan and said, eyes downcast and gleaming with unshed tears, "Ruiha. The rebellion needs her, especially if Akrysanth beats us."

"And Ihazan," Mettan whispered.

Fen nodded numbly. "It would be cruel," she said slowly, "to separate Hahru and Naijima. We can't bring back one without the other."

They found Alekhai staring out the window of Fen's room, gazing at the same view she'd looked out on last night. But instead of cool grays and blues, the day had baked the desert into blazing gold. On the low table were four small, bloodstained pouches and four Senmavaris weapons from Oshyeva's armory. It was everything he'd need. Fen's stomach twisted as she looked at the glinting edge of the nearest sword.

"The Accusers envy us, you know," Alekhai said. "Our time is fleeting, and thus precious."

The comment caught them all off guard, jolting them from the net of misery that ensnared them.

"*Envy?*" Sijara scoffed. "They eviscerate us whenever we step out of line."

Fen had to agree—murderous discipline was the Accusers' very purpose, carved into them by their alien creators.

Alekhai shook his head. "They love us for the brief flashes of beauty in our lives. Diamonds are just rocks. And yet we drive ourselves mad over them, because they are rare." He turned around then. He looked impossibly sad. "Whom shall it be?"

☾

It took much longer this time, to build bones from nothingness and spin sinew from air. Slower than tar, Alekhai's ichor trickled back into the gaping wounds he'd made. Fen had turned away when he'd carved into his own flesh, and she could barely look at him now, knowing that soon he'd do it all over again.

Five hours later, Ruiha was sitting up from the table, gasping and trembling and more afraid than Fen had ever seen her. Fen half flung herself at their captain, dragging her into a bone-crushing embrace. Ruiha froze as Mettan and Sijara threw their arms around them both. She let out a broken, silent sob, and for a moment they just held each other.

Then Ruiha looked up at Alekhai, slumped silent and still in the far corner, and said, in her most stern voice, "Alekhai."

"Ruiha Khotol," he replied.

The rebel snorted. "I saw flashes of what you did for us, as I was coming back. Get over here."

The princeling's brows shot into his hairline. "That's not supposed to happen," he said, but then he joined them.

As they pulled apart, Ruiha said to Fen, "I'm sorry I refused to accept you, at first."

Fen swallowed hard. "I know. I understand."

Ruiha shook her head. "You don't. You have so much of your

fathers in you, Fen. I was worried Barra would show you preferential treatment and become distracted."

Fen stared at her, her hands balled so hard it hurt. *My fathers were traitors.* The words were on the tip of her tongue. It took everything in her not to glance at Alekhai.

"You were only looking out for your friend," she said instead.

"Yes." Ruiha let out a mirthless chuckle. "But how could I have considered turning you away? Your fathers died for Kira. In the end, I hoped that saving your life would in some way absolve Barra of his guilt. I think it did. But even if it hadn't, I am so, so glad you joined us."

Fen might've burst into tears right there, but then she felt Sijara throw an arm around her shoulders. She sank into the touch.

"My fathers—" She wasn't afraid of damaging their memory, but she realized how it could affect the rebellion, how it could reopen old wounds for Ruiha, who'd finally made peace with her friends' deaths. The truth wouldn't bring them back. "They died for what they believed in."

Ruiha gave a firm nod. Fen finally let herself look at Alekhai. He was already picking up the next weapon. Five hours after that, Ihazan took the first breath of their second life. They all wept. They all wept and clutched each other and shared their stories. Fen and Mettan brought up some food from the kitchens, and as they ate, they spoke of their pasts and the Broken Masks they'd never get back. They spoke of the future and the future of their world.

When they finished the last of their dinner, Alekhai stood.

"This is where we part ways," he said. His face was a smooth mask, but his voice was drawn tight as a garrote. "I'm going to say my goodbyes to Oshyeva, and then—"

Sijara nodded as if she hadn't heard the first bit. "And then we'll head out to Ivytra."

Alekhai's mouth thinned. "No. You're not coming with me."

"Oh," Mettan said sweetly, "that's not up for discussion."

"You need to look out for yourselves," said Alekhai.

Sijara smiled lopsidedly. "Is that a threat?" she teased.

"Please. I'm being serious."

"So are we. We started this journey together, we're finishing it together." Sijara glared at him. "Sit. Down."

Alekhai whirled around to Fen. "Talk some sense into your friends!"

She held his gaze. "I'm sorry," she said. "I can't help you."

Alekhai let out a ragged, irritated sound before drawing himself to his full height and taking a deep breath. "The rebellion needs all of you," he said. "If I fail and the Broken Masks wage war, they'll break the imperialists, but it will be brutal."

"He's right." Ihazan's mouth twisted. "The bloodshed would be unfathomable."

Fen went statue-still with rage. "So what do you want us to do? Crawl in a hole and wait it out while more people die?"

Alekhai reached out with a beseeching hand, but she ducked out of the way. He looked down at the table.

"My father understood that the quick slash of a knife often suffices. So did Kira. But the warriors of today can only imagine the blunt force of the hammer, so that's all they'll use. This empire must end, but it won't do so prettily."

"We know how important your mission is," Mettan snapped. "That's why we need to go with you."

Ruiha sighed. "I wish Ihazan and I could go as well, to fight by your side."

But the rebellion needed them, the captain especially. They'd hardly argued when Sijara had begged them to guide the Masks. Ruiha was a leader, through and through. She knew she had to go back.

Alekhai still hadn't given up. "Stay," he begged the others.

"There've been too many sightings of the three of us," Fen said. "We can't stay in the city and endanger Oshyeva."

Alekhai drew in a sharp breath. "And you can't force me to bring you. You're too valuable—"

Fen rolled her eyes. "Come now, we're not—"

"To me," Alekhai snapped. "You're too valuable *to me*. So no, I'm not going to let you get murdered by my brother. I promised Ying."

Out of the corner of her eye, Fen saw Ruiha flinch.

"And if we told *you* not to go?" said Mettan. "What if we told you we need you, too?"

"If that were true," Alekhai said slowly, "then I'd stay."

"Then we—"

"Don't." He looked down. "Don't say something you don't mean."

Sijara sucked in a gulp of air. And then she began to laugh, great, heaving peals of incredulity tearing themselves out of her.

"Eternal Mother, Alekhai," Fen snapped. "You're a fool if you think the pitiful woe-is-me sad-sack ploy still works on us."

Alekhai shrugged with something close to a smile. He sat down. "Well, I tried. But I will not permit—"

Sijara's wild laughter snapped. *"Permit?"* she echoed. "We weren't asking for your permission! Who do you think you are?"

"A life under the Sovereign is no life at all," Fen said softly. "Especially if we lose you and know we could've done something about it."

They stared at Alekhai. Alekhai stared back at them, his mask fracturing. There was a little tea left in the communal pot. Fen watched as Mettan poured Alekhai the last cup. As he handed it to the prince, Mettan trapped Alekhai's fingers between his own and the warm stoneware.

"Don't underestimate us," said Mettan quietly.

Alekhai tugged away and looked up at the ceiling. "You know," he said, "not caring about anyone is how I survived my family. I didn't shed a tear when Akrysanth killed Sona, because I knew her days were numbered since birth. I knew you can never save everyone." He drew in a long, shuddering breath. "But I know now that you still have to try."

Fen grabbed his hand and gave a gentle squeeze.

"If we all survive this," Alekhai said, "the rest of your squad will be returned to you. I'm sorry I can't promise more right now." He swallowed thickly and was silent. His next words were all but a whisper. "Thank you."

"You don't have to thank us." Fen leaned back on her cushion with a hard smile. She had her own promises to fulfill: to her lost friends, to herself.

"This fight has always been *ours*, Alekhai," Sijara said. "And we're going to end it for good—together."

☾

The only reasonable thing to do after that was get well and truly drunk.

Somehow, the liquor made Alekhai's first proposal more attractive, except Fen wanted them all to flee together. The urge to ask her friends to run away with her burned like the alcohol going down Fen's throat. At the end of the day, they were just one small part of the struggle. People were fighting the good fight in every corner of the empire. Someone else could try to avert the war. Others could do the hard work . . . But she knew that was exactly the sort of thinking that made the first rebellion's defeat linger as long as it did. They had to see this through. Nothing had changed, except for . . .

Everything.

They'd finally gotten Ruiha and Ihazan back. They had each other now, a whole world left to lose. Shame absorbed some of Fen's alcoholic haze.

"I can't believe you thought you were going to take on Akrysanth all by yourself," Sijara murmured, grinning blearily at the princeling. "Think of how lonely you'd be on the way there, to start."

"I'm alone without you three, not merely lonely." Alekhai sat back, arms loose at his sides like he didn't know what to do with them. "You don't understand," he said. "My brother is a monster."

Sijara lifted her eyes to the ceiling. "We know."

"No, he's . . . " Alekhai's hands tightened. "He's the one who massacred all those villages."

At first Fen thought it was just a bad joke. But when he wouldn't meet her eyes, she knew he was telling the truth. Horror slammed into her gut, sharp as an axe and heavy as a hammer.

Mettan's mouth opened and closed before words finally got through. "But you said there was no secret weapon. And the bandits—"

"Yes, they destroyed some of the settlements, but most of the initial slaughter was at my brother's command, and at the hands of an Accuser bound to our genetic line. *That* is what he's been wielding."

"Why didn't you tell us?" Fen choked out. Her vision was flickering at the edges.

"I'm sorry. I am so, so sorry."

White-hot anger, spiced with shame, burst within her chest. She was no better with secrets—she knew it, and yet. "*Why didn't you tell us?*"

"I had to lay the groundwork for a transition back to self-rule by the tribes," Alekhai said. "I had to resurrect my allies first."

"You didn't trust us," said Fen.

"Not at first," Alekhai whispered. "But even once I did, I never meant for you to follow me after your side of the bargain was fulfilled. Please, stay here. He'll kill you all."

Mettan's hands had formed fists. "Then I'll die knowing I fought for something better," he said.

"No, you'll die catatonic with pain in a torture chamber!" Alekhai shouted. "Akrysanth can keep his victims alive for weeks!"

Fen was touched by his outburst, so much that it hurt. "If your brother wields his Accuser like a weapon, all the more reason to face him together—"

Alekhai cut her off with a quick sweep of his arm. "No. *This* is why you need to hide. I cannot let you sacrifice yourselves." He looked them all in the eyes. "You're my only true friends." He said it softly, haltingly.

Fen stared at him. She'd been manipulated all her life, but never with pure earnestness.

"Don't look at me like that." Alekhai rubbed awkwardly at his arm. "We can go back to pretending we can't stand each other in the morning. It'll make parting easier."

"You're our friend, too," said Fen. "Our family. We're not letting you go alone."

"Obviously," added Sijara.

"Why do you look so shocked?" asked Mettan.

Alekhai just blinked at them. Fen could see the whole of his irises—gold circled by burning white.

"When we face Akrysanth, be safe," Fen said. "Swear this to me, all of you."

It was ridiculous, she knew. They were vastly outnumbered and unprepared. They could all die. They probably would.

"Only if you promise first," said Alekhai. His voice was spidersilk over steel.

Fen took one of Alekhai's hands in hers. He did the same with the other. She mirrored him as he set a kiss upon the inside of her wrist, an oath sealed. They turned to Mettan and Sijara and did the same, forging four links in the chain binding them together.

Ruiha and Ihazan, blearily observing the dramatics, shoved

their glasses to the side and started drinking straight from the bottle, but Sijara tugged them in.

"You too," she demanded, smiling. "Even if you're taking a different path, you have to swear like the rest of us."

Ruiha scoffed, but Fen thought she saw tears shining in the captain's eyes as she leaned in.

# 47

## ALEKHAI

Later, much later, Mettan found Alekhai in his borrowed room. The princeling was seated at the little central table, nursing a cup of tea.

"I've finally figured it out," Mettan said. "Sijara and Fen. They think we're . . ."

Alekhai tilted his head at him.

Mettan sputtered on: "I don't even know when they think we'd be—the four of us are always together."

"*They* manage," said Alekhai. "But also, they're joking." He paused, considering. "Does it bother you?"

"No. No, I don't think so."

Alekhai patted the cushion next to him, and Mettan sat. It did not escape Alekhai that the rebel's gaze fell almost immediately to the expanse of skin left exposed by his loosely tied robe, where two thin, barely visible lines curved over his chest like cupped hands—the only scars he'd kept from his youth. The only scars he'd ever wanted. He and Mettan had, of course, seen each other in various states of undress by then, but this felt different.

When Mettan's gaze slid back to Alekhai's, he turned anata-seed red. "I'm not—it's just that I wanted to see how you were healing. I'm not ogling you, I promise—Eternal Mother, I'm bad at this."

He really was. Alekhai smiled. "You're welcome to ogle me as much as you wish."

"I wasn't! I would never—"

"You know," said the princeling, "there was once a plan to style emperexes as gods, human manifestations of the Eternal Mother herself."

Mettan made a face. "I'm not going to worship you, Alekhai."

"Good. I don't want you to. What I want, Mettan, is to worship *you*. If you'd let me."

Mettan let out a slightly strained laugh. "What does that mean?"

"It means whatever you want it to mean." Alekhai smiled—or tried to. "Your heart is beating so fast. Is this too much?"

" . . . No, that line was very smooth. How long did it take you to come up with that?"

Alekhai pursed his lips with great gravity. "Only a few days."

"I'm still impressed."

"How impressed?" Alekhai touched a fingertip to the inside of Mettan's wrist, just under the edge of his sleeve. To where he'd pressed his lips earlier. And even inebriated as the princeling was, his touch was one of reverence.

"It depends," said Mettan. "Did you come up with that line just for me, or for general use?"

In a moment of startling lucidity, Alekhai stared up at him and said, "What do you think?"

"I think . . . " Mettan swallowed. "I think that I'll tell you when this is all over."

Alekhai made sure to maintain his attempted smile as Mettan

drew back and wobbled to his feet. "I await your answer with bated breath, then."

"Good night, Alekhai."

"Sleep well, Mettan."

And then he left Alekhai alone for the night, praying to all the gods he'd never believed in that his own heartbeat would slow.

## ALEKHAI

They said their farewells near Astawen, the remnant of yet another once-great city. A single wide road passed through the ruins, one end stretching toward Makhan, the other rolling back out through the Ata desert. Ruiha and Ihazan would find Ying waiting for them in the roving tent village of Meseria.

Standing beside his friends on a sand-scoured rock, Alekhai watched the captain and the young rebel beside her disappear into the dunes. As the winds swept away their footprints, and as he turned toward the capital and his brother, he was almost surprised to feel that he'd left something with them.

They moved quickly into Makhan. Once, long ago, this region had been covered in lush forest and creeping lagoon. But the botched terraforming had dragged the Ata desert over it all like a smothering blanket. And yet, for the first time in his life, Alekhai appreciated the beauty of his tribe's ancestral lands, even altered as they were. The yellow glare of the sun sank into the sands until they glowed. Even ruined, Newearth was lovely.

Fen joined Alekhai as he prepared food for the group each evening. In retrospect, it was shocking that the rebels had ever let him do it when they'd first started out; the opportunities to poison them had been endless, which had yet to occur to anyone but him. He imagined that, as with him, caring for others had been a foreign concept to Fen for most of her life. She'd protected others, but against her will. And now she laughed and hummed and—when she thought no one was looking—smiled softly at their companions as she rehydrated packets of stew and rice.

That night, Fen roasted the sand beetles Mettan had collected over the campfire, ground them into a rough powder with a precious pinch of stolen spices, and sprinkled them over their dinner as a delectably crunchy garnish. They huddled in around the flames as the sun began to set and tucked in with gusto.

"So," Sijara began, spooning stew over her rice, "what's new in the bag?"

"I have no idea what you're talking about," lied Alekhai, who was a liar.

Mettan gave him a kind, patient look. "What are you possibly going to do with all the shit you're hoarding?"

"They're keepsakes," Alekhai said. "To remember this journey by." The teasing smirks evaporated. Mettan's mouth opened and closed without a sound. Alekhai groaned. They were all so Motherdamn *annoying*. "I despise you all."

"Still haven't answered my question," Sijara said, her eyes soft.

Alekhai dragged over his satchel and pulled out the day's finds. Fen's gaze latched onto the board in his hands. The realwood base was splintering apart, and the painted tiles were faded almost to gray, but recognition dawned in her eyes immediately.

"Mefabo?" she asked. "I haven't played in years."

Alekhai gave her a long, considering look. A bright new thread wove through the plan that had been stitching itself together in his head over the last week. "Then we should go a round or two, while we still have a little daylight. Half the pieces are missing, but we'll make do."

Fen looked hesitant.

Alekhai summoned up his best shit-eating grin, alongside a glowing page of rules from his omnichip. "Shall I refresh your memory?"

She narrowed her eyes. "I remember well enough." She sat opposite Alekhai, shifting on the sand until she got comfortable. "Ready?"

They played as night trickled down around them. Alekhai lost the first round and demanded a rematch.

Fen couldn't hide her smirk. "So eager to taste defeat again, are you?"

"That's not—" Alekhai cut himself off and set to work resetting the board. "I won't lose twice."

"You won't get the chance to," Sijara cut in. "Move over, princeling, I want to play the winner."

One more day.

One more day until all his plans finally came to fruition. Until he could leave the world in better hands than his family's.

One more day until the end. Well, *an* end.

As dusk stained the rings, Alekhai found Fen perched on a rock, looking out over the chapparal ahead. In the far distance, the familiar gold-brown grasses of the steppe unfurled along the horizon.

"It feels so strange to be back."

Alekhai clambered up and sat down beside her. "It hasn't been that long," he said quietly.

"Feels like it has." Fen leaned into him, dropping her temple to his shoulder.

He let his head fall atop hers. When his gaze fell to her lap, he saw that she hadn't been looking at the grassland at all, but a shimmering holoimage of her parents from her omnichip.

"I'm sorry, Fen," he whispered.

"You said that already." Her voice was steady when she spoke, but he saw a tear fall through Juma's flickering chest and roll down into her palm.

"Still."

Mettan and Sijara joined them moments later. And together, they watched Newearth's stars blink to life, one by one, in the sky above.

Fen closed the holoimage and uncurled her fingers, revealing the tiny green jar sitting at the center of her palm.

Mettan let out a small gasp when he saw.

She twisted the jar open. "Please."

The white river was meant to be drawn by family on one's face when a young Ataa person came of age, at the very end of their declaration ceremony. Without a word, Mettan dipped a finger into the jar and drew it gently over one cheek. Sijara painted across the other. Finally, Alekhai drew close, connecting the two lines over the bridge of her nose.

Fen had come of age years ago. She didn't know what it meant to get her markings so late. All she knew was that her family was giving them to her now.

And really, nothing else mattered.

After so long traveling together, they'd gotten dismantling their camp down to a science. Typically, they packed up and set out on autopilot, silently going about their agreed-upon tasks. But today they took their time taking everything apart. This would be the last camp they'd break down for a long while, if everything went well. The last camp they'd ever make, if things went badly. They talked and joked and teased as they worked, but there was a tense undercurrent threading through it all. They were stalling and they all knew it.

But no amount of delay could shield them from the impending last stretch of their journey. They came across a village soon enough. Under the cover of night, Alekhai led them to a thatched hut. He knocked on the door thrice, and the slab of realwood swung open so fast it nearly bashed Mettan in the face. In the shadows within stood a woman with smile lines so deep they looked carved into her. She was not smiling now.

"When a king's palace burns down . . . " she began.

"The rebuilt one outshines the old," Alekhai said.

"Fine, then," said the woman. Her gaze slid to the others.

Alekhai gestured to the rest of the group, something tender in his eyes. "My friends," he said, and offered no more.

The woman grunted. "Lady Fox," she said, by way of greeting. She did not bow, nor did she extend a hand to shake. She did, however, jerk her thumb at the covered hovercart parked at the side of the hut. "Let's get this over with."

A sudden lurch jolted Fen awake. She sat up and rubbed the sleep from her eyes, jerking as the cart hit another rut in the pockmarked road. A glazed stoneware vessel knocked her knee, its carved face grinning up at her vindictively. The vase was fashioned from nearly translucent porcelain, decorated with incredible care. Fen considered kicking it out onto the road, despite the attention doing so would call. Rubbing her leg, she slumped back down onto the hard wooden floor. She met the eyes of her friends as the cart lurched again and began to move, rattling a box of slip-painted tea jars. They were on a flat, smooth path now, the imperial road slashing through the Makhanish woodland.

Only a few hours later, Alekhai mouthed, *We're here.*

Fen's heart gave a hard kick of anxiety.

Ivytra.

The capital of the empire. Fen peered through a crack in the cart's side, squinting against the glare. Under the evening sun, the yellow-glazed tiles crowning each curled roof gleamed so brightly she was nearly blinded. The cart carried them past the gates and into the congested heart of the famed gilded city.

Ivytra was home to an endless, brilliant array of new sights and new sounds and new scents. It was too much. The city was massive, perhaps two hundred times larger than Talishminn. Packed lines of houses, shops, and inns were laid out across the land in a grid, clutching the dirt and stone beneath like a second skin. The aroma of roasted insects and fried roots filled the air, mingling with the stench of sweat and refuse. Thousands of ribbons danced in the pungent breeze, and Fen could only just make out columns of characters extolling the virtues of the imperial family.

And then, of course, their ultimate destination: the palace. A city all on its own. Its magnificent walls concealed it entirely, save for its glittering rooftops, each sporting a set of intricately carved sphinx figurines. The back of the cart swung open, and Lady Fox's lined face appeared in the shadow of the vehicle.

"This is as far as I can take you," she murmured. She pulled a vase into her arms and turned away.

They slipped out from the cart and landed on stone tiles behind a worn market stall. Fen's legs nearly gave out from under her, weak and aching after being folded up for hours.

Mettan moved to help Lady Fox unload her wares, but she waved him away sharply.

"Don't you have better things to do, boy?" she snapped. And then, with a sharp smile, "Good luck, all of you."

As Alekhai led them down a dizzying sequence of streets, they recounted everything they'd observed on the way in: heightened Senmavaris numbers, overflowing housing, and—for all the overwhelming sights and smells—less food and wealth than the capital had ever had.

Finally, they came to a dead end. In one shadowed corner, beside a single withered potted plant, sat a large unsuspecting white tile. It was unadorned, save for the tiny claw carved into one corner. Alekhai knelt and worked his dagger underneath the ceramic square. Crawling back, he hefted it aside, revealing a staircase spiraling far below.

"Are you sure Akrysanth doesn't know about this?" Mettan whispered.

He'd asked before, but Alekhai nodded. "I'm certain. My father wanted us all trapped in the palace, so he destroyed records of any escape routes. I came across this only by chance, and my brother never bothered to explore far beyond his rooms."

Sijara stepped in first, activating the light feature of her omnichip, followed by Mettan. Fen stopped the princeling just before he went in.

"Alekhai," she whispered, reaching out and taking hold of his shoulder. "If something happens, if this goes wrong . . . " She pressed her lips together. There was so much she wanted to say. "If something happens to me—"

"It won't. I won't allow it. Enkaiia needs you."

Fen lifted her eyes upward. "Princeling."

"I know. I'll take care of them." Alekhai let out a breath. "Let's go."

They darted into the shaft without further words. The stairs dropped them into a series of tunnels that wound beneath the city complex. Darkness filled the space like oil, broken only by the burning blue-white glow of their omnichips. The globelanterns on the rough-cut walls hadn't worked for months if not years; a thick film of dust had settled over their dull shells.

As Fen crossed the age-old tiles lining the tunnels, her friends silently at her side, she braced herself for soldiers leaping from the shadows, for the cracked walls to crumble and crush them. Nothing happened—Alekhai had already hacked the palace's security to accept their presence—but still the sickly sweet tang of fear filled her mouth. It remained even as she followed Alekhai up a set of smooth steps.

She could die tonight, but dying was easy. The world had shown her living was not. Her real fear was what would happen if Akrysanth simply cut them all down and crushed the rebellion. The thought that everything they'd done might be for nothing sat on her chest like some horrible creature, shoving her wrists down and grinning into her face.

But Fen had faced monsters before, and she'd won.

Alekhai reached up and pushed aside a slab of rock. And then they emerged into another world.

They stood on a mossy mound in the middle of a vast lake. Fen spun a full circle, scanning the blue-roofed pavilions and blushing flower gardens at her sides. Enormous braziers stood in solemn formation over gleaming marble steps, splashing warm golden light over the still water of the lake. A perfect reflection of the palace gazed serenely back up at her, framed by a ring of trees bowed in obeisance. Pink blossoms spiraled through the air, weightless.

Rage scorched away half of Fen's fear. She couldn't begin to imagine how much water was required to maintain this paradise. Official reports declared the ocean desalination efforts too exorbitant to expand; the freshwater plants produced just enough to keep the empire alive—or somewhat alive. People were dying of thirst not two weeks' travel from here, and the royal family had *this*.

With scarcely a splash, they stepped in. They cut through the dark water, sending ripples through the reflected palace so that the lake resembled a bolt of embroidered spidersilk, crumpled by a careless hand. They clambered over the opposite bank, ducking low when a line of the emperor's honor guard marched by.

It was said their armor had been a gift from the Accusers, though that was obviously a lie. Still, the gliding metal, shifting like fabric with their movements, was magnificent. Their breastplates and greaves shone like the sun itself, but their shields and helmets were another thing entirely. The guards carried upside-down teardrops of bronze, tin, and gold, the surfaces hammered into delicate depictions Fen could make out even from this distance: the night sky, whole cities and fields, feasts and festivals, bloody war and pleasant peace—all of human life beneath the stars. The shimmering helmets atop their heads were each adorned with stiff silver stripes of realhair, plucked from an atrox's mane.

Alekhai gave a sharp wave of his hand after they passed, and then scrambled up the bank, leading them into the protection of a half-open hallway. He rounded a corner and stepped through an unadorned red door. Up ahead, a servants' path snaked behind a line of verdant potted shrubbery, twisting and turning around the marble halls of the inner court.

The inner palace reclined atop a lattice of gilded realwood, connected by a mazelike web of roofed walkways. Luckily, they had a resident on hand to guide them. Still, Fen etched entrances and exits into her mind as they went, memorizing and tucking away possible escape routes as best she could.

In single file, they clambered up a low wall and onto a roof, melting into the swelling darkness of the approaching night. They dashed over covered passages, the sounds of laughter and clinking dishes rising, until they came to a vast sunken courtyard, so richly appointed it made Redya's look like a garden pit. According to Alekhai, if Akrysanth followed the traditional schedule, he'd be taking his supper now. All they had to do was sit and wait for him to leave, and then they'd corner him on his way back to his chambers.

Fen couldn't help but stare at it all as they peered over the roof's crest. She'd never seen such food—or so much food—in her entire life. There was a small army of soups, dumplings both pan fried and steamed, fresh berries, round spice cakes, candied nuts, and buns adorned with scarlet pepper flakes. Realfish and realmeat poached in sweet-smelling sauces, slathered in mashed vegetables and aromatics. Translucent noodles spun with paper-thin root slices. Elaborately sculpted pies, savory and sweet, glazed in real-egg yolk and dressed in gold foil. Shallow dishes of rare candied insects glistening with spiced syrup. Bowls of black grain pudding, swirled with cream and glittering with slivers of fruit. All of it so natural it was unnatural, alien. And that wasn't all. The dishes and cutlery alone would've sustained Talishminn for a year: plates of beaten silver, knives sporting miniature sapphire sphinxes, cloisonné dishes glinting with ivory and pearls. Fen spotted a wine jug fashioned to look like an Oldearth lion, complete with enamel fur and a fearsome maw for a spout.

The dishes were placed on samite-smothered tables one at a time by silent servants. There were dark half-moons under all their eyes, and many moved as if injured. What Fen didn't see, however, was the Sovereign. His seat at the place of highest honor, when she finally found it, was empty.

"He's not here," Alekhai muttered, as if it were sacrilege for the emperor to skip dinner.

"Well, where is he?" Sijara hissed back.

"The only other places I can think of are the throne room and the south tower—his private hall," Alekhai said. "Former's more likely."

Sijara's smile was almost genuine. "Then what are we waiting for?"

Alekhai scampered along the cobalt tiles, slipped down a wall of painted clay, and crept back toward the servants' exit. The others followed, weaving through agate-crowned columns.

The pylons framing the throne room's entrance towered over them as they crossed under. The massive blocks sported fine carvings: age-old rulers dominated the limestone, racing chariots and clubbing foes' heads in. Dead tyrants watched the rebels as Alekhai commanded open the doors with his omnichip.

The chamber itself was a simple one. Up ahead, atop opalescent steps, a throne stood tall like a sentinel. And on the throne sat a figure in purest green.

Kharakh.

Fen froze, pulse skittering. "How?" she gasped.

"Easily." Kira Moru's son smiled down at Fen. "You were right about one thing, Mekantai. Your prince's allies are useful indeed. Of the countless numbers that serve this city, Chinonso, Oshyeva, and Hetarian recruited thousands to the rebellion. The new Masks snuck in their fellow rebels over the past few days. Just enough to try cutting off the head of this wretched empire. Ruiha and Ihazan's plan, by the way. They managed to convince the Sworn to hold off the war."

"Why weren't we told?" Sijara demanded.

"Because your captain's messages to you were blocked," Kharakh replied. His gaze flicked to Alekhai. "Both the Sworn and I know *he* will never cleanse Enkaiia."

"What does that mean?" Mettan asked.

"Those who served the Sovereigns must die, along with their kin." Kharakh rose from the throne in a single smooth motion. "As we speak, my soldiers are headed for the imperial apartments. They will bring the emperor to me. I will hack off his head, and then I will do the same to every aristocrat in this city. I was ordered to kill you all, but I have no wish to harm my fellow rebels. As a last and final favor, I will permit you three to leave. But the prince must stay behind."

"We're not going anywhere without him," Fen said lowly.

"I'm happy to pay for my family's crimes," Alekhai said, ignoring Fen's outraged glare, "but I won't let you massacre half the empire to end it."

Kharakh's grin evaporated. He drew his sword and laid it over one shoulder. "Go now," he said, "before I do something we'll all regret. In minutes, the palace will be soaked in blood."

Sijara drew her own blade. "And as she said, we're not leaving Alekhai."

Kharakh sighed. "Fine, have it your way."

Ten shadowed figures swept in from behind carved columns, flanking the bandit lord.

"We don't want to fight you!" Fen shouted. "You're not our enemy!"

"Forgive me." Kharakh dashed down the steps, followed closely by his guards. "I did warn you."

The two sides crashed into each other, waves blown by opposing winds.

The first warrior to attack Fen swung too wide. Her quick responding jab landed, quarterstaff sinking into a kidney. The man doubled over in pain but still managed to lash out. Fen hissed as a blade slashed across her shoulder, nipping at her skin. She spun and struck him in the head.

At the corner of her vision, Fen saw Sijara slip as Kharakh unsheathed a needlelike blade. The dagger swung upward and into her arm. She cried out, and somehow, that hurt worse than Fen's own oozing wound.

Rage and fear swept through her. "Sijara!"

She would not, *could* not let her family be taken from her again. She'd tear out the bandit-rebels' throats first.

But before she could reach her friend, boots thudded across the polished marble toward her. She swept the warrior's legs right out from under them and knocked them on their back. She stomped on the hand still holding a sword. But they were replaced just as quickly—the edge of an axe flew past Fen's face, nearly scraping the bare skin of her throat. She flung herself away, but then the rebel's hand swung up from below and connected with her jaw.

The blow sent her careening backward, agony blooming up from her chin. Ignoring the pain, Fen swung at him, but he spun away from her quarterstaff. He slashed at her again and again and again, but she evaded each blow. He switched tactics, spinning and swinging at her sides. She yanked herself back, guided by desperate reflex alone. The warrior's leg flew up to knock her down, but she dodged and returned the strike. But the man slipped out of range at the last second, and her quarterstaff struck only the surface layer of skin.

As he wheeled away, Fen glimpsed Alekhai crossing blades with Kharakh just before he could strike Sijara again. The bandit lord lashed out savagely, forcing Alekhai to the ground. But the princeling speedily flipped back to his feet, and Kharakh's sword thudded into the wood where his head had been a mere moment ago.

Then Fen's opponent was on her again. Lunging forward, he sidestepped her swing and hooked the edge of his axe around her weapon. He twisted, but Fen held on tightly, and when he jerked the axe back, both weapons went flying.

*Fuck.*

Without pause, the warrior advanced with a volley of striking fists and feet, forcing her to take the defensive. She parried as many of the blows as she could, but he was no mere brigand; he was more weapon than man. Barely managing to block a barrage of punches, she shoved the heel of her hand into his throat. Wheezing, the warrior wrenched himself aside as she struck again, but this time he was too slow. She made a fist with one hand, middle finger braced against her thumb so that the knuckle jutted out, and drove it into the center of his chest. She felt a sick snap as the tip of his sternum broke.

The warrior stumbled back, eyes wide. She'd struck true—the bone fragment had punctured a lung. Wasting no time, Fen dove for her quarterstaff and struck up toward his skull. But not before he kicked out, heel sinking into her knee. She screamed.

And with that cry rose others. Not her friends'. No, the screams were coming from beyond the throne room, torn from the throats of armies. She heard the screech of stun bolts through the air. The crunch of rock against bone. And then—

"*Stop.*" Kharakh. His command cut through the tumult.

In that second, everything ground to a halt. Fen spun, despite the pain tearing up and down her leg.

Kharakh was on his knees before Sijara and Alekhai, one sword at his neck and another at his heart. Mettan stood facing the last of Kharakh's guards. The others were all incapacitated or unconscious.

"Lay down your weapon," Kharakh barked, and with a savage curse, the last of his warriors threw down her sai.

"What do we do with them?" Mettan asked. His eyes never left the fighter before him. "Kill them?"

"I have a better idea," Fen said. She limped over to Kharakh, grip tightening around her quarterstaff. "A last and final favor," she said, and then she hit him across the head.

He crumpled. The last bandit's jaw flew open, perhaps in a roar of anger, but she scrambled back when Mettan lifted his sword. Hands raised, she crossed the room to join her leader.

Fen took a step—and then nearly bit through her tongue as her knee gave out. Alekhai caught her just before she fell and gently lowered her to the floor. Mettan knelt beside her, prodding gently at the injured leg.

"Your knee is dislocated," he said, brow furrowed. "We'll have to pop it back in."

"I'll do it," Sijara said grimly, dropping down next to Alekhai. "Ying showed me how."

Fen gritted her teeth. "How much is it going to hurt?"

"Less than it did going out," said Sijara. She placed both hands on either side of Fen's leg. "On three."

Fen counted with her. "One, two—"

Sijara shoved the knee back into its socket with a nauseating crunch.

"You said three!" Fen screeched.

Sijara's lips formed a weak smile. "It hurts less when you don't expect it."

Alekhai leaned forward and tucked a stray curl behind Fen's ear. The touch was so careful it hurt. "Can you keep going?"

Fen smacked his hand away and forced a grin. She wobbled to her feet. "Of course I can. Where to now? The tower?"

Alekhai dragged in a ragged mouthful of air. He clearly didn't believe her, but when he let the breath out again, he merely nodded. "The tower."

They stepped into a maelstrom of clashing swords and scythes and spears. Fallen soldiers littered the cobblestones; blood pooled over glazed tile. Senmavari packed together against an unyielding tide of Kharakh's bandit-rebels. Those who attempted to escape the frenzy of steel and crackling stun bolts screamed as vats of burning oil were tipped over them.

The imperialists were being slaughtered. They outnumbered the rebels, but Kharakh had been prepared, thanks to the Masks and Alekhai's allies. Fen saw rebels in sharp green uniforms fighting alongside brigand warriors. Akrysanth's Accuser was nowhere to be seen—no strange shimmer swam across the battlefield, no bodies were flung up into the air and hacked apart by unseen blades. The Makers, it seemed, had truly forsaken the Sovereign.

The group dodged axe blows and stinger fire as they scrambled toward the south tower. Panting, Fen followed her friends up the low-hanging branches of an age-old tree and onto a wall. She let herself tumble over and only just managed to land on her feet without breaking them. She scanned the path ahead for immediate danger and, finding none, let herself regain her breath for a moment.

"We need to keep moving," rasped Alekhai, out of breath for the first time Fen had noticed. "The others will find their way here soon enough."

And neither the Senmavari nor the Broken Masks would spare them.

Fen let out a faint string of profanity, but when Alekhai took off, she pushed herself up and raced beside him. At last, they came to a pair of towering blue doors, each studded with eighty-one hemispheres of solid gold and sporting a pair of sphinx-shaped knockers. They dashed up the lapis lazuli steps and into the tower, slipping past the six carved sphinxes guarding the doors.

The household hall of the emperor possessed seven stories. There were no lifts, so they took the stairs. Each floor of the keep was decorated with a different set of flora and fauna, powerful mortals, Oldearth gods, shifting Accusers, and—of course—Makers. Clear changes had been made to the imperial apartments. Sections of the tower had been stripped bare, the darkness broken only by the rare globelantern. Where the rest of the palace was a riot of gold and blue, the corridors stretching before them were all dark shades and clean lines.

They stormed the bedchamber, weapons drawn. Fen's eyes plundered the silent room. Gem-scaled animals frolicked through the cobalt tiles of a flower-pond mosaic. The gleaming wood of lacquered furniture reflected untold lights, casting a warm golden glow that only made the twisting feeling in her gut swell. Nothing was hidden. Gone were the painted alien saviors of their ancestors. Here there was only the Sovereign. And an utter, swallowing silence.

Something crashed behind Fen. She whipped around, quarterstaff gripped in both hands.

Akrysanth.

For a long moment, he merely regarded the group.

He looked like he'd been readying himself for bed. His shoulders carried a rich purple robe, dyed with the prized secretions of rare sea snails, but beneath that and the herringbone chains circling his neck, he wore a spidersilk shift. He was as pale as Chinonso, but his hair was gold, and his eyes were a green as bright as faceted peridots.

Fen hadn't known what to expect. She'd anticipated beauty—and he *was* beautiful, nearly Alekhai's equal despite all the differences between them. Besides that, perhaps some indication of cruelty, of loathing. Perhaps even the dull apathy Alekhai had once worked so hard to perform. But Akrysanth merely looked tired. Sorrowful, even, like a child watching the curtains close on his favorite play. Still, there was something under it that was not quite right.

Barefoot, the Sovereign stepped through the shards of the porcelain bowl he'd just dropped. Wine spread across the polished floors, dark as blood.

"Spare me," he whispered. His too-fine features were as frozen as the golden faces mounted on the wall behind him, the ceremonial masks of past Makhanish kings. Beneath them hung an array of age-old weapons: scimitars and spears and swords polished to a mirror shine. "Spare me and I'll go. I'll never come back, I'll never breathe a word—"

"*You,*" Sijara growled. "You have lain here among your riches, well-fed and draped in finery, as your people starved. Then there's your Accuser, the *slaughter*. How dare you ask for mercy now?"

Fen's gaze darted about the chamber. Where were his guards?

Akrysanth lifted his hands placatingly, but there was a sharpness in his eyes. "The drought can be addressed only with the tribes unified. What have *you* and your saintly Broken Masks done, besides pillage my cities and incite my people to violence? Those villagers were destined for death anyway."

Fen took one painful, angry step forward. "Pillage? The Masks *liberated* those cities; their people welcomed the rebels with open arms. And who are you to decide who should live?"

"Please," Akrysanth snapped, fear sloughing away as the charade dropped entirely. "Liberated? Those people will have even less now than they did before, since you fools decided to break open my stores and gorge yourselves for a day, rather than save it for the coming years. My way is kinder, cleaner than mass starvation. I'm told it happens so swiftly, the victims feel nothing."

"Of course their deaths mean little to you," Mettan snarled, "when the only commoners you see are your servants. When you and your court feast day and night."

Akrysanth spread his arms wide. "Did you see me gorging with the ungrateful creatures I call my nobles? If I don't keep them well-fed, as you put it, slow starvation will be the least of our worries. A civil war amongst aristocrats would make Moru's uprising look like a schoolyard brawl."

Fen exchanged a glance with her friends, a thorn of hesitation digging beneath her skin. She'd never truly thought of Akrysanth as a real king before now, only as a cruel boy with too much power in his hands. But in this moment, she realized she'd been fighting a Sovereign willing to sacrifice everything, including his family, to preserve the empire. If only his sacrifice hadn't included his own people. If only there had been no empire at all.

"I have no hope of convincing you, do I?" Akrysanth's robe flowed like water as he moved behind a gilded desk. "You came here to kill me, after all, and you've already doomed Enkaiia. Did you even think about the consequences of removing me? The anarchy that would follow? I suppose my dear brother has some clever scheme. Do you know what it is?"

Mettan raised his sword. "Yes."

"Do you? Really." Akrysanth shook his head. "Let me tell you something. This world has only two kinds of people: the aggressors—"

"And let me guess," Sijara drawled, "the victims."

The Sovereign's gaze grew distant. "I saw our father laugh when Sona pushed Alekhai into the fire. She was always his favorite. I confronted him. And do you know what he did to me?"

"Of course not," Sijara snapped.

"Of course not," he echoed. "But you've been traveling with my brother for some time, so you can imagine. The servants had to scrape me from the floor. And while my spine was regenerating and the physicians were growing me a new set of hands, I came to a decision: One day soon, no one would ever be able to hurt me ever again."

Fen drew in a deep breath. The man before her had suffered greatly, but then he'd gone and passed on that pain a thousandfold. "Where are your guards?" she demanded.

"Fenyyang Mekantai." The emperor smiled at her. "It's an honor to finally make your acquaintance. Well, properly this time. I knew your fathers. They were good men. Wise, careful—"

"*Silence*," she said.

He went on, almost apologetically: "I would've traded my family for yours in half a heartbeat. Their only mistake was overstepping one time too many. I am truly sorry, but I couldn't keep my father's lackeys around."

Fen's vision flashed red. "*Where. Are. Your. Guards?*"

The Sovereign laughed. "Right behind you."

A cold chill ran its fingers over Fen's skin as a sharp click sounded. She spun just in time to see the back walls of the chamber slide up and away, revealing two shimmering rows of honor guards.

"It took you all long enough to get here," Akrysanth drawled. "Don't worry, I'll try to give you clean deaths, despite the wait."

When Fen turned around again, her back pressed to Mettan's, she saw it.

The guards' armor gleamed unnaturally in the light. But the gilded enemy didn't shine half as brightly as the Accuser that now loomed over the Sovereign, glittering tendrils shrinking and unfurling and shrinking again around him. Meanwhile, the emperor leaned a hip against his desk, running a fingertip over the taut string of a nearby duruqin. Iridescent pieces of mother-of-pearl inlay danced over the instrument's dark wooden belly. When he looked up at them, there was a keen, gloating savagery in his eyes.

"Kill them."

After a moment, the imperial Accuser replied, in a voice that made the walls tremble, "I THINK NOT."

Akrysanth's left eye twitched. He didn't, however, look surprised; the Accuser, as Fen had suspected, must've already refused to eviscerate the rebels now making a ruin of his palace.

"WE HAVE NEVER INTERFERED IN YOUR FAMILY'S SQUABBLES," said the Accuser. "WE HAVE NEVER INVOLVED OURSELVES IN YOUR LITTLE WARS. WE PUT YOUR SUBJECTS OUT OF THEIR MISERY ONLY BECAUSE WE WERE ASSURED IT WAS THE ONLY WAY." It shifted, and suddenly Fen felt Its burning attention on her and her friends. "WHY SHOULD I LET YOU TRY TO KILL YOUR KING?"

"*Why?* He's killing us!" Fen threw out her hands, beseeching. "He's destroying this planet. And every second you stand back and watch him, so are you. It's this or a war that might end us all."

The Accuser rose into the air, tendrils flexing, and . . . did nothing. "YOU MAY ENGAGE HIM IN COMBAT."

Akrysanth rolled his shoulders, shrugging off the construct's blunt refusal to obey him with regal grace. "Fine," he said. "We'll do this the hard way." He flicked a hand at the rebels. "Try not to kill them all. I'd like to take at least one prisoner."

Fen and Mettan and Sijara and Alekhai. They moved around each other like currents in water, twisting and turning as they switched opponents. When a guard slashed at Sijara's throat, she leaned back, and the blade whistled just over her face. Mettan lunged. His sword slid against the guard's and into his neck. A spray of blood stained Fen's tunic.

Guards replaced the ones they'd cut down just as swiftly,

yanking free their stingers. All in one breath, Alekhai knocked the weapon from one woman's grip, snatched it from the air, and fired in rapid succession. A guard ducked below the slash of Fen's quarterstaff, only to face Sijara's blade. Their head went flying a moment later. When Mettan's next blow went wide, Fen ducked in and struck the soldier square in the chest. The rebels looked around the chamber as the next line advanced.

They were completely surrounded, the exits all blocked off. They were carving through Akrysanth's forces, but they couldn't fight forever. Two spear-wielding guards managed to separate the four, and then they were on their own, facing four soldiers each.

With a grunt, one guard swung a silver-plated energy axe at Fen's face. She leapt back, narrowly missing the brazier behind her. Something glinted at the corner of her vision. Fen spun, and her quarterstaff ground to a halt against a short sword. The second guard leaned in, so close Fen could smell the tang of fine soap and sweat.

She saw Mettan go flying back at her right, losing his sword as he struck the ground hard. A hammer-wielding guard pounced at him. Fen cried out his name, barely managing to beat her own opponents back. But before the next blow could land, Mettan rolled. The hammer smashed into polished tile. He flung out his arm and found the hilt of his sword. He kicked back upward and rushed forward, unleashing a quick series of strikes. The guard crashed to their knees, blood drenching their tunic.

Fen tried to reach her friends, hoping against hope that they could squeeze into formation again—then stumbled back when a hulking guard materialized before her.

His mace struck her quarterstaff so hard it ripped through her fingers. She flung herself around the nearest column when he swung at her again. The blunt weapon slammed into the pillar, splintering the gilded realwood. When she forced her head upward, dragging in a breath, she was confronted with her reflection, trapped within the polished gold panels of the ceiling. Time seemed to slow as she met her own eyes.

The woman, the warrior.

The war had killed her: That was the cold, sharp truth of it. She squeezed her eyes shut for half a second, the sounds of battle melting away. When she opened them again, they landed on the imperial weapons hanging beneath the golden masks.

Her breath caught in her throat.

She was Fenyyang Mekantai. The last of her traitorous bloodline. And if today was her day to die, then she would die a rebel.

She whirled around the pillar, throwing herself back into the fray. The guard's eyes went wide. Fen dodged two strikes from the mace and snatched an ancient sword from the wall. But she was not quite fast enough to fully avoid the third blow as she faced him.

Everyone heard the low snap of two ribs breaking. But only Fen felt it—her mouth flew open in a silent scream ripped from her lungs. Stars scattered over her vision. Everything was agony; her whole body felt like it was being torn asunder. But the pain, in the end, sharpened her focus. She would not let the emperor take her friends, not so near the end. Not only for her own sake now, but for the tribes'.

Fen twisted, shoving the sword beneath the guard's chin. Blood gushed down the length of the blade. She slumped against a column and pressed a hand to her abdomen, wheezing hard through clenched teeth as she surveyed the chamber. There were only two guards left.

With a short, bitten-off swear, Akrysanth shoved between his sworn protectors. He pulled a sword from the wall, a perfect match to Fen's.

"Enough!" he yelled to the pair of guards. "Go to your families. I'll finish this myself." The sword flashed as he gave it a few experimental swings.

Alekhai smiled. "Come on, then."

Akrysanth lifted the sword and charged. Alekhai raised his own blade and swung. They both moved preternaturally fast, each lightning-quick movement perfect and precise. Finally, the self-proclaimed heirs of Oldearth were facing equals. For every strike there was a parry. For every parry there was a riposte. Akrysanth countered each of Alekhai's attacks with a strength and speed that amazed and terrified Fen. And every slash of Alekhai's blade was increasingly brutal.

"You've gotten better," said the emperor, lips stretched into a too-wide grin.

Alekhai hacked at him. "And you've gotten worse."

"Still think you're clever?" Akrysanth deflected the next blow with a biting laugh. He was winning. Fen knew it, and from the acceptance in Alekhai's eyes, he knew it, too. His own deterioration had caught up to him. "Still think you're strong? No, brother. You're nothing without me, without your family. *Nothing*."

"You're wrong!"

"Am I?" Akrysanth feinted and slashed. "Will it matter, when I'll kill you either way?"

Alekhai knocked aside the blade, but barely, nearly losing his nose and left ear in the process.

"I'll burn you to ash this time," Akrysanth drawled, dodging another blow with scarcely any effort now, "and once I'm done with you, I'll do so much worse to your friends—"

He never got to finish that sentence. Alekhai let out a ragged yell. Steel struck steel with stunning force. Fen saw Alekhai's arms began to shake as he tightened his grip on his hilt. He twisted on his heel, too swift for unaltered eyes to catch, and then—

The emperor's sword clattered to the floor. Akrysanth's arm hung limp, a line of glittering red trailing down his arm, seeping up from where Alekhai's sword bit into his shoulder. His mouth opened and closed twice before sound escaped.

"You were supposed to be dead," he whispered.

Alekhai's eyes were cold and lifeless, gold coins that had been dug up from wet earth. "Oh, but I am. Stand down, brother. It's over. Let the blood we've spilt already be enough."

Akrysanth looked at the four of them, one by one. "I'm your scapegoat. The target for all your ire. Your disappointments and your failures and all your mistakes. But when there's democracy, you'll have only yourselves to blame." He let out a broken laugh. "You'll soon learn that the only thing worse than a tyrant you didn't choose is one that you did."

Then he moved, a hair faster than his brother. In a blur of movement, he unsheathed the dagger at his hip and threw it. The blade flew past Alekhai as he reared back and slit his brother's throat.

Akrysanth keeled backward. His fingers flew to his neck, cocooning the exposed flesh as if attempting to coax the bloody ruin back together. Scarlet froth bubbled up over his tongue as he struggled in vain to form his final words. His eyes met Fen's over Alekhai's trembling shoulder, wide not with shock, rage, or agony, but something she could not name. And then Akrysanth, Sovereign of Enkaiia, breathed his last.

Delayed pain exploded across Fen's chest. She stared down at herself, watching in silent, screaming horror as the front of her tunic went dark and wet. There, sticking out from between two broken ribs, was the hilt of Akrysanth's knife. Blood spurted over her lips and down her throat. A string of strangled coughs racked her body. She stumbled wildly before crashing to her knees.

Alekhai rushed forward. He caught her as she collapsed. They fell, tangled together. An awful cry clawed its way out from his chest. It was a broken sound, somewhere between screaming and weeping, and not quite human.

And then Fen heard nothing at all.

# 52

## *ALEKHAI*

"This will be my last resurrection." Alekhai took a breath. "I love you," he said. "I should've said it sooner. But I love you both, and I *will* love you to my last breath."

"She wouldn't want this," Mettan said.

"I don't care what she'd want."

"Alekhai—" Mettan began.

"I have to. You know I have to. I am nothing but my oaths and my duty, after all."

Sijara reached for Alekhai's hand. Mettan took the other.

Alekhai squeezed once before letting them go. "Mettan, Sijara, you have my devotion."

"And you ours," said Mettan, without hesitation. The corners of his lips twitched, as if he wanted to smile but had forgotten how.

"Alekhai," Sijara said slowly, rolling the syllables in her mouth. "I love you. We love you."

He limped over to Fen. He pulled free the dagger as gently as he could. It was still dripping with her blood when he pressed it to his heart. Already he felt it, tasted it. Technomancy, pulsing in a low, steady beat—the call of a hundred war drums in his chest as the tang of blood and salt filled his mouth.

Alekhai looked back at his friends, one last time. "I know. And one more thing: When Fen returns, the throne is hers."

He pressed his fingers over the hilt and pushed inward. The blade sank deep into his flesh, easy as anything. And then Alekhai crawled into Fen's arms to die.

☾

The soul stood at the banks of a lake, hands clasped firmly behind her back.

"Well," said Alekhai, "it was nice while it lasted."

"You shouldn't be here," said the soul. She wouldn't meet his eyes. She knew. Of course she knew. There were no secrets in death.

"There is no place for me *but* here," he replied. "I'll follow you anywhere."

"Don't do this," said the soul.

He saw now that she was trembling. So was he.

"I must," he said. "I'd ask you to forgive me, but you wouldn't."

"You're not sorry," the soul said.

"I'm not," he conceded. "But I am ready to die. At least it's for you."

"I wish it wasn't," she said. "You're so willing to bleed for me and die for me, but I would rather that you lived for me. I don't understand."

"Oh, it's quite simple," Alekhai replied. "I refuse to exist in a world you aren't in."

"But I would've killed you if you took a single wrong turn," she said. "I promised Kharakh."

"All right."

"Alekhai, *please*. What is the *point* if you die?"

For a long time, he said nothing. He merely stood by her, trying and failing to find the words that would make this all hurt less.

In the end, he said, "The world is a duruqin, our lives the

strings. We can pull and pluck at them as much as we please, but once the playing stops, their shape remains the same." He sighed. "For a short while, though, there is music."

She let out a broken sound: half a laugh, half a cry. "You missed your calling as a poet."

"You'll have to make up for the loss, then. Write a good verse or two for me."

The soul gave a hard sob, dragged herself together enough to say, "How should it end?"

"Oh, Fen," he said, "it's only just beginning." He stopped himself for a moment, gathering his resolve. He hated himself for doing this to her. He looked down at her and smiled weakly. "Forgive me."

"I can't. We've been over this."

"Not for what I did. For what I'm about to do."

"And what," Fen forced out, "is that?"

"I cannot leave Enkaiia without a hand to guide it." He tried to map her face, tried to commit her to memory. But looking at her like that was akin to staring straight into the sun, so he shifted his gaze to her shoulder. "You'll be Sovereign. That's how the crown will pass."

"You can't." Fen sniffled, wrapped her arms tightly around herself. "*Alekhai*, I can't."

"You can. You've shown me that a thousand times over." He beamed at her. "I know you, Fenyyang Mekantai. You love so easily. You care so deeply. It's the most beautiful thing about you. And you have so much strength. You are the greatest of us all."

"I'm not."

"You *are*," said Alekhai, cupping her cheek. He could barely feel her now. "Nothing's changed, not really. I always knew my love for you and Mettan and Sijara would outlast the universe itself. And it will. Listen to me. I love you, I love you, I love you."

The soul rocked back and forth on half-transparent feet, shaking her head.

"You're not alone, Fen. You never have been." Alekhai brought his other hand up to frame her face. "Will you remember that?"

"Yes," she whispered. "I'll remember."

Alekhai made to move, but the soul's arms swung out and yanked his face toward hers. For a specter, she had unnatural strength. Or perhaps he had simply tired of fighting. She pulled him down to her, until his temple met hers. He could smell blood and smoke and sweat on her skin as he forced himself to finally meet her gaze. He looked at her then—really looked at her—for the first time in his life. Her eyes were hard and sad and honest enough to hurt. An ocean of words unspoken and actions unrealized and hopes unmet stretched between them. Drowned them.

"You've cursed me," said the soul.

Alekhai felt himself fray at the seams. "I know."

"Come with me," she said.

"You know I can't." The time had finally come for him to pay the price for his power.

"Then walk with me to the edge." She reached for his hand and tangled their fingers together.

"Of course," said Alekhai. His eyes were already starting to shine sun gold; he could see the light falling over her face. "Of course I will. And when you cross it, don't look back."

"No promises," said Fen.

"I know that, too," said Alekhai.

*You have so much strength. You are the greatest of us all.*

But Fen didn't feel great or strong. She just wanted it all to stop, so that she would never have to lose him.

She didn't get what she wanted, in the end.

Perhaps it was the last few drops of Alekhai's soul evaporating from hers. Perhaps not. But when Fen doubled over, opened her mouth, and screamed, she shook the very world.

Her friends helped her sit up. A trail of crimson ran over Sijara's forehead, across her brow, and resumed its bloody path down her left cheek. She'd almost lost an eye. Fen pushed herself upward, struggling to her feet.

Alekhai's Accuser was a newly solid shape at the corner of her vision, swaying back and forth beside the blurred angles of Akrysanth's construct. It had a head like an anvil, hammered from black pearl. A body like fire. She turned to face It.

It spoke. "HE SWORE YOU WOULD HAVE THE REST OF YOUR COHORT," It said. "SO I WILL LEND YOU HIS POWER."

Fen held a hand out to Mettan. Wordlessly, he gave her the satchel containing what little they had of Hahru and Naijima. She pulled the pieces from the worn cloth and set them on the ground before her. For Naijima, she hefted the sword she'd brought down her last opponent with. For Hahru, she pulled a spear from the wall.

Then she brought them back.

When it was over, she stared up into the Accuser's shifting, eyeless face. "Let us have him."

She knew the answer before it came: "NO."

"Please," she whispered, hopelessly. "Please."

"I HAVE SAVED A THOUSAND WORLDS AND BROUGHT RUIN TO COUNTLESS MORE," It said. "THERE ARE MANY WHOSE LIVES I WISH I COULD TAKE." A pause. "STILL MORE WHOSE LIVES I WISH I HAD NOT. *NO.*"

Fen shook, swallowing hard.

"What did it say?" Mettan whispered the words over Ihazan's shoulder. He was still holding Alekhai's wrist, waiting for a pulse that would never resume.

Sijara was staring at her. "You can bring him back, right? Right, Fen?"

She made herself speak. "I'm sorry."

The four of them—Mettan, Sijara, Hahru, and Naijima—were crushed to each other in a bone-breaking embrace. She did not join them. The shame in her chest, in her revived heart, was far too great.

She repeated the same words over and over again in her head, a kind of prayer: Breathe in, breathe out, breathe in, breathe out. Push back your shoulders, stand up straight. And for the love of the Eternal Mother, stop crying.

The tears welling up in her friends' eyes when she finally met them didn't make it any easier.

"It refused," she said again.

Distantly, she heard Mettan make an odd hiccupping sound as he sobbed. "I thought we'd have more time."

Slowly, Fen looked over to where Akrysanth's two remaining guards stood, near the far edge of the room. They'd never left. Lined up behind them were a dozen unmasked imperial officials.

Still more flowed in from behind golden curtains. Someone in the cyan robes of the Synedria stood at the head. Kharakh's forces had won. The rebels had taken the palace, and the people here didn't want to die.

"Please," Fen said. But there was nothing else to say.

This could not be victory; it was too hollow, too empty. She'd won. She wished she hadn't. Gaze never leaving her, the councilor lowered themself to the floor. Behind them, row after row of officials knelt. To her—and to the two Accusers she could feel looming at her sides, both suddenly as solid as stone.

"No," Fen whispered. "No, please. Stop."

They did not.

"The old Sovereign is dead," said the councilor. "Long live the new Sovereign!"

Fen bit the inside of her cheek so hard she tasted iron. Black spots exploded across her vision like a hot spattering of ink. Perhaps if she closed her eyes now, she'd never have to open them again.

But.

Alekhai had given her a gift she could not give back.

She looked up to where the Accusers were quickly fading. "I will do what my friend has asked of me. I will serve Enkaiia until my last breath. But know that I will spend every spare moment till then plotting a way to tear you apart. I swear it."

"AND IF WE STRUCK YOU DOWN WHERE YOU NOW STAND?"

"You should," Fen said. "It's the safest option. But I have to help the people of Newearth first."

And then she got to work.

# EPILOGUE

Onath came when Fen called for him. The magistrate had always been an enigma; even after two decades as his ward, she sometimes felt she knew strangers better than him. But they trusted each other in their own odd way, and he was an enormous help. The moment the news slipped through the palace gates, the corags of Enkaiia descended on Ivytra, ready to feast on the scraps of whatever imperial power remained under the new peasant empress. Onath helped Fen keep the scavengers all at bay long enough for saner, wiser voices to prevail.

All their throats would've been slit, no doubt, without Alekhai's Accuser looming over the proceedings. It remained for some reason, wavering over Fen's head like an eldritch halo, and its presence alone was threat enough to keep even the most violent nobles and bandit lords in line.

The construct remained by her side as the worst of Enkaiia's monsters were brought to justice. The tribes elected their own leaders once more, and those leaders formed a council that replaced the Synedria. The palace was stripped of its riches to support aid efforts across the tribes and clans. The first seeds were planted in razed forests. And when Fen asked the Accuser to lend its strength to the new government's efforts, it built new infrastructure and transported food and water so quickly, scientists argued whether it could teleport.

At first Fen served as a figurehead, reciting speeches for broadcasts and sitting in endless ceremonies, while the pan-tribe council carried out the real work. Occasionally they involved her and her friends, but she knew it was more out of generosity than anything else. Naijima was the exception. He shined in meetings, and Fen thought privately that he had a good chance of being elected chieftain of Eira one day, especially now that he was training as a cleric under Chinonso.

Meanwhile, Ihazan ran off with the wife of a popular omnichip app developer and returned two weeks later declaring they were going to become a civil rights lawyer. Hahru briefly considered going into politics, but then decided to start what rapidly become a popular local martial arts school instead.

Mettan and Sijara refused to leave the capital, even after Fen's abdication. The Masks' dream, Alekhai's mission, was all they had left of their fallen friends, rebel and royalty both, and they would not abandon it now. Besides, Alekhai's Accuser went wherever they went, and half the reason the councilors were so effective was because there was an alien construct present. That, and the law that let Enkaiians vote representatives off the council whenever they wanted. Sometimes, though, measurable progress on the scale of the former empire seemed forever out of reach. For every rapacious tycoon and callous aristocrat ousted and fined, a hundred aspirants materialized to take their place.

More than once, Fen found herself certain that nothing was ever going to change. That nothing could get better, only worse. Because everyone wanted money and power, the two things that corrupted most. She wondered whether humanity was ever meant to leave Oldearth, much less the savannahs the species arose in. Fen didn't know what to call the thing inside people that made them monstrous the moment they had means and opportunity—"greed" was insufficient—but she was certain civilization fed that hunger, that wrongness.

And yet.

She held on to hope with all her strength. She had to. Because if not for her friends, if not for her dream that if they all worked hard enough for long enough, then perhaps things could change, she'd find poison or a good sharp knife, and join Alekhai in whatever happened after.

☾

"What is death?" Onath asked her once.

"A curse," Fen said, a hand over her eyes. "And a gift."

"Perhaps," he said thoughtfully. "I think it is a lesson. And only once you've learned it do you know the importance of life. Of memory. Of time with those you love."

Ying proposed to Ruiha a little less than a year after the rebels took the palace. The pair had retired from active work, but popped in to help however they could whenever they were asked. And so when Ying presented to her lover the mask she'd carved for her at the steps of the capital's temple, Fen, Mettan, and Sijara were there to see it.

Naijima officiated the binding ceremony. Fen wept as her friends kissed each other's wrists. She tried her best to believe that it had all been worth it.

☾

The realization came to her, one year later.

When it did, she ran straight to the Maker's sanctum. She'd been summoned there the night after her coronation, but she hadn't gone since. She didn't trust It, not after what It had allowed Akrysanth to do. Not after she'd learned what It and Its people had done to the worlds they'd deemed beyond salvation. The less It interfered here, the better. But now, she fell to her knees before the alien and Alekhai's Accuser. She made her demands.

"I AM THE DESTROYER OF A THOUSAND WORLDS,"

thundered the Maker. "I HAVE PAINTED WHOLE STAR SYSTEMS IN COUNTLESS COLORS OF BLOOD—"

"Yes, yes, I know," Fen snapped. The dagger was already in her hands. "But your creature *will* do as I ask."

Her words were fact; both creator and construct knew it. And so they granted her final wish.

"THIS RESURRECTION WILL BE THIS WORLD'S LAST." The Maker lowered Itself to her as she unsheathed the blade. The air hummed with Its power. "AND YOUR GENERATION WILL BE THE LAST TO KNOW MY KIND. AFTER THIS, I WILL RETURN TO THE STARS WITH THE ACCUSERS."

"Good." Fen pressed the tip of the dagger to her chest. "I thank you for saving our ancestors, but you've meddled long enough."

☾

She found his soul sitting at the bottom of Umut Pass.

"How?" he whispered when he saw her.

She extended a hand to him, her eyes glowing gold, and he took it.

"Your first oath," she told him. "You swore no lasting harm would come to my friends. And at the end of it all, you were one of them."

When it was all over, she grabbed him by the shoulders and pulled him to her.

"Alekhai of the last empire, of the fallen empire, of golden blood and bone," she whispered. "I hate you. And if you weren't half of me, I'd strike you down where you stand. Well, where you sit."

"Fenyyang Mekantai." Alekhai clicked his tongue. "You always say the sweetest things."

"How . . . how could you leave me? Leave all of us?" Her shoulders tightened.

"It was the only way to save you," he said simply. "And I didn't plan on being alive to deal with the consequences."

Fen drew away just far enough to glare at him. "You were wrong, you know. I don't love easily. But you won me over, and you brought me back just to take yourself away."

"I had to." His eyes glittered with a light all their own. "I could've lit a match and set the world aflame if I'd really wanted to. It's what I would've done, had I not been able to restore you. I would've relished the burning. But I wanted to save you more than anything. I would choose you, Sijara, and Mettan. Every time."

"Alekhai—"

"So I didn't do this for you. I did it for myself. For the world."

"*Alekhai.*"

"Don't be angry with me." He smiled then, full and bright and beautiful, as if it were the most natural thing in every world.

Fen cursed, then pulled him back into an embrace. "Come on," she said then, standing and offering him a hand. "Everyone's here for the Night of Two Moons. I can't wait for you to meet the others."

The work ahead of them would never end. There was so much to do: to mend and replace and revive. The imperialists hadn't vanished with the last true emperor, and the remaining bandit lords, Kharakh foremost among them, wouldn't disband their forces without a fight. The last remnants of the empire would never accept the council. If the elected tribe leaders all died natural deaths, it would be a miracle from the Mother.

Fen didn't know if it was too late to save Newearth, but they would try. And for now, she had this. Her friends, her family. She'd hold them close in the time they had. Together they watched the sun rise.

She found herself smiling as the sky burned gold, her arms outstretched to greet a new day in a new world.

# ACKNOWLEDGMENTS

*THE KING MUST DIE* is the book of my heart, as they say. It's a love letter to my friends and so it feels fitting to thank them first. To old chums from elementary and before: Liana Brydle, Nico A., O.R., and Rachel. To besties from high school: Melodey Soong, Lianne Quek, Caitlin Lee, Olivia Mestas, Hannah Rivera, Liyue Chen, Liri Chen, Mary A., E.P., Julia N., Elizabeth N., Laura Searcy, Isabella C. To companions from college: Ivy Tran, Julianna Kim, Celina, and Sohan. To dear pals from grad school and Friday Harbor: Andrea, Julia, Simone, Jasmine A., Ariel S., Kai D., and Maggie. To writer buddies Ehigbor, Yume, Julia Vee, Karen Jialu Bao, Hana Lee, Annie, E. J. Lee, Victoria, and Julie. I love you all so much. Thank you for being my friends.

Of course I'd also like to thank my agent, Trish, and editor Amara, along with the whole team at Saga Press, including Jéla Lewter, Karintha Parker, Savannah Breckenridge, Camryn Johnson, Crystal Watanabe, Kayley Hoffman, and Yvonne Taylor. They're incredible, and I'm so grateful for the work they put into this book.

I'd been writing various versions of pretty much the same story since 2014. How times have changed! The edition you're holding now is essentially the science fantasy reboot of two combined rewrites from college. (The first was called *The Match-*

*breaker*, which sounded very cool to me when I was eighteen. If that title seems familiar, it's because I left a silly little reference in *The Splinter in the Sky*.) My roommate at the time, Julianna Kim, read the earliest version of that story and provided the first real critique I ever received of my longer work. Without that feedback, bestowed with all her signature snark and skill, *The King Must Die* probably wouldn't exist today. And if it did, it certainly wouldn't be as good.

This book, and its previous incarnations, benefited from the input of many other wonderful critique partners and beta readers over the years. Thank you to Alan Agostinelli, W. J. McCane, Shane Simonsen, Nihar Sonalkar, Viola, Renée K. Reeves, Jacen Atlas Wolfe, and J. S. Morrison.

Thank you to my PhD advisors, Erik and Jon; my labmates, especially Andy, Lucy, and Jood; and professor Steve. This story leans a little more toward the fantasy end of the science fantasy spectrum, but was very much shaped by research and coursework, and I'm quite lucky to be part of not one but two wonderful labs. Also, I revised the last chunk of the first rough draft while on a class field trip. During the car rides between sites, Steve kindly answered my hundred or so questions, some of which were secretly for this book's world-building, ha! I'm grateful for his expertise.

Finally, thank you to my family. We've had a tough year, but we're still here.

# ABOUT THE AUTHOR

KEMI ASHING-GIWA IS A WRITER and graduate student from Altadena, California. Her work, which includes *The Splinter in the Sky* and *This World Is Not Yours,* has won the Compton Crook Award and has appeared on the *USA Today* bestseller list. Her short fiction, which has been nominated for an Ignyte Award and featured on the Locus Recommended Reading List, has been reprinted in collections including *Some of the Best from Tor.com: 15th Anniversary Edition* and *The Year's Top Tales of Space and Time*. She studied integrative biology and astrophysics at Harvard University, and is now pursuing a PhD in the Earth and Planetary Sciences department at Stanford University.